About the Author

Tasneem Abdur-Rashid is a British Bengali writer and podcaster born and raised in London. Having recently completed a Master's degree in Creative Writing, Tasneem spends her days writing in coffee shops and her nights co-hosting the podcast *Not Another Mum Pod*. In between, she's busy trying (and often failing) to be super mum, super wife and super chef.

 @TasneemARashid
 @tasneemarashid

Finding Mr Perfectly Fine

**TASNEEM
ABDUR-RASHID**

Finding
Mr
Perfectly
Fine

ZAFFRE

First published in the UK in 2022 by
ZAFFRE
An imprint of Bonnier Books UK
4th Floor, Victoria House, Bloomsbury Square, London, England, WC1B 4DA
Owned by Bonnier Books
Sveavägen 56, Stockholm, Sweden

This is a work of fiction. Names, places, events and
incidents are either the products of the author's
imagination or used fictitiously. Any resemblance to
actual persons, living or dead, or actual
events is purely coincidental.

A CIP catalogue record for this book is
available from the British Library.

ISBN: 978-1-83877-815-6

Also available as an ebook and an audiobook

1 3 5 7 9 10 8 6 4 2

Typeset by IDSUK (Data Connection) Ltd
Printed and bound in Great Britain by Clays Ltd, Elcograf S.p.A.

Zaffre is an imprint of Bonnier Books UK
www.bonnierbooks.co.uk

For my Nani. I miss you every day.
May your soul rest in peace. Ameen.

Part One

Winter

Chapter 1

My stomach churns as I type in 'Muslim Marriage Websites' on my laptop and I'm not sure if it's out of excitement or shame. Probably a bit of both. Although it feels empowering to take charge of my destiny instead of waiting around for things to happen, I can't help feeling embarrassed. Looking for a husband online isn't exactly the dream, is it? Anything else would have been preferable. Meeting him at uni, work, or even on the Tube would have been better than filling out a form and putting myself out there for public scrutiny. Yet here we are. Desperate times . . .

I hit 'search' and I'm immediately inundated with countless sites claiming to be the best and to do what my mum, aunts and social network have failed to do: find me a husband. As the pointer hovers over the first link, my youngest sister, Yasmin, peers over my shoulder, scrunching up her nose at the choices.

'This is like, a bit old-fashioned, isn't it?' she says after I've clicked on the first option and we are assaulted by hot-pink branding and images of airbrushed, light-skinned brown people.

'Huh? I thought internet dating was in fashion?'

'Yeah, ten years ago. Now it's all about apps. Look.' Slamming my MacBook closed, she grabs my phone, enters my passcode and starts browsing. Despite being the youngest sibling and still at uni, she's clearly so much more knowledgeable than I am. I didn't even realise she knew my passcode, for God's sake.

I let her do her thing, and mull over how my life has got to this stage. I know everyone does it. I know it's not a big deal. It's barely any different from a traditional arranged marriage scenario, only instead of a meddling aunty being the mediator, it's a website. But I can't help feeling ashamed about it all, like I've somehow failed because I'm still single at twenty-nine. Bengali years are a bit like cat years, so in my community, I might as well be thirty-nine.

In the end, 'we' decide to download an app called MuslimMate, because according to Yas, 'That's where all the cool people are'. She goes on to tell me that she has friends that use it, and I'm aghast that twenty-year-olds feel the need to go online to find husbands. Not just because online dating can be soul-destroying, but because now I'm going to have to compete with women a decade younger than me as well! How is that even fair? And why do they want to get married so young anyway?

'You're so naïve sometimes,' Yasmin giggles. 'They're not looking for husbands, they're looking for hook-ups. Boyfriends. You know, *fun*.'

Bloody hell. So it's a dating app disguised as a marriage one, to make it more respectable and 'Islamic'. I keep my opinions on the matter to myself though, as I already look like an ignorant old granny next to my younger, cooler sister.

'I really don't feel comfortable about this,' I mutter as Yasmin snatches my phone out of my grasp and scrolls through my photo gallery before selecting what she thinks is the right picture; a selfie I took in a park a few months ago. The sun was beaming down on me, its rays illuminating my face and making me look radiant.

'Let me fix this up a bit,' she mumbles to herself, opening up an editing app and then playing around with my face until she's zapped away a spot and blurred out a laugh line from the corner of my eyes.

'Isn't this deception?' I ask, partly in awe, as I try to grab the phone back.

'Chill out!' She rolls her eyes. 'Everyone does it. But look – you have to take a selfie now so they can verify that it's actually you and you're not a catfish.'

'No way! Not looking like this!' I haven't washed my hair in three days and the evidence of yesterday's chocolate binge is sitting on my cheek right now, all red and painful.

'No one's going to see it! They'll use facial recognition technology to make sure that it's you.'

This is getting worse by the second but I reluctantly comply. It's either this or a Biman Bangladesh flight

5

straight to Shahjalal Airport. A spot of online dating is definitely the lesser of two evils.

The selfie shows me in all my true glory – messy hair, a bit of uneven colouring, a sunspot or two, dark circles that are bigger than my friend circle – and I'm convinced that they're not going to let me submit the other, manipulated photo.

'Who's "they"?' Yasmin sighs. 'It's not going to be an actual person doing the verification, Zara. It's some software that will see that you've got the same features and that's it. Please. Relax.' Shaking her head, she goes back to the phone and starts typing away. I have no idea what she's writing but she won't let me see until she's finished. Leaning back with an accomplished smirk on her face, she hands it over and I read her intro warily.

Fun and friendly twenty-nine-year-old Londoner here, finally biting the bullet and exploring the mysterious online Muslim dating scene in the hopes of finding a like-minded someone who's looking to settle down. I'm after someone kind, funny, intelligent and successful to join me on this adventure, to laugh, explore and learn with me. If you think you could be my match, you know which way to swipe!

'I can't do this.' I gulp, staring at the words directly below the image of my face smiling back at me. 'Am I really about to put myself out there for a bunch of nameless, faceless strangers to ogle at my picture and tear me to pieces? What if no one picks me? What if someone I know screenshots my profile and shares it? What if someone takes my picture and photoshops it onto a glamour model's body and shares it around? What if—'

'Relax, Z,' Yasmin soothes me in her most calming voice. 'Your pictures are already on every social media platform that's out there. If someone wants to turn you into a glamour model, they don't need MuslimMate to do it.'

'True,' I squeak, reaching over for my stone-cold hot chocolate to moisten my throat. 'Is the intro too flippant though? Maybe I need to sound more serious?'

'No way! Serious means desperate and you are *not* desperate. It's fine. It's chill. See how the responses go, you can always switch up the photo and intro in a week's time, if you want.'

Sometimes my twenty-one-year-old sister's social and emotional maturity is shocking.

So, I take a deep breath, whisper, 'Bismillah' and hit 'save'.

It all started a couple of hours ago, with my mum digging her elbow into my ribs and my grandma breathing down my neck as I reluctantly put together a biodata – aka a Bengali marriage CV – under their strict direction.

I tried to ignore them both as I comprehended the magnitude of what I'd agreed to do, but I would have had to be deaf to tune out Mum and Nani's excited ramblings; Mum was reeling out a list of people to send my biodata to, and Nani kept chanting 'Alhamdulillah' – Praise be to God – over and over again. A biodata: a piece of paper that describes me in my most basic, no-longer-a-human-just-a-bunch-of-stats form. And according to the Bengali community as a whole, knowing my height, education and family background is pretty much all they need to determine whether or not I'm an adequate fit for their precious son/nephew/brother. If it wasn't for my name right there on the top, this document could have been describing anyone.

While a part of me still can't believe I've let my mum put together the most archaic of arranged marriage resources (it's not exactly the romcom-worthy love story I had envisioned for myself), the other, more realistic part, knows that I don't really have much choice. It's not like I have a queue of tall, dark and handsome suitors lined up outside my house. Or any sort of suitor at all, in fact.

When you look at it logically, I suppose it's not really that surprising that I've yet to find a match. After all, how many single Bengali men do you really think there are in the UK that are older than me, taller than me, educated, respectable, relatively religious, from the right part of Sylhet, the right family background, and somewhat attractive? And how many of them are going to magically cross my path so I can fall in love with them organically?

Last week, I turned twenty-nine. Along with the usual home-made Victoria sponge, helium balloon and

Selfridges' gift vouchers, my mum's birthday present to me was the ultimatum that if I'm not engaged by my thirtieth birthday, she's sending me off to the Motherland to find a fresh-from-the-Desh husband.

So there you have it. With a threat like that (picture a short, skinny engineer with a grizzly tash and dubious English) looming over my head, it's no surprise that I was sitting there in my jammies, nursing a hot chocolate and a headache, putting together a Bengali version of a dating ad. Only instead of it being uploaded online, my parents would share it with friends and relatives.

'So you're going to be sending my personal information to every aunty, uncle and grandma in the British Sylheti community?' I asked, nauseated by the very prospect.

'Of course not!' my mum responded primly. 'I know we're desperate, but we don't want everyone to know that, do we? We'll only share it with trusted middle people when, and only when, we've seen and vetted the potential suitor's own biodata.'

It sounded pretty complicated to me but, apparently, it's completely normal in our culture.

BIODATA
Bride's Name: Zara Choudhury
Age: 29
Height: 5' 8"
Complexion: Fair

'Mum,' I began tentatively, my finger poised over the backspace key. 'Is it really necessary to describe my skin colour? I'm hardly "fair" and even if I were, why should it matter?'

'Of course it's flippin' necessary,' Mum snapped back at me, the grin turning into a scowl. It's quite scary how my mum can go from deliriously happy to majorly pissed-off to brandishing a rolling pin in seconds. 'People need to know what they're getting into. You might like to think that no one cares about complexion any more, but trust me, no one will look twice at a biodata that has "complexion: dark" on it.'

'So what are "dark" people supposed to do?' I retorted, disgusted. I didn't really want an answer. I got one, though. You always get an answer from my mum.

'They say that they're "medium",' she responded matter-of-factly, adjusting her saree. 'Overweight people also call themselves "medium" build, before you ask.'

Nani murmured her agreement from her place on my bed as she twiddled with her glow-in-the-dark prayer beads.

'Are you telling me that I'm going to have to describe my body on this?' My hand instinctively moved on to my belly and my eyes darted to the hot chocolate I was about to gulp down, which now looked horribly unappetising. I couldn't believe it. It was like I'd accidentally gone back two hundred years, before feminism, BLM or even common decency.

'Stop moaning and get on with it,' Mum said, rolling her eyes and muttering something in Bengali about girls these days being naïve and difficult. 'We've still got Amina to think about, and we can't even begin to look for her until you're engaged at least.'

'Good luck finding someone for Amina. She'll never be as compliant as I am,' I grumbled under my breath.

'That's *my* problem. Go on, carry on typing.'

And so I did. I swallowed my pride, dignity, self-respect and self-doubts, and continued to type. Slowly.

Build: Slim

Education: BA (Hons) English Literature. Upper Second-Class Honours. King's College London.

Occupation: Community Engagement Manager. Haringey Council.

Father: Abdul Aziz Choudhury

Occupation: Director of Finance

Mother: Jubeida Choudhury

Occupation: Homemaker

Brothers: None

Sisters: Amina, 25, MSc in International Relations, London School of Economics. Yasmin, 20, Brunel University, Marketing.

The CV had details about my maternal and paternal grandparents, what they did, the village and district they were from in Bangladesh, my aunts and uncles, what they do . . . It was my entire family history on a screen and in a couple of hundred words.

'What about my interests? What I'm looking for in a husband?' I implored when Mum finally stopped dictating and smiled at herself, pleased with her efforts.

'Oh, none of that's important. You don't want to give away too much. Plus, you're the girl, so you can't look like you're too keen. Now we need to choose a couple of pictures. Thank God you're photogenic.'

By that point I'd given up on feeling like a human being. The fastest way to get this entire ordeal over with was to oblige with minimal fuss, so I opened up my photo gallery, handed my laptop over to Mum and collapsed on the bed next to Nani who gave me a reassuring smile.

'Gosh, you have a lot of selfies here, don't you?' Mum mumbled, adjusting her reading glasses and squinting in concentration.

'I take one before I go anywhere to make sure I look presentable,' I explained through gritted teeth.

'But why are they on your laptop? Do you know how long this is going to take? There are thousands of pictures here!'

'It automatically syncs with my phone when I connect it!' I exclaimed in irritation, resisting the urge to snatch my laptop back. Everyone knows that looking through a woman's photo gallery is akin to rummaging through her underwear drawer.

'All right, calm down.'

I closed my eyes and practised the deep breathing techniques I saw on a mindfulness TikTok the other day. Not that I could remember how to do it properly, so I winged it and focused on getting my heartbeat to slow down. As Mum muttered to herself while browsing through my 7,489 photos, Nani stroked my hair and whispered to me to be patient, it would all be worth it in the end. I stifled a snort and continued with my deep breathing but I was secretly pleased to have Nani in my corner. OK, so she agreed with this biodata malarkey but I knew she would never pressure me into marrying someone I didn't want to.

'Here, this is a good one.' Mum's voice startled me out of my thoughts and I opened my eyes, still breathing slowly to calm my nerves.

'Mum, that's from my graduation.'

'So? You look sensible. Not like all these silly, pouty—'

'So, it was eight years ago. I look nothing like that now!' I felt my pulse racing again. So much for the deep breathing. Nani squeezed my arm and I lowered my voice. 'I can't use that.'

'You look exactly the same.'

I didn't. I looked young in that picture. My complexion was fresh, plump and there wasn't a pore in sight. My black hair was still silky and shiny, yet to be abused by GHDs and hair dye. I have better eyebrows now, though. The thin arches from my youth looked positively anorexic.

'And here's the second picture. This one from Nasima's wedding. You look lovely in that saree.' She was right. I looked happy in the photo and peach always complemented my colouring. But I didn't feel right sending a picture of me in a saree when I didn't even know how to wrap one. The last time I wore one it unravelled as I ran up a flight of stairs and I had to ask a random woman to fix it for me before I exposed my modesty.

'Mum, I only ever wear sarees at weddings. Isn't that deceptive?'

'No more than an eight-year-old picture. And what do you propose then? Sending one of you in jeans and trainers like some sort of, what do you girls call them? A "roadman"?' Mum did the whole exaggerated air quote thing, and I stifled a giggle at the look of confusion on Nani's face.

'What have the road cleaners got to do with it?' she asked in Bengali.

Mum ignored her and carried on. 'I don't think so. Right, email it all over to me, OK? And copy your dad in. He's got three people waiting to receive this.'

With that, she clambered out of the chair and waltzed out of my bedroom before I could even process what had happened. Nani got up from the bed as fast as her arthritic knees would permit and planted a kiss on top of my head.

'Don't get cross with your mum, moni,' she said in Bengali, using the same term of endearment she's used for me since I was a baby. As she slowly made her way to the open bedroom door, she added, 'She's worried about you. As soon as you turn thirty, the proposals will stop coming. You'll be old. We don't want you to be all alone forever.'

Letting out a big sigh, I fell backwards onto the duvet and stared up at the ceiling, my eyes filling with tears I begged not to spill over. Because that would have been really pathetic.

I thought back to uni days and how my best friend Layla and I would talk about the guys we fancied. The prospects were endless. There was tall Mohammed, blue-eyed Mohammed, Omar, Rafiq, Jamal ... So many to choose from. We really thought we would have our pick. And then she met Hasan, fell in love and got married. And me? Well, I met someone but that obviously didn't work out. So here I was, five years after we broke up, putting together a bloody marriage CV with the help of my mother.

I honestly never thought I would find myself in this predicament. According to Mum it's because my expectations are too high. Well, excuse me for wanting someone who respects me, makes me laugh, challenges me, looks after me – and who I happen to fancy. Is that really too much to ask? Is it my fault that the few proposals that have passed my mum and nani's stringent criteria have been a foot shorter than me, fifteen years older than me, or still living with their parents and ten siblings?

As I sat there, pondering where the hell I went wrong, I suddenly had a vision of me still living with my parents and grandmother at forty, while my younger sisters' kids wreaked havoc around me. I imagined my mum moaning at me for shopping too much and wasting my money. I heard her hypothetical voice screech, 'You've got no husband to look out for you so you can't afford to throw your money around!' I saw my dad looking pityingly at me and my bedridden nani wailing to God to have mercy on her and find me a husband. *Any* husband. Even a divorced, balding father of six would have been fine.

I worked myself up into a bit of a tizzy, looking into the future like that.

I can't become the moral of a 'look what happens if you reject all your proposals' cautionary tale. I can't become the spinster aunt who dedicates her life to her nieces and nephews because her eggs have dried up. I can't live with my overbearing parents forever. I won't!

I'm not going to rely on my mum and her limited network of aunties and uncles from a certain part of Sylhet to find me a husband. I'm twenty-nine, not sixty-nine. I have an entire year to find someone and if I put enough energy into finding a husband as I did in finding the latest celebrity lipstick, I'm sure I can be engaged in six months and married in twelve. I'm taking matters into my own hands: I've already signed up to MuslimMate, I'll attend a bunch of Islamic conferences, attend a speed-marriage event or two, and basically walk around with a MARRY ME henna tattoo on my forehead, if that's what it takes.

Chapter 2

It's Monday; I'm back in the office and apart from joining MuslimMate, putting together the biodata, and wearing more makeup than I usually would to work, I've done little else to find Mr Right. Judging from the calibre of candidates I've seen so far, though, I should probably lower my standards and settle for Mr All Right.

My department, Community Engagement, has the best corner in the open-plan office space on the third floor. There are only three of us at the moment; me, Adam the graphic designer and Francesca the events coordinator, and we sit facing each other right by the window, with Adam's posters and hand-drawn sketches covering the wall next to us.

My desk, like my bedroom, screams my personality. There are Polaroids of my friends and family stuck everywhere and all my stationery is stuff I've bought myself, not nicked from the supply cupboard. I'm one of those saddos who has a thing for stationery. I can spend hours stroking pens, checking out highlighters and eyeing up notebooks.

I absolutely *love* my job. I have a fantastic team, my manager, Kevin, is supportive, and all day I get to do things I enjoy; like writing articles for the community newspaper, contributing to the website, and coming up with events and ideas on how to bring the local community together. I get to meet new people all the time, which is one of my favourite things, and boss my little team around. Admittedly it's not the most glamorous of jobs, and my 'team' comprises only two other people, but the hours are decent, the salary is OK, the benefits are amazing and I can even walk to work if I want to.

My best friend Layla doesn't get it, though. She's constantly on at me to aim higher and either go completely corporate to earn loads of money, or go into the non-profit sector and use my brains for the greater good. But I'm honestly well and truly happy here. She's always ranting about her crappy boss and how her workplace isn't diverse enough, how all the old white men don't take her seriously because she's a young woman of colour. I don't have that problem. I'm respected here, I feel challenged and I genuinely enjoy what I do. OK, it's comfortable and safe, but what's wrong with that? Not everyone wants to save the world like her. Some of us are still trying to save ourselves.

The only downside is the lack of potential suitors. All the guys are either too old or (no offence) too white. When I first joined three years ago and learnt that Adam was Turkish, for a fleeting moment I thought he might have been a possibility. He's actually quite attractive in that North London 'rough around the edges' way. As I got to know him better, I realised that he's not really what I'm looking for in a life partner. For starters, he's a not-very-practising Muslim. I know I have a long way to go myself, but I do want to become more God-fearing. I want my kids to grow up in a household that prays regularly. The only thing *he* does five times a day is smoke those cheap fags you have to roll up yourself.

Adam's religiousness (or lack thereof) isn't the only thing that has prevented me from considering him. He's also a year younger than me, which isn't that big a deal, but he's pretty immature and looks quite young. The last thing I want when I turn forty is a husband that still looks thirty and thinks farting in public is funny. There's also the fact that I'm his line manager, which would make things super-awkward if things ever went wrong.

'What did you get up to over the weekend?' he asks a couple of hours into the workday.

'I put together a marriage CV,' I reply blithely, continuing to edit the community newsletter.

'You what?' he splutters, spinning his swivel chair around to stare at me. 'Why?'

Francesca, who, despite the Italian name is actually from Essex, also turns around.

'Because I need my family to hurry up and find me a husband, that's why.' I answer without looking at either of them, already regretting being so forthcoming. Adam is completely unpredictable and part of his boyish charm is that you never know what's going to come out of his mouth.

'Isn't actively "finding" a husband a bit contrived? Aren't you supposed to meet someone, fall in love and then get married?'

I roll my eyes. 'Don't get all coconut on me. You're Turkish. You know exactly what I'm talking about.'

'Yeah, but that hardly happens in our community any more.'

'Whatever.' I turn to look at him. 'Most women at some point start actively looking to settle down. She might call it looking for a boyfriend. Or dating. But what she really hopes is that it will one day lead to a life partner. All I'm doing is cutting out the time-wasting stages that happen before.'

Adam turns to Francesca for backup and she shrugs. 'Sorry, Adam, I'm with Zara on this one. It gets tiring, not knowing who's serious and who's messing about. I think it's pretty cool that you can cut out the bullshit and get to the point.'

'Thank you.' I smile at Fran. She smiles back and I relish this moment of sisterhood and experiences that transcend culture and religion.

'Well, it sounds unnatural to me,' he says, giving me a haughty look that I don't care for.

'Good thing I don't really care about what you think, then,' I retort.

'Good thing I don't care that you don't care.' See what I mean about him being immature?

I turn my back to him pointedly and take out my phone to act like I'm busy but I don't really have anything new

20

to check. Except . . . I haven't logged into MuslimMate since yesterday. I'm quite curious to see if I've managed to get through the verification process despite the not-entirely-accurate picture I submitted, so I open it up and sure enough, I've passed. And not only have I passed, I have over 300 new 'likes'!

I stare at the screen in shock. How can that possibly be true? My profile has only been live for a few hours. There are no messages and I deduce that only people I 'like' in return will be able to have that privilege.

'Zara, do you have a minute?'

My boss, Kevin, appears in front of me like an apparition and I stuff my phone into my pocket nervously, hoping he hasn't seen what I've been doing. I always think the worst when he asks to see me.

'Sure!' I reply with faux cheeriness, getting up to follow him to his office. As we walk across the room, all the possible worst-case scenarios play out in my mind; from being put on a performance management programme to getting fired. I force MuslimMate to the back of my mind. The 300 men all waiting to hear back from me are going to have to wait a little longer.

It turns out that Kevin only wanted an update on our upcoming community event. We usually have cross-departmental meetings on a Monday, but a few of the senior managers were off sick or in meetings, so it was cancelled today. Still, I decide not to open MuslimMate again during work hours, since 'Finding a husband' isn't a part of my job description.

After my satisfying lunch of yesterday's leftover chicken pulao that Nani kindly packed for me, Layla emails me asking if I want to attend a swanky Muslim networking event in the City. She hasn't told me much, just that I need to be in London Bridge by six thirty and I need to look 'hot'.

In an effort to do her proud, I nip off to Boots straight after work and pile on even more makeup. I also buy a cheap pair of earrings and a necklace from Primark to jazz up my dark jeans and jumper. Not exactly *Vogue* but I decide I will have to do.

Emerging from the Underground at London Bridge, I start walking down Tooley Street, where I am surrounded by imposing glass towers juxtaposed against classic English architecture. People who look as if they've jumped straight out of a fashion shoot, with their cashmere coats and monogrammed briefcases, hurry past me. It's a far cry from Wood Green High Road, I can tell you that.

As I wait for Layla outside the PwC offices – a really cool, modern glass building that curves in the middle like it's come from the future – I begin to wonder if I was too hasty in accepting her invitation. This morning I thought I looked pretty decent but now, at dusk, at the heart of the City surrounded by glass and lights, I wish I was wearing heels. And silk. And diamonds.

'Assalaamu Alaikum!' Layla calls out to me, her arms outstretched.

'Wa Alaikum Salaam,' I respond with a smile. We hug and, as always, I feel better by her energetic presence. She's always hopping around, laughing or cracking a joke. We were introduced by a mutual friend, Ezra, in Wood Green Library during our first year of A Levels, where we would go to 'study' every weekend. By 'study' I mean gossip, check out boys and generally mess around. We bonded over our love for Garage music and playing pranks and have been best friends ever since.

'You look so hot,' Layla says with a wide grin. 'I bet at least one guy asks for your number tonight.'

'It's not about numbers though, is it?' I reply as we sit on a nearby bench to kill the ten minutes before the event starts.

'What is it about then?' she asks, adjusting her loosely tied headscarf. 'I mean, I know your mum threatened you, but is it really about that?'

I think for a moment. I've been asking myself the same question and although I've been a bit difficult about the whole biodata thing, the truth is, I *want* to get married.

'Not really,' I admit. 'It's been so long since you-know-who. He was a piece of shit, I know, but apart from that, I enjoyed being in a relationship. The feeling of having someone there for you, no matter what, the companionship. Right now, I feel so . . .' My voice begins to wobble slightly. '. . . Lonely.'

23

'Ah, sis, don't say that! You have me, and Ezra, and your sisters. You're definitely not alone.'

'I know. But I still need more, you know? I want what you have with Hasan.'

Layla scoffs at this and rolls her eyes. 'Are you serious? I want to kill him half the time.'

'Yeah, but the other half of the time you can enjoy the fact that you married your first love. He has your back, no matter what. You never go to sleep alone.'

'Honestly, Zara, going to sleep alone is the best thing! No duvet-hogging, no snoring, no dribble on your pillow-cases. I don't go on about it, but I often wonder if I married Hasan too soon. We were only twenty-four . . . Well, I was twenty-four and he was twenty-three, for God's sake. Who the hell gets married that young these days?'

'So? You got to grow together!' I insist, beginning to feel a bit panicky. In my eyes, Layla and Hasan are the perfect couple and the image I have of them is currently teetering on the edge of a precarious cliff, about to topple over and shatter into a million shards.

'More like grow apart,' she mutters. 'Look, Zara, all I'm saying is that things aren't as rosy as they seem. I wish I'd waited, but I was desperate to flippin' shag him, wasn't I?'

What? I stare at her and the shock is quickly replaced by giggles. 'Are y-you telling me that you were in such a hurry to marry him because you wanted to *sleep* with him?' I manage to choke out in between fits of laughter.

'I wanted to make it halal, didn't I!' she wails, covering her face with her hands.

I lean over and give her a hug, still chuckling. 'You're such a horny cow. He's a lucky man.'

'But that's the thing: now I can't be arsed most of the time. He feels like I lured him into marriage under false pretences.' She looks both embarrassed and pissed off as she admits this but one look at me struggling to contain my laughter and she lets it all out. We're still laughing as we wobble into the building like a pair of drunks.

'What exactly is tonight about, other than networking?' I ask once the giggles subside and we are assaulted by more glass, chrome and marble. For a moment I wish I worked in Finance so I could wear high heels and a power suit every day. Then I remember that I rarely wear heels because I'm already tall and they hurt my feet.

'It's a chocolate-making night!' Layla squeals as we head towards the lifts. She's one of those people who can rarely conceal her emotions, be it excitement, anger or pain. I feel my spirits begin to lift. You can't go wrong with chocolate.

We walk into a spacious conference room with glass walls and floor-to-ceiling windows overlooking the Thames. Layla spots a noticeboard at the entrance of the room with our names and table numbers on it.

'Damn,' she whispers, her hazel eyes wide, 'we're on different tables! I didn't think they'd do that.' So much for having a wingwoman. She is at the other end of the room and will be of no use to me.

There are five men and four other women on my table and, despite the odd wing person, it's painfully obvious why we're here. 'Networking' my arse. I can smell the desperation in the air as the women casually play with their hair or their headscarves and the men try to look indifferent.

Everyone looks so high-class in their tailored suits and expensive shoes and I'm the only one in jeans and Primark accessories. I shrink into myself as I wonder what to say when I reach my table.

I opt for a simple, 'Assalaamu Alaikum,' with a bright smile. There is a chorus of 'Wa Alaikum Salaam's as everyone turns to smile back at me. I can feel all of them, men and women, sizing me up. They're probably wondering how I got past security.

I write my name on a label and stick it onto my jumper. On my right is a tall, OK-looking guy with trendy geek-chic glasses and a quirky tie. On my left is a petite woman in hijab. Sitting opposite me is a really tall hench-guy with brown hair and green eyes, who, according to his name label, is Hamza. He's so big he looks like a tree, and I feel even smaller than I already did.

I can feel Hamza appraising me as I make small talk with Wahida on my left. Maybe I don't look that bad after all. Feeling a bit more confident, I pretend not to notice.

'What do you do?' Wahida asks me with a bored expression. The way she has wrapped her plain black headscarf tightly around her bare face makes her look quite severe and I doubt she'll be successful tonight. I notice that she's wearing what looks like a designer watch, so I don't feel too sorry for her.

'I work in Community Engagement for my local authority,' I reply.

'Oh,' she says with – hang on, is that a sneer on her face? 'That sounds . . . relaxing. I'm an auditor for E & Y.'

Before I can control myself, I retort, 'That sounds . . . boring.'

I'm relieved when the facilitator finally starts talking and I can turn away from Wahida. When we're told to get into pairs and introduce ourselves, I hesitate. I don't feel like talking to either of the people closest to me. I decide that the guy on the right is the more appealing option, so I turn towards him. Except I'm too late and he's partnered with a tall, skinny girl on his right.

Feeling deflated, I turn to my left and find that Wahida has been replaced by Hamza. How he managed to shuffle over here without me noticing is beyond me.

'Hey, I'm Hamza,' he says with a strong American accent. Up close he's all-right looking, with his clear, fair complexion, flushed cheeks, light-brown hair and green eyes. He looks a bit too clean-cut and fresh for my taste and his cheeks are smoother than mine. I tend to go for the tanned and dark-hair type with facial hair.

'Salaams, I'm Zara,' I respond with a friendly smile. I'm not interested in him but we're stuck together for at least an hour so I might as well enjoy myself.

'So, what brings you here, Zara? Making new friends? Networking? The possibility of finding "the one"?' He says this with a cheeky grin.

'Actually, it was the chocolate,' I reply flippantly, looking him straight in the eye. He lets out a hearty laugh and I can't help but giggle along with him.

'A woman after my own stomach,' he guffaws, clutching his belly. He makes so much noise that despite the hum of voices around the room, people turn to look at us. I spot Layla grinning at me. She gives me a thumbs up and I glare at her and try to shake my head subtly. She carries on smiling so I look away before Hamza notices.

Once we get talking, I find he's quite fun. We decide to make a dark chocolate bar with hazelnuts and a white chocolate swirl going through it. As Hamza gets on with melting the chocolate, I start chopping the nuts and I'm surprised at how well we work as a team.

'So, what do you do?' he asks after we finish talking about our favourite foods. 'I'm pretty sure you don't work in Finance.'

'What makes you say that?' I ask with interest as I chop the nuts haphazardly. 'Because I do, actually.'

'Oh really?' he smirks, measuring out the white chocolate. 'What's eight multiplied by seven?'

'Er . . .' I turn red as my mind blanks out. He laughs again, and before I can stop myself, I dig my elbow into his ribs. Bloody loud Americans. All the other eligible bachelors – and I spot a few decent-looking ones – probably think I'm into Hamza now and won't even bother with me.

'Sorry,' he says, still chuckling. 'I can't help it. This is how I laugh.'

'Well, stop taking the piss out of me, then,' I grumble.

'Sorry,' he says again, looking slightly apologetic. 'This is why I'm still single. I find everything and everyone funny.'

'Fine,' I concede with a sigh. 'Go on then, how could you tell I don't work in Finance? I could have been some hotshot auditor, you know.'

'None of the auditors I know wear jeans to work,' he muses, raising his eyebrows. 'And none of them look as glamorous as you, either.'

Even though I don't fancy him, I can't help feeling tickled. Don't judge me, OK? It's not every day a girl's called glamorous.

'I mean, look at you compared to everyone else here,' he continues. 'Yes, there are some attractive women, but they all look so serious and boring, whereas you look like you looted Ernest Jones with all that bling.'

I smile at that and find myself confessing that I actually stopped in Primark on the way here. He laughs again and this time, instead of admonishing him, I join him.

'See Wahida over there?' he says in a stage whisper. '*She* looks like an auditor.'

Now we're both in hysterics and we don't even care if people stare. Wahida turns and gives me a dirty look and I'm feeling so giddy from the chocolate and giggling that I smile stupidly back at her.

Layla rushes up to me as soon as the activity is over and everyone's free to mill around and talk to people from other tables.

'I can't stay for long, Hasan has texted me, like, ten times already. Tell me quickly – what's going on with you and that guy?' she whispers, stealing glances at Hamza who is rummaging through his goody bag.

'Nothing!' I say with a laugh. 'I think I've made a new friend, that's all.'

Chapter 3

As I get ready for work the next day, I revert to my usual trampy self and pull on my favourite old tatty jeans with the frayed hem, a baggy cream-coloured jumper with a hole in the elbow, and my trusty trainers. Scraping my hair back into a greasy ponytail, I forgo the contacts for my glasses and only decide to put on a bit of blusher because I don't want to scare anyone.

'I take it you're no longer looking for a husband?' Adam observes with a raised eyebrow when I quietly take my seat at my desk and open up my calendar and task list.

'I take it you think you're at some grungy gig?' I reply, looking his scruffy hair and falling-off jeans up and down.

The morning passes quickly, and I'm so absorbed in writing an article about diversity in the borough that I don't notice the email that's come through from a 'H. Hegazi' until it's time for lunch.

> Salaams, Zara, hope you're good. Sorry for not emailing sooner, wasn't sure if you wanted to hear from me or not. It's taken me a while

31

to realise that unless I get in touch, I'll never find out. Are you free for coffee/dinner/shisha today after work? Hamza.

Sooner? It's been less than a day!

'Shit,' I squeak, reading and then rereading the email as Adam approaches our corner balancing two mugs of tea and a packet of Hobnobs in his hands.

'What's up?' he asks, placing a mug in front of me and opening up the biscuits.

'I needed this! Thank you!' I exclaim, grabbing a biscuit and shoving it in my mouth to calm me down. 'This American guy from the chocolate-making event last night has emailed me. He wants to meet up tonight!'

'So?'

'So I don't like him like *that*. He was fun and everything but . . .' I trail off, not sure if I really want to go into the intimate details of my lacklustre love life with a bloke. Yes, we're friends . . . sort of. As friendly as you can be without hanging out, outside work.

'But what?' Adam asks, taking a gulp of his black tea. He always drinks it black and sickeningly sweet, Turkish style.

'But I don't fancy him?' I avert my eyes. I feel as if our relationship has moved onto another level and we're crossing the boundary of colleagues. I hear my nani's ominous voice cautioning, '*No man from a good family wants to marry a girl who is friends with boys, moni.*'

'Why not?' he asks with genuine curiosity.

'He's not my type.' He doesn't need to know that I usually like guys with a bit of an edge to them. Hamza is so . . . proper. Where's the excitement in that?

'Don't meet him then.' He shrugs, as if it's that simple. As if I might not regret it five years down the line when I'm still single and alone, but it's too late because he got married to Wahida the auditor instead.

I say something to this effect out loud, my voice getting smaller and smaller because I know how silly I must sound to a man who never has to worry about growing old alone.

'That's the weirdest thing I've ever heard,' he says, sounding completely baffled. 'You can't meet him purely because you've got no one else on the horizon. What's going to happen if you do meet him, and then tomorrow, someone better comes along? You can't lead the poor bloke on like that.'

Deep down, I know he is right, but hearing him say it out loud makes me feel dirty. What the hell does he know about being a Bengali woman in Britain today? What does he know about familial and societal expectations? What does he know about eggs, and expiry dates, and diminishing beauty? In fact, what the hell does he know about anything? He's a good-looking, practically white guy with limitless options, no pressure and all the time in the bloody world.

So what if I don't fancy Hamza right now? Fancying someone isn't the be-all and end-all of a relationship. I could grow to fancy him. One day. Right?

'You know what? I think I *will* meet him,' I say stubbornly, partly to piss him off. 'Thanks for your advice.'

His eyes narrowed, Adam mutters something under his breath and turns back to his screen. I don't know what his problem is and, quite frankly, I don't care. I do the same and, for the rest of the day, we ignore each other.

Hamza and I have agreed to meet at Leicester Square at six thirty. Since I finish at five and it's only half an hour away on the Tube, I have more than enough time to go and sort my face out in Boots before I head over. But I don't. Instead, I stay on at the office to get some work done. Adam also stays behind, giving me sidelong glances every so often. I know he's itching to say something but is too proud to be the first one to break the silence.

'Aren't you going to go and freshen up before your big date?' he jeers as he gets up to leave.

'Nope.' I continue typing and don't bother looking at his condescending face.

'Well, that says it all, doesn't it?' He puts on his leather jacket, grabs his motorbike helmet and walks out of the office.

When I'm sure I'm not going to bump into Adam and his stupid logic by the lift, I pack up my things and make my own way out into the chilly evening.

Leicester Square, as always, is buzzing with tourists, lights and traffic and I weave in and out of groups chattering away in different languages as I make my way to the restaurant Hamza has suggested. There's something about this place that always energises me and by the time I arrive, I'm feeling a lot more positive. So much so, that I pull out a lipstick from the depths of my handbag and put it on in an effort to look like I care.

'Salaam Alaykom,' Hamza booms out from behind me in a thick Arabic accent and I chuck my lippy back into my bag before turning around to see him striding towards me with a huge grin on his face. His excitement is infectious and as we enter the warm, dimly lit restaurant, my spirits begin to lift. He helps me out of my coat and even pulls out a chair for me before the waiter can. The gesture is sweet and chivalrous, something I've never experienced before.

'The steak here is halal,' Hamza informs me, surveying the menu with uncontained glee.

'Yay, I can't wait.' I grin. 'I hate ordering vegetarian or pescatarian options at nice restaurants. It's all about meat.'

'Thank God,' he responds, putting the menu down. 'You're not the limp salad type then?'

'Hell no. Do I look like a no carbs sort of girl?' I scoff, gesturing to my stomach. 'I'm getting the steak for mains. With the sweet potato fries. But I'm not sure whether to get the mini mac 'n' cheese for starters or the baked camembert.'

'Get both, if you want. No judgement here.'

I look at Hamza's expressive face; so simple and unassuming. What you see is definitely what you get with him and it's really refreshing.

The evening passes smoothly and I'm surprised at how much fun I'm having. I find out that Hamza is Egyptian, which explains the Arabic accent whenever he says Arabic/Islamic phrases. He was born in the US and lived there for most his childhood, hence the American accent but the British turn of phrase. His dad was the personal cardiologist to a Saudi sheikh, so ended up moving from Egypt to Saudi, the US and then the UK when Hamza was twelve, just to work for him.

'How the other half live,' I say a little wistfully. 'I'd love to live abroad.'

'It's not as fun as you would think,' he replies. 'We moved around a lot, even while we were in the States. It was hard to make friends and fit in, over and over again. I never quite knew where I belonged.'

'Even without moving around I'm not sure where I belong,' I admit. 'I always feel that I have one foot in each culture.'

From what he tells me about *his* culture, it doesn't sound much different from mine, and we swap stories of the things our families have done in order to find us a spouse. He keeps making me laugh out loud, especially with his wicked Egyptian aunty impression.

He tells me about his family. His dad is a doctor, his mum is a teacher and they live in West London. He has a younger sister, also a doctor, and a younger brother, who he speaks fondly of, and generally he seems to have a good relationship with them all. His dad, apparently, was disappointed in him for becoming a chartered accountant instead of a doctor and reacted as badly as he would have had Hamza become a gamer.

In return, I tell him about my own parents, sisters and, of course, nani. He thinks Amina sounds hilarious and Yasmin a little intimidating. I find myself wondering what they would think of him and if they would get along. Yasmin would definitely like his good manners. I'm not sure what Amina would think. She'd probably be impressed by his career and income. Nani would love the fact that he is 'foshha' (light-skinned), Abbu would like that he's educated, but I don't know about Mum. In fact, I don't even know if they'd allow me to marry someone non-Bengali. Mum's always dropped threats about disowning me if I ever considered a non-Muslim man, but she's never said anything about Muslims who aren't Bengali.

You know what's really weird? As the evening has been progressing, he's becoming more and more attractive in my eyes. In fact, with a different haircut and some strategically sculptured facial hair, he might be considered cute. I look into his twinkly green eyes and wide smile and search for a sign that I fancy him; a tingly feeling in my gut, a fluttering in my heart, a butterfly in my belly. But so far, there's nothing.

When the waiter brings the bill over, Hamza won't even let me look at it, let alone get my wallet out, despite my protests.

It's almost ten when we finally walk out of the warm, cosy restaurant and into the cold January night. Walking through London at this hour, with a man by my side, feels strange, but I have to admit that it feels comforting as well. I don't know if it's the magic of Leicester Square, or it's the fact that I've spent most of the evening laughing, or it's because of the delicious meal, but right now, I feel pretty content.

'This is me,' Hamza announces when we stop in front of the entrance of the Tube station.

'It's me too,' I reply after a moment, still lost in my thoughts. 'We're going on the same line remember, but I'm going in the opposite direction to you.'

'Oh, er, about that,' he stammers, shifting from one foot to the other. 'I hope you don't mind, but, er—'

'What?'

'I hope you don't mind but I ordered an Uber for you.' The words tumble out of his mouth, as if the faster he says them, the less likely I am to be offended by the interference. 'I didn't know your address, though, so I scheduled it for Finsbury Park Station. You can give the driver your postcode.'

'You what?' Now that's unexpected.

'I know it's a bit presumptuous of me, but it's quite late and it isn't safe for you to be getting the Tube at this time.'

I stare at him as I try to figure out what to say. He looks back at me sheepishly.

'I can't let you do that, Hamza,' I say once I've finally got my words back. 'Thanks, but I'm perfectly capable of getting the Tube.'

'I know you're not some damsel in distress, Zara, but I don't feel comfortable with you having to take public transport at this time. You're out late because of me, so let me sort out a safer way for you to get home.'

Once again, I give up and accept the gesture as gracefully as I can. He looks relieved; and when the car pulls up, we stand awkwardly for a moment, unsure of the correct etiquette to part ways. He leans in for a hug and I half reciprocate it and half jump into the car.

It's only once we're a good few minutes away from Leicester Square that I lean back against the seat and let out a deep breath. Making the most of having phone signal over ground, I call Layla to get her advice on Hamza.

'Wagwan, sexy one,' she sings down the phone when she picks up – like she's been doing every time I've called her for the past twelve years.

'I'll tell you "wagwan",' I respond dramatically. 'I went for dinner with Hamza.'

'Omigod! You didn't! How did it go? Wait, who's Hamza again?' I hear her shushing Hasan in the background.

I remind her who he is (the tall guy from the chocolate-making event) and proceed to explain how, although I like him and he ticks a lot of boxes, I don't think there's that spark. And I really don't fancy him. Layla is married to the love of her life, so I expect her to tell me to lock him off and move on. I'm surprised when, after listening carefully, she tells me to give it a go.

'Relax and see where this goes, Zara. Not everyone experiences fireworks from the get-go. Sometimes things take a while to brew, you know, like a good cup of tea. What have you got to lose?'

'For starters, I might miss out on more appropriate prospects while I'm exploring this. My family are in the middle of sorting out some people for me to meet.'

'So? Carry on meeting whoever you want, what's wrong with that? Hamza has no claim over you.'

'Isn't that unethical?'

'Are you serious?' she scoffs. 'You barely know the guy. You don't even know what his intentions are. I bet he's still going to meet other women. Why shouldn't you?'

Anxious for a second opinion, I seek out Yasmin the moment I get home. She's in her room, typing away on her laptop, when I burst in.

'Why is it that no one knocks in this flippin' house?' she grumbles, closing the lid of her computer.

'Whatever. I need to talk to you.'

'What's happened now? How's MuslimMate?'

'Forget about that, I haven't even checked it yet. I had a date tonight. With Hamza from the chocolate event.'

'And . . .? How was it?'

'I actually had a really good time,' I admit reluctantly.

'So why do you look like you've just found your pet hamster, dead, stiff and cold in its cage?'

'Wtf, Yas? What sort of imagery is that? You've been hanging out with Amina for too long.'

Yasmin shrugs unapologetically and I flop down onto her bed and sigh dramatically.

'He's a really nice guy and everything. I mean, he paid for the meal, opened doors, booked me a ride home. He's a proper gentleman.'

'But . . . ?'

'I don't fancy him. I really don't. Surely I would know if I did, right?'

'Uh, yes. You would know,' Yasmin says wryly, rolling her eyes. I push her gently but I'm not annoyed. I'm well aware of how ridiculous I sound.

'But how can I be sure? It's not like I can trust my instincts. I've been so wrong before.'

The smile disappears from her face when I say this, and she leans over and puts her arm around me.

'Hey. There's no way you could have known that he would turn out like that. That was *so* not your fault. But this is separate from you knowing whether you fancy someone or not. This isn't the same thing.'

That night, I mull over Yasmin's words as I get ready for bed. She's right. Just because I was wrong before, doesn't mean I can't trust myself at all. My brain knows this. But even so, I go to bed feeling weary and wary, because every time I think I'm over him, over *it*, something triggers me and the memories all come flooding back.

Chapter 4

I usually go out with friends on Saturdays but I'm feeling wrecked after the week I've had. Trying to find a husband is tiring business and it shows. And I really need it *not* to show by the time I make my grand entrance at tomorrow's wedding. By tomorrow, I need to look fresh and sprightly, because nothing says 'dried-out ovaries' like puffy eyes and dehydrated skin, which will be even more apparent next to the plump youthfulness of my cousins and sisters.

This is why I'm lying on my bed with my third Korean face mask on and fresh cucumber slices on my eyes, listening to calm spa music. I'm hoping that the soothing atmosphere I've created will coax all the negative energy and toxins out of my body and give me an aura of confident nonchalance tomorrow.

'I think you need to chill out,' I hear my younger sister Amina scoff over the sounds of the sea. 'This whole finding a husband thing is so anti-feminist.'

'This *is* me chilling out,' I mumble, trying not to move my mouth as I speak. 'At least, it was until you came along.'

'Leave Zara alone,' I hear my mum say in the background somewhere. 'She needs to take this marriage search seriously – and unless you want to end up in the same situation, you could do with a face mask or two yourself.'

I sigh. I should have just booked myself into an actual spa, but after spending a fortune on a new saree, I didn't want to spend any more on this wedding of a person so distantly related that I'm not even sure *how* we know each other.

'Do you guys mind? I'm trying to relax here,' I say from between clenched teeth.

'All right, I'm going! Just wanted to give you girls your sarees, that's all. Your dad's brought them back from the dry cleaners, so they're lovely and pressed now,' she says. 'Here take yours, Amina. I'll leave Zara's here.'

'Thanks, Mum,' I reply, my eyes still closed. Ironing sarees encrusted with gems is a mission, so it was nice of my parents to get them professionally steamed for us. There are some things I'm going to miss when I eventually leave home.

'Seriously, Zara, I don't know why you're letting Mum pressure you like this,' Amina continues once our mother has left the vicinity. 'You don't *have* to get married you know. You're not going to turn into a khodu when the clock strikes twelve on your thirtieth birthday.'

'No one's pressuring me,' I reply. 'I want to get married. The older I get, the harder it's going to be to find someone, so I need to get cracking.'

'Do you know how ridiculous you sound? The older you get? You're twenty-bloody-nine! I bet men never worry about getting old! The double standards make me sick!'

'Amina! My trying to get married doesn't mean that I'm complicit in upholding the bloody patriarchy, OK? I want a life partner. I want kids one day. That's it! It's not that deep!'

Amina mutters something about failing feminism under her breath and stomps out of my room. The door slams closed and all the tranquillity I felt moments before disappears with her.

Despite yesterday's mishaps, the bit of pampering I did has refreshed my complexion and reduced the puffiness around my eyes. A good thing too, because today is going to be a golden opportunity to parade myself in front of potential in-laws. According to Mum, the crème de la crème of the UK's Bengali elite will be at this wedding and I need to make it count.

'Zara, I need your heeeeeelp!' I hear Amina screech from her bedroom next door. Before I have the chance to answer, she bangs on the connecting wall in case I've developed hearing problems overnight.

Amina, Yasmin and I may be sisters, but not only do we look nothing like each other, our personalities couldn't be more different. Amina is like a volcano ready to erupt at any moment, and it could be over something as minor as losing her favourite lipstick or something as complicated as Middle Eastern politics. She is also extremely loyal and has a heart of gold, and I can say with the utmost confidence that she would kill for me. No joke.

Yasmin, on the other hand is really, really chilled. Nothing fazes her and she's often the one who rushes to placate Amina. And me, to be truthful. She's very mature for a uni student and while she works hard, she plays harder. She's rarely at home and has a social life that is far more active than any of ours. I'm supposedly a cross between them both.

'What's the emergency?' I ask as I walk into Amina's meticulously tidy sea-green room. Mum thought that a soothing colour would help calm her. We're yet to notice a difference.

She looks up at me from her cross-legged position on the floor in front of her full-length mirror. 'I need help curling my hair. I can't do the back properly.'

'Can I do it later?' I say, trying to put her off from hijacking my getting-ready time. 'It's only ten thirty and we're not leaving until one.' *And I need every second to make myself look desirable since I'm the one whose eggs are drying up as we speak*. I don't say this out loud, though. I'm well aware of Amina's thoughts on the topic of marriage and old age.

'So? You know it takes me ages to do my makeup!' Her voice goes up an octave so I give in and sit down to get on with it as fast as I can. As I curl her hair around the heated tongs, she talks about the Muslim charity she works for and how all the old men don't take her seriously, and I 'umm' and 'ahh' in the right places. When her maroon hair is suitably bouncy, I leg it out of her room and go back to my comfortably cluttered haven with only an hour and a half to turn myself into an irresistible goddess.

'Oh, you look beautiful,' Mum gushes as she enters my room to put my new coral-coloured saree on for me. The border has pearl and crystal embellishments and I've tailor-made the blouse so it has long sleeves and a long top that doesn't expose my stomach. I may be ready to start making an effort with my appearance again, but there's a limit to how much attention I like drawing towards myself.

Mum gets to work with wrapping the saree around me. It isn't easy because I'm tall as it is and with three-inch sparkly heels, it's just about long enough. Once she's finished, she takes out three industrial safety pins and pins together parts of the saree that are likely to come undone. I honestly don't know how my nani lives in them with no safety pins. She even jumped into the pool wearing one when we were on holiday in Dubai. You should have seen her backstroking away with her headscarf on and everything.

'There, let me see.' Mum pushes me back to observe her handiwork. 'Stunning!' A strange expression crosses her face and I frown, wondering what's wrong now.

'What is it?' I ask warily as I check myself out in the full-length mirror and, to my surprise I agree with her. Sarees are amazingly slimming and I look as though I'm in proportion for a change.

'Nothing, nothing,' she mumbles, wiping the corner of her eye.

'Mum! What is it?'

'Nothing important! I . . . well . . . you're probably not going to be around much longer and I felt sad for a second. You know I love you and want the best for you, don't you?'

I stare at her, not sure if she's serious or winding me up. She ignores me and takes out her phone, ordering me to look demure while she takes pictures of me, muttering something about replacing the one from my biodata.

'Omigod you look so sexy!' Yasmin squeals, stomping her way into my room, her chin-length hair swishing like she's just stepped out of the salon. She has no problems showing off her skin and her mint-green saree has tiny sleeves and a low back. Although Nani has wrapped it to cover her flat, toned stomach, the material is slightly sheer so you can make it out through the fabric.

'So do you,' I say raising one eyebrow. 'A bit too sexy, perhaps?'

'Oh, leave her alone, she's still young,' Nani chides as she shuffles into the room, out of breath from climbing the stairs. 'Let me go and see if Amina needs any help.'

We hear Amina grumbling in the next room while both Nani and Mum sort her out. She finally emerges in a hot-pink saree. Like Yasmin, she's also gone for the exposed look. Her newly dyed maroon hair clashes with the pink, but I say nothing. I value my life, after all.

At last, we all trundle into my dad's eight-seater car, arguing over who has to climb into the back. None of us want to risk messing up our outfits. In the end, Mum shoves us aside and gets into the back herself so the three of us can sit in the middle whilst Nani, as always, rides shotgun.

Thankfully, the drive is short as the event is at a banqueting hall in Wood Green that every other Asian in a ten-mile radius hires for their wedding reception. There's lots of squealing, hugs and air kisses as we enter the main hall and bump into relatives we haven't seen since the last family wedding in December. Everyone is dressed in their finest with jewellery dripping from every available outlet; big, dangly earrings, headpieces, forehead tiklis, rings, bracelets, armlets, anklets and even jewellery you can clip onto your hair.

You know how at English weddings it's considered bad form to wear white? Well, Bengalis have no such qualms and you'll always find one woman dressed in her own wedding outfit. Sometimes you can't even notice it because it looks like another red saree. Today, however, it's glaringly obvious because not only is the woman wearing a red and gold saree that is so heavy she can barely move, but she is also wearing what is clearly her wedding gold, right down to the nose hoop that is connected by a gold chain to her earlobe.

My sisters, cousins and I grab a table in the middle of the hall as it's the perfect location from which to spot potential suitors. Mum and Nani head off to mingle with guests their own age.

There are ten of us at the table; us three sisters, three of my elder uncle's four children (Kamal, Madiha and Ridhwaan) and all four of my younger uncle's children (Rashid, Jannah, Samia and Ameera). Within minutes we're all laughing away at Kamal's jokes and Rashid's one-liners and, for a moment, I forget that I'm supposed to act respectable and demure like a suitable prospective daughter-in-law. The only cousin who's missing is Sabina, who lives in Dubai.

I'm sitting next to Samia, my twenty-five year-old cousin, who I'm closest to after Sabina. Although Samia's closer in age to Amina, the two of them seem to rub each other up the wrong way. They're both too ambitious and highly strung, always competing or arguing. They also both work for non-profits, and Amina can't seem to help dropping in the fact that she's more qualified than Samia, whenever they talk turkey.

Samia and I don't see each other that much since she lives and works in Luton, but we chat on the phone pretty much every week. We start catching up on every-thing that's happened since we last spoke, and I fill her in on the biodata, MuslimMate and the chocolate event.

'To be honest, you should have let Fufu make you a biodata a long time ago,' she says and, as always, I feel as though she's older than me, instead of four years younger.

'Yeah, well, it's taken me a while to get my head around marriage again after what happened,' I say quietly, so the boys on the table don't overhear.

'You think you're ready now?'

'Yeah. I am. I'm nearly thirty. If I want time to find someone, get married, and have a couple of years together before kids, I need to do it now.' She nods, and I ask her if her parents have started looking for her, as she's the eldest of her siblings.

'Not really,' she replies vaguely. 'It's on their radar, but I'm not in a hurry. Anyway, I'm off to Zimbabwe next week for two months, so I'm not even gonna think about it until I get back.'

It doesn't take long for other relatives to start dropping by our table to ask intrusive questions or make distasteful comments. At first, it's not too bad and I handle it like a boss. But they keep coming and each remark is beginning to feel like a bullet. One granny tells me that I'm getting old, one tells me that my colouring has become 'dirty' and another tells me that I've put on weight. And that isn't even the worst of it.

The worst is when Mum brings an aunty over and not-so-subtly presents me to her, rambling on about how great I am at cooking and how I'm such an obedient and perfect daughter. My cousins all snigger and giggle as mum tells lie after lie to try and sell me to this woman. She might as well stick a price tag on my face, the way she pitches me to her.

'Boish khotoh?' the aunty asks, and Mum stumbles a little before plastering a fake smile on her face and telling her that I'm twenty-nine.

'Yallah go mai, ita oitoh nai,' the aunty exclaims in dismay. 'Damandor boish matro shataish!'

The groom is only twenty-seven? So why is my mum even putting me through this ordeal? My cheeks have turned red. I know they have because the heat is so intense that I'm certain my makeup is about to melt off. Oblivious to the embarrassment she's inflicting on me, the aunty peers at Samia and asks my mum how old *she* is. Mum's expression freezes, and when she tells her that she's twenty-five, the aunty beams and starts quizzing Sam about her future plans.

The confidence I felt this morning begins to seep out of my pores. Who was I kidding, trying to make myself look attractive? I've met three distant cousins a similar age to me who, last year, were single and this year are either engaged or married. There's obviously something wrong with me. Why else am I still alone?

'Excuse me,' I mumble, getting up. 'I need the bathroom.'

'I'll join you,' Sam gathers up the folds of her saree so she can also get up. Then, 'Ignore them,' she says as we walk across the hall. 'You know what busybodies they are. Always sticking their nose in other peoples' business.'

I say nothing.

As we approach the doors to the foyer, I catch the eye of a tall, very good-looking guy in a three-piece suit. He must be from the groom's side because I've never seen him before. Even though I'm still reeling from all the questioning, I feel my spirits begin to lift. From the way he's looking at me, maybe I'm not such a hideous old hag after all.

So, I do what every girl at a Bengali wedding would do in my situation; I look away, force my expression into one of aloof indifference, push my shoulders back and catwalk past him like a Brazilian supermodel.

At least, that's what I try to do. I end up stepping on Samia's saree, causing her to buckle and let out an ungodly shriek. Gasping in horror, I try to grab her arm but she falls to her knees and I stumble. My first instinct is to let go of Samia and run. Anywhere. But if I do, someone else is going to have to help her up and she will never forgive me.

My face bright pink, I pull her back up and she glares at me, too angry to say anything. Her hijab and head jewellery askew, she grits her teeth and limps out of the room, clutching on to the parts of the saree that have come undone. I follow her, but not before I spot the look of amusement on the guy's face.

'What the hell was that!' Samia explodes the minute we enter the restroom. She whips around to look in the mirror and upon seeing her dishevelled appearance, turns a scary shade of purple. I gulp and offer to help sort it out.

'You don't even know how to put on a saree!' she hisses and starts fixing it herself. I'm too scared to start reapplying my lippy now, so I hang back with a guilty look on my face.

'Sorry,' I mumble when she's finally sorted herself out. 'I got a bit carried away.'

'Carried away doing what?' she demands, giving me a look. She appears to be slightly calmer now so I tell her about the guy and my epic fail to ignore him and look cool and mysterious.

'Well, the illusion is shattered,' she sighs, and I smile wryly back, dreading the fact that I have to walk back in there.

We leave the bathroom and linger around the foyer for a while, still working up the courage to head back into the hall. On one side there is a drinks station set up with fresh juices and mocktails, and a gelato stand with a range of different flavours. On the other, there are two stalls, one with a lady dressed in a bright green saree wrapping up fresh paan with betelnuts and all the traditional accompaniments; and the other, a skinny man frying up chana choor mixed with lemon juice, chilli, fresh onions and coriander. The fragrance of the chillies and lemon is too good to resist, and since it's already two and neither lunch nor the bride are anywhere in sight, I help myself to a little cone and dig in. Samia doesn't want to look greedy or drop any on her clothes so decides to swallow her embarrassment and go back to our table.

A group of drummers dressed in white sherwanis burst into the building and start pounding a traditional Punjabi beat. Their energy is infectious and immediately everyone in the hall (apart from the really old or really religious) stands up and starts clapping to the beat.

The huge bridal party follows in a haze of pink. In the middle of all her siblings and cousins is the bride, looking absolutely breathtaking in a white raw silk lengha covered in crystals, carrying a pretty floral bouquet. I have no idea how she's managing to walk with the stone-encrusted dupatta weighing down on her complicated updo and the long train of her skirt. She is clutching on to her dad for dear life and is looking downwards, as is the custom for Bengali brides. You can't look too happy, you see. If you do, everyone will think you've had a love marriage and couldn't care a toss about leaving the safety of your parental home.

After the bride and groom unite on the stage and exchange flower garlands, we finally get to eat. The food, as always, is the main event at our weddings and everyone tucks in as though they haven't eaten in days. Except me. I'm too afraid of dropping curry onto my expensive saree and humiliating myself even more than I already have done.

The happy couple also eat during this time, and I notice how ecstatic they both look. There was a time in the not-so-distant past when Bengali girls didn't meet their future husbands until their wedding day; and even then, they were too shy/respectful/scared to glance at the man they would be expected to share a bed with. They would sit there, dressed in beautifully adorned red silk sarees with red dupattas draped low over their heads and faces. Their vision obscured, they wouldn't dare to look up even when feeding their new life-partner mishti. I've lost count of the number of wedding photos I've seen where the bride is looking in one direction, and her arm is pointed in another as she reluctantly brings rasmalai to her husband's lips.

By the time my siblings and cousins have stuffed their faces (and I mean stuffed – they had to refill our platters twice), everyone can barely move. Kamal and Rashid undo their trouser buttons as they sit back with huge grins on their satisfied faces.

The speeches are lame as they always are. I don't know why Bengalis bother with speeches. You can never hear a thing over the endless chatter of all the elders, the kids running riot and the servers clanging cutlery as though they're playing steel pans. Half the people in the room don't get the 'English' humour either and most of the jokes fall flat. When the bride and groom finally cut the cake, somehow, we all manage to find space in our stomachs to eat a slice or two.

When Mum and Nani drag me over to yet another table to meet yet another aunty I've never seen before, I'm well and truly ready to go home. My feet are hurting, my makeup's melting and I'm tired of smiling. I'm tired of telling people I'm twenty-nine years old only to see instant judgement and pity in their eyes. I'm tired of no one understanding what I actually do for a living, and I'm *bloody* tired of this whole stupid wedding with its stupid forest theme and stupid perfect bride.

There is a flurry of activity in the hall and I look up to see that it's the part of Bengali weddings that I hate – the 'biddai' – which literally translates to 'farewell'.

This is always the most emotional part of the day. It's when the girl officially leaves her parents' house to join another family; when she's no longer a daughter, but a wife and daughter-in-law; when she's traditionally expected to prioritise her husband and her in-laws before her own family.

With all that looming ahead, it's no wonder the entire bridal party is in tears. When the bride's dad kisses her on the forehead and whispers something to her while she weeps, even I feel like crying.

There are more tears and finally the bride, with mascara-streaked cheeks and bloodshot eyes, climbs into the Rolls-Royce Phantom where the groom is sheepishly waiting. He's supressing a massive grin in an attempt to be sympathetic, but he is clearly besotted and cannot wait to get out of here with his new wife. I mean, if he's anything like Layla, then there's a reason why he's so eager to fast-forward to the wedding night.

As the car doors close, I see him hand her his white silk handkerchief and give her arm a gentle squeeze. She looks at him gratefully and her sadness slips away when he says something reassuring to her.

The moment is intimate and beautiful and I feel guilty for noticing it. A lump swells up in the back of my throat. Will I ever find a love like this? Actually, forget love, I'm not naïve enough to think that I'll fall in love with my husband before we get married. Will I ever find a person who cares enough about me to hold me while I wipe my waterproof mascara all over his expensive white clothes? Will I ever find someone who will look at me as if I'm the most beautiful, precious thing in the whole world? Will I ever find someone who will look after me more than my parents?

And then, right there, in the crowd of people waving goodbye, I burst into tears.

Chapter 5

I feel a huge sense of relief when Monday rolls along. If I ever have to look at a saree again, I think I might strangle someone with it. On the way home from the wedding, Mum and Nani kept exchanging worried looks and then glancing over at me, as if they were afraid that I had officially lost my mind. I kept reassuring everyone that I was fine and when that didn't work, resorted to the old PMT excuse. Even though I'm not due on for a while.

Monday mornings are usually pretty hectic at work. We have a cross-departmental meeting with Marketing and PR, followed by our own quick huddle setting out our priorities for the week. That doesn't stop Adam, Francesca and me from sharing a packet of biscuits and having a long chat about our weekends, though. It's become an important Monday tradition, almost as important as the meeting itself.

'How was your weekend then?' I ask Fran as Adam goes to refill our tea mugs.

'Wild,' she admits. 'I think I slept about three hours in total. I feel like shit.'

She doesn't look like shit. She never does. Everyone can tell when I haven't slept by the grease in my hair and the circles under my eyes. Not Francesca Robinson, though. Her blonde mane is as glossy as if it's been combed a thousand times with a brush made from unicorn fibres, and the only things that ever rim her baby blue eyes are expensive designer glasses, which I recently found out are purely for fashion purposes.

'Mine was a mad one as well,' Adam says, catching the last part of her story as he rejoins us, carefully balancing three mugs of steaming tea.

'Why, what happened?' I asked, dunking a Hobnob into mine.

'It was my cousin Aygul's thirtieth birthday party. It started off normal, you know, loads of food, the kids running around the house wrecking everything . . .'

'And then?' I probe, looking forward to hearing the rest. Adam always has the best stories.

'Then, my bastard sixteen-year-old cousin Ahmet, spiked the mocktails, so when we thought we were taking a break from the alcohol, we weren't. Everyone got completely smashed, even my mum. Even my gran! I haven't seen her like that in years! She got up and started dancing like it was 1973, then knocked into the birthday cake and ruined the whole thing!'

Fran and I laugh as he pulls out his phone and shows us videos of destroyed cake, sitting on the floor in a heap of fresh cream and vanilla sponge.

When it's my turn, I 'fess up about the wedding, how I burst into tears like a hormonal adolescent, and how people said I had put on weight and that my complexion was 'moila'. I omit the bit about my cousin being chosen over me.

'What does "moila" mean?' Adam asks, confused.

'It literally means "dirty," bu—' Before I can explain the meaning in this context, he interrupts me.

'I can't believe people came up to you and told you you've put on weight! And that you're dirty!' he exclaims indignantly. I expected him to laugh or take the mick, but he actually looks horrified.

'Hang on a second,' I cut in, before any rumours of my hygiene start circulating. 'They didn't call me dirty. They said my complexion is "moila". In Bengali it doesn't sound that bad.'

'Well, it sounds bad in English,' Fran looks perplexed in that way politically correct white people do when they don't want to offend you or your culture. 'You have a nice colouring. I pay good money and spend hours under sunbeds to look like you!'

'And you're not fat, either, so get that out of your head,' Adam adds.

'Er, OK.' I'm not used to Adam saying anything nice to me or about me, so I'm not sure how to take it. I study his face, wondering if he's winding me up, but he looks serious.

'And you're not old,' he continues, clearly on a roll. 'I've got loads of aunties in Turkey who are, like, in their forties and unmarried and childless—'

Spotting the startled look on my face, he hurriedly adds, 'I meant, you're not even old. You're twenty-nine, big deal. Who wants to marry an immature kid who doesn't have a clue about life, anyway?'

'When did you become such a Zara fan?' I tease, when he finally stops ranting.

'Shut up,' he grumbles, swivelling his chair around and opening up InDesign on his Mac. 'Be thankful I'm looking out for you.'

'And maybe you need to find a husband a different way?' Francesca adds. 'That wedding sounds like a complete circus!'

'Don't worry, I am. I've actually signed up to a Muslim marriage app,' I admit before I can stop myself. As soon as it's out of my mouth, I regret it. One nice moment doesn't mean I can trust Adam with this sort of info about my personal life. He swivels back round again, his mouth agape.

'You're seriously going to date men online? You know they're all after one thing, right?'

'It's not a *dating* app, it's a *marriage* app,' I say slowly, enunciating every word like I'm talking to someone thick. 'The guys on there are looking for wives, not hook-ups.' *Well, most of them*, I say in my head, remembering what Yasmin told me about her friends.

'Give me a break,' he snorts. 'It's horse shit dressed as manure.'

'Pretty sure horse shit *is* manure, Adam.'

'Speaking of which, I need the loo,' he says, getting up and stretching dramatically before leaving the room. I roll my eyes and turn back to Francesca.

'He's got a point, Zara,' she says. 'You should see the guys I come across online. As soon as they get my number, boom! They feel the need to show me pics of their bits.'

Now it's my jaw's turn to drop. 'That's disgusting!' I gasp. 'Why would they do that?'

'Oh, they do it all the time.' She shrugs breezily. 'All men are the same, babes. They're all narcissists, gagging for positive affirmation. Haven't you had any from that Muslim dating app you're on?'

'No! But then, I've only been on it once since I created the account and I've not checked out the profiles or anything.'

'What? No way! Open it now!'

'Right now?' I look around the office to see if Kevin is nearby. It's only been a week since I swore never to open the app at work. 'What if Kevin comes in?'

'So what? He doesn't care what we do, so long as we get our work done.'

'Oh, all right then.' With one last furtive glance around the room, I open up the app and stare in shock at the thousands of 'likes' I have.

'Ooooh, look at you, Miss Popular,' Fran teases. 'That's a LOT of likes!'

'But they can't even see my photo,' I tell her, completely confused. 'Why would they like my profile if they haven't even seen what I look like?'

Francesca shrugs. 'I dunno, but you need to press the tick or cross, I think. If you press the cross, their profile vanishes and if you tick it, they probably get to message you.'

One thing that becomes increasingly clear as I sift through the profiles is that all these men who supposedly 'like' me haven't even bothered to read my profile properly. The privacy is set so that men can't see women's pictures unless a woman 'likes' him back and then agrees to reveal the image, so I'm beginning to think that whenever a new female profile appears on the site, they all go wild and hit 'like' randomly in the hopes of receiving one back.

And you know what that means, right? More than half of them are way too old or young for me, most are shorter than me, and the ones that are the right age and height admit that they drink or don't eat halal food. So now I'm inundated with profiles of unsuitable men that I have to manually check out one by one before I can hit 'no' and remove them from my sight. I do this for about ten minutes, getting more and more pissed off as I do, but there are still hundreds to go.

'Bloody bastards,' I mutter under my breath, my agitation increasing with every 'x'.

'Talk about slim pickings,' Francesca muses, peering over my shoulder. 'There's not one decent prospect here.'

Adam returns from the toilet and he also joins in, making rude comments about every single man.

'He looks like a serial killer,' he says when the first half-decent profile comes up, of a clean-shaven guy from Uzbekistan with bright blue eyes and thin lips.

'No, he doesn't,' I protest weakly, glancing up to check Fran's opinion.

'He does,' she confirms. 'He looks like the type that will smother you in your sleep.'

A good thirty minutes of declining later, just as I'm beginning to go cross-eyed, I stumble across a profile that looks interesting. Both Adam and Francesca have grown bored and gone off to do what we're paid for. I'm relieved because if Adam says he looks like a drug addict, and if Fran agrees, I'm likely to throw my phone out of the window and become the Muslim equivalent of a nun. Not that there is one. Getting married is considered to be half of our faith.

I read the profile.

MrMoneyMaker. 31. London. 5'10". Bengali. Sunni. Moderately practising. Always eats halal. Never drinks or smokes. Sometimes prays.

He's not the best-looking guy on the planet but he's definitely attractive in that sharp, brooding kind of way. I decide to read on.

I don't care how beautiful you are, if your personality is ugly, you're ugly simple!

> Like banter. Not on here for time-wasters.
> Sleep is for tortoises. Into kickboxing and foot-
> ball. Shoots zombies in spare time. The word fun
> has been ruined. Films and food is life. Slightly
> smarter than a sophisticated root vegetable.

Erm. OK, then. I'm not really sure of what to make of that. The guy sounds like he's had a bad experience, and is a bit unhinged. But he's taller than me. The right age. Doesn't drink. Eats halal food. All-right looking. And he doesn't look like a murderer. After a moment's hesitation, I decide I have nothing to lose, so I hit 'like'.

I've had enough of this cesspit of a dating pool, but as I'm about to close the app, a notification comes through. It's a message, from MrMoneyMaker. As much as I loathe to admit it, I feel a stirring of excitement, wondering what his opening line is going to be.

> Hi, Zara, I'm Mo. You made the right choice in
> liking me. What are you up to? Can I see your
> picture?

OK, so he's decided to get straight to the point then. I feel a bit put out that there's no banter, no flirting, but I guess he doesn't want to waste time.

'Have you found a good profile?' Francesca pipes up from across the room and I hush her, my eyes darting over to Kevin's closed door. She casually comes up behind me and looks over my shoulder, pretending to look at some work. Adam glances at me with narrowed eyes, but doesn't get up, and I'm glad.

'Ooh, he's a bit of an all right, isn't he?' she whispers. I show her his message, unsure of whether or not I should share my picture.

'Do it!' she hisses. 'Why wouldn't you?'

Sure, I reply back and then go through the options until I figure out how to 'un-blur' my image so he can see what I look like – in good lighting, with my spots and lines edited out.

MO: You're gorgeous.

ME: Thanks

MO: Do you want to meet up?

ME: Um, can we talk a bit first? I don't really know that much about you.

MO: Well you liked my profile . . .

ME: Mostly because you're taller than me.

MO: Mostly?

ME: Well, you're all-right looking as well, I suppose.

Oh my God! Have I flirted with a random stranger online? A blush creeps up my neck as I eagerly await his reply, completely forgetting that Francesca is standing right there.

MO: I'll take that as a compliment.

'Oooh, look at you!' she teases, going back to her seat. 'Our Zara has graduated to the first base of online dating,' she tells Adam.

'What the hell is first base?' he demands, a look of disgust on his face.

'Flirting via messages, duh,' she responds, like it's the most obvious answer in the world. They start bickering and I ignore them and look back at my phone instead.

And that's how I find myself drawn into a never-ending text conversation with a total stranger. Call me a late bloomer, but it's the first time I've experienced anything like it. I was never the type to go on chatrooms as a teenager or speak to randoms over MSN Messenger, and boy, do I regret it or what? I was completely missing out.

We message each other throughout the rest of the work day. Not every second – I do some work and I think he does too – but every so often, my phone pings and my heart lifts just a little. We chat on the bus home, throughout dinner, and while I'm watching TV with Nani. She's too engrossed in the Hindi drama she's watching about an evil daughter-in-law trying to murder her mother-in-law, to realise that I'm paying more attention to my phone than the show.

Now, snuggled up under the covers in the middle of the night, I'm finding the whole experience oddly liberating and I wish I had done more of this during my youth. This guy doesn't know me. He doesn't have my number or my email address. The anonymity is refreshing and I find myself slipping into the romance and anticipation as I lose my inhibitions with each cheeky innuendo, anxiously awaiting the next message to come my way.

I find out that MrMoneyMaker is in fact called Mo, aka Mohammed. He's thirty-one. An investment banker. Bengali. Lives in Cambridge with his mum, who's a widow. But aside from all the important stuff, he also writes well, which surprises me given his badly written profile intro.

Adam texts me at some point that evening, asking me how it's going with Mo, but I'm too engrossed to reply. At four in the morning I decide to call it a night.

ME: Mo. I need to sleep
MO: Can I join you?
ME: Er . . . – no!
MO: ☹ dream of me then, beautiful. Night x

Chapter 6

'What base are we on now?' Francesca asks as soon as she comes into the office the next day. I yawn in response and she laughs before heading off to the kitchen for a round of tea. Adam turns and stares at me and I shrug at him.

'What?'

'Been sexting all night, have you?' he jibes and I narrow my eyes at him. There's something in his expression – judgement maybe – which is making me feel defensive.

'No, it's not like that, thank you very much.'

'If you say so.'

When Francesca returns with three steaming mugs on a tea-stained tray, I take one from her in relief and she deposits Adam's one on his desk before coming back to my desk and hovering over me.

'So? How's it going? Met any more potentials?'

'Nah, just been chatting to Mo,' I admit, and she gasps in mock horror. 'Well, Hamza texted this morning as well, asking me how I am, but that's it.'

'Zara, that's really not the point of online dating. You're supposed to bang it out, you know? Date 'em quickly, and chuck 'em aside if they're not the One.'

'I don't know if I can do that, it feels wrong.'

'It *is* wrong,' Adam chimes in.

'It's *not*,' Fran insists. 'Trust me, he's doing the same thing.'

I'm exhausted when I get in from work that evening, not least because of the online shenanigans that lasted half the night. We've got an event coming up in the spring, and some stallholders have cancelled, so Francesca and I spent most of the day trying to entice businesses into booking a space.

Kicking off my shoes and leaving them haphazardly in the hallway, I start making my way to the sanctuary that is my bedroom, but Mum hears me and pulls me into the kitchen. She's in the middle of cooking dinner and is wearing an apron with her greying hair pulled back in a severe bun. The hairstyle, together with the way she's waving her chopping knife around makes me feel a bit anxious. Why can't she wait until dinnertime to talk to me, when I have the safety of the others around should things get a bit dangerous?

'Right, Zara, we need to have an important talk,' she announces, staring down at me.

'Erm, OK,' I begin warily. 'But can I take my coat off first? And change my clothes? I don't want them to smell of curry.'

'Fine. But come right back down.'

'What's up?' I ask nonchalantly when I return in my trackies and collapse onto the dining chair. I study the plastic tablecloth with the odd curry stain that won't come out as I wait for Mum to join me. She gives the three curries she's whipped up for dinner a quick stir and then sits down across from me. She doesn't speak for ages though, and when I peek up, I see that she looks about as uncomfortable as I feel.

'How are you?' she asks, a small frown on her face. Mum's always frowning, which is why it's quite miraculous that her complexion is relatively smooth and youthful. People are always mistaking her for our older sister. Beige don't age, and all that.

'Er . . . fine,' I reply, stifling a yawn. All I want to do is have my dinner and go and collapse onto my bed and maybe chat to Mo, instead of being held hostage in the kitchen. 'Why? What's going on?'

'Look, I know I've put a lot of pressure on you by suggesting that we start looking at grooms from Desh before you hit the dreaded three-oh—'

'I think you mean "threatening" not "suggesting",' I interject, my eyebrows raised.

'I didn't threaten you! I just said that we need to broaden our search, that's all. Time being of the essence, and so on. Anyway, your dad seems to think that your tears at the wedding were because I'm pressuring you too much.'

She stops talking and pauses, as if waiting for me to jump in and tell her that Abbu's wrong and she has done no such thing. I don't.

'Well. Anyway. I wanted to have a chat with you because there are a few candidates in the pipeline and if you want to slow down or anything, now's the chance to let me know. Once I've confirmed with them, that's it, there's no going back.'

'Look, Mum,' I begin, breathing deeply to calm my agitated nerves. 'I got a bit emotional at the wedding because it had been a really challenging day, but I'm OK now. I'm not some delicate flower that's going to crumple at the thought of sitting through a few awkward meetings. I'm also well aware of the fact that I'm growing older every day, OK? Just so you know, I've got my own things in the "pipeline" too.'

I throw in that last bit to show her that she's not the only proactive one in the room. She looks surprised.

'What do you mean, "things in the pipeline"? You can't go around meeting people willy-nilly without my approval!'

'Yes I can, Mum. I'm nearly thirty, as you pointed out. I can't rely on you and Network Aunty to find me someone. What if you don't find anyone? Then what will I do? Live with you forever?'

There is a silence as Mum ponders my reasoning. I can tell by her expression that she knows I'm right, but she'll never admit it.

'OK, well if anything gets serious you must let me know,' she reluctantly agrees after a while. 'And in the meantime, your dad and I will carry on getting the word out.'

'Fine.'

'Great! On that note, we've received a couple of biodatas and need to decide whether or not we want your one sent to them, too. Your dad has one on his phone and I've got the other one here.'

Mum hands me an A4 sheet and goes back to the cooker to check on her curries. The fragrances wafting out of her stainless steel saucepans are making my stomach rumble, so I join her and lift a piece of lamb out of one pot and stuff it in my mouth before she can tell me off. It scalds my tongue and I squeal. Serves me right for being so greedy.

'Serves you right for being so greedy,' Mum says, handing me a glass of water, and I'm reminded of how alike we are at times, a thought that sends a shiver down my spine.

I go back to the table and feign reluctance as I take hold of the paper, but I'm secretly quite curious to see who's on offer. I feel as though I'm at a fine dining restaurant and the waiter has come to tell me what today's specials are.

Scanning through the page, I read that Iqbal is a thirty-year-old computer engineer. He's 5'9", has four sisters and is the only son. His dad is a retired business owner (code for ex-restaurateur), and his mum is a housewife. I turn the page over to be assaulted by a collage of pictures of him. There's a cringey selfie, one full-length one of him posing alone in a three-piece suit and another one of him in the same suit, but this time with a group of girls who I assume are his sisters. They're all short, skinny, really fair-skinned with huge hijabs on their heads that make them look like little lollipops. They're wearing matching sarees and look so perfect that I immediately know I won't fit in.

Feeling queasy, I study the smug expression in all his pictures. He looks like a typical Bengali boy from East London, with shiny black hair, slick with gel, a little goatee and smooth, dark skin. For a second I wonder why he's darker than his sisters. Are they all wearing foundation that's three shades lighter? Or perhaps they edited themselves in the picture. Or maybe he's their half-brother because their dad has multiple wives. None of those scenarios are acceptable to me.

I say all this out loud and Mum gives me a deadly look.

'You know there are people out there judging your biodata and picture the way you're judging them, right?'

'It's different if I do it,' I mutter a little illogically. 'I'm a woman. I'm more vulnerable and I will always be judged ten times more harshly than a man.'

'Only God can judge,' Mum sniffs.

I look at the picture again. I can tell that he loves himself. I turn the paper over to check where he lives. Yep – Tower Hamlets. No surprise there. So much for fine dining, this is more like our local Perfect Fried Chicken.

'Well, what do you think?' Mum asks as she gets started on the usual salad of finely chopped tomatoes, cucumbers, onions, green chillies and coriander to accompany the curries. 'And don't give me any nonsense about his sisters being a different colour to him. Take this seriously please.'

I shake my head, taking a huge gulp of water. 'Mum, look at his hair! Look at his tight suit! Look at his over-dressed sisters! I'm really not feeling it.'

Mum sighs. I can tell that she's dying to give me a shake but she needs to appeal to my logic to get me on board. 'I know it's not the perfect proposal and he's not even from a great family (which, in Mum-ish, is code for not being from a good caste), but it's not bad. What's the harm in meeting him? He might be completely different in real life. Not everyone photographs well.'

'He's a computer guy,' I continue with growing fervour. 'I hate computers. The only thing I know what to do on a computer is open up Word and Chrome!'

'Well, maybe it's time you learnt more about them,' Mum responds primly, taking out dishes to set the table with. She gestures for me to help her.

'But he's from Tower Hamlets,' I whine, a pained expression on my face as I begin to set the table. 'I can't even speak Bengali properly. You can tell by looking at him that all his friends are Bengali.'

'So what? Do you think you're better than him because you're from North London?' Mum whips around from the cooker and gives me a look so dirty that a weaker person would probably turn into stone.

'No,' I lie, looking away. 'We're from two different planets.'

'Well, right now you're on Planet Nearly Thirty. Unless you want to stay there forever, you need to keep your options open.'

'I don't see what the big deal is about turning thirty!' I reply, crossing my arms defiantly. 'Why has it got you in such a tizzy? There are loads of people older than me who aren't married!'

'And why do you think that is? It's because they left it too late.'

'What if I don't want to ever get married?'

'Don't you?'

'I didn't say I didn't, I said "what if"! Are you going to disown me or something?'

'Of course not, stop being such a drama queen.' Her dismissive tone pisses me off even more. Noticing the two spots of pink growing on my cheeks she sighs, putting down the dish she's carrying.

'Look, Zara, it's not that we don't want you around, there's nothing I would love more than keeping my girls with me forever. But it's not about me, it's about you. I know you think you know more than me because I never studied and never had a career, but if there's one thing I know about better than you, it's our culture and community.'

I snort, and she continues. 'As soon as you hit thirty, that's it – the proposals will start dwindling. Whereas previously you had five, now you might have one. It'll get harder and harder and then before you know it, you're thirty-six and then you'll agree to marry the first semi-decent man who's interested, even if he's not from a good family, even if he doesn't have a good job, even if he lives with his whole family, even if you're not particularly attracted to him. Remember what happened to Fahima? And I don't want that for you. I want you to have options.'

As she goes on and on, I find my resolve wearing thin. Because deep down, I know she's right.

'Fine. Send my biodata to them,' I mutter, pushing my chair back and standing up. 'I don't know why you even bothered to ask me.'

Unable to meet my mum's triumphant gaze, I turn around and go back upstairs.

I've been moping about in my room for over an hour. I feel silly for letting my mum's words affect me so much, but at the same time, I feel angry. Why is my family so messed up sometimes? You'd think after living outside Bangladesh for so long we would have evolved a bit, that women would be seen as more than wives and mothers. To be fair, not all families are the same. In fact, mine is much less traditional than many. But even so, we still eat Bengali food, wear Bengali clothes, follow Bengali traditions. Look at my mum: she grew up in the UK but even she doesn't believe that my life is *my* life. Our lives are only partly ours, the rest belongs to our entire family, extended included. And when we get married, they belong to our husbands and in-laws as well.

My phone beeps and I summon the energy to glance at it. When I see that the sender is Mo, I perk up instantly.

All right gorgeous, how's your day been?

I wonder if I should make something up to sound interesting and alluring, but I find myself being honest.

Pretty crap, I type back. I'm not expecting him to reply immediately, so I go to toss the phone onto the bed when I see that there's a response. The feeling that he's been waiting for me to come onto the app is empowering and my mood begins to brighten.

What can I do to make it better?

Ooh, er. A slow smile spreads across my face but before I can even think of a witty reply, there is a sharp rap on the door and Yasmin comes in holding two mugs of hot chocolate. Plonking them down onto my dressing table, she throws herself onto the bed next to me. I quickly exit the app and rearrange my smile into a scowl.

'You missed dinner,' she states, shoving my legs to one side so there's more room for her. I grunt in response, staring at the hot chocolate. I'm starving but I don't want to admit it.

'What do you want?' I ask after a while. I'd rather she gets whatever it is that's bothering her off her chest so she can go away and leave me in peace.

'Abbu wants me to show you a biodata,' she admits. 'He and Mum are too scared to show you themselves so they sent me.'

'So now the little runt is braver than the pack leader?' I say with a wry smile, turning to face her. She's eight years younger than me, but somehow seems so much more mature and sorted than I am. She's always on top of everything; uni, internships, family stuff, her social life, and she makes it look easy, she's always chill. Unlike Amina, who despite being utterly brilliant and one of the smartest people I know, is always stressing about something or another.

I say this out loud and she chuckles.

'Me? Sorted? That's only because I'm at a stage where I know what I'm doing and I don't have to think beyond my next exam. Once uni's finished, if I can't find a job, or if I'm single in a few years' time, I'm sure I'll be as fagol as you are.'

She's probably right. I wasn't as crazy at twenty-one as I am now. At twenty-one, I was on top of the world. I was doing well at uni, I had loads of great friends, I was attractive and guys were always asking me out. I thought I had my pick. I thought I had all the time in the world.

'You *still* have time,' she reassures me, shifting over and putting her arm around me. 'Don't let Mum and

Abbu pressure you into doing anything you're not comfortable with.'

'Well, to be fair, I'm not comfortable with any of it; biodatas, marriage meetings or even dates.' I sigh, nestling into her. 'Especially after Tariq. But I need to be.'

We sit in silence for a while, sipping our hot chocolate and enjoying the rare stillness of the evening. Up here at the top of the house, you can't hear a thing that's going on downstairs. Mum has probably forced Amina to wash up, and she's passive-aggressively demonstrating her reluctance by clanging the dishes around. Abbu will have retired to the living room where he'll be watching Al Jazeera, while Mum puts all the food away since Yas and I are up here. Nani is more than likely sitting with Abbu folding up a little paan triangle filled with chopped betelnut to munch on. She'll offer one to Abbu as she always does, and he'll refuse and take some of the fillings instead. My dad isn't your standard old Bengali man. He doesn't chew paan, doesn't smoke, doesn't even drink tea. My mum is the same – except for the tea part – but then, that's the Brit in her, not the Bengali. She came to the UK when she was only six and is one of the few Bengali women her age that speaks the Queen's English and prefers roast dinners over curries.

'Go on then, let's have a look,' I concede. Yasmin hands my dad's phone over to me and, bracing myself, I open up the file and scan through the words. Farook Chowdhury. Thirty-three. 5'10". Dentist. Blah blah blah.

He's OK-looking, a bit nerdy with his old-fashioned glasses and dodgy haircut. His outfit choice is dubious, too. He's wearing a white lab coat with a stethoscope round his neck. Hang on, I thought he was a dentist? What does he need a stethoscope for? To listen to people's teeth?

I show the picture to Yas, who starts cracking up.

'He's like the dentist from *The Hangover*, who keeps saying he's a doctor,' she splutters. I shove her but can't help giggling myself.

'Watch it, this could be your future dhulabhai,' I tease, and she makes a mock horror face.

'No way, you can do better than that! Even Hamza must be better than him!'

'Oi, don't talk about Hamza like that, he's not that bad!' I thump her with the pillow while she holds up her arms to block her face, still laughing.

My bedroom door swings open again and Amina stomps in.

'What's so funny?' she demands with a scowl. 'I thought you were too depressed to even eat? I had to do all the bloody cleaning up.' She squeezes herself onto the bed and we show her the biodata. She's not impressed by the guy or our amusement.

'You're not going to send your details, are you?' she exclaims, tossing the phone aside and looking at me intently. 'You're more than some ovaries, Z. You don't need a man to complete you.'

I'm not surprised by Amina's reaction. She's made it clear to everyone – Mum and Abbu included – that she has no interest in marriage until she's had a fulfilling career, and will only do it for love, not something as insignificant as dehydrated ovaries. That won't stop my mum from hounding her the moment I'm married, though.

'Er, I totally will send them,' I admit with a shrug as both my sisters exchange pitying glances. 'Look, he's a Choudhury. He's educated. He's taller than me. He's not bad looking once you get over the glasses and the hair style – both of which can be rectified. He ticks a lot of boxes.'

'Since when did you become so pragmatic?' Amina says, folding her arms across her chest. Everything about her oozes disapproval and I feel my skin prickling defensively.

'Since I turned twenty-nine,' I snap. 'I hope neither of you have to go through what I'm going through when you get to my age.'

'I don't even want to get married!' Amina retorts haughtily. 'I don't need a man bringing me down, telling me what to do, stopping me from progressing in my career to have his offspring. No thanks.'

'I'll go and tell Mum and Abbu the good news, shall I?' Yasmin interrupts, jumping off my bed and making a swift exit before the conversation turns into an argument.

'I hope you know what you're doing,' Amina says darkly before leaving the room herself.

Of course I bloody don't. But at least there are now three prospective husbands on the scene, four if you include Mo. I'd better write a list before I get confused between them all. I take my phone out and get creating said list when it buzzes; a message from Hamza. I'm a little surprised since I still haven't replied to this morning's text. I thought that the ball being in my court would buy me a little time. Evidently, he doesn't play by the rules.

Salaam, Z, you OK? What are you up to this weekend?

I'm not sure if I want to see him this weekend. Once the high from eating all that delicious food and coming home in an Uber I didn't have to pay for wore off, I was back to feeling like Hamza and I weren't suitable. Anyhow, now that there are three other men on the scene . . .

Adam's sneery voice asking me if I'll drop Hamza like a hot potato the moment a better opportunity arises comes back to me. Is that what I'm about to do?

I write back,

Hey, Hamza, Good, thanks, how are you? I've got a lot of stuff going on this weekend. Maybe the week after?

That sounds nice enough, right? It's friendly, not an outright rejection as I've suggested an alternative, but makes it clear that I'm nowhere near head-over-heels.

His response comes within seconds.

Sure, next week sounds great!

Chapter 7

The following Monday, I'm really feeling the hours of sleep I've missed out on because of my text convos with Mo. The weekend was no exception – in fact, it was even worse because I tried to do what Francesca advised and speak to multiple men on the app at the same time. This drained *hours* of my time and it all got really confusing. I started mixing up where Ahmed lived with what Khalid did for a living and what Wassim liked doing for fun. It got even messier when I replied to Mo instead of Khalid and then had to backtrack and work my way out of that one. It was exhausting and in the end, I gave up. It's hard enough having three guys on the scene in real life. I don't need to complicate it further by adding another three online.

I'm not a morning person anyway but today, it's worse than ever. My alarm starts going off at seven but it takes me a whole hour to persuade myself to get up: *Should I get up? Do I really have to get up? When was the last time I pulled a sickie? Can I get away with pulling another one? Can I pretend I had a morning meeting and go in at noon instead? Can I switch off my phone altogether and make up an excuse tomorrow?*

By eight, I've reasoned that I can't pull a sickie as it hasn't been long enough since my last one. I can't pretend I have a morning meeting because Kevin has access to my calendar. I can't *not* go in – not unless I want to lose my job anyway. Seeing as I'm lucky enough to be one of those rare people who actually enjoys what she does, in the end, I leap out of bed and do my morning stretches and deep breathing.

Yeah, right. Ha. I literally roll out of bed, fall onto the floor with a loud thud, and drag myself across the thick, grey carpet in my room and go to my en-suite bathroom to get ready.

Mum has given me strict instructions not to apply my makeup in my room in case any debris should fall from a palette onto her beloved carpet. I don't blame her. It took a whole year of moaning at my dad before he agreed to change the ten-year-old carpets in the house and she is very protective over them. How would she know if I defied her, you might be wondering? She won't, but the one time I ignored her, I dropped my eyebrow pomade everywhere. I almost stopped breathing. Half an hour of scrubbing later, the marks had almost disappeared and my hands were left red and raw.

As I go through my usual morning routine, I decide to spend a little longer on my face, to make it look as though I haven't been awake most nights over the past week. Back in the day, I could slap on a bit of blusher and lippy and hope for the best, but that just doesn't cut it anymore. My imperfections are even more apparent when I'm next to Insta-perfect Francesca.

When I'm done, I spray on my lucky perfume, throw on a long jumper and dark skinny jeans and make my way down the three flights of stairs to the ground floor. Today is Monday, I remind myself. It's a new day, it's a new week, and I'm going to make it count. So far, I've been to a matchmaking event, joined MuslimMate and I've agreed to send my biodata to two potential suitors. This week, I have to think of a new way to meet someone.

'Salaams, Nani,' I say to my grandmother as I enter the kitchen and spot a plate of scrambled eggs, avocado and wholegrain toast waiting for me on the kitchen table, along with a Thermos of hot tea and a Tupperware with my packed lunch. I walk over to her and give her a big hug and kiss and then plant myself in the chair next to her and dig in while she daintily sips her tea and nibbles on Ryvita with low-fat spread.

Before you ask, yes, she does do this for me nearly every day. And no, she doesn't do it for anyone else.

'Tumareh ayzku oto shundor lager kheneh?' Nani asks, pouring me a glass of water.

'Thanks, Nani.' I grin at the compliment, my mouth full of food. 'I've decided to make an effort so boys notice me more.' Nani almost chokes on her tea.

'Toubah ostoghfirullah,' she splutters, her eyes wide with horror. This, by the way, is her favourite phrase, a Bengali version of the Arabic, 'I seek forgiveness from Allah.'

'Not like that, Nani,' I laugh, giving her a squeeze. 'I can't sit around and wait for Ammu to find someone for me. I need to look out myself, too. And while I do, I need to look presentable.'

I love my morning chats with my grandmother. As my sisters both leave for uni/work an hour earlier than me, and my dad leaves half an hour before me, it's usually just the two of us eating and talking together. Nani has lived with us since my granddad died when I was fifteen. I have uncles she could have lived with, but we have the biggest house so Mum insisted that she moved in with us. Sometimes it can become a little stifling, having three adults in the house to answer to, but mostly I love it. Nani is like a little 4' 9" mother hen, always flapping about, making sure we're fed, warm and happy.

The February air is crisp as I walk to the station, wrapped up in my winter coat, thick-knit scarf and knee-length boots over my jeans. I'm lucky enough to be able to wear casual clothes to work so long as nothing is ripped or too provocative. Not likely with a mum like mine. I bought ripped jeans once. There was only one, tiny, modest tear at the knee – just one – and she went ballistic. The next morning, I decided to rebel and wear them with leggings underneath. I found them folded up on my dresser with the tear neatly sewn up.

Now do you see why I need to do whatever it takes to get married and get the hell out of this house?

I usually take the bus to work as the W3 stops right outside the office, but I've cut it too close today so need to get the Tube. As I hurry towards the station, Hamza's text the other day plays on my mind. I wonder if I should have been more cut-throat with him and told him I'm not interested. Or maybe I should have just ghosted him and saved myself the awkward conversation altogether. But the thought of completely ignoring someone without having the decency to tell them why makes me feel sick. I couldn't do that to him, or anyone really.

The eastbound Piccadilly Line train towards Cockfosters is almost always empty by the time it gets to Finsbury Park. I'm only on the train for a couple of stops so whether or not I get a seat is pretty irrelevant, but it is nice to be able to sit down, pull a book out and read instead of standing squashed against other commuters.

I step into the carriage and do a quick scan of where to sit when I realise that my Tube crush, Mr Piccadilly Line, is in the same carriage but right at the other end. As always, he looks like he's stepped out of a men's magazine. He's tall and broad with a head full of thick, wavy hair and a small beard. And there's no ring in sight. The only problem is . . . I don't know if he's Muslim or not. He looks it. Sort of. Back in the day, it used to be easy to tell if a guy was Muslim by his facial hair. Now that beards have become fashionable and every man that grooms himself fancies himself as a hipster, it's bloody impossible.

Mr Piccadilly Line and I have been 'bumping' into each other every couple of months for the past two years. We've made eye contact a handful of times (and, damn, his gaze is unnerving) but that's about it. This is the London Underground, after all, where you ignore everyone around you as much as you possibly can. Even if they're crying in front of you and staring at you like they need help.

He hasn't seen me get on the train as his (perfect) nose is buried in a book. If this coincidence had occurred before my birthday, I would have sat down in the nearest empty seat and stolen the occasional glance at my little Tube crush from afar.

However, today is not just any day. Today is a new week, a new beginning. Today is the day I'm wearing my lucky perfume and most of the makeup I own. Today is the day I'm wearing my magic jeans that almost make my bum look sexy.

Today, my friends, is the day I will do more than accidentally catch his eye. Today I will find out whether he is Muslim, and therefore, marriage material. Today is not a coincidence – it's fate.

I can't bring myself to pass the empty seats nearby and walk all the way down the carriage to sit near him, though. I do have a bit of shame. By some stroke of good fortune, the doors haven't closed yet, so for once, I act fast. I jump off the carriage, run down to the other end and, as the doors are about to close, leap back onto the train. Panting unattractively, I plonk myself down in the seat directly opposite him.

My abrupt movements startle Mr P into looking up from his book and into my slightly manic, grinning face. Oh Lord, he is even better looking up close, if that's possible. Everything about him is sheer perfection, from his full, but not-too-thick eyebrows and super-long eyelashes that frame his chocolate eyes, to his straight nose and neatly trimmed beard.

I need to say something to him. Anything. While I still can. Because the minute he starts reading again, that will be it. My chance will be over for another few months. I'm not lucky enough to have lightning strike in the same place twice while I'm looking this good.

'Sorry, didn't mean to disturb you,' I say, still wheezing from the rare exertion of running ten metres. 'I didn't want to miss this train and be late for work.'

As soon as the words leave my mouth, I regret it. It's such a boring thing to say and it's not even a question. How am I going to keep the conversation going if he replies with something like, 'It's OK'?

'No problem,' he says with a smile. He appraises me for a moment, a curious look flashing across his face before it becomes impassive again. Gosh, even his teeth are perfect, sparkly white and straight. He looks back at his bloody book.

What am I supposed to do now? I have no legitimate reason to interrupt his reading. If I do, I'll look like a complete idiot. A desperate idiot. I know I am, but he certainly doesn't need to be aware of that yet.

I decide to wait until the train pulls up at Manor House before attempting round two. He's bound to look up to see what stop we're at and I'll seize the moment then.

While he's reading, I take the opportunity to study him properly. Sinking back into the soft, worn, dark-blue seats and inhaling the familiar scent of soot mixed with the unfamiliar fragrance of an earthy male perfume, I analyse everything I can. His forehead is furrowed slightly, which means he must be taking whatever he's reading seriously. I glance at the jacket and am surprised to see that it's the latest crime novel to have been turned into a movie. He doesn't strike me as the contemporary crime fiction type; I thought he would be more into philosophy or history, but then, what do I know about him anyway? He's wearing a dark grey coat and black leather shoes with what looks like suit trousers. So he must be going to work then. Phew. Imagine if he was a uni student – that would have been really embarrassing. His fingers are long and slender and I'm happy to see that his nails are short and neat.

As I continue to observe him and the tingly sensation that's brewing in my gut spreads through me, I wonder why it is that Hamza doesn't have the same effect on me. He's a nice guy. He's not bad-looking. I think he might be successful as well. Why can't the chemicals and hormones in my body react to him in the same way they're reacting to Mr Piccadilly Line right now? If Mr P had texted me the other day asking to meet up, I would have been out the door before you could say 'Piccadilly'.

But that's the thing, I guess. You can't control who you're attracted to. It's not something you can think about, analyse, or persuade yourself into. Those feelings are completely disconnected from your brain. Attraction, I decide, is not like love, which can grow over time. There's no logic, sense or explanation behind attraction. It's either there, or it's not.

The train slows down and I brace myself to meet Mr Piccadilly Line's gaze again. And as I do, I have a brainwave. I know *exactly* how to find out if he's Muslim.

'Achoo!' I fake sneeze, loud enough for him to notice and look up. I'm careful to cover my mouth daintily. 'Alhamdulillah,' I say, the customary Islamic phrase to use after a sneeze.

If he replies with the Arabic response 'Yarhamukallah' (which means 'May Allah have mercy upon you'), I'll know that he's a Muslim. If he doesn't? Well, there's a chance he still is but said it in his head. Or didn't want to say it. Or is too irreligious to know that's what you're supposed to respond with. OK, I see now that my plan is majorly flawed.

Mr P glances up at me for a split second, smiles the briefest of smiles, and continues reading. He doesn't say a word and I'm none the wiser about his religious preferences. What is slowly becoming clear though, is that he has zero interest in me. Because if he did, surely he would have made a move by now?

Deflated, I wonder if I should admit defeat and let this one go. I'm practically throwing myself at him, yet he remains unresponsive. But I can't, because of all the days for us to be on the same carriage, it's happened today. When I'm right in the middle of my manhunt. That is a cosmic sign if I ever saw one.

I have two more stops – approximately four minutes – to make a move.

Taking a deep breath, I count to ten to calm my nerves and say a small prayer. It's now or never.

'Enjoying the book?' I ask, my voice shaking slightly. It is at that precise moment that the train goes through a particularly noisy part of the track and my words are completely drowned out.

Mr Piccadilly Line looks up, puzzled.

'Sorry, did you say something?' he asks, looking straight at me. My smile falters and I feel a bit sick. Did I really disturb him to ask him about his book? There's no way I can repeat that again.

'Erm, I said, do you know where I can get off for Wood Green High Road?' I lie weakly. I'm pretty sure my smile is beginning to look like a grimace now.

'Er, Wood Green?'

'Yes, Wood Green High Road.' I repeat.

'No, I meant, you get off at Wood Green.' His expression is completely deadpan and I feel like throwing up.

'Oh! Right, of course. I wasn't sure if that was the best stop. You know, like how Arsenal isn't really Arsenal. Anymore.' I swallow nervously and look down. This really isn't how I expected our first conversation to go.

'Well, Wood Green is still very much Wood Green,' he says wryly, raising an eyebrow.

What the hell did you expect? an annoying voice whispers in my ear. *A deep conversation about the meaning of life and a proposal by the time you reached Oakwood?*

'Just shut up,' I hiss at the annoying voice in my head, turning red.

'Excuse me?' Mr Piccadilly Line is looking taken aback. 'Did you tell me to shut up?'

'Of course not! I wasn't talking to you!' I exclaim, barely able to get the words out. I need to get off this train. Now. This is *not* going according to plan. The entire plan was stupid anyway.

The train pulls into Turnpike Lane. Praise the Lord! I jump up and hurriedly stuff my arms into my coat.

'OK, this is my stop!' I manage to say, grabbing my bag and my Thermos. 'See you around!' I look at Mr P one last time and I wish I didn't. He looks part-bewildered, part-annoyed, and still looks bloody good while doing so. Idiot! I hate his pathetic guts.

'I thought you wanted to go to Wood Green?' he says, raising an eyebrow.

Oh, for God's sake! What is his problem? Can't he see that I need to get as far away from him as possible before I make myself look like an even bigger weirdo?

'I didn't say that, you must have misheard. Bye!'

Before he can say anything else to incriminate me, the doors open and I leg it off the train without looking back.

Chapter 8

I'm more than a little flustered when I enter the office fifteen minutes later. There is a reason why Londoners ignore each other on public transport. I am never, ever going to shun social norms and strike up conversation with a random stranger on the Tube again. Ever.

'What's got your knickers in a twist?' Adam says as I stomp into the open-plan room, fling my bag onto my desk and slam my Thermos next to it.

'Nothing,' I snarl, throwing myself into the chair. 'And you can't say words like "knickers" to me, all right? Have some respect.'

Well accustomed to my occasional outbursts, Adam rolls his eyes and turns back to his screen. Not that he's working. I can see quite clearly that he's messing around on Facebook and, as his manager, I feel like telling him off. But I can't because he's my friend too and since I'm going to spend half my day on social media, I'd be a total hypocrite.

The morning's events still making me feel nauseous, I decide to take a moment to myself before I sit down to work. I gulp the last drop of tea from my Thermos and then head off to the kitchenette for another. At times like this, I wish I drank. I could do with a strong shot of something right about now. Oh well, piping hot tea with about ten biscuits is going to have to do.

As the kettle boils, I replay what happened on the Tube over and over again. Each time I do, the scenario gets worse and I feel like an even bigger loser. Maybe I should just leave the husband finding to my mum? But then, that's what I did the first time, and look how well that turned out.

'Do you want to tell me what's going on?' I turn around and see Adam lurking in the doorway holding a packet of chocolate Hobnobs. 'I come in peace, bearing a friendship token from my planet.'

I grudgingly take his token and, against my better judgement, proceed to explain what happened. By the end of it, he is practically rolling on the floor with laughter.

'I'm glad to see that you find my humiliation so amusing,' I grumble, dunking a biscuit into my tea and licking the chocolate off.

He snorts. 'I can't believe you told him to shut up at the end!'

'I didn't! I was telling myself to shut up! I didn't realise I said it out loud!' I turn red at the memory.

'That's even worse. He must think you're a total psychopath.'

'Well, thanks for pointing *that* out!' I snatch up the rest of the biscuits and head back over to my desk to nurse my wounds.

For the rest of the day, I struggle to concentrate on my work, mostly because I've got Mo DMing me throughout. It's becoming a bit annoying now. The messaging was fun at first but now I just want him to call me and the fact that he hasn't makes me wonder if there's something wrong with him. Or me?

As I start winding down for the day, I get a different unexpected call. Mum never bothers me while I'm at work, so I can't help but feel a nervous stirring in the pit of my stomach when the theme tune to Alfred Hitchcock's *Psycho* starts playing. In the eight seconds it takes me to locate my phone and answer it, I've already gone through various scenarios in my head (Nani has fallen and broken her hip; Amina has had a nervous breakdown in public and has been institutionalised; Yasmin has run off with a Jehovah's Witness), and have consequently worked myself up into a bit of a panic.

'Hello?' I answer, my palms sweating. 'What's going on? Is everything OK?'

'Everything's fine! Why wouldn't it be?' Mum quite rightly responds, her voice so loud that I have to adjust the volume. I take a sip of water in relief and notice Adam shift in his seat. From the way he's tilting his head, I can tell he's trying to listen in, the nosey git.

'You never phone me when I'm at work,' I explain, lowering my voice to just above a whisper.

'I know, but this is important. You know your dad told the mediator to go ahead and send your CV to the dentist and the Tower Hamlets boy? Well, he got back to your dad and said that the dentist wants your email address.'

'That's odd,' I muse. 'Why?'

'We won't know unless we give it, will we? But the thing is, I don't really want to tell them that it's Norf-LandanGyal. Sounds a bit . . . "street", doesn't it? You really ought to think about getting a more mature email address. You're not fourteen anymore.'

'Er, good point,' I admit. 'You can give my work one then.'

'Oh, that's a good idea . . .' She trails off and I feel my nerves begin to rattle again. I can tell that something is up and I'm about to find out.

'Anyway, it's too late for that, I've already made a new email address for you,' she says so quickly that I almost miss it.

'You what?'

'Calm down, it's only for this purpose. I'll text you the password and I won't access it without your knowledge.'

'Dare I ask what it is?' I sigh. I don't know why I'm even surprised by my mum's behaviour these days.

'Well, "Zara.Choudhury" was taken everywhere unless we added lots of numbers to it, which is a bit unimaginative. We wanted something a little different and intriguing . . .'

My mouth turns dry and I swallow nervously. I really don't like where Mum's going with this. I take another sip of water and brace myself.

'. . . so in the end we went for ZaraTheExplarer.'

'*What?*' I screech, forgetting the fact that I'm still in the office. Water spurts all over my computer monitor and Adam and Francesca both turn to stare at me, as do about twenty other people in the open-plan workspace. I mouth 'sorry' to them, wipe my lips with my sleeve like a sloth and continue my call outside.

'*Mum! How could you?*' I shout the moment the lift doors close. '*Zara the what?*'

'Oh, stop getting so worked up. It's funny. Creative. A great conversation starter.'

'For a six-year-old who can't spell, perhaps!'

'Don't be rude to me, young woman. I'll speak to you later. Bye.'

Mum hangs the phone up on my face and it takes all my willpower not to throw it against the wall. Zara the Effing Explorer? Where the hell does she *get* these things from? He's going to think I'm an illiterate nutjob before I even meet him. *If* I get to meet him. He'll probably run for the hills once he sees my supposed email address, inspired by a backpack-wearing, adventure-seeking Spanish-speaking infant with a bad haircut. So much for a more 'mature' email address!

I feel my blood pressure rising. In an attempt to calm down, I decide to go outside and passive smoke in the alleyway where the smokers congregate.

The icy air strikes me as soon as I open the emergency exit door. I nod to the only other person crazy enough to venture out in the freezing February cold and go and stand near enough to him so I can breathe in his second-hand smoke. He shuffles away from me and I inch closer again, inhaling deeply. Within minutes I'm shivering, my flimsy jumper more of a fashion thing than a keeping-warm thing. Maybe this wasn't such a good idea after all.

'What was all that about?'

I turn to see Adam next to me, two mugs of fresh hot tea in his hands and I almost hug him in relief. Instead, I grab a mug from him and hold it tight to warm up my hands.

'N-nothing! N-none of your b-bloody business,' I stammer, my teeth beginning to chatter.

'Well, it sounded like something,' he says reasonably. 'You look like you're freezing. Here, take my jacket.' He hands me his mug to hold while he shrugs his jacket off. I start to shake my head but I don't want to catch pneumonia for the sake of my pride, so I accept it grudgingly and pull it on. It's surprisingly warm considering he's only been wearing it for a few minutes, and smells like soap, lemons and a tinge of aftershave. It's also pretty big, so I wrap it tight around me. I've never worn a man's clothes before and it feels quite nice, if I'm honest. I wonder if Mo smells this good?

'Thanks,' I mutter, taking a big sip of tea which makes me feel better instantly. He's made it just how I like it, milky but strong with the bag still inside and two heaped teaspoons of sugar.

'Well?' He looks at me expectantly so I take a deep breath and tell him all about the dentist's biodata, his picture, and my new email address. I recount all this whilst examining the countless dots of old chewing gum embedded in the pavement, but when there's no reaction from Adam, I peek up at him. He has a solemn expression on his face but the glint in his hazel eyes suggests otherwise.

'Go on, laugh and get it over with,' I grumble, and not a moment too soon, as the laughter erupts.

'ZaraTheExplarer!' he gasps, holding on to his sides. 'I don't know what's worse – your email address or his stethoscope! Maybe it's a euphemism for . . . something else?'

His laughter is infectious and I start to giggle. When he isn't being an idiot, he's quite fun to be around. He asks me if I have the biodata on my phone, and I nod and show it to him. He studies it intently and I can tell he's reading it all, word for word. He smiles at the picture but his mood seems to have altered slightly.

'You've agreed to meet him?' he asks, handing my phone back to me.

'Well, I agreed for the middle person to send my own biodata to them,' I explain with a shrug. 'If he likes mine then we'll probably meet. But since he's asked for my email address, I guess he's seen it and wants to correspond for a bit over email before meeting.'

'Hang on, so you have one of these as well?' Adam's eyes light up and I shake my head vehemently before he asks.

'No way, you're going to take the piss,' I moan, covering my eyes. 'It's so embarrassing. My mum wrote it all and it's awful!'

'Go on, I promise I won't laugh.'

'Like hell you won't!'

'I can tell you what it's like from an outsider's perspective,' he reasons.

'Fine, but if you so much as snicker, I swear I'll have you fired,' I threaten, handing my phone over once again. I feel a bit self-conscious but it's not like he doesn't know me already. I analyse his face as he reads it all carefully but his expression gives nothing away.

'Well? What do you think?' I ask impatiently after he's been staring at it for a while.

'Erm . . . all that village and district stuff is pretty meaningless to me but it's obviously important to you lot. Why is that?' he asks, his face impassive.

'I dunno, I'm not really bothered. I want someone I get along with who believes in the same things I do. But my mum and grandma want me to marry someone from a similar district and background as there's a better chance of our families getting along. It's more likely that we'll all have the same expectations, similar upbringing and basically be on the same wavelength.'

He takes a moment to digest this, and I ask him what happens in his community.

'None of this!' he says drily. 'Yeah, you sometimes get aunties and stuff trying to matchmake but not to this scale.'

'Does it matter where in Turkey they're from?'

'Not at all. I reckon my mum would be pleasantly surprised if I brought a Turkish girl home, but she knows I've never dated one so she won't be too shocked if I don't.'

'My parents would have a thing or two to say if I chose someone from a different culture,' I admit.

'So how come you're dating Hamza then? He's not Bengali is he? So why—'

'Hang on, we're not dating,' I hurriedly interrupt. 'We've been out once, that's it. Twice if you include the chocolate event. Which you can't. So it's just once.' I know I sound defensive but I can't help it. I don't want people to think that Hamza and I are more than we are.

'You know what I mean. He's not Bengali so how come you're considering him?'

'Well, desperate times and all that,' I try to joke, smiling at Adam. He doesn't smile back, so I figure he wants a real answer.

'We've never explicitly discussed it,' I say. 'But members of my extended family have started marrying outside our culture and the older I get, the more lenient my parents are becoming. I get the feeling they won't mind. But obviously, being Muslim is the main thing. Non-negotiable.'

He ponders this for a minute and I appreciate the fact that he's not jumping down my throat for a change. He glances down at my biodata again and I can see he's struggling to make sense of it all. I guess our traditions can be a bit difficult to understand.

'So? Would you meet me after seeing my biodata?' I ask playfully, trying to lighten the mood.

'I dunno about that, ZaraTheExplarer,' he says with a resigned smile, gesturing at me to follow him back to the office. 'Your pictures don't exactly do you justice.'

Chapter 9

That evening, dinner is a solemn affair with me scowling at Mum every few minutes, her huffing and puffing and everyone else waiting for one of us to explode. I don't, though. I eat my generous portion of shepherd's pie as quickly as possible, help with the tidying up and then excuse myself. As I make my exit, I hear Abbu grumbling to Nani about still being hungry and if there's any 'real' food around (i.e., rice and curry).

I don't know why, but I keep replaying my conversation with Adam over and over in my mind. I know I'm a bit of a ditz sometimes, but I am astute enough to realise that something changed between us today. Apart from when he acts like a judgemental git, we've always got along quite well. Our conversations rarely go beyond superficial topics, though; office politics, films, TV shows, restaurants. Now we're suddenly talking about the things that matter. And his coat was so warm and smelt so good.

I wonder what my parents would say if I wanted to marry a Turkish guy . . .

Argh!

This isn't good. This isn't good *at all*.

Looking for further confirmation of what I already know, I find myself on Adam's various social media pages. It's the first time I've looked at them since he added me two years ago. On Facebook he doesn't have many profile pictures, so it doesn't take long to go through them. None of them are too posey, which I like. There's one of him on top of a mountain with some guys, another in the desert with a falcon on his arm, and one of him holding a fishing line on a boat. I hadn't realised he was so outdoorsy.

My phone pings with a message from Mo and I start, feeling ever-so-slightly guilty; texting one guy, seeing another, whilst stalking the social media of someone else. A year ago, I would have scoffed in your face if you'd told me that I'd have three men on the scene simultaneously. And yet here I am. According to Yasmin, Layla, and even my inexperienced cousin Samia, this is what dating in this decade is all about.

I go back to Adam's profile and, after a little poking around, find quite a few photos of him that other people have added, which mainly consist of him in different bars and clubs with various scantily clad women hanging off of him.

The butterflies I got from his beautifully fragranced, manly jacket flutter away as quickly as they appeared. I can't compete with these women, with their fake tans, big hair, bigger boobs and strategically placed tattoos. I doubt he'd ever be interested in a girl as plain as me. The closest I've ever got to a tattoo are the henna ones we get done before weddings.

'Zara! Quick!' Mum bursts into my room with my sisters close at her heels and Nani panting behind them.

'What?' I look up with a bored expression. I do this intentionally because I know my mum hates my resting bitch face. But she's too wound up to notice, let alone care.

'You have an email from the dentist!' she exclaims, practically dancing with excitement. 'See! I knew Zara-TheExplarer was a good call!'

Yasmin chokes as she tries to contain her laughter and I give her my most lethal death stare.

'I thought you said you wouldn't check that account without letting me know?' I say, raising an eyebrow.

'I'm letting you know now, aren't I? Quick, open it up!'

All of them gather around me on the bed as I let out a theatrical sigh and quickly open a new tab before they see what I've been doing.

'Read it out loud then,' Mum commands as I open up the email from 'F. Chowdhury'. I read in a monotone,

Dear Zara,

I hope this email finds you well. I have perused your biodata; thank you for sharing it with me. However, before we proceed, in order to determine whether or not we are compatible, could you kindly complete the attached questionnaire.

Do take your time with each question and remember – there are no right or wrong answers! All the best and I look forward to hearing from you soon.

Dr Farook Chowdhury.

There is a silence so deafening that my ears begin to ring.

What. The. Hell?

Like seriously. What the hell? I don't know what's worse – the questionnaire or the fact that he's signed himself off as 'Dr'.

Yasmin is the first to break the silence by clearing her throat. 'Erm, it's a bit like when you apply for a job, Z,' she says in a strangled voice. 'You sent your CV in and now he wants you to complete the application form, so he knows whether you're the right candidate to be invited for an interview.'

I stare at her, not sure if she's taking the mick or being serious. I think it's the former, and judging by the dirty look she shoots Yasmin, Mum obviously does too. She chooses to ignore the sarcasm and steps in before I get my voice back.

'Exactly, that's all it is, nothing wrong with that,' she says chirpily with a huge fake smile. 'Open the attachment then. Let's fill it in together, shall we?'

'Don't open it!' Amina bursts out, her face red with fury. 'Who does this *Doctor* Farook Chowdhury think he is, exactly? Unless he's Zayn Bloody Malik, how dare he belittle you like this? Actually, you shouldn't jump through hoops even for Zayn! You don't need him or his shoddy questionnaire, thank you.'

'I thought you were a Riz Ahmed kinda girl,' Yasmin says to Amina, going off topic. 'Zayn is a bit obvious don't you think?'

'Don't listen to your sister,' Mum interrupts, flapping her arms about. 'What does she know about getting married these days? Open—'

'Don't do it! You need to start how you mean to go on. He's going to think you're desperate and he can ask anything of you if you fill that thing in!'

'No, he won't, he'll respect you for taking the time!'

Mum and Amina argue at the top of their voices while Yasmin tries to intervene to get them to calm down.

'What's a questionnaire?' Nani asks, looking lost while she tries to keep up with the conversation.

Hands are flailing around as all four of them gesture wildly and carry on arguing. They're doing my head in, so I open the attachment and try to tune them out.

1. Name:
2. Age:
3. Height:
4. Weight:

Excuse me?! How dare he ask how much I weigh? What's it got to do with him? Am I a suitcase that has to be below a certain allowance?

Too busy staring at the questions in undisguised abhorrence, I don't notice that the room has fallen silent and that they are all reading along with me.

'Calm down,' Mum quickly intervenes before I lose it completely. 'It's a fair question.'

'Oh, really?' I snap. 'And I guess it's fine for him to ask for my bra size as well?'

'Toubah ostoghfiruallah!' Nani exclaims, her wide eyes darting around the room in horror. 'Ita kita mati rai? Is this man talking about undergarments?'

'You've lost the plot, Mum,' Amina spits, absolutely livid. 'What is she? Cattle that's being sold to the highest bidder?'

'Let's all just calm down,' Mum implores weakly. 'The rest may be less . . .' I watch her face contort as she struggles to find the correct word.

'Intrusive?' Yasmin offers.

'Obnoxious?' Amina counters.

'Invasive?' I add.

With a sigh, Mum lets her sentence hang limply and we continue to read the questions.

5. Occupation:
6. What do you do in your spare time?
7. Please describe what you are looking for in a husband.

8. Please describe yourself in six words.
9. How many children do you want?
10. On a scale of 1 to 10, please rate your religiousness.

'Rate my religiousness?' I scoff. 'How does a person rate how religious they are? What am I supposed to do? Add a mark because I eat halal food, another because I fast, another because I wear modest clothes, but deduct one for not praying five times a day?'

'Knock off another point for not wearing hijab,' Amina adds, unhelpfully. I feel the vein that occasionally pops up on my neck throb in rage.

Angry tears well up in my eyes. I can't believe what I'm putting myself through for a man who is barely attractive and walks around with a stethoscope round his neck, *when he's not a doctor!* I can't believe that there are men out there that think it's OK to send intrusive questionnaires to a woman they haven't even *met*. But worst of all, I can't believe I'm entertaining this. I have officially crossed the line from anxious to desperate.

The whole of Thursday passes without me hearing back from the dentist. I try not to let it bother me because it's not as if I was dying to meet him in the first place. But it does bother me. It bothers the hell out of me, because I pushed my pride and dignity aside and actually filled out his blasted questionnaire. I wrote out my weight (well, my 'approximate' weight minus a few pounds) and rated my religiousness. I made myself look like a desperate fool in front of my younger sisters. And, after all that, he hasn't bothered to acknowledge receiving it.

Maybe the actual test was seeing if I would be low enough to entertain his mind games. Maybe he's only agreeing to meet women who don't fill it in.

Whatever. Who needs him when I have sexy Mo the Money Maker keeping me company every night? Virtually, of course. I replied to him after the whole dentist palaver wound down, and we ended up texting until 2 a.m. It's becoming a bit of a regular thing, and I'm dying to speak to him but he's yet to call me or ask to meet up again.

Now that I think about it, it is a bit worrying, really. Why doesn't he want to meet up with me? He's mentioned that his previous relationship was a bit traumatic – without going into much detail – so I've been assuming he wants to take things slow. But what if that isn't the case? What if he's already got a girlfriend and I'm a side ting for a bit of a laugh?

I haven't heard from Hamza either, not since he asked me out again and I told him I would get back to him. And I didn't.

I feel so down about it all – Mo, the dentist and even Hamza – that on my way home from work, I find myself taking a detour and venturing into a world I have only witnessed on TV and read about in books. Somewhere so far out of my comfort zone that previously, the mere thought of entering one, let alone joining one, was enough to send me running for my duvet whilst clutching an extra-large Snickers bar.

All the way over here I've been telling myself that joining a gym has absolutely nothing to do with having to lie about my weight on that questionnaire. Nor is it about wanting to get married or the fact that my mum has started dropping hints about my weight gain. It's about getting healthy – mind and body. It's about feeling strong, inside and out. I've hidden inside baggy clothes for long enough and maybe it's time to get my confidence back?

I have no idea what to expect when I walk through the shiny, smudge-free glass doors and fearfully take a few furtive glances around. On one side, I see a room full of skeletal exercise bikes, on another I see an empty studio surrounded by mirrors and, in the distance, I see a bunch of scary-looking machines that I know I will never be able to work out how to use.

A couple of women walk past me in leggings and vest tops, showing off their perfect derrieres and toned legs. I picture myself panting away in a baggy tracksuit on one of those machines while my various bits and pieces jiggle around and everyone sniggers.

I haven't started exercising yet and I'm already sweating. What on earth was I thinking, coming here? I should exercise in the privacy of my own home, where no one cares if there are wobbly bits flapping around; or that I have sweat dripping from every inch of exposed skin; or that I forgot to shave my legs, so my ankles look like they're wearing fur scarves.

'Hi, can I help you?'

A voice startles me just as I'm about to slink out, and I turn around to see the hottest guy *ever* behind the reception counter. My jaw drops. I don't know if I can bring myself to talk to this creature, he is that beautiful. Not only does he have a face that belongs on *America's Next Top Model,* his muscled arms are gorgeously smooth and brown and I can see his sculptured abs through his tight black T-shirt.

I'm so astounded by his beauty that, for a moment, I lose all my senses and when I open my mouth to speak next, an American accent comes out.

'Uh, I'm just having a look around,' I croak in said accent, giving him a shaky smile and quickly averting my gaze before he sees the lust in my eyes.

'Well, if you're thinking of joining, let me give you a quick tour,' he says gamely, before sauntering over to me and standing so close that I can smell his magnificent aftershave.

Oh. My. God. My heart starts dancing a jig and I somehow mumble something coherent, while trying to stop my pupils from turning into hearts.

'So where in the States are you from?' he asks me genially as he starts showing me around the gym. Good question. Where *am* I from? I can't think of anything!

'Um, Sweet Valley,' I say in the end, because nothing else comes to mind but the fictional town I spent years reading about as a teenager.

'Sounds like a cool place,' he says innocently and I nod in agreement, feeling a bit sick. *What the hell is wrong with me? What if he looks it up and knows I lied?*

The next fifteen minutes are a blur. I barely absorb a thing he says as he shows me the various workout rooms, the pool, the spa facilities and juice bar. All I do is give him sidelong glances when he's looking the other way and try my best not to drool. I do, however, notice that he isn't the only good-looking man in these ends. There's one over there at the machine that you run on, there's another down by those big weight thingies, and there's one coming out of the changing rooms. They are absolutely everywhere. I pinch myself to see if this is some sort of twisted, yet beautiful, dream. *Ouch.* OK, this is definitely real then.

Forget going to Muslim matchmaking events, why have I never thought about joining a gym to find a husband? Well, probably because I'm horrifically un-athletic. But who said I have to work out that hard anyway? I can casually stroll on the running machine and watch the scenery as it goes by.

It's no surprise that in my intoxicated state, I find myself signing a contract and I have absolutely no idea what it's about. I could have signed away my kidneys, for all I know. But they can bloody well have them if it means I can stare at talent like – hang on, what's his name? – *Jordan* every day. In my daze, I also sign up for five personal training sessions with the man himself.

I'm so excited about my newfound discovery that I text my sisters to tell them what I've done. Yasmin replies immediately, asking for evidence so, when Jordan is busy putting together my welcome pack behind the vast reception desk, I discreetly take a photo of him.

'I need your emergency contact number,' he says, coming over to me with my joining gift of a towel, water bottle, headphones and rucksack.

'Sure, I'll give you my mom's, hold on a sec while I pull it up,' I reply, giving him a dazzling smile.

Now that I'm slowly getting used to his beauty, I have relaxed in to my American voice and can finally look him in the eyes without my knees buckling. I unlock my phone to get my number out, and there, on my extra-large screen, is the picture I took, right in Jordan's line of vision. I quickly close the gallery and glance over at him, praying he didn't notice. His amused expression tells me he has.

I feel the blood rush to my face as I struggle to think of a legitimate reason why I would have his picture in my phone. So I blurt out the first thing that comes to my head.

'You look like a famous Bollywood actor,' I say, my eyes wide with innocence. 'I thought I'd take a picture and show my grandma.'

'I do?' he asks, his own eyes twinkling. 'No one's ever told me I look Indian before.' I'm not surprised. He's obviously mixed-race, with his honey-coloured complexion, dark brown tight curls and cool grey eyes that you want to swim laps in.

'Well, that picture is crap. Why don't we take a selfie instead?'

'Sure,' I squeak as he grabs my phone, stands right next to me and before I know what's happening, puts his arm around my shoulders and pulls me close. I think I have died and gone to heav – er – probably hell after that.

'Much better.' He smiles, looking at the picture and handing my phone back. 'When shall we pencil in your orientation meeting and first PT training session? We've got a couple of slots open tomorrow evening and early morning?'

I have plans tomorrow night but something about this Jordan makes me do and say silly things so I find myself agreeing to come in at half six in the morning.

This is the first time in my life that I'm going to do something that will make me healthy and strong. I've never exercised properly (unless you count a couple of half-hearted online yoga sessions), I can't swim, and apart from a crash diet when I was sixteen, have never thought much about the food I put in my body. I've heard that once you pass thirty, your metabolism slows down and before you know it, you're waddling around with Type 2 diabetes and rheumatoid arthritis.

Not me, though. I'm taking control of my life – and my future. With a massive grin on my face and a spring in my step, I leave the gym feeling motivated and excited.

When my alarm goes off at quarter past five the following morning, all I want to do is punch Jordan in his stupid, perfect face. What sort of voodoo did he do on me that had me agreeing to come in at half six? Who in the world decides to go to the gym *before* work, when they could be catching up on much-needed beauty sleep instead?

I roll over, cover my head with my soft, warm and oh-so-cosy pillow and bury myself deeper under my duvet. Jordan can get lost; there is no way I'm waking up and leaving the house when it's still dark. My alarm goes off again so I grab my phone, turn it off and close my eyes for the second time – and then I remember exactly how much I've paid for these personal training sessions.

With a groan, I force myself out of bed and into the shower. It's already five thirty and I have only half an hour to make myself look presentable and leave the house. I curse Mo for making me stay up until midnight talking to him as I hurriedly apply my makeup in the dark and hunt around for attractive workout gear. I begin to realise that exercising with someone I fancy is a really, really daft idea.

'You're seriously doing this?' Amina smirks from the kitchen table as I scoff down a banana, fill up my water bottle and head for the front door.

'Why are you up?' I ask as I catch a glimpse of my ashen complexion in the hallway mirror. Waking up this early really doesn't suit me.

'I have a meeting at our head office in Birmingham,' she replies. 'Why didn't you book sessions in after work?'

I turn and give her a massive, fake smile and repeat my dad's favourite saying: 'Early to bed, early to rise, makes one healthy, wealthy and wise.' And with that parting wisdom, I turn around and head out into the cold, dark street.

There's a tingly feeling in my stomach as I walk up to the bus stop. I don't know if it's because it's so quiet and eerie, if it's because I know I'm about to be tortured, because I get to spend an hour in close proximity to Jordan, or because I'm actually excited about doing something new. Whatever it is, I pull my coat tighter around me, recite Ayatul Kursi, an Arabic prayer for protection, and quicken my pace.

When I get to the main road, I'm pleased to see that it's quite busy. But despite the bustle, there is a sort of calm serenity at this time of the morning. No one seems to be in a rush yet, and all along the bus route I watch lights turn on in Victorian terraced houses, people coming out of their front doors wrapped up in thick coats and scarves, and little grocery shops and newsagents rolling up their shutters.

By the time I get to the gym, not only am I fully awake, I'm finally feeling like myself and I can't wait to get started.

'All right, love?' Jordan calls out as I enter the warm, brightly lit reception area. 'Changing room's that way – meet you out here in five minutes.'

Gosh, talk about cutting straight to the chase. I sort of hoped I'd have a moment of small talk with him while my makeup is still perfect and my hair is in place.

'Sure, see you in a minute!' I reply freakishly chirpily, remembering in time to put on the American accent. I skip over to the changing area and, to my surprise, there are at least five other women in the communal area of the room in various states of undress. There's a woman wearing a towel with wet hair dripping down her back, indicating that she's already finished her workout, and the others look like they're raring to go.

I pull on a pair of brand-new black jogging bottoms, a black long-sleeved top and spray myself with deodorant for the second time, hoping the double protection and dark colours will disguise any sweat or unpleasant odours appearing on my person. With a deep breath, I urge the butterflies in my tummy to settle down and then head back into the unknown.

'Let's start with the initial assessment,' Jordan says as he ushers me into a little office with various bits of equipment. 'Can you take off your trainers and stand on the scales over there?'

'Erm, is that really necessary?' I stall, my eyes darting between him and the dreaded scales. 'I know how much I weigh, so can we move on to the next part?' Jordan smiles patiently at me and leans forward so I can smell his fresh, enticing scent. I inhale deeply to calm my nerves but I end up breathing in more of him, which makes me a bit giddy.

'I know, but it's for my records. The scales don't just tell you your weight – they tell you your BMI, how much fat there is on your body, how much water weight and how much muscle as well. It's really useful so we can make sure you're building muscle, burning fat and not only losing water.'

I really don't want to do this. But then I don't want to look like a wimp either, so I find myself taking off my shoes, my watch, my earrings and even my hairband before tentatively getting onto the scales. My hands are clammy and I'm too scared to look down at the number, so I don't. Jordan makes a 'hmm' sound and writes something down on my chart. What sort of reaction is 'hmm'? Is it a good 'Oh, she's actually lighter than she looks' 'hmm' or is it a 'Oh shit, how am I going to sort this lump of lard out' sort of 'hmm'?

'Right, you can come down now,' he says, and I leap off it as if it's turned to hot coal. I sit back down and he asks me what sort of exercise I usually do.

'Well, I walk to the bus stop every day,' I reply hesitantly, looking down at my barely scuffed exercise trainers. He nods encouragingly, as if expecting me to continue.

'Erm, that's it,' I admit when the pause starts becoming uncomfortable.

'Oh, right,' he says without missing a beat. 'Is there any sort of fitness goal you're aspiring towards?'

'What do you mean exactly?'

'Like, are you training for a particular event? Do you want to run a marathon? Are you going on a hiking holiday? Do you want to be able to run 5k easily?'

'Well, it would be nice to be able to run for the bus without giving up halfway,' I explain, examining my shoelaces. This is so excruciating. When I signed up for Personal Training I didn't realise I would be cross-examined. Apparently the 'personal' bit is literal. 'And it would be even better if I could run for a long time, and fast. Really fast. You know, in case someone is chasing me.'

'Chasing you?' There is an alarmed look on Jordan's face and I quickly continue before he thinks I'm a victim of domestic violence.

'You know, by a murderer, or a rapist, or some guy I've met online . . .' My voice trails off when I realise that the alarm has been replaced by a 'she is bloody insane' expression. 'Anyway. Yes. So I'd like to be able to run for long distances. Fast.'

We talk for a little longer and I try and keep my answers short, so he doesn't figure out that I don't just *talk* crazy, I *am* crazy. When it's finally over, I let out a massive sigh of relief and take a sip of water. This gym business is already really stressful and I haven't even started exercising yet.

Following Jordan back out into the main area, I spot my reflection in a huge mirror. Despite being a little flushed from the interrogation, I look quite good in my form-fitting Adidas trackies and simple, yet effective, makeup. My hair is still out and is behaving for once and looks quite glossy and voluminous.

'Zara?' Jordan's voice snaps me out of my thoughts. 'Let's start with the treadmill,' he says, gesturing for me to join him at a long row of formidable-looking running machines. Taking a deep breath, I give him my megawatt smile and confidently hop onto the belt as he begins pressing various buttons while explaining something about heartbeats and fat burning. Truthfully, I'm not paying much attention – it's difficult to, with Jordan's beauty constantly distracting me. The belt begins to move and I'm forced to start walking, slowly at first and then a little faster as Jordan presses the buttons to make it pick up the pace.

The machine speeds up again and now I'm walking so fast that I feel as if I'm about to topple over. It's impossible to walk gracefully when you're moving this fast and I look like a meerkat being chased by a fox.

'Start jogging,' Jordan instructs as he adjusts the speed again. I don't really have a choice but to oblige, and as I do, my bum and boobs start bouncing in synchronisation. I look in the mirror again and suddenly I don't look like an Asian model for Adidas anymore. My bits are leaping around all over the place! My boobs are practically hitting me in my face and my hair has gone from sexy volume to dragged-through-a-hedge volume.

While I'm lost in thought with my hair obscuring my vision, Jordan decides to speed things up even more, only I'm not paying attention so I buckle, land on my knees, get carried to the end of the belt and flung off.

'Zara, are you OK?' He runs over to me as I quickly get up and plaster a smile on my face.

'I'm fine!' I squeak, teetering precariously from the sudden rush of blood to my head. Jordan grabs my arm to steady me and leads me back to the office where he hands me a cup of cold water and tells me to sit down while he checks me over. I'm beyond embarrassed now. What happened to me out there is far more humiliating than Jordan weighing me.

'OK, you seem to be fine. Does anything hurt?'

Only my battered ego. 'No, honestly, I'm fine. Just feeling a bit embarrassed, that's all.' By this stage, I can't bring myself to look him in the eyes anymore. Not only does he think I'm a lazy, unfit nutcase, I'm now a lazy, unfit, clumsy, *vain* nutcase who can't break into a light jog without falling over.

'Great, so let's get back out there then. We'll give the treadmill a miss for today but let's see how you fair on the stepper, cross trainer and resistance equipment.'

We spend the next half an hour on various machines as he tests my stamina, strength and core strength, all the while writing notes. By the time we get to the final machine – a resistance one for my upper arms – I think I'm going to die. Every part of me is throbbing in agony, my face is dripping with sweat that I feel too embarrassed to wipe because my makeup keeps leaving brown streaks on the new white towel, and I am panting like an excited Labrador. Even my bum is sweating and has been leaving wet patches on the leather seats. I am beyond grateful that my black top is concealing the pools of water collecting under my arms.

The worst part is, I can't even pretend that I look OK because there are bloody mirrors everywhere. What is it with gymmers wanting to look at themselves while they curl their biceps and run on a conveyor belt? Everywhere I turn I see my ridiculous reflection; my red, shiny face with countless strands of hair sticking on to it, and my foundation streaked like war paint. My lipstick has almost wiped off entirely, but somehow my lip liner has remained intact, the outline reminding me of The Joker from Batman. I can feel that my scalp is drenched and even my boobs are sweating. I. Am. Going. To. Collapse. Any. Second.

'I can't do this anymore,' I rasp when Jordan tries to get me to lift some weights over my shoulders, my eyes about to pop out of their sockets. My arms are shaking like jelly and I feel the vein in my neck bulging dangerously. 'Seriously, Jordan, my arms are going to fall off. Please don't make me beg!'

My voice starts wobbling and my fake accent starts to waver. I think Jordan is afraid I'll burst into tears because he takes the weights and smiles kindly down at me. I'm so exhausted that he doesn't even look good anymore. In fact, every time he says, 'Go on, Zara, one more time', his face turns into the devil emoji.

'OK, that's enough for today then. Let's get you stretched out and we'll call it a day.'

As if I'm not humiliated enough, Jordan then makes me lie down in my own pool of sweat and starts contorting my limbs into unnatural angles. I resist, tensing all my muscles, because I'm scared that if I let go even an inch, something worse than just sweat will escape from my body. I'm sure I stink, despite the deodorant I doused myself with, and I don't want to know what my face looks like right now.

'Relax, Zara, I can't work the tension out otherwise,' Jordan says, looking down at me, worried. I can't meet his gaze so I squeeze my eyes closed and just pray for all this to be over.

As soon as it is, I hobble out of the workout area as fast as my aching legs let me and lock myself into a toilet stall and just sit on the loo for ages, trying to gather up the strength to get into the shower.

I make it to the shower and avoid looking at the fully naked woman who has just emerged from a cubicle. I'm so done with this place and all these exercise-obsessed freaks. I scrub off all the grime, sweat and crusty makeup, cursing myself and Jordan the entire time. My arms are so wrecked that they shake when I try and wash my hair. When I'm finally done and ready in my work clothes, I take a moment to sit in the juice bar to regain my strength. Scouring the menu, I try to find something that doesn't sound like a bloody salad. Kale, avocado, nuts, ginger, wheatgrass, spirulina. The thought makes me turn as green as the drink the man in front of me is happily slurping. In the end, I go for a banana, blueberry and avocado drink, which sounds tolerable, apart from the avocado bit. Whoever said that exercise before work is invigorating, is a total bullshitter. Forget feeling ready for the day – I'm ready to go to bed and never get back out.

As I sit there sipping my smoothie and waiting for the sugar to give me enough energy to get to the bus stop, I check my phone and am surprised to find a text from Mum. This early? For a second, I contemplate deleting it without reading it. I've had enough stress this morning to last me the rest of the week. But then I worry that something serious may have happened so I take a big swig of my banana and blueberry concoction and open it up.

> The dentist replied to your email and said he wants to meet at the weekend. I've taken the liberty to confirm on your behalf. You and a chaperone are meeting him at Ladurée in Covent Garden on Saturday. Get ready!

Chapter 10

'I can't believe what you're wearing,' I chuckle as Yasmin and I leave the house on Saturday to meet the dentist. Mum and Nani are waving furiously from the gate, as though we're off to our first day at school and we wave back genially, as if today's meeting isn't one of extreme magnitude.

'Me neither,' Yasmin admits with a laugh, linking her arm into mine, forcing me to match her long strides. 'But what Mum wants, Mum gets!'

On my mother's strict instructions, under my mac I'm wearing a white silk shirt and navy straight-legged jeans that I haven't worn since 2006, which are so tight around the waist that I can't do them up anymore. I've had to leave them undone and have covered the gaping gap with a brown belt. Brown leather boots and a white cashmere cardigan Mum pulled out from God knows where complete the look, along with Nani's real pearls that rest daintily on my collarbones. My nana gave them to her when they first moved to the UK in the seventies and she's treasured them ever since. My makeup has been laboriously fashioned to look like I'm not wearing any and I've doused in Mum's Chanel No. 5. I look and smell like a Surrey soccer mum – her interpretation of what a dentist's wife should wear on a leisurely Saturday. And nothing like me.

Yasmin doesn't look like herself either and every time I glance at her, I suppress the urge to snort. In all honesty, the fact that everyone – especially my mum – thought my sister had to uglify herself in order to keep the attention on me, the older, less-pretty sister, isn't funny, it's pathetic. I'm not completely naïve; I know that I'm not as young or trendy as Yas but I didn't think I was that bad. I'm still all-right looking. I'm still a decent person, still an attractive prospect. I think.

Not only is my sister's face barren of a single swipe of makeup, she's wearing one of Nani's old-fashioned triangular white headscarves with a lace trim, the type people would buy from Saudi Arabia back in the nineties. She has pinned the scarf under her chin so that the two ends hang down over her chest. Not that you can tell she has a chest, under the baggy black jumper she's wearing that's about four sizes too big. Without her usual glossy bob on display she doesn't look like herself, but together with the outfit, she could pass as my mother – or worse, Nani.

'Are you OK?' Yasmin asks me, examining my expression as we wait on the platform. She stands close to the edge which makes me nervous, especially because of the way she's dressed. What if an Islamaphobe pushes her onto an oncoming train? I pull her away from the yellow line and explain that the fact that Mum thought she needed to dress like this is a really harsh reality check.

'Z, you can't let Mum's warped view affect you,' she replies as we get onto the train and grab two empty seats.

'It's a bit hard to ignore her,' I say. 'Especially when there's some truth to it.'

'The only thing that's true is that you're twenty-nine – and there's nothing wrong with that. It's our culture and community that's the problem, not you. Next time anyone says you're too old, remind them that the Prophet's first wife was over forty when they got married. And she was way older than him.'

'Yeah, like that's going to change anything. You know how they love to pick and choose the bits of Islam that suits them.'

'Well, they need to get with the times because no one cares about these outdated traditions anymore. When it's my turn to get married, there's no way I'm going to go through all this. I'm finding my own husband.'

'That's what I thought as well. And yet here I am.' I lean back against the grimy seat and close my eyes; Yasmin, as emotionally intuitive as she always is, swiftly changes the subject to uni, and some drama with one of her tutors.

'I'm sure she's racist,' she says, after moaning about how her presentation was far superior to her white class-mates, but she got the worst feedback.

'That's a pretty serious accusation to make,' I warn her. 'Don't throw that word around unless you have evidence, or your life could be over. You'll become the girl who cried race.'

'How do you prove something so subtle? You know when you just *know*?'

'I do know. We *all* know. But knowing isn't going to hold up in an investigation. You need something tangible, otherwise you need to keep quiet and work harder than everyone else. That's the shitty reality of being a woman of colour.'

We arrive at Covent Garden and, as always, I'm thankful that we live so close to Central London. For a moment I wonder what it would be like to commute in from Rayner's Lane – where Hamza lives – every day. I barely know anything about West London, other than that it's where most of London's Arabs live. Anyway, today is not the day to be thinking about Hamza.

But I am, because he texted me last night, which led to a phone call and a conversation that went on for over an hour. At first, the conversation was great. He's attentive and his accent is really endearing, not at all like the one I put on for Jordan, which is so bloody cringey that I haven't told my sisters about it. But then he started talking about work and he droned on, and on, and on. I also found out that his idea of a fun night is staying in and playing on his PlayStation . . . whereas mine is a night out on the town. How can a relationship last forever if I'm already experiencing a twinge of boredom – and it's barely been a month? Not that it *is* a relationship. What is this process even called, the period of time you spend getting to know someone to see if they're suitable for marriage? It's not dating either. A 'courtship', perhaps?

There's other stuff that's niggling me about him as well, but I don't know if I'm imagining it. Last night, while we were talking, he asked me what my career plans were.

'Plans? Erm, I'm not really the type to have plans, per se,' I said like a planless idiot. 'Do *you* have plans?'

'Sure do,' he replied confidently, before explaining his five and ten year goals from manager to director and one day, partner. I felt tired just listening to it.

'What about you?' he asked. 'You could do so much. Comms skills are totally transferable. Have you thought about leaving the public sector and going private? There's more money in it.'

'Yeah, my friend Layla's always telling me to, but I'm happy where I am,' I replied, stifling a yawn.

'It's not all about happiness though,' he continued. 'Don't you want to earn enough money so you can save up for the future?'

'I do save,' I said a bit defensively. 'I live with my parents, so I have no overheads. I save most of my salary and the rest I'm either eating or wearing.'

'But you could save more if you earned more,' he insisted and went on about mortgages and the property ladder, blah blah blah.

To be fair, I could see his point but given the fact that we've met twice and spoken once on the phone, I found his pushiness a bit overbearing. But then, I guess that's what the arranged marriage scenario does – it accelerates relationships so that the conversations that would usually take place over a course of a year, happen in just a few weeks.

Stepping out of the dark Underground into Covent Garden is like stepping into another world. The pedestrian-only cobbled streets are full of tourists taking pictures with living statues and Londoners pausing to listen to the beautiful classical music that a string quartet is playing outside the market.

The weather is surprisingly mild for March and although there's definitely a chill in the air, the temperature has improved a lot from last week's iciness. I've put away my winter coat and I'm happy to see the back of it. While I love winter with its dark, romantic nights, luxurious hot drinks and magical Christmas spirit, I love spring more. I love the yellow daffodils that have already started to pop up, I love the cherry blossoms on our road creating a pretty canopy for us to walk under, and I love the little bursts of sunshine that provide the right amount of warmth in the otherwise cold air.

Yasmin and I start walking towards the café and I have to grab her arm to force her to slow down as nerves start taking hold of me.

'Stop!' I squeak as we're about to round the corner that is between me and my fate. Yasmin stops and looks at me, concerned.

'Are you OK?' she asks, taking in my pale face and the way I keep fidgeting.

'No,' I whisper, my heart pounding. 'I can't do this. I want to go home.'

'We can't go home, Z, there's someone waiting for us,' she says patiently, taking my hand in hers. I snatch it away because it's clammy and she laughs and reaches out to hug me.

'This isn't Tariq,' she whispers into my ear as she holds me. 'I know you had a horrendous experience before, but it doesn't mean that it will happen again. Maybe Dr Farook is the one, maybe he isn't. But whatever is going to happen is going to happen. God's already written it. You won't know unless you walk in there with your head held high and find out. It's time to face your fears, Z.'

'I said I would never let Mum set me up again. I swore that I would find someone myself,' I say in a small voice, my face burrowed into her shoulder.

'So what? No one's judging you. Mum might have set you up with Tariq, but what happened wasn't her fault. She couldn't have known what he was going to do. And this dentist has nothing to do with Mum. The biodata came from someone else, and it was sent to Abbu, not her. If you don't give it a go, you'll always wonder.'

I know she's right, so I give myself another moment to compose myself and then pull away. For a second, I had forgotten what she was wearing and looking at her barren face with the tight hijab amplifying all her features makes me smile.

'All right. Let's do this,' I say and with a deep breath, venture around the corner.

We enter Ladurée and make our way up the narrow, rickety stairs. When we get to the top, we stop and scan the room, trying to see if we can spot a tall Asian guy with a dodgy haircut.

'Is that him?' Yasmin whispers, nodding towards the back of a man sitting alone in the corner. He is hunched over his phone and I stare at his narrow back, a sinking feeling in the pit of my stomach.

'I don't know,' I whisper back, swallowing nervously. 'This dude's bald. Dr F has a weird haircut remember? And this one looks like he's on the skinny side, too.'

'He could have shaved it,' Yasmin replies. 'He's brown, it must be him. There are no other brown people here.'

We walk over to the table and stand next to it, unsure how to announce our arrival.

'Er, Assalaamu Alaikum,' Yasmin says and I hide behind her, my gaze firmly on the floor. My palms are still sweating and I can feel my hands trembling so I clench my fists, hoping they will stop. We sit down and I continue to avoid looking at him.

'Wa Alaikum Salaam,' he replies in a low, gravelly voice. My spine shudders as if I've heard a fingernail scratching a blackboard.

'So!' Yasmin begins brightly, smiling a wide, fake smile, before launching into mindless small talk in the poshest accent that I've heard. I don't know where she musters up so much confidence from. I guess it's because it's my future on the line, not hers. Dr Farook Chowdhury hesitantly starts talking to her, darting looks at me every so often. I can tell he's taking in Yas's severe look compared to my own, less religious attire and wondering how it is that two sisters are so different. I try my best not to look back at him and spend my time pretending to study the menu instead.

This is excruciating. More than I imagined it would be, and it's not because of what happened with Tariq. It's uncomfortable and contrived and completely unfit for purpose. We're supposed to be figuring out if we can be life partners; but the whole meeting is like one big act, from my pearls to Yasmin's hijab and even the conversation. I'm sure not all marriage meetings are as off-putting as this. If they were, the world would be full of unmarried Bengalis and our entire race would die out.

Yasmin and Dr Farook talk about the weather, travelling and dentistry without me having to do more than 'hmm' or nod in the right places. I'm using the word 'conversation' very liberally here; it's more of a monologue with him talking and Yasmin barely getting a word in. He doesn't seem to care that I'm hardly speaking, either. From what he tells us, it sounds like he's got a full and varied life with all the places he's been to, but he manages to make it sound *boring*. There's no passion in his voice, no excitement, no life.

With the spotlight away from me, I take the plunge and discreetly study Dr Farook Chowdhury's unfortunate looks. He's so different from his picture that I feel slightly catfished. The whole purpose of the picture element of a biodata is to avoid these situations. In his photo, he wasn't good looking, but he wasn't *bad* looking either and had a full head of hair. But I think his dodgy haircut in the biodata picture was actually a wig to hide his alopecia. He can't help it if he has no hair, and I almost feel bad for noticing.

Anyway. It is what it is, and I'm not going to hold that against him. But what is entirely his choice is how he has decided to dress; completely unbuttoning the top half of his shirt. Peeking from beneath the folds of the creased linen are tufts of thick, wavy chest hair. Having that on display is something he has chosen to do, and I know some women dig that look, but it's just not my thing. Then, if that's not bad enough, he keeps reaching for a tuft of chest hair and twiddling it while he talks.

You know how you can't help but stare at an accident as you drive past? Even though it's horrible, scary and messed-up? Now that I've noticed the foliage on his chest, that's it, I can't tear my eyes away. I try – I really, *really* try – but when I think I've got over it, I find myself drawn back to the jungle that is Dr Farook's chest.

Chapter 11

'Why do you look so depressed?' Adam says, strolling over to me with the long sleeves of his T-shirt rolled up and his hands stuffed in his pockets. He is smiling in that cocky way of his and looks like relaxation personified. Unlike me. I was up super-early because I've been struggling to sleep the past few nights. I even got to the gym before it opened because I was already awake and I needed a distraction. I thought it would help me recover from my horrific meeting with Farook Fudging Chowdhury, but it didn't. I get the feeling nothing will.

After I dragged my eyes away from his chest, we managed to have a conversation, but it was stilted and forced. He pretty much said that women who didn't work full-time were lazy, and women who worked but didn't do all the housework and child-rearing, were also lazy.

'What's the point of having a partner if you're left to do it all alone?' I said from between clenched teeth, the anger rising in me like hot lava about to erupt.

'What's the point of getting married if I'm expected to do housework?' he retorted. We left soon after and I then spent the remainder of the weekend hiding under my duvet in between texting Hamza and WhatsApping Mo.

Today, I feel mentally and physically exhausted. It's not Dr Farook's shitty personality that has got to me, though (although that's obviously a part of it). It's more the fact that I wasted so much time on him; filling in that bloody questionnaire, fighting with my mum, enduring a long family meeting to discuss how to go about meeting him, dressing up, pretending to be something I'm not . . . I went through all that for a rude, arrogant, chauvinistic and stingy piece of shit who made me feel like something stuck to the bottom of his M&S loafers. The tight-arse even left us with the bill!

'Just meet him again!' Mum begged when we got home and Yasmin relayed the entire meeting to her, word for word. Including his very specific expectations of a woman and her place in a marriage.

'He basically wants an unpaid servant who also works, Mum,' Yasmin explained patiently as Mum desperately tried to make it out like his demands are normal.

'All men want women who will take care of them!' she insisted. 'Look at your dad. Does he ever lift a finger around the house?'

'But he doesn't expect you to work and contribute financially, as well as do it all at home!' Amina said indignantly, coming to the rescue. 'This dentist sounds like a complete misogynist! There's no way Zara can meet him again!'

'And he was butters,' Yasmin added. 'A million times worse than his picture. And God, his voice!'

'What was it like?' Amina asked, eager to find out as much bad stuff as possible to add to her growing bag of ammunition.

'Hoarse. Like he'd spent the morning screaming at underprivileged children in between fag breaks.'

'You three are unbelievable,' Mum interjected at that point. 'He is a dentist *and* a Choudhury and you're tearing him to pieces because of his voice? If Little Miss Twenty-nine thinks she can do better, then she's completely deluded!'

With that parting compliment, she stormed out of the room and slammed the door shut behind her. Now I know where Amina gets her theatrics from.

'Will a cuppa make you feel better?' Adam asks, a look of concern on his face when he waits for more details that I don't provide. I lived through Dr F once and relived it once already. I don't have the strength to go through it all again.

'Yes,' I say in a small voice, still facing away from him. 'With biscuits, too.'

'Well tough, I don't believe in indulging your wallowing,' he replies, throwing himself into his chair in glee. I decide that ignoring him will be the correct response, so I turn my face away and continue to work. My event is only a fortnight away now, and I have too much to do without the likes of Adam Yazıcı disturbing me.

I'm in the middle of organising my paperwork – my least favourite part of my job – when a text pings through; a welcome distraction from the all the receipts I've been tallying up against an Excel spreadsheet. I take a moment before I check it, wondering if it's Mo or Hamza and I realise that I'm not quite sure who I'd rather it was. Things have gotten a little repetitive with Mo. The flirting has become boring when it isn't building up to anything, and he still hasn't initiated a meeting. I'd rather stay single forever than make the first move with him. There's something about his confidence that's unsettling me and a part of me wonders if he's dating loads of women and waiting to see how things pan out with them before taking the next step with me.

As for Hamza; although our last convo wasn't exactly great, at least I know he's interested and isn't messing me around.

I finally check the text and it's from Hamza, with a simple, *Hey, Zara, what are you up to after work? Wanna go for a coffee?* No beating around the bush, no innuendoes, just straight up – a vast contrast to the message I got from Mo last night, which went something like, *What are you thinking about?* The reply to which he probably assumed was him, but it wasn't. At that precise moment, I was wondering if I could get away with having three donuts for dinner without Jordan realising.

I don't reply to Hamza immediately. Instead, I decide to take a lunch break at my desk and reassess the situation once I'm less hangry. I unwrap my sandwich to find that Nani's prepared me one of my fave Bengali sarnie combos; chilli omelette and ketchup. The omelette is made with eggs, onions, coriander, green chillies and salt and fried in a bit of ghee. The sweet ketchup is a welcome contrast to the spicy omelette and it tastes *amazing* in a sandwich. Trust me.

'What are you eating?' Adam asks, sidling over to me and sitting on my desk. I shove him off.

'Nuffin',' I mumble, my mouth full of food.

'It doesn't look like nothing. It looks tasty. Smells it too.' Then, before I can stop him, he grabs the other half of my sandwich and takes a massive bite out of it.

'Oi!' I moan, snatching it back and examining the teeth marks. 'How am I going to eat the rest of that now that you've slobbered all over it? I was proper hungry as well.'

'You're always proper hungry.' He shrugs. 'And that was bangin'. I didn't know you could cook.'

'I can't. My grandma made it for me.'

'You having a laugh? Your little old grandma packs your lunch for you?'

'So what? She likes doing it.'

'Yeah, like Dobby liked serving the Malfoys.'

'I can't believe you're comparing me to a dark wizard!'

It's while we're in the throes of this squabble that my dad calls me to let me know that the Tower Hamlets guy has rejected me because, according to the middle person, I'm too old and don't wear hijab. And they heard that I've been engaged before.

I feel as though I've been punched in the middle of my chest. It's all my darkest fears vocalised in one phone call. In the minutes after the call, I excuse myself to the prayer room and sit there, sobbing, for ages. I hate my dad for calling me at work with this news instead of waiting until I get home. I hate him for telling me the reasons why they said no. And I hate him for making me feel that I'm nothing because I can't secure a husband.

'Are you OK, babe?' I look up from my position on the floor to see Francesca peering around the door, her eyebrows knitted together in concern. I try to answer, but the words get caught in my throat. She slips into the room and sits down next to me in silence until I'm ready to talk.

'I'm all right,' I whisper. 'Just feeling so drained from all this marriage business.'

'All that stuff your parents are making you do?'

'Yeah. My dad called to tell me that I've been rejected by a man I wasn't interested in to begin with. And it hurts a lot more than I expected.'

'It's his loss, hun. And I know it's a cliché, but there are loads of men who would kill to be with you.'

I snort unattractively. 'Where are all these mystery men? I can't see any.'

'What about that guy you're dating? The Egyptian one? And the one from the app?'

I look down at the worn carpet and sigh. 'The guy from MuslimMate has made no move to meet me, and yeah, there's Hamza but we're not exactly dating. We've only met twice and I'm really not sure about him.'

'So meet him more so you can decide,' she says simply. I think back to the text that I still haven't replied to. She's right. How can I decide for certain if we've only met up once after the chocolate event? I take my phone out and shoot him a reply: *Hey, I'm free tonight. Let me know where to meet you.*

I sit there for a bit longer, and Fran, the sweetheart, goes and gets me a baby wipe so I can clean up my smudged mascara before I head back to my desk and pretend that I haven't spent the last half an hour crying in the prayer room.

'A few of us are going to the pub after work,' Adam says, loitering by my desk holding a gigantic sub sandwich and offering me the half he hasn't touched. That guy doesn't stop eating. I refuse the sub; my appetite seems to have disappeared along with my self-esteem. 'Why don't you come out with us for a change?'

'Have we seriously never had this conversation before?' I reply, probably more harshly than I should have. After what's happened, I'm not in the mood for Adam's judgement. We've been working together for what, three years, and he's only now realised that I never go to pubs? 'I don't go to pubs.'

'Oh. Why not?' He looks genuinely confused and once again I'm reminded of how different we are. How is it that a Muslim man is asking me such an obvious question?

'You know I don't drink,' I say simply.

'So? You don't have to drink.'

'Please don't say something as cliché as "have an orange juice",' I scoff, rolling my eyes.

'Well, yeah. Or a Coke.'

'Why on earth would I want to be surrounded by people getting drunk and acting stupid when I'm perfectly sober? You might not remember that you've slobbered all over Harriet from Housing in the morning, but I will.'

'God, judgemental much? Not everyone who drinks is a raving drunk,' he exclaims, his face turning pink with indignation. 'It's a social thing. Lighten up.'

If there's one thing I can't stand it's being told to 'lighten up'. Or 'chill out'. It has the completely opposite effect and makes me furious, even if previously I was only mildly irritated.

'Well, excuse me for having values,' I retort, my own cheeks heating up.

'Are you trying to say I don't? Because I drink?' Adam splutters. 'I might not be a perfect Muslim but it's not your place to judge me. I'll take my chances with God, thanks.'

'You go ahead and do that!' With a final glare I look pointedly at my screen. As in, 'this conversation is over'. I can feel him still fuming as he stomps out of the office entirely.

The thing is, I honestly don't care if Adam and the whole world drinks. That's their business. It's *my* business to decide whether I want to participate or not, and if I choose not to, why does it make me judgemental, boring or holier-than-thou? The worst part is that Adam, as a so-called Muslim, should get it. I've never had a non-Muslim colleague or classmate give me grief over avoiding the pub, so why is he?

Anyway, I have too much to do so I try not to dwell on Adam and his warped mentality. For the rest of the day I ignore him and his huffy back and get on with ploughing through my mammoth task list.

'Zara, are you going to join us tonight?' Francesca asks me late in the afternoon. 'You could probably do with a pick-me-up today.'

I'm so engrossed in my work that I hadn't realised that it's already nearly five. I look up from my computer to see that she's put on cherry-red lipstick and lots of mascara since I last looked at her – not that she needs the extra support. Francesca is your classic English beauty, with masses of glossy golden hair, really thick eyebrows and super-long limbs. Everyone in the building from Tom in Social Services to Rakesh in Finance fancies her. I know this because at least twice an hour, some stray male winds up in our little corner and makes up an excuse to talk to her. She does a good job pretending she doesn't know that she's the office beauty queen, making her all the more desirable.

I stare blankly at her, still lost in my world of confirmation emails, itineraries and down-payments.

'Drinks at the Duke? A few people from Housing, Education, and Social are going to be there.' She starts gathering up her things and I see that Adam is also shutting his computer down. Early, I might add, but today isn't the day to bring that up.

'Thanks,' I finally respond with a smile. 'I've got plans tonight. Have a good time, though.' Adam stops shoving his things into his messenger bag and turns to look at me.

'Aw, you don't have to pretend you have plans on a Monday, Z. You don't want to go to the pub with me, I get it.' His tone is jokey but there's a mocking undertone that I don't like.

'Well, there's that, but I also have a date,' I retort.

'Oh, really? Who's the lucky guy then?' I can tell by the sceptical look on his face that he doesn't believe me and I stare blankly back at him, refusing to react. Francesca looks at the two of us, confused by the tension. She opens her mouth, closes it, opens it again – and closes it. I would laugh if I wasn't so annoyed.

'Hamza. And judging by our texting last night, I think he *does* consider himself quite lucky.'

'Poor bloke doesn't know what's in store for him,' he says eventually, putting on his jacket.

'Well, let's let him be the judge of that, why don't we?' I mimic his line from earlier. 'He seems to like what he's seen so far.'

We glare at each other. I honestly don't know what his problem is. One minute he's a nice guy that I consider a friend, and the next he's this awful teenager that relishes bringing me down.

'The Duke's only around the corner from here,' Francesca finally interrupts. 'Why don't you come for a bit?'

'She doesn't drink like us,' Adam interrupts, grabbing his helmet and I can't tell if it's another jibe or he's merely stating the obvious. Is it really an 'us' and 'them' situation? I'm already sensitive because of my traumatic weekend, followed by the blow from the Tower Hamlets guy, and Adam's stinky attitude makes me feel worse. A lump forms in my throat.

'Don't listen to him, Frannie. I really do have a date. Tell me all about it tomorrow, yeah?' I give her a small smile and quickly turn away before either of them can see the droplet of water that's gathered in the corner of my eye.

Hamza has decided he wants to come all the way to North London for our coffee to check out my ends. I know it's going to turn into dinner so I text him that we should go for a meal instead, my treat.

North London is home to the best Turkish food in the whole of the UK. And maybe even the world. No joke. Wood Green has a fair few restaurants but the real action is further down the road on Green Lanes where there are countless Turkish restaurants, cafés, bakeries and grocery shops, all selling the most delicious grilled meats, soft breads and flaky pastries.

As I wait for Hamza on the High Road, the intoxicating fragrance of charcoaled lamb wafts out of the restaurant and starts tickling my nostrils and I feel better because of it. I breathe in the scent and close my eyes, trying not to think about what Jordan would say if he knew I decided to follow up my morning workout with an evening feast.

'Salaam 'Alaykom!' I turn to see Hamza striding towards me, grinning from ear to ear, looking like a big cuddly teddy bear. It's been a while since I last saw him and a lot has happened between our first 'date' and today, but still there's an air of familiarity about him that feels comforting.

'Is it Casual Monday at work today?' he says, checking out my look with amusement as we wait for the waiter to show us to our table. I'm wearing an oversized hoody, boyfriend jeans and high-top Jordans, topped with an unzipped bomber jacket because it's still a little chilly in the evenings.

'It's Casual Monday every day in my office,' I reply with a grin. 'Not what you're used to in the City, eh?' His cheerfulness is intoxicating, and I feel the dark cloud hovering over me begin to pass.

'I never knew sneakers could be so sexy,' he says, wiggling his eyebrows suggestively.

'You mean trainers,' I correct him playfully. 'A sneaker is someone that sneaks.'

'Are you planning on sneaking around with me, Zara Choudhury?'

'Do I look like the sneaky type?' I gasp, mock offended. The waiter arrives and takes us upstairs. My thighs are still aching from my torture session but I don't want Hamza to know about my new gym obsession, so I keep my mouth shut and soldier on.

Hamza gives up looking at the menu and lets me order for us both. I choose a shared mixed platter of tender lamb chops, juicy ribs, crispy chicken wings, charcoaled lamb and chicken chunks, buttery rice and Turkish couscous. We are given complimentary bread, three types of salad, humous and yoghurt dip, so when the main course gets here, I'm already stuffed but Hamza is delighted by how generous the portions are. He packs away more than half the dish and there's no way I can even try and keep up. He urges me to ditch the cutlery and dig into the ribs with my hands. Laughing at his enthusiasm, I oblige. God knows what I look like with bits of charcoal stuck between my teeth but I get the feeling that I could walk around with my front tooth missing and Hamza would still make me feel like the most beautiful girl in Wood Green.

'Come on, Zara, you can do better than that,' he teases when after one rib, one chop and two wings, I declare myself as incapacitated.

'I honestly can't eat another morsel,' I moan, rubbing my bloated tummy. 'How are you managing to eat all that?'

'Well, I have a manly appetite, being the alpha male that I am.' He says this with a completely serious expression and I burst out laughing.

The remainder of the night flows as smoothly as the first time we met and so much better than our awkward phone conversation. I realise that he's the type of guy who's better in person. Technology seems to dull his energy.

We talk about everything; work, family, friends, movies, books, music, and I have a such a good time. His cheerfulness is contagious, and I almost forget the shitty day and shittier weekend I've had. He's so engaging that the more I laugh, the more attractive he becomes. I wonder if I'm going to have to start taking our 'thing' a bit more seriously. Look what else is out there: amidst the limited fish in the sea, there are sharks, jellyfish, and other unpleasant creatures that I don't want to become entangled with. Would a simple, stable – and sometimes a bit serious – tuna really be all that bad?

He's also taken my mind off Adam and our snarky exchange, and I love that he knows exactly what to say to make me laugh. And unlike Adam, his jokes are never at my expense.

'I've had a nice time tonight,' I say, as we sip our strong, super-sweet Turkish black tea while enjoying the complimentary crispy baklava, sweet syrup oozing out of every bite and dribbling down my chin. Hamza looks so elated by my admission that I instantly regret being so forthcoming. I don't want to lead him on; not when I'm completely unsure about us and exploring every other avenue for someone I'm more compatible with.

I gesture to the waiter for the bill and then force myself to look into Hamza's expressive eyes that are full of warmth. I'm not sure what he sees in my eyes in return. Probably wariness laced with a bit of guilt.

'Sister, your bill was already paid by the gentleman,' the waiter announces, his sudden appearance making me jump.

'What?' Guilt goes flying out the window and I glare at Hamza. 'You promised I could pay this time!'

He shrugs, a small smile on his round face. 'Sorry, not sorry.'

'If you keep doing this, I'm not going to meet up with you again!' I warn him, my irritation fading the more I look at his pleased expression. It's pretty hard to stay annoyed at someone so guileless, but the nicer he is, the worse I feel about leading him on.

'I'll take my chances,' he retorts, still smiling. 'How are you getting home?'

'Don't worry, I'll book a complete waste-of-money Uber,' I sigh, smiling to let him know I'm not actually pissed off. 'Even though my house is like, five minutes from the bus stop and it's completely unnecessary.'

'I'm glad.'

Hamza gets up and helps me put on my jacket. It's the first time a man – well, *anyone* – has done this for me and I'm not sure if I like the gesture. For starters, getting my padded arms into the sleeves is tricky, and then, during the struggle, our fingers brush and once again, I yank my hand away from his accidental touch. I sense him stiffen from the rebuke. I'm sure my rebuffs will stop being charming at some point and start becoming offensive, but I don't know how to stop myself.

We walk downstairs to where my car is waiting. Hamza opens the door for me and this time he doesn't lean in for a hug or even a handshake. With a wry smile, he bids me farewell and when I'm safely deposited into the back seat of the car, he closes the door firmly behind me, gives me a little wave and then walks away.

I lean back into the leather seat, still as muddled as ever. His goodbye seemed a bit on the cold side and I wonder if this is it, if I've screwed things up between us. And that's when I realise that if Hamza were to walk away right now, I would spend the rest of my days wondering if I made the biggest mistake of my life.

If this were a romcom movie, I would jump out of the Uber, chase Hamza up the High Road and throw myself into his bulky arms, and he would swing me around as if I were as light as a feather. But it's not a movie and I can't do stuff like that. For starters, I can't run, remember? I'll need more than two gym sessions before I can start literally chasing men. And also, there's no way I would let anyone try and pick me up, not unless I'm bleeding to death and need to be lifted onto a stretcher.

I turn away from the window and decide not to fret over it tonight. What's done is done. If Hamza and I are meant to be, if our fates are entwined and God has written it for us to be together, it'll happen.

On that positive note, I take out my phone to distract my wandering thoughts. There are a few unread messages from Mo, but I ignore them and open up Instagram instead, half-heartedly scrolling through carefully filtered shots of elaborate meals, pretty scenes, pouty selfies and edgy fashion, pressing 'like' even when I don't particularly care for the image, for the sake of being polite.

Layla at a fancy restaurant with her husband; some faceless fashionista showing off her designer handbag outside a Central London townhouse; one of those perfect, Muslim married couples hugging and staring at each other with pure happiness. How is it that they've succeeded in making me feel inadequate, even though I'm mature enough to realise it's all pretence? I wonder how many naïve Muslim teenagers aspire to nothing more than finding a perfect husband based on all this nonsense. Anyway. Moving on. Adam and Francesca hugging; Amina and her friends at a . . .

Hang on a second. I scroll back up to the picture of Adam and Francesca. I don't know what happened to the demure outfit she was wearing at work, but there she is, in a seriously low-cut vest, pressed up against Adam as if she can't stand without him propping her up. He is grinning, a beer in one hand and the other firmly around her narrow shoulders, his hand dangling dangerously close to her ample bosom.

I look back at the Cheshire cat grin he's wearing in place of his ethics and feel like slapping it off him. Adam was the *one* guy in the office who didn't drool all over the resident English rose, and I know it sounds stupid, but I kind of thought he preferred me. But why would he? Look at her, she's tall, slim, young and perfect. White. And she doesn't mind going to pubs with him. And look at me. The old, brown, flabby, judgemental prude.

The bloody picture already has forty-three likes and it's only been an hour. Well, you know what? Adam isn't the only one who can post a picture with a good-looking creature.

I feel my blood pressure begin to rise, and before I persuade myself otherwise, I scroll through my photos and find the one of me and Jordan. You know, Jordan, my super-hot, buff and all-round perfect-looking personal trainer. I play around with the filters and editing tools until I look radiant and flawless (Jordan doesn't need any extra help) and then post it with the slightly mysterious caption, 'Having a fab night with my BAE'. Thank God my account's private and Hamza isn't following me. I don't think he does social media.

With a satisfied smirk, I put my phone away and close my eyes. Ha. Let's see what Adam makes of *that*.

Chapter 12

I am so late for work that I don't have time to deliberate on what to wear, let alone iron anything. Hoping no one will notice, I throw on yesterday's outfit, pull my greasy hair into a bun and rush to the station as fast as I can without a scrap of makeup on. That's the last time I go to bed without showering; I feel, look and smell like rotten doner kebab.

When I got in last night, I went upstairs before anyone could interrogate me and climbed straight into bed. I couldn't sleep, though. I lay there, in the dark, staring at my ceiling and wondering where I would be in ten years' time. I went through all sorts of scenarios: marrying Hamza and having a sexless marriage; marrying a freshie – short for 'fresh from the Desh' – and having to support him financially for years and years; not getting married at all and growing old, bitter and alone . . . I must have nodded off though, because I had a disturbing dream that I can vaguely remember snippets of. In it, Hamza had Jordan's face but his own body, and kept making me do push-ups while screaming at me for not going to the pub with him.

Adam and Francesca stare at me when I stumble into the office at ten thirty, panting from running up the stairs instead of waiting for the lift as I usually do.

'I'm so sorry I'm late!' I gasp, jumping into my seat and switching on my computer, my face glossy with perspiration. 'Adam, I know you're waiting for approvals on the new roll-ups so they can go to the printers. I haven't missed the deadline, have I?'

'Er, not yet,' he says quietly, still staring at me with a bewildered expression on his paler-than-usual face. Must have been all the drinks he was guzzling away with his beloved Francesca.

'We've been trying to call you,' Francesca blurts out, also looking at me strangely. Unsurprisingly, she doesn't look worse for wear in the slightest. In fact, she looks like she's come out of the spa, all glowy and radiant in minimal makeup, a beige slouchy jumper falling off a perfect bony shoulder, wide trousers and white trainers. You'd never catch her coming into work in yesterday's battered ensemble.

'Oh, my battery died last night and I couldn't charge it. Sorry. Was it something urgent?' I rummage around in my desk, pull my USB cable out and connect my phone to my computer so it can charge up at last.

'Um, no, nothing urgent,' she mumbles, exchanging a knowing look with Adam. I have no idea what their problem is. It's as though I've shown up with my hair shaved off. And then it hits me. They're acting weird because something happened between them last night and they're worried that I'll pick up on the shameless vibes they're emitting and report them to HR for having an inter-departmental love affair. OK, I know I'm being a cow, but the thought of them getting together bothers me. I don't know why, but it does. I decide to ignore their nonsense and get on with sorting out my event.

I'm dying for a cup of tea to calm me down, but after rolling up an hour late and almost missing my print deadline, I can't wander off to make one. My stomach lets out a tiny growl, protesting the lack of a Nani-prepared breakfast. I could really do with some biscuits to accompany the imaginary tea. If Adam and I weren't sort-of fighting, I could have asked him to get me some. But we sort-of are. I have to sit here, parched, sweaty, smelly and hungry, and make sure that my tardiness hasn't screwed up the event I've been planning for the past two months.

With a huge sigh, I ignore my rumbling stomach and get to work, blocking out all distractions. I go through the artwork I have to approve, make sure there are no embarrassing spelling mistakes or incorrect sponsor logos, and send it all to the printers. Adam's done a great job with the designs – very Banksy-esque with hand-drawn sketches and a pop of colour – and I hope to God that people show up.

By lunchtime, I've worked through more than half of my task list so I allow myself a quick break to recharge. Grabbing my revived phone, jacket and handbag, I let the gruesome twosome know that I'll be back in half an hour and make my way down some back streets to a greasy spoon caff that does the best jacket potato with cheese and beans.

I settle down on a plastic chair, brush away some sugar granules on the Formica table, and cut through the crispy, perfectly-baked skin to find moist potato drenched in butter underneath. After a couple of massive mouthfuls, I begin to feel more like myself.

As I eat, I pull out my phone to see what I've been missing while it's been out of action – and nearly choke on a baked bean when I see that I have 176 WhatsApp messages and a hundred other missed calls, texts and notifications.

My appetite disappears. Something has happened, I know it has. *Please God, don't let it be Nani.* She was complaining of a headache this morning and I was too stressed about being late for work to pay attention. What if it wasn't a headache? What if it was a brain tumour and I'm so self-absorbed that I've missed all the signals?

I start reciting the prayer 'Inna Lillahi Wa Inna Ilaihirraajiuun', over and over, trying to calm my pounding heart. *We belong to God and it is to Him we shall return.* Throat dry, I take a big swig of my drink and force myself to open the first unread WhatsApp conversation. It's from Layla.

OMG WHO WAS THAT HOT GUY ON YOUR INSTAGRAM LAST NIGHT?

OK. That wasn't what I was expecting. What hot guy? The only guy I saw last night was Hamza, and I wouldn't classify Hamza as 'hot'.

> ZARA!!! Answer me God Dammit! Who is this BAE? I thought I was your BAE?

I have no idea what Layla's on about, so I ignore it and move to one from Amina, split up into about twenty lines. I hate it when people do that. No wonder I had 176 unread messages. Half of them are from my sister, the serial return-key presser.

> Zara
> Mum heard me gasp
> She grabbed my phone
> She's having hysterics
> Luckily
> Her and Dad
> Have gone to Uncle Mujib's house
> Just go to sleep
> Before they come home I mean
> Otherwise
> You're gonna be in deep
> S
> H
> I
> T

And there's one from Mum. Bracing myself, I open it.

> ZARA!
>
> Why is there a picture of you and a good-looking black man on your InstaSnap?
>
> I don't think it's very appropriate given that we are trying very hard to find you a husband here.
>
> Please delete it.
>
> Before I show your dad.

InstaSnap? Does she mean Snapchat? I don't remember snapping anything last night . . . Oh, but I did snap the food, I think. Was Hamza in the background? He's hardly a good-looking black man, though.

And it goes on, and on, and on. Even friends who I haven't spoken to in ages, have messaged me asking me who the 'hot/fit/sexy/buff/banging/peng' guy is.

My head throbbing from the lack of sleep and my mind confused from all the pending work-related tasks, I can't, for the life of me, figure out what they're talking about.

I rewind back to yesterday. Tower Hamlets rejecting me. Crying. Fighting with Adam. Meeting Hamza. Our weird farewell. The atmosphere changing. I remember sitting in the Uber, feeling tense and confused after Hamza's chilly goodbye, and discovering Adam's cosy picture with Francesca. There was that little twinge of envy that, as the seconds passed, grew into full-fledged jealousy and a bit of rage.

And then that moment of true madness when I posted the selfie of me and Jordan and pretended that he was last night's date, to get back at my colleagues.

Bingo.

'Bloody hell,' I groan, covering my face with my hands. This is so embarrassing. If the truth ever comes out, I'm going to be completely humiliated. I will forever be known as the single desperado who pretends that her personal trainer is her boyfriend.

On and on it goes. WhatsApps, DMs and comments demanding to know who my 'BAE' is.

Reading through all the gushing comments, I can't help but begin to enjoy the attention. This must be how influencers feel, except better, as I don't have any haters on my account, only my friends and family. A part of me has secretly always wanted to be a famous influencer. But I don't have the confidence to get up there, flaws and all, and have everyone pick away at everything I say and do. Besides, my mum would kill me if I decided to parade myself online. She's a huge believer in black magic and the evil eye, and is always telling us off for posting pictures on social media, even though our accounts are private.

Ah yes. Mum. I'm going to have a lot of explaining to do when I get home this evening. She probably won't believe that Jordan's my trainer, and even if she does, I know I'm going to receive a good telling off for hiring a male trainer. Oh well, it's worth it. Adam hasn't liked the picture but he must have seen it because he spends half the day online. He's probably in the loo right now, inspecting his lack of upper body muscle in the grimy mirror. In my picture, Jordan's ripped biceps are very obvious, and his arm around me is more obvious. Ha! Let's see what he makes of that.

I skip back to the office, enjoying the warmth from the sun that has finally fought its way through the thick clouds.

Adam and Francesca exchange another glance as I saunter past them and head to the kitchen to make myself a well-deserved cuppa. Before the kettle has a chance to start boiling, Adam slips in and quietly fetches his plain black mug and places it next to my hot-pink personalised one. If that's supposed to be an apology for yesterday's appalling behaviour towards me, it's a pretty crap one. But I'm in a benevolent mood so I say nothing and add two heaped teaspoons of sugar to his mug, and one in mine.

'Only one sugar?'

'Yeah, I've decided to cut out the crap in my life,' I reply pointedly, giving him a 'look'.

'Touché. Point taken.' He takes the kettle and pours the boiled water into my mug first, and then his. I stir the sugar until it dissolves while he takes the milk out of the fridge and pours a generous amount in mine.

'Biscuit?' he asks, offering me a packet of chocolate Bourbons.

'No thanks.'

'Wow. A lot has changed in your life, hasn't it?' he notes, looking a bit dejected.

'A bit.' I know he's dying to know more about my post but there's no way I'm offering any information unless he swallows his pride and asks me. I sip my tea and look at him coolly. His complexion is still pale and he has greenish-blue shadows under his eyes. His jaw is usually adorned with fashionably sculpted facial hair, but today, the hair has jumped over the fence from stubble to full-on beard. He looks rough.

'So . . . how was your date last night?' he eventually asks, shifting his weight and not quite meeting my eyes. *Aha!* I knew it was coming. While the moralistic part of me thinks that now is the chance to 'fess up and admit that the Instagram post had nothing to do with my date, my wild side does a little flamenco dance. Forget confessing. This isn't church and I'm not Catholic. Now is my chance to get my own back on him and his secret lover for rubbing their dalliance in my unmarried-at-twenty-nine face.

'Oh, it was amazing,' I gush with a huge smile. 'We had a lovely dinner and even though I made Hamza promise to let me pay, when I went to get the bill, he had already sneakily paid for it. He's a proper gentleman, you know?'

'Sounds disrespectful to me,' he grumbles. 'If he can't respect your wishes now, you can bet your life that he won't respect them later.'

'We have *sooo* much in common,' I continue, as if he hadn't spoken. 'The evening flew by, we had that much to talk about. We're on the same wavelength about *everything*.'

'And this is the same guy you told me about before? The one you don't fancy?' By his befuddled expression, I can tell that he's trying to figure out if BAE is Hamza or someone else.

How do I get out of this one? Any woman with even the slightest ounce of oestrogen – no, let me start again – any *human*, male or female, gay or straight, would have to be blind not to fancy Jordan.

'Omigod, no, of course not,' I reply as convincingly as possible. 'That was someone else. Someone completely different. Whose name also starts with H.'

'It all sounds too good to be true,' he concedes grudgingly, staring morosely into his mug.

'It's perfect,' I fib, beginning to feel a bit sick, the lies leaving a slight bitter taste in my mouth. This suddenly isn't so fun anymore.

'Well, I hope you know what you're doing,' he says ominously, walking over to the sink and rinsing out his mug without scrubbing it with liquid. No wonder he has a black mug; he doesn't want anyone to see the thick tea stains defacing it. As he opens the door to leave, he turns around and adds, 'I bet he wasn't that good. You're not even glowing.'

The door closes and I stare at it slightly confused as I try to decipher what he said. What did he mean by 'I'm not glowing?' Why would I be glowing right now?

Realisation dawns on me and I lean against the kitchen cabinets and take a deep breath. He thinks I *slept* with Jordan?

All the knowing looks Adam and Francesca have been sharing all day make sense now. They've obviously been talking about me and what they think happened last night. Did I say that I was enjoying the attention? I'm not anymore. And when I get home and face my mum's wrath, it's going to get worse.

Part Two

Spring

Chapter 13

'God, this place is a dump,' Adam grumbles as he, Francesca and I walk into the creepy old church hall we've hired for tomorrow's 'We are Haringey' bash. It's six on Friday night, and while the rest of London will be gearing up to all sorts of debauchery to celebrate the start of the weekend, the only excitement I'm going to get is if a ghost from the adjacent graveyard pays us a visit.

'It won't be once we've finished with it,' I reply unconvincingly, placing the cardboard box of supplies I'm carrying on a table. A cloud of dust rises from the surface and I cough. This place *is* a dump, but we've got a long night ahead of us and I'm determined to stay positive. Besides, I managed to get it for free which meant we had more money to spend on other stuff, like the entertainment and decorations.

'What do we need to do tonight?' Adam asks, glancing at his watch as though he has somewhere else to be. Francesca's no better; she's wrinkling her nose and looking down at her expensive ensemble in concern. I'm in old jeans and a hoodie because I knew what my Friday night was going to consist of, and I have no desire to ruin my good clothes cleaning a dilapidated church hall. She, however, is in a white silk shirt tucked into beige tailored trousers, more suited to a coffee shop in Milan.

I'm still a bit miffed with Francesca for being so flirty and tactile with Adam, although I know I'm being irrational. And it's not just because of that cringey Instagram post. Ever since their night out, she's been all over him like a rash; creating excuses to go up to him and touch his arm or leg, giggling at all of his lame jokes and constantly flicking her hair. I've never seen her behave like this, and I feel like I'm in a L'Oréal photo shoot half the time, the way she's posing and carrying on.

As for how I feel about Adam . . . I'm still upset with him for the awful way he spoke to me, and to be honest, if he wasn't my colleague, I would probably cancel him, but seeing as he is, I'm stuck with him for the foreseeable future.

'We need to brush the floor and dust down all the tables,' I begin, looking pointedly at Adam before checking my to-do list and rattling out the long list of things we need to get done.

'All right, let's do this,' Adam declares once I've finished reciting, rolling up his sleeves gamely and marching off in search of a brush and mop, while Francesca and I get the balloon pumps out and start pumping air into colourful balloons.

'How is it that you're not even sweating?' she asks half an hour later, her face pink and covered in a sheen of perspiration.

I shrug and blow up my fiftieth balloon. 'It's the gym life, babe.'

The night is long and tiresome and at some point, Adam has the genius idea of listening to music. He digs out his iPad and we take turns choosing songs on YouTube and singing along half-heartedly. Francesca bows out at eight, her usually fresh face looking weary and her clothes covered in dust, dirt and PVA glue. We're almost done anyway, so for the next hour, Adam and I work silently until the hall is gleaming and looking festive.

'This place looks amazing. Thank you, Adam, I really appreciate it.' I beam, taking a long swig of water and wiping my wet mouth with my sleeve. I'm too tired to get up and look for some tissue.

'Don't be daft, you don't have to thank me, it's my job.' Adam shrugs, looking bashful for a change. 'Anyway, let's get out of here. I'm starving. Do you wanna grab something to eat?'

'I don't know, it's getting late.' I get up and stretch out my stiff muscles, my back cracking as I do. 'I don't fancy getting the bus in the middle of the night.' More importantly, things are going so well with Adam that I don't want us to push it and end up arguing again.

'I'll drop you home, don't worry.' He looks at me with puppy dog eyes framed in long, thick brown lashes. 'Go on, please. Don't let me starve to death.'

'Oh, all right then.' I'm hungry too and could do with a good meal in me, especially as I was too busy to have lunch.

We make our way back to the office building which is halfway between the church hall and the restaurant, so we can dump all the bags and supplies until the morning. I don't have the energy to go all the way upstairs with him, so despite it being dark and late, I wait for him down by the main entrance.

It's actually been a really nice day and the first time in ages we haven't bickered or fought. We've always had a bit of banter going on, but that's all it's been, innocent banter, nothing serious. Lately, however, it seems as though we've crossed the fine line from jokes to insults, and it feels as if all he does is jump down my throat at every little thing. I don't know how our relationship degenerated so quickly but tonight it's beginning to feel that perhaps it can still be salvaged.

When he returns, we walk towards my usual Turkish restaurant in Wood Green, and grab a small table upstairs, away from the raucous crowd on the ground floor. Unlike Hamza, Adam doesn't pull my chair out for me, let alone attempt to help me with my jacket. In fact, he almost lets the door close on my face before he remembers himself and grabs it at the last second. A gentleman he most certainly is not, but it's not like this is a date, so his bad manners are no skin off my back. He also orders a beer and I bite my tongue, not wanting to get into another argument over the topic of drinking. When it arrives, though, I think something changes in my expression despite my best efforts to keep my face impassive.

'What? No comment on my choice of beverage?' he asks, slightly confrontationally as he takes a long swig, staring me defiantly in the eye.

'Nope,' I say evenly, refusing to rise to the bait. We've had such a good evening and I'm not about to ruin it all now; especially when we have an event to pull off tomorrow.

'You know, Zara, you've gotta realise that this whole religion thing is different for me,' he begins. 'For me and my family, religion is more of this old-fashioned cultural thing, you know?'

I bristle at his choice of words but still, I resist the urge to comment. It might be 'old-fashioned' to him, but it's not to me. 'OK. Got it.'

'Come on, don't be like that.'

'Be like what? I'm not saying anything. How, why, or *if* you believe in God is not really any of my business.'

'You don't care at all?'

'I don't,' I affirm. 'Why would I?' Then I realise that I *do* want to know what he believes, and I try and backtrack a little. 'I mean, yeah, I'm curious to know your stance on it, but that's it. It's not going to change our friendship, is it?'

'So whether I'm an atheist or agnostic makes no difference to you whatsoever?' He narrows his eyes slightly as he says this, like he doesn't believe me for a second.

'None.'

'Well, I do believe in God,' he says when the nibbles arrive and he digs in without offering any of it to me first. 'I believe in the spirit of Islam, but not the dogma, if you get what I mean. I guess it's different for you.'

'It is. People assume that because I don't wear a hijab I'm irreligious, but I'm not. I believe in God, and I believe in the rituals, and I believe in the way the Prophet set out for us to live our lives.'

'You don't find it controlling?'

'No. I find it liberating. I can't imagine getting through life thinking that this is it, there's no greater purpose to our existence than just . . . living.'

He ponders this and nods. 'Yeah, I get you. Anyway,' he says, tearing off a piece of warm bread and dipping it into hummus, 'enough of the deep shit. How are things with you and Hamza?'

'Seriously?' I raise an eyebrow, too tired to react any further. 'You really want to go there?' First religion and now Hamza? The two most contentious topics between us?

'Sorry, just making light conversation,' he mumbles, his mouth full of bread.

'If you must know, everything's fine,' I answer shortly. 'I invited him to the event but he's got plans so he can't make it.'

'You know,' Adam begins slowly, 'I honestly don't get why you're so fixated on finding a man, as if it's difficult for someone like you.' He says this nonchalantly, his eyes focused steadily on the salad he's loaded his plate with.

'What do you mean?' I have no idea what he's getting at, but right now, I'm too distracted to analyse it. The food has arrived and I'm so hungry that I grab my plate which is piled high with succulent lamb doner and buttery rice and take a huge mouthful. It is at that precise moment that Adam chooses to reply to my question.

'Are you telling me that you honestly, hand on heart, don't know that half the guys at work fancy you?' he says, completely straight-faced.

'What?' I gasp, forgetting that my mouth is full of food. I take a gulp of water and somehow manage to choke out, 'What the hell are you going on about? No, they don't!'

'Yes, they do,' he insists with earnest. 'Why do you think they're always hanging around our corner, offering to help at our events?'

'Er, to chat to our resident next top model, perhaps?'

He laughs at this and shakes his head. 'What? Francesca? She's already slept with most of the single guys, and probably a couple of the married ones as well.'

'She hasn't! Don't make up shit about a female colleague Adam, that's a nasty rumour to spread!' Bloody hell, this evening is full of revelations. A few minutes ago I was about to nod off, but now I'm wide awake.

'I'm not! I heard it from the horse's mouth. She tells me everything.' Adam leans back, grinning. He loves shocking people and I'm reacting exactly as he hoped I would.

'Good for her,' I croak, taking another long swig of water.

'Yeah, so getting with Fran isn't much of an achievement,' he continues. 'You, however, are a bit of a mystery. Everyone's wondering about what our Bengali beauty gets up to in her free time.'

'Oh, shut up,' I say, part-annoyed, part-embarrassed. 'You're chatting rubbish now. I know you like shocking people, Adam, but I'm not that gullible.'

'Seriously. You never come out with any of us, you never get too close to anyone. You never go for lunch with anyone. You're like this chatty loner. You're an oxymoron and it doesn't make sense to them.'

I shake my head in disbelief; partly because I didn't think he knew what an oxymoron was. 'Me? A loner? I talk to you and Fran, don't I?'

'*We* know you're not,' he explains. 'But you're aloof with everyone else. The thing is, at the same time, you don't come across as shy, either. No one can figure you out. Some of the girls think you're stuck up, but the guys find it hot.'

There's an uncomfortable silence while I try and digest everything he's told me. I don't know whether to be flattered or offended by it all. Maybe it's time I actually went to some of these stupid social gatherings, pubs or otherwise.

'How come Francesca confides in you then? Have you and her . . . ?' The unfinished question hangs in the air like a dead body hanging off a noose and my voice trails off as I realise that it isn't really any of my business.

'What?! Me and Fran? No flippin' way! She ain't my type.' Now it's Adam's turn to look affronted and, weirdly, I'm pleased by his reaction.

'Your Instagram paints a different picture,' I reply primly, playing with the food on my plate so I don't have to look him in the eye.

'Aw, have you been stalking me online?' he teases, digging into his doner and grinning simultaneously. This guy seriously has no table manners – or any sort of manners, actually. It's no wonder Francesca hasn't added him to her list of conquests.

'Get lost! I haven't been doing anything of the sort. It's not my fault your crap is always showing up on my feed. I'm not in charge of algorithms.'

Adam laughs and, to his credit, doesn't dwell on my little blunder. In fact, he swiftly steers the conversation away from what people at work think of me and I grudgingly concede that I'm having a good time. If there's one thing Adam excels at, it's making me laugh, and he alternates between having me in stitches, shocking me, and winding me up. He's the type of person who has no filter and you never know what's going to come out of his mouth next. We talk about anything and everything and, slowly but surely, the memory of him having a massive go at me the other day dissolves in the peals of laughter. In fact, he reminds of Layla and her inability to keep her thoughts to herself. My phone buzzes a few times with texts from Mo, but I don't want to break our flow by reading and replying to them now, so I put my phone away and ignore it for the rest of the night.

'So you live at home with your parents? And aunt?' I ask, a little surprised when he mentions who he lives with. I always assumed that extended families living together was a South Asian thing.

'You judging?'

'It would be a pot and kettle thing if I were. I live with my parents, sisters *and* my grandmother.'

'Yeah, well, I don't have a dad so it's me, my mum, her sister and my older brother at home.' He looks subdued when he says this, and I feel a pang of sorrow. I mumble an apology, not knowing what to say next.

'Hey, it's OK,' he says, smiling a sad smile. 'He died when I was six. I don't remember much of him. But apparently I look like him.' He scrolls through his phone and shows me a picture of a man who looks exactly like him holding a chubby baby.

'Wow, he was proper good-looking. And that baby is so cute.'

'That's me, of course.' He grins, a bit of the fire returning to his eyes. 'I've always been cute.'

We carry on eating, talking and eating some more. Adam finishes all his kebab and the rest of mine as well, not to mention all the bread, dips and salad. I have no idea where he packs it all away. He's wearing one of his usual T-shirts with a long-sleeved top underneath and when he stretches I catch a glimpse of tanned torso. If it wasn't for the bits of doner grizzle on his chin, he would be quite fanciable. I quickly avert my eyes before he notices me checking him out and makes a big deal out of it.

'Right, that's it, I seriously need to get home,' I say after we've polished off all the complimentary baklava and sweet Turkish tea. 'My mum's gonna kill me if she catches me rolling up after midnight.'

'Really? What did she say when you didn't come home the other night?' As soon as he says it, I can see in his eyes that he wishes he hadn't. But Mr No-Filter couldn't help himself, could he? I take a deep breath. I'm not going to let his throwaway comment ruin what's been a surprisingly pleasant evening.

The pause is so pregnant that it's practically in labour. I wonder if I should correct him and tell him what really happened that night, but in the end, I decide to let him think whatever the hell he wants.

After splitting the bill, we trudge back up towards the office where Adam's parked, too full and too tired to hurry, each step making my bones ache with fatigue.

'Here we are,' he announces when we get to a quiet side road. I look around for his car, eager to climb in and turn the heating on full blast, but instead of pointing out his car, he points to a black motorbike and then opens up his rucksack and pulls out a matching helmet.

'What the hell? Adam! I thought you meant you'd give me a ride in your car!' I shriek, staring at the monstrosity, my hands beginning to get clammy. Am I supposed to trust him and hop on? Adam, who has no regard for his life or limbs and likes to participate in all sorts of life-threatening activities, like bungee jumping and sky diving? Adam, the most immature and unreliable man-child in North London?

'Why did you think that?' he asks, a blank look on his thick face. 'You know I ride a bike. I bring this helmet with me to the office every day. It sits on my desk, right in front of you!'

'I thought it was a prop to help you look sexy! I didn't think it was actually being used!'

'Are you serious?' Adam stares at me as though I've completely lost the plot, so I shove him in response and take my phone out.

'That's it, I'm getting an Uber. I'm not risking it with you and your deathtrap.'

'What's wrong with you? Are you scared? I thought you would be up for a bit of excitement.' I know he's goading me into giving in but I'm not going to fall for his transparent tactics.

'Of course I'm not scared,' I scoff. 'I just don't trust you. You're going to show off and speed like a maniac.'

'I won't,' he says with a smirk. 'I promise I'll take it nice and slow.' He sings this last part and he almost sounds as good as Usher.

My cheeks flare up at the innuendo and to hide my face, I grab the helmet from him and push it down over my head. It's big for me and I fiddle with the straps, my nervousness making me clumsier than usual. Damn Adam and his shameless comments, and damn me for letting him get under my skin.

'Here, let me.' Adam pries the straps out of my reluctant fingers and leans in close, adjusting it in one swift motion. He pauses for a second and stares into my eyes, his own completely unreadable. They really are the most beautiful shade of brown. I feel like I'm in a Nespresso ad and I'm suddenly going to fall into a pool of Dulce de Leche coffee. Butterflies flutter in my stomach, and I tell myself it's the imminent bike ride doing this to my innards, not Adam.

'Come on then, let's go,' I say gruffly, turning away and climbing onto the bike, trying to distract him from the fact that I'm a hot mess right now. He clears his throat and does the same, and I lean away from him as much as I can without falling off altogether. Things are getting a bit intense already, without me adding to the tension by pressing up to him. And there's no way I'm going to hold him either. I've found these little handle thingies and I use those instead. This evening is becoming far too romantic. Well, it would be if I wanted to be there, and if it wasn't Adam but someone I really fancied, like Jordan, perhaps.

'Look, Zara, you're going to have to hold on to me unless you want to fly off.' Adam turns around to look at me with his eyebrow raised and I smile thinly.

'It's OK, I'm fine. I'll hold on to these handles. That's what they're here for.'

'All right, don't say I didn't warn you.' He puts the key into the ignition and the bike roars to life, like a lion awakening from a deep slumber. My throat dry and my hands still clammy, I hold on to those tiny little handles as tight as I can, praying that I'm not flung off as soon as he moves, all the while whispering Ayatul Kursi, the travelling prayer, and then all the other prayers I can think of, over and over again.

'Ready?' he calls out, turning to look at me again and catching me mid-prayer. I hold up my hand, finish my prayer and then squeak that I'm ready. I'm not, by the way, but I've left my fate in God's hands. Although I don't think God is very impressed with me right now, sitting on the back of a bike with a non-related man, our bodies close enough for me to smell his Eau de Parfum.

Adam pushes the bike forward with his feet as he checks for oncoming traffic, and I brace myself as he joins the road and whizzes off like a bullet. The force throws my body back, and I let out a glass-shattering scream and grab on to him for dear life; all previous reservations disappearing as fast as we do down the busy street.

'You piece of shit!' I yell, burying my face into his back as my stomach does somersaults and threatens to release its contents. 'You promised you wouldn't go fast! Slow down!' I hear him laugh and he eases the speed. When I'm certain that he's not going to accelerate again, I slowly work up the courage to release my demon clutch a little and force myself to open my eyes and look around.

I'm so glad I did. There's something wonderfully exhilarating about riding a bike through these dark, quiet streets, the wind tearing through my hair and all the twinkling street lights blurring into a pretty, hazy glow. I relax my grip a little more, a massive smile on my face. Why was I so scared? This isn't scary, this is amazing. I'm like Princess Jasmine, soaring through the sky with Aladdin showing me all the wonders of the world. OK, so I'm in North London, and instead of flying amongst the stars we're riding through grimy, damp streets, but it's still bloody amazing!

We've almost reached my house but I'm not ready for this magical carpet ride to be over, so I ask Adam to take a detour. He obliges with a stupid know-it-all grin, and we carry on riding past my house, down to Seven Sisters and up Holloway Road. Not the most glamorous of locations for this midnight adventure. In fact, it's pretty dingy, but I don't care about the scenery because I'm having way too much fun on this bike. I feel powerful and strong and I'm not even the one controlling it. No wonder Adam has such a huge ego, I would too if I was claiming the streets of London on this monster of a machine.

As we come up to the roundabout by Highbury and Islington, he speeds up and spins around it so fast that I'm once again clinging on to him, my face pressed against his back. I inhale deeply and take in his warm, masculine scent and it leaves me feeling strangely giddy. The only guy who's got this close to me (apart from He-Who-Shall-Not-Be-Named) is Jordan, and that's because it's his job. I've never even had a male doctor before. Yet here I am, squished up to Adam as though I do this sort of thing every day.

My mind races as fast as the bike as I wonder what this broken barrier means. Will Adam now think it's OK to hug me hello and goodbye? A couple of hours ago he thought I was mysterious and different from all the other girls he knows. Does he now think I'm yet another girl who quivers at the sight of his lean muscles and cheeky grin? He does feel amazing, though, and probably even better under the leather jacket.

He heads back down Holloway Road and I'm glad we're going towards my house. This is all getting a bit too impassioned and confusing. It must be the excitement of it all that's clouding my judgement and turning my insides to mush. No rational, logical or sensible twenty-nine-year-old Bengali girl would ever go for someone like Adam; who's not only rude to me half the time, but the complete opposite of what I want in a husband.

But then, look at Hamza; he ticks all the boxes and I'm hardly ready to run up the aisle with him either. I don't think I *know* what I want.

'Which one is your street?' Adam asks when we reach Nando's, and I reluctantly direct him to my quiet road with its long row of Victorian terraced houses, the engine shattering the silence. I look up at my house, praying that no one hears it. For a second, I think I see a curtain on the first floor twitch slightly. My heart in my throat, I check again but there's nothing there.

'Nice house,' Adam says, looking up at it as I climb off the bike and take the helmet off. The top of my head is sweating and my hair is stuck to my scalp, while the bottom half is wild from the wind ripping through it. I probably look like something the cat dragged in, and I self-consciously run my fingers through the tangles.

'Thanks,' I reply shyly. 'And thanks for the ride. It was pretty awesome.' I look at him from beneath my lashes, and then look away, scared that the dodgy feelings that have been stirring away in my stomach might manifest in my expression.

'I knew you'd like it,' he says with a smirk as he takes his helmet back. 'No one ever complains after I take them for a ride.'

Before I can articulate a witty response, he zooms away and I'm left standing at my gate watching him become a little speck in the distance. Idiot boy with his idiotic comments.

I open the gate and walk up the path, unable to wipe the stupid grin off my face. As I'm digging around in my bag for my keys, the front door swings wide open and there's Mum in her cotton nightie, her expression furious.

'You better have a flippin' good explanation for coming home at this hour *on the back of a motorbike* like a behaya,' she fumes, grabbing my arm and pulling me into the dark hallway. 'What were you thinking? Don't you care that the whole street can see your shenanigans? First that ridiculous picture with your personal trainer and now this? How am I supposed to get you married now?'

'He's my colleague,' I yawn, still smiling. 'You know I was working late tonight. Did you want me to get on the bus at this time?'

'Oh, really? You expect me to believe that you were working all this time, do you? I'm not one of those village mums, all right. I can smell the kebab from here.'

Mum's famous 'I'm not one of those village mums' line is one I've heard countless times before: when she discovered that I had a secret mobile phone at thirteen; when she read through my diary and learnt of all the naughty things Layla and I were getting up to at seventeen; and that one time I snuck out to go clubbing when I was at uni, she was waiting for me with the rolling pin when I got back at two in the morning.

How I wish she *was* one of those mums that grew up in a rural Bangladeshi village and was too naïve to figure out what their kids were getting up to. Instead,

I'm lumbered with a mum that is the worst of both my worlds; tech savvy and cynical like a Western mum, but still clinging on to old traditions like the village mum she claims she isn't.

'So what if I went for dinner with Adam after we finished working? Maybe I was trying to be proactive about finding a husband like you desperately want?' I retort insolently, to piss her off more. I'm aware that I've placed Adam in the husband category, but I don't mean it. I want to wind her up and turn the spotlight back to her, but it has the complete opposite effect.

'Give me attitude again and *Allahr Kosom, I swear to God*, I will book your ticket to Bangladesh right now!' she hisses, as she grabs me by my ear and pulls me towards the stairs. 'Now go upstairs before I take off my slipper and show you who's proactive!'

'Ouch, that hurt!' I moan rubbing my ear, the grin well and truly wiped off. And then stop abruptly when I see the thunderous look on her face. So I turn around and leg it up the stairs as fast as I can. I guess when you're Bengali, you're never too old for a good ear-yanking or a slipper-slap from your mum.

Chapter 14

It's just gone 1 p.m., my event is in full swing, and so far, everything is going really well.

The dingy church hall doesn't look dingy any more; it's vibrant, colourful and absolutely buzzing with people from all walks of life; exactly how I envisioned it to be. Scattered around the room are various stalls celebrating the diversity of the people who live in the borough and, at the far end of the hall, kids are going wild jumping around and squealing happily on the bouncy castle. The third act of the day is on stage: a West African drumming group, pounding away on their drums, the beat so infectious that a group of uni students have started an impromptu dance. Adam, who has been doing a fantastic job compering, gets up and joins them, effortlessly moving to the music. I laugh as I watch him grab a Nigerian stall lady and persuade her to dance with him.

I turn to see Francesca by my side, holding a bottle of water in her perfectly manicured hand. Lord knows when she had time to do it – her nails were a wreck when she left us last night. To be fair, she's been fantastic today, weaving in and out of the crowds making conversation, taking photographs and even going outside to entice more people to come through our doors and have a good time. I decide to stop dwelling on her infatuation with Adam and put it behind me.

'You're doing a great job today,' I say sincerely, giving her a warm smile. 'Thank you.'

'No problem,' she replies, barely registering what I'm saying. Her response is uncharacteristically lacklustre, so I follow her gaze and see what's got her attention. Surprise, surprise, it's Adam, laughing and dancing away as he mimics all the moves of his dance partner. His energy is infectious and more people get up to join him. Francesca isn't smiling, though, she looks a combination of wistful and forlorn.

The more I watch Adam lark about, the more yesterday's goings on fade away until the memories take on a surreal, dreamlike quality. There's something about the darkness that stirs up emotions that are better left unacknowledged.

Thankfully, when I woke this morning and drew back the curtains, the bright rays of sun killed off every silly romantic notion that had been playing on my mind, and I've since realised that last night's flutterings and tinglings were nothing to do with Adam, per se. It was more about being in such close proximity to a warm, hot-blooded man, the excitement of riding a powerful motorbike, the thrill of speeding through the dark London streets, and the magic of being under the moonlight. And that's it. It could have been anyone, I told myself – even Dr Farook Chowdhury – and I would have reacted in the same, carnal way. I'm almost thirty, after all, and yet to get laid and find out what all the fuss is about.

I give Francesca's arm a squeeze and then turn away from her to see what else is going on. Kevin, my boss, is beaming from ear to ear, also watching Adam. He's here with his wife and eight-year-old daughter, who's currently munching away on freshly spun candyfloss, her freckled face sticky and pink with melted sugar while her mum gets an intricate henna design done on her palm. My mum, Nani and Amina were here for a while too, but Nani gets tired if she stays out too long, so after buying up half the goods on sale and sampling an array of delicious home-made snacks, they bade their farewell. My phone buzzes a couple of times: a call from Hamza and a text from Mo, but I'm too busy to read the messages or take the call.

At three, the local youth choir takes the stage. The loud chattering stops almost as soon as they start singing, their angelic voices aweing everyone into reverent silence. I take the opportunity to have a little break and, as I sit down with a bowl of jerk chicken and rice and peas, I spot Hamza tentatively walking through the arched wooden doors, peering around as if he's looking for someone.

'Habibti,' Hamza calls out when he spots me. People turn to look at the commotion as he strides towards me and pulls me into a hug. I stiffen in his embrace, my arms hanging limply on either side. What is he doing here and why is he *touching* me? He said he couldn't make it. Is this supposed to be a surprise?

In my peripheral vision I can see Adam, but I have no idea if he's noticed our exchange. Not that I should care. Or he would care. But obviously I do. I don't feel comfortable with him witnessing this behaviour from me.

As Hamza rambles excitedly about the event and how amazing it all looks, I glance over at Adam and our eyes lock. I expect him to break contact immediately, but he doesn't, so I stare back, a dull ache forming inside my chest. Then Hamza grabs my hand and pulls me towards one of the food stalls, and the eye contact is broken.

I hope and pray that Hamza's visit is a courtesy thing and that he'll disappear as suddenly as he appeared. He doesn't, though. He takes it upon himself to try out every single food item from every single stall whilst bopping along to the music. He's having such a good time that I hate myself for being pissed off with him. I wish I could relax, but it's impossible with my two male friends at such close proximity to each other.

'Aren't you gonna introduce me to your mate?' Adam asks, casually sauntering over and draping an arm across my shoulders. I jump as if stung, and push him off me, glaring at him as I do. Hamza notices my reaction and then smiles his usual warm, open smile at that git, extending his hand.

'Hi, I'm Zara's boyfriend,' he introduces himself, shaking Adam's hand with vigour. I nearly choke on my own spit. *Boyfriend*? Since when? We've met, what, three times? And that's when I remember that I told Adam that Jordan, my personal trainer, was Hamza. *Shit*. What if he mentions his name?

'Oh really? I didn't realise Zara had a boyfriend,' Adam replies almost mockingly, and I feel Hamza tense up beside me. 'You didn't mention that when we had dinner last night and I dropped you home.'

Hamza lets go of my arm abruptly and I try, awkwardly, to laugh it off.

'Ha ha, er, shut up, Adam. Stop chatting nonsense!' I turn to Hamza with a forced smile. 'He loves provoking people. Ignore him.' With that, I tug him away, shooting Adam one last filthy look as I do and exhaling the breath I had been holding in.

'What's up with you and this Adam?' Hamza asks as soon as we step outside. Despite the April sun shining down on us, there's still a chill in the air. I wish I could go back inside and grab my cardigan to wear over my short-sleeved cotton shalwar kameez, but there's no way I'm letting that idiot interact with Hamza again.

'Nothing! He likes getting a rise out of me,' I reply, rubbing my bare arms to keep them warm. 'What are you doing here? You said you couldn't come.'

'Are you sure? It looked like he was jealous.' There's a strange look on Hamza's face; a hardness I've not seen before.

'Jealous? Adam? Ha! Trust me, it's not like that at all!'

'What was he talking about, him taking you home?'

'Oh my God, Hamza, chill!' I exclaim, beginning to get annoyed by the interrogation. 'He's my *colleague*. We worked until late last night, getting this event sorted. We went for a meal and then he dropped me home. It's no biggie!'

A prickly silence follows as Hamza digests what I've told him, and honestly, I don't get why he's acting like this. He still hasn't explained why here's here, when he told me he couldn't come today. Contrary to what he told Adam inside, he is *not* my boyfriend. We're considering each other for marriage, the Islamic way, but we're not dating. We're not in love. We're not committed. We're not exclusive. We're figuring out if we're compatible and *that's it*.

It's while we're both sitting there on the cold brick wall in sullen silence that I notice someone who looks vaguely familiar walk up the path to the church. Instead of walking past me into the hall, he stops right in front of us and smiles down at me.

'Zara?'

I stare up at him, but it takes me a second to reconcile the man in the flesh, with the man on the phone, and for a moment I think it must be someone from the council here to check out my event.

'It's me, Mo. From MuslimMate?' He sounds a bit unsure now and his smile falters, but that's the least of my concerns. I shoot a quick glance at Hamza who remains silent, but the flush creeping up his neck says it all. Panic sets in as I desperately try and figure out a way to get out of this mess. Damn Layla and her stupid advice! Why am I talking to more than one man at the same time? What did I think was going to happen?

'Oh, Mo! Of course,' I say with a strangled laugh, trying to maintain my composure. 'Hi, thanks so much for coming!' I get up and extend my hand for him to shake as if he were a client, and he looks at it like I'm dangling a dead rat in front of him.

'Er, that's a bit formal.' He laughs and pulls me close for a hug instead. I think I'm going to die. For five years I've managed to avoid physical contact with the opposite sex, and in the space of thirty minutes I've wound up with three different men thinking it's OK to manhandle me.

And that's when I realise that Mo, who all this time I thought was 5'10" is shorter than me. Much, much shorter, even though I'm in my flats. But I don't have the time or headspace to process this information, because the short-arse liar has just gone and hugged me, with Hamza right there, and I don't know what to say or do to redeem myself.

'This is my f-friend Hamza,' I stutter, for want of anything better to say, as I extract myself from his unwanted embrace. 'Hamza, this is Mo. He's, er, also a, er, friend.' My voice trails off now, as I realise how bad this all looks and sounds. The term 'friend' has never felt so loaded.

Poor Hamza is now forced to acknowledge what's going on. He gets up from the wall and towers over us both, looking between my pained expression and Mo's slightly defensive one.

'Hey, nice to meet you bro,' he says easily, shaking Mo's hand. 'I'll catch you later, Zara.' With that, he turns and walks down the path towards the main road. I stare at his retreating back, feeling sick. A part of me thinks I should run after him, but how can I with Mo still here, and my work event in full swing? So instead, I watch as he disappears from sight, my heart sinking with every step that takes him further away.

'You OK? Who's that bloke?' Mo asks, sitting down at the spot Hamza has vacated, which somehow feels like a bigger act of betrayal than chatting to him for the past few months.

'A good friend of mine,' I reply limply. I sit back down and turn to look at him. He looks like his pictures – with big, dark brown eyes and beautiful jet black silky hair – but now he's in the flesh, I see how petite he is. His shoulders, though defined, are narrow, and his fingers are small and slender. I feel well and truly catfished, and I can't believe I might have messed up my relationship with Hamza over a man who's half my size and makes me feel huge and awkward. I decide that instead of dancing around the topic, I'll face it head on.

'So . . .' I say, deflated. 'It's good to finally meet you, but I'm a bit surprised.'

'Why?' he replies, with a look of genuine confusion on his face.

'Well, firstly, I didn't know you were coming today. You should have told me. I'm at work right now and this event is really important to me.' As soon as I say it, I know it's the wrong thing because of the shadow that flits across his face.

'Event?' he replies, his thin lips curled into a sneer. 'You call this an event? It's some poxy little fair in a shitty little hall in a shittier part of North London. Calling it an "event" is a bit generous, ain't it?'

You know how sometimes you're so blindsided by someone's behaviour that you focus on the mundane to help you get through it? As he rips into me, I focus on his voice which seems too deep for his stature. It was this stupid voice that got me. From what he's told me about his past, I know he had a tough childhood and got into a lot of trouble when he was a teenager. At the time, I thought he was trying to impress me with his street cred, but now that I'm seeing him in the flesh, I know that all the stories were true. I can tell by the way he's looking at me right now, as if I'm nothing and my job is nothing, and he's entitled to gatecrash whatever he wants whenever he wants.

This isn't the first time I've felt like this; as if I'm nothing. As if the man I'm with thinks he can say – or do – whatever he wants to me. The last time I experienced this feeling of losing control of a situation was when

I was with Tariq. Déjà vu ripples through me and my heart begins to pound so hard that I barely hear what he says next. I see the scowl though.

'What?' I ask, my mouth dry. He continues his tirade as if I hadn't spoken, more and more venom appearing in his tone.

'And anyway, how long did you think I was gonna sit around texting you all night without meeting you? I had to make sure you weren't wasting my time or sending me your sister's pictures, pretending it's you.'

Now I'm pissed off and I'm thankful for it because adrenaline finally kicks in, smothering the fear. '*Me* wasting *your* time?' I exclaim. 'More like the other way round!'

'What's that supposed to mean?'

'Well, your profile said you're 5'10" for starters.' I fold my arms and stare him straight in the eyes. They're so expressive that I can practically see them effing and blinding at me.

'So what? Yours said 5'8"! Everyone exaggerates on their profiles.'

'But I am 5'8"!'

'Not without them massive heels you're not. There are no Bengali girls that tall, so don't chat shit, yeah?'

'Heels? Are you blind? My shoes are flat!' I stand up in indignation. The more Mo tries to defend himself, the more intent I become at proving him wrong.

'Go on, stand up and see for yourself!' I can't believe that I've been blindly flirting with this catfisher all this time. And the thing is, his height is the least of my issues. It's his attitude that really stinks.

Mo gets up, glowering at me. He's at least four inches shorter than me but the stubborn little shit refuses to admit it. I've spent five minutes in his presence and I'm already regretting how much energy I wasted on him. How many hours of sleep I lost. How is it that people who appear so charismatic online, can turn out to be total dicks in real life?

'Take off your heels, then we'll see the truth,' he demands. I look down at the ground covered in pigeon poo, chewing gum and probably dried dog wee as well. But I'm too invested in this argument to let it go, or let him win, so gritting my teeth, I take off my ballet pumps.

'Zara! Where have you been? You're late for your closing speech!' Adam bursts out of the church, and then stops dead in his tracks when he comes across Mo and me standing back-to-back and barefoot. 'What's going on?'

'Adam, hi,' I say in a fake chirpy voice. 'Who's taller? Me or Mo?'

Adam looks at us like we're a couple of sandwiches short of a picnic. 'Is this a joke?'

'Answer the bloody question!' I plead. 'Quickly.'

'Obviously it's you. Your mate Frodo is like, at least three or four inches shorter.'

'Thank you,' I respond primly. 'Mo, it's been a pleasure but I don't think it's going to work out.'

'Whatever,' Mo mutters, putting his trainers back on. 'You're an ugly bitch in real life anyway.'

I gasp, too stunned to reply and he turns and jogs away, surprisingly quickly for someone with such short legs. But instead of feeling hurt or worried the way I did when it was Hamza making his escape, this time, I feel relieved. I know I've dodged a bullet.

'I don't want to know,' Adam huffs, grabbing my arm. 'Come on, everyone's waiting for you.'

'Hang on, my shoes—' I turn around to get them, and step right into a piece of dog poo.

'SHIT!' I stare down at my bare foot that's now entrenched in a fat turd, and try not to cry. I've been working on this event for months and now I'm about to mess it all up, right at the last moment. How am I supposed to clean this off and get back inside quick enough to give my speech? I don't even have any tissues on me. I turn to look at Adam, my eyes full of tears and he sighs.

'I'll make the speech. I'll get Fran to bring you some wipes.'

He turns and leaves and I close my eyes and try and focus on my breathing instead of the sticky sensation on the sole of my foot. The phrase 'shitting on your doorstep' has never felt more real.

Chapter 15

'I can't believe that bastard said that to you,' Yasmin is appalled when I relay what happened to her later that night. As relieved as I am to have realised how nasty he is before anything truly bad happened, now that the shock and anger has worn off, I feel quite shaken by the whole thing.

'I know,' I reply, unable to meet her sorrowful stare. 'I can't believe it either. I mean, I knew he was a bit of a bad boy and there were parts of him that reminded me of Tariq, but I don't know why I kept overlooking it.'

'Overlooking what?' Amina asks, ambling into my room like it's her own. 'Can I borrow your new lippy please? The Huda Beauty one?'

'Yeah, take it,' I reply. I don't have the strength to retell the story for a second time, so Yasmin gives her an abridged version and Amina is beyond horrified. She is livid.

'Give me your phone,' she demands, snatching it from my bed before I consent, and opening up MuslimMate. 'I'm gonna report his bastard arse.'

'Be my guest,' I mumble, burying myself further under my duvet.

'His profile's gone. Look.' She hands my phone back to me and sure enough, his profile has completely disappeared from the app. I check our WhatsApp chat and find that I can no longer see his profile picture, either.

'He's blocked you,' Yasmin the Wise says gravely.

'I'm glad,' I reply brightly when, inside, another part of my heart withers away.

I know it shouldn't bother me, but the fact that he rejected me first (in the virtual world at least) plays on my mind for the rest of that evening, and the following day at work. Once again, I seek refuge in the prayer room where I can gather my thoughts in peace. Since when did human interaction become so transactional? Forget chivalry and good manners; where the hell had common decency gone?

'But am I any better?' I ask Francesca in the kitchen as we make our third teas of the day.

'What do you mean, babe?' she replies, grabbing the box of Yorkshire Tea and depositing two bags in our mugs.

'Look what I did to Hamza. He basically got ambushed by two other guys at the event, and I haven't even called him to apologise. I mean, I texted him, but when he didn't reply, I should have called. But I didn't know what to say.'

Francesca makes a face and remains silent as she pours the boiled water into the mugs.

'What?' I ask. 'What's that face for?'

'What face?'

'The scrunched-up, constipated-pug face you just made,' I say rudely, yanking my mug towards me and adding a generous splash of milk to the brew. She laughs.

'My mate's always telling me off for making that face.'

'Just come out with it, Fran!'

Francesca takes a deep breath, giving her tea one quick stir before pulling the bag out, barely giving the flavour a chance to develop. 'If you ask me, you're the one that was ambushed.' She turns away as she says this, as if looking at me is too discomfiting for her.

'I don't get it,' I say slowly. 'How was I ambushed?'

She sighs loudly and then turns to face me. 'Your man Hamza, he said he wasn't going to come, right? And then he did? Why didn't he tell you?'

I pause as I digest this. 'I guess he wanted to surprise me?'

'Maybe,' she says, her tone suggesting anything but 'maybe'. 'Or *maybe* he wanted to catch you off guard?'

'Why would he do that?'

'I don't know, I don't know the man, do I? But think about it. Does he often say one thing and do another? Or just ambush you in other ways? Push you into things?'

I think back to our interactions. 'Well, the first time we met he made me take an Uber home . . . and since then I always have to, and if I don't, he threatens to book it for me. And there was one time when he said I could pay the bill and then sneakily paid for it behind my back.' *Hardly incriminating stuff, in my opinion.*

'There you go,' she says smugly, folding her arms across her chest. 'That's got control written all over it.'

'Um, I think he was just being a gentleman, hun,' I respond as gently as I can. Francesca, I decide, has had too many bad experiences with men and now even the nicest gestures come across as narcissistic to her.

'If you say so,' she says ominously. 'If you say so.'

We walk back to our corner silently, and I'm so engrossed in my thoughts that I don't notice Kevin lurking around near my desk. It's not until I sit down and take a sip of my tea that he coughs to make his presence known. I jump, knocking over my mug and spilling the scalding hot tea all across my desk.

'Shit!' I cry, leaping up and grabbing a handful of tissues. 'You scared me, Kevin!'

'Sorry. When you have a minute, come to my office so we can chat, please,' he replies.

'Sure,' I say chirpily and I don't think anything of it until I catch the grave look Adam exchanges with Francesca.

Once I'm done cleaning up the mess, I go into Kevin's small, dull office with its eighties wooden furniture and ancient box files everywhere and look at him blankly with my red-rimmed eyes, waiting for him to speak. I can tell from the pained expression on his face that he's not about to praise me for the amazing event I just threw. I shift nervously in my seat. *Are we going through a restructure? Am I about to lose my job? Is this because I spent half an hour in the prayer room again?*

'Zara, I hate to do this because I know how hard you worked on the event, and it really was fantastic . . .' he begins awkwardly and, as he struggles to find the right words to fire me, I feel my body turn cold with fear.

'I'm so sorry!' I blurt out. 'I know my mind's been all over the place recently, and I've not been at my best, but I promise it's all over and I'm going to give this job everything! No more loitering in the kitchen ten times a day making tea, no more crying in the prayer room, no more passive smoking outside. I've just been going through some stuff but I won't let my personal life affect my work anymore. I promise!'

I stare at Kevin desperately, my eyes once again beginning to water. 'I love this job so much, Kevin. I *need* this job. It's the only thing keeping me going right now. Please don't get rid of me!'

'Er,' he falters, looking nervously at me, and then at the door, as if he wishes he could make a run for it. 'I was actually going to ask you why Adam did the closing speech instead of you.'

'Oh, right.' I swallow nervously. Why didn't I let him say what he wanted to say first? Why am I always such an idiot? 'That.'

'Yes. That.' He smiles wryly. 'Drink as much tea as you want, and passive smoke as much as you want. I don't care so long as you get the work done. But that event was yours, and it should have been you closing it, not your graphic designer. Did you get cold feet?

Do I need to send you on some sort of public speaking training? What happened?'

I wrack my brains for an answer that would be acceptable, but I can't think of anything. 'No, I'm fine with public speaking! I just had an incident outside the venue which momentarily incapacitated me,' I ramble, as I cling on to the lifeline I've just been given. 'It's sort of gross, I don't know if you want the details, but if you do, basically—'

'No!' Kevin almost shouts, looking panicked. 'No, it's OK. I don't need the details. I just need your head in the game, OK? You three are my dream team. Let's keep it that way, all right?'

'Yes! Absolutely! Thank you and sorry. It won't happen again!' Before he can change his mind, I jump out of my seat and out of his office, well aware that I've just been given a second chance and I can't mess up like this again.

I keep my head down for the rest of the day, feeling both ashamed and relieved. Adam and Fran try to engage me in convos but soon give up when they see that I'm not in the mood. How can I be? Despite my love life being in complete shambles, I've always prided myself on my work, but I nearly screwed it all up, and for what? A narcissistic midget with a nasty mouth on him?

Francesca's analysis of Hamza's pushiness bothers me as well. Has she got a point? Was his visit more of an ambush than a surprise?

Throughout that week, I take my phone out multiple times to call him. Even if he did ambush me, he still didn't deserve to be confronted by two strange men acting like they had some sort of claim over me. He deserves an apology. But no matter how many times I tell myself that and hype myself up for a phone call, when it comes down to it, I can't press the call button. Instead, towards the end of the week, I send another feeble text message.

> Hey, Hamza, I hope you're OK. I'm really sorry about last week. I swear to God that Adam is just my colleague and a friend of sorts. I don't know why he was goading you like that. As for Mo – he was someone I used to talk to. We don't talk anymore. Call me whenever you're ready so we can sort things out x

He still doesn't reply.

On Saturday morning, Mum sends Amina to my room to wake me up and force me to join them on their bi-annual trip to Luton, where both of my mum's brothers live. When Nani lived in Luton we would visit every weekend without fail, but after she moved in with us about fifteen years ago, the trips dwindled to a couple of times a year.

'I'm not in the mood for this impromptu visit,' I moan at Amina as she pulls the covers off me.

'You have to. Samia got back from Zim last night. Don't you want to see her?'

'Crap, I forgot about that,' I mumble, rubbing my eyes and sitting up. Has it been two months since she left already?

'Yeah, well, you've been a bit self-obsessed recently,' Amina points out wryly.

As usual, we stop for tea and nastha, which can mean either breakfast or snacks in Bengali, at my elder uncle's house before heading over to my younger uncle's flat. Samia's dad is two years younger than my mum, and whenever they get together, they spend hours singing old seventies music and reminiscing about the 'good old days' when they first came to Britain and things were 'simple' and life was 'easy'. Mate, I've heard the stories and there's nothing easy about going for a wee in an outhouse infested with spiders in the middle of the night, being one of three brown kids in a sea of white faces at school, or having to travel two hours to get hold of halal meat.

Straight after a massive lunch of ten different curries, Sam and I make our excuses and go and chill in her room, leaving the clearing up to Yas, Amina and Sam's little sister Ameera. Well, I'm chilling and she's unpacking, having returned from a two-month stint in Zimbabwe, volunteering in an orphanage.

'What's happening with your whole husband-hunting plan?' she asks as I lie back on her single bed and sip my mug of masala chai.

'You've come back from an epic adventure and we're seriously going to talk about my boring life?' I ask, rolling my eyes. 'No thanks. Tell me all about what you got up to. I still can't believe Suto Mama let you go.'

'Well, you know what he's like, he always gives in eventually.'

At her insistence, I give her a rundown of all the men I have and haven't been meeting over the past few months, leaving out my own emotions. I don't need my younger cousin pitying me. As I talk, she continues to sort her suitcase out, occasionally murmuring something in solidarity. When I tell her about the rejection from the Tower Hamlets guy, I pause for a second and wait for her outraged response but she seems to be too busy with her unpacking to pay much attention to me.

'Did you hear what I said?' I demand. 'They said I was too old when I'm bloody younger than him!'

'That's crap,' she replies flatly. 'But to be fair, you know what Bengali families are like. They think bigger age gaps are better.'

I snort. 'Of course they do. God forbid a bride is too mature and experienced to know her own mind. Those mothers-in-law like them young so they can groom and manipulate them.'

'It's true though, isn't it? The older a woman gets, the more set in her ways she becomes. Marriage is all about compromise.'

'And what about men? Doesn't the same apply? Don't they get more set in their ways?' I stare at Sam, agog, like she's grown a third, Masonic eye in the middle of her forehead. I can't believe that this is what she thinks. I'm no Amina when it comes to feminism and dismantling the patriarchy, but even I can see that this is messed-up.

'Men have to get married when they're older,' she says matter-of-factly. 'So they can establish their careers and all that.'

'OK, so if all the older, established men, marry younger women. Who do the women in the middle marry?'

Samia smiles sagely, as though only she is privy to the inner secrets of marital structures. 'There's someone for everyone. Allah knows best.'

'You sound very well versed on marriage for someone who isn't planning on getting married any time soon,' I say after a long pause. This whole conversation has not turned out the way I expected it to. I'd expected her to have my back, tell me that the world, and our community with its expectations should all go to hell. Instead, she basically agreed with it all.

'I need to be ready when the time comes.'

There's a rap on the door and Nani hobbles in and tells us to go back downstairs for dessert. She frowns when she sees the open suitcase on the floor, and I know what's about to go down.

'Dekhrayni kilan amareh nah zikaya, Africat gya addo marso,' she scolds Samia, telling her off for 'gallivanting' around Africa without getting her permission. Serves Sam right for hiding her trip from Nani until she landed. I chuckle to myself as she continues to berate her, about how she'll never get married now because she's too independent, and what has happened to her previously lovely colouring? Can't she scrub her tan off?

'Marriage isn't on the cards now,' Sam snaps at Nani. 'I'll wait for Zara to go first, thanks.'

I sneak out the room and let Sam deal with Nani. I hear enough of it on a daily basis.

'How come Sam got to go to Zimbabwe but you won't let me?' Amina says on the way home. 'She's only a year older than me. If she's allowed, I should be, too.'

'Samia's life is her dad's problem, not mine,' Mum replies, turning around from her position at the front passenger seat to glare at us. 'And by the way, the only reason he agreed was because of their arrangement. If you're happy to make the same deal, then by all means, we can discuss you living abroad for two months.'

'What deal?' Amina scowls, her arms folded across her chest. I lean forward, eager to hear the gossip myself.

'That if she went to Zimbabwe, as soon as she got back she had to get a biodata written up and start meeting candidates.'

'Oh.' Amina slumps further into her seat and Yasmin and I exchange glances. It's the first I'm hearing of such a deal.

'And they've already got a meeting lined up. So unless you want to follow the same path as your cousin, don't make comparisons.'

'Did Sam mention anything to you?' Yasmin asks me quietly when the conversation moves on. She and I are sitting right at the back of the eight-seater, in our usual seats.

'No. She went on and on about how men should marry women that are more than just a couple of years younger than them,' I admit. In fact, I'm pretty sure she acted as though marriage wasn't on the table at all. Didn't she tell Nani that she was waiting for me to go first? I stare out of the window, tuning the rest of the conversation out as I try to figure out why Sam basically lied to me.

There's only one possible, albeit heart-squeezingly painful conclusion, I decide. My cousin – who I thought was one of my closest confidantes – has hidden the fact that she's looking to get married because I'm older, still single, and she thinks I'm going to give her nazar. She's always been a massive believer in the evil eye.

Layla gets straight to the point, when I call her to ask her what she thinks.

'Who cares what your cousin is up to?' she says bluntly. 'Forget about her and focus on yourself.'

'How? I don't know if I even want to marry Hamza.'

'Why are you trying to make such a massive life decision on your own? If you need help on deciding whether or not to progress things with Hamza, you need to let either your friends or your sisters meet him. Get our opinions. See him through our eyes.'

This is probably why Layla is a lawyer and I work in local government.

'He probably wants nothing to do with me anyway,' I whisper. 'I've ruined my chances with him.'

'Well, the longer you air him, the worse it's getting. Call him, text him, do something to make him realise you're not messing around.'

After we hang up, I brace myself and text Hamza a simple, *Hey, you OK?*

I spend the rest of the night waiting for his reply. It never comes.

Chapter 16

It's one of those rare, super-quiet days in the office. Kevin's on leave so we've taken the opportunity to spend most of the day drinking tea and playing games. Francesca's infatuation with Adam seems to have been short-lived as she's back to acting like her usual self around him instead of flirting and giggling whenever he's in the vicinity. When I mention that she seems a bit different lately, she reveals that she's met someone via some new dating app.

'What, just him and no one else?' I ask. 'I remember you telling me that the point of online dating is to simultaneously date as many people as possible.'

'Yeah, I know, and I was,' she says with a smile, coming over to my desk and perching on it. 'Until I met Nathan. We've been out a few times now and I want to see where it goes without clouding my headspace with other men, you know?'

'Makes sense. I can't wait to hear all about him! Hang on, let me make some more tea. Do you want some?' She nods, so I grab her mug. I move to take Adam's as well – he never says no to a cuppa – but he decides to join me in the kitchen instead.

'What are you doing this evening? Do you want to go out for shisha?' he asks me as the kettle boils and I prepare our mugs. I look at him, the surprise evident in my expression. This is the first time he's asked me to go out with him, apart from the time he asked me to the pub. And we all know how that went down.

'Let me guess, shisha is haram and you don't do it?' he sighs, misinterpreting my reaction.

'I *do* do shisha, but I'm not sure about tonight. I could do with a night in.'

'Granny,' he teases as we walk back to our workspace, him carefully balancing the three mugs while I carry the biscuits and snacks.

'I am a bit of a homebody,' I admit. 'And proud. Are you still going to go out?'

'Yeah. I need to get out the house.' I look at him, waiting for him to elaborate, but his eyes darken and he doesn't say anything further. I don't feel right prying, so I let it go.

'Right. Nathan.' I say to Fran when we're back at our desks and munching through a packet of chocolate Hobnobs.

'Well,' she begins, a starry look in her eyes, 'he's really tall. Like six feet two or—'

'I'm six three,' Adam interrupts. We both roll our eyes, for the millionth time that day.

'Really built, with like, tattoos all the way up his right arm,' Francesca continues, 'which is *not* like you, Adam.'

'How would you know? I might have tattoos in places you can't see.'

'Ew!' Fran and I exclaim in unison, wrinkling our noses. We start to laugh, realising that we've basically reacted the same way to Adam's antics for most of the day.

'Ignore him!' I groan, dipping my biscuit into my tea and licking the chocolate off. 'Carry on!'

'Anyway. He's a builder, so, you know, good with his hands and all that . . .'

Now it's Adam's turn to screw up his face. 'I don't really want to hear this,' he mutters.

'Don't then.' I shrug. 'But I do. He sounds really hot.'

With a scowl, Adam puts on his AirPods and Francesca continues to describe all the 18-rated ways Nathan fulfils her, physically and emotionally.

Fran finding love online plays on my mind the rest of the afternoon, and I wish I'd had better luck on Muslim-Mate. I wonder if I should log back in and try again, seeing as Hamza hasn't replied to me. But then Mo's parting words echo in my ears and I can't bring myself to go through that whole palaver again.

I'm idly reading through various news sites when my phone hums and I nearly fall off my chair when I see it's a text from Hamza. My reaction doesn't go unnoticed by my colleagues, so I fill them in and stare at my phone in trepidation.

'Open it!' Francesca instructs. 'How can you move on until you know what he's thinking?'

'I'll do it if you can't,' Adam butts in, grabbing my phone out of my hands. It's already unlocked and he opens it up without waiting for my permission. I'm so nervous that I don't try to stop him.

'Well? What does it say?' I demand.

'It says ... "Piss off",' Adam replies, reading the words slowly. I feel heat flare in my cheeks.

'*What?*' I snatch the phone off him to see for myself, and almost weep in relief when I see that the actual message is an icy, 'What's up?'

'You're such a piece of shit!' I wail, chucking a tissue box at him. 'Not that "What's up?" is much better.'

'It *is* better,' Fran intervenes. 'He's got back to you. If he wanted nothing to do with you, he wouldn't have replied at all. This shows he's still interested, but wounded. You need to tread carefully.'

'What shall I say?'

'Ask him if you can talk. And be humble about it, babe. Don't get all snarky like you do, sometimes.'

I look at Adam to see what he thinks and he shrugs. 'I say you cut your losses and aim higher.'

I raise an eyebrow. 'Higher than a chartered accountant who works for one of the Big Four, who also happens to be over six foot and really sweet and generous?'

'Whatever. I'm six three.'

Fran and I look at each other, and yawn, 'We know!'

It's the end of the day when I work up the courage to text Hamza back with, *I'm really sorry for what happened the other day. Can we please talk?*

His reply comes within seconds. *OK.*

It's obvious he's pissed off, and I don't blame him. I know we only met three times, but we spoke on the phone quite a bit, and it wasn't nice for him to come all the way to North London to support my career, only to be antagonised by Adam and then Mo. At the very least I owe him an explanation, if not an apology.

I call him when I get out of the office and he answers on the third ring.

'Hey,' I say, forcing myself to sound upbeat as I walk towards the bus stop.

'Hey,' he replies quietly.

'Are you free? Do you wanna meet up in Central?' I feel a bit nauseous suggesting this. I wasn't planning on chatting to him face to face – it would be too excruciating – but it kind of makes sense that we do.

'I can't, sorry.' He doesn't sound sorry. He sounds vexed.

'OK, then.' I take a deep breath. 'Look, I'm really sorry about what happened at the event. I'm mortified and I can't imagine what you're thinking.'

'Can't you?'

'Well, I can. I have a pretty overactive imagination, after all. But obviously I don't know exactly what's going through your mind.'

'I'll give you a clue. I feel like you've been taking me for a ride, talking to me and a million other guys at the same time.'

Ouch. He's not going to hold back then. 'OK. I can see why you feel like that.'

'Am I wrong?'

'Yes. Sort of. Not a million, one other, but it was an online thing. I never invited him to come to my event. I was as surprised as you were.'

'Yet he felt comfortable enough to turn up.'

'Hamza! Come on, be fair. We've only met three times! You know I'm looking to get married. It's normal to talk to a few people at the same time – until things get serious, anyway. Are you telling me you stopped looking elsewhere the moment you met me?'

'Pretty much.'

'Oh.'

'Well, it's good to know where I stand.'

The conversation continues in a similar manner, so much so that I start to wonder why I'm trying to get through to someone who doesn't want to listen. Has he always been this black and white about everything, and I hadn't noticed?

By the time we hang up, I've been standing at the bus stop for over an hour and he still doesn't understand where I'm coming from.

Part Three

Summer

Chapter 17

The holy month of Ramadan comes and goes. Like most Muslims around the world, for the past month I've been participating in Ramadan activities. This includes loads of things, like extra night prayers at the mosque, fasting from dawn to dusk, and reading the Holy Qur'an. But it's not just about the rituals, though. Ramadan is also about reflection, spirituality, charity, compassion, forgiveness and self-control. And as part of the whole self-control aspect, I've been abstaining from unnecessarily communicating with all the men in my life. Including Hamza, Jordan and Adam (outside of working hours).

Hamza and I have texted occasionally but we both agreed that it wasn't a good idea to meet up whilst fasting, and since sunset was around eight, with Tarawih prayers starting at nine thirty, there wasn't any time to meet in the evening either. Well, it was actually his idea more than mine. After what happened at my event, he pretty much said he wanted some time out to reconfigure, and I suppose I needed the space too.

During our time apart, I realised that I have missed him a bit, although it isn't a heart-wrenching longing that would inspire a sonnet; more like a vaguely wistful type of emptiness that would inspire a meme.

I really, *really* want to fall madly and deeply in love with Hamza. Everything would be so much easier if I did. I know I would have a simple, stress-free life with him. He's so happy and unassuming, and he seems to genuinely like me. I could breeze through life with him at my side and I know he would be a great dad as well. I can tell he loves kids by the way he talks about his cousin's children, not to mention the way he always stops to coo at babies whenever we've been out.

Anyway, maybe today will bring some clarity to the situation. Throughout Ramadan I prayed for God to help me come to a decision about him so I don't waste his or my time anymore, and I'm hoping that today will push me towards the path I'm supposed to take.

The sticky, humid air assaults me as I jump off the bus and hurry towards Nando's, where Hamza has been waiting for me for about half an hour now. I got stuck at work waiting for PR to come back with the final version of a press release they're sending out tomorrow.

This summer has been an odd one so far; blistering one week, chilly the next. Today is hot; so hot that my cotton dress is sticking to me and I have to keep dabbing at my face with blotting paper to absorb the excess sweat. Not the ideal climate to reunite with Hamza but it will have to do.

'I'm so sorry I'm late!' I say as I enter the cool, air-conditioned restaurant and approach him.

'It's OK, Eid Mubarak, habibti,' Hamza replies with a warm smile as he gets up and knocks into at least three tables while walking towards me. This is the first time we're meeting since the event and I've been a bit nervous about how he'll act around me, but it seems as if I had nothing to worry about.

'Eid Mubarak to you too,' I reply with genuine warmth. He leans in for a quick hug and before I can pull away, kisses me on the top of my head, sending a jolt through my body. I know it's not a sexy kiss, and it could easily have been an exchange between relatives, but I could feel the emotion in that gesture and I know it wasn't something he did without thinking. He probably did it to let me know that what happened at the event is forgiven, but even so, my stomach starts to churn as I'm overcome with a sensation of déjà vu. *That was how it started last time.*

I'm too embarrassed to pull away, so I stand there limply and comply without fuss, even though I'm uncomfortable. On the outside, I look as cool as a cucumber in a sunhat, but on the inside, I'm a wreck. Within seconds I've worked myself up into a panic. What is he doing? It was the holy month of Ramadan mere hours ago, for crying out loud! I thought he respected my need for distance? I *knew* I should have said something after the event. By shoving it under the rug, he seems to think I was OK with it, with him showing up unannounced and hugging me in front of all those people. But how could

I have brought it up, when his embrace was trumped by my surprise online flirtation appearing in the flesh?

The fact that we're in my ends doesn't help the situation. I feel clammy and panicky, and I keep scanning the restaurant to check if there's anyone I know. What was I thinking, suggesting coming here? Well, I do know what I was thinking. I was thinking how nice it would be to walk home in five minutes without having to get an expensive Uber or endure a long train ride in this heat. In my defence, I didn't expect respectful, sensitive Hamza to suddenly start touching me up.

'How was your Ramadan and Eid?' he asks, returning from placing our order with his arms full of plates, cutlery and sauces. I stare at him warily, but his face gives nothing away, so I decide to play it his way. I'm probably overreacting. Maybe the kiss wasn't as orchestrated as I assumed and he did it without thinking. In fact, maybe he does it to everyone, and the fact that he *hasn't* been kissing my head all this time is what's weird?

'It was good,' I say, helping him unload the plates as I launch into what I've been doing for the past month. He does the same, making me chuckle with his accounts of how hungry he was, and how he fell asleep every night during Tarawih prayers, right there in the mosque. I start to relax in his presence and try to forget about the earlier awkwardness. Until his hand brushes mine, and I snatch it away, accidentally knocking my fork onto the floor as I do. I jump up and go and get another, but when I return to the table, the mood has changed and Hamza's expression has darkened.

'You OK?' I ask lightly, sitting back down. He grunts in response and busies himself with taking all the chicken off the bones, his movements so harsh that it looks like he's decapitating the bird.

'Are you sure?' I try again, trying to keep my voice from betraying my irritation. All this passive aggression is a bit uncharacteristic for Hamza. He says nothing, but sighs loudly instead.

'Oh, for God's sake, what's the problem?' Exasperated, I put the fork down with the chicken still pierced into it, a little louder than I had intended. It clangs against the plate, and I wince, hoping that no one has noticed that I'm about to experience my first domestic. I'm not one for public scenes, and judging by the look on his face, neither is he.

'Do we have to do this here?' he says from between clenched teeth, and I'm surprised by the sharpness of his tone. It's the first time I've seen Hamza with his feathers this ruffled, and to be honest, I'm not sure I like it.

'If you don't want to talk about it, why are you huffing and puffing and sighing then?' I demand, my voice rising a notch.

'I'm not "huffing and puffing", he huffs, crossing his arms defensively and staring down at his plate.

After a minute of awkward silence, I take a deep breath and tentatively reach over to him, placing my hand on his arm. 'What's going on, Hamza?' I say gently. 'You don't seem like yourself.'

There's another silence as he pushes the food around on his plate and then he finally puts his fork down and looks up at me.

'So it's OK for you to touch my arm, but I can't touch yours?'

Fire burns in my cheeks as the sympathy I was previously experiencing flies out the window. I snatch my hand away.

'Is this what your little mood is about, then? Me not wanting to touch a non-mahram man?'

'Not related? Seriously?' he says this with such a look of incredulity that I know that he's thinking I'm a complete phony, using Islamic terminology when I barely practise the basics of Islam.

'Yes, seriously! Do you have something to say about that?' I seethe, daring him to throw in my face that, until this Ramadan, I rarely prayed, and I don't cover, so why am I acting like I care about getting too close to a non-related man?

Because I *do* care. Does me not wearing a piece of cloth on my head mean I'm fair game to maul and grab? Life isn't black and white, and neither are people, so why would my faith and how I practise it be any different?

Hamza looks at my clenched fists and the water gathering in my eyes and doesn't take the bait. Instead, he lets out a long breath and, as he does, his shoulders sag slightly.

'I need to talk to you about something,' he begins, the confusion and hurt in his eyes painfully obvious. His expression and his tone are softer than before, but still, my pulse starts to quicken in nervous anticipation.

'OK,' I respond, taking a long gulp of my Diet Coke in a feeble attempt to calm the anxiety that's bubbling away inside me.

He looks at me in silence for a few seconds. 'How long have we known each other?'

'Er . . . I'm not sure exactly. Three months?'

'Five months today, actually.'

I swallow. 'Is that why you're upset? I'm not good with dates.'

'Fair enough.' There's another painstakingly long pause and I'm tempted to get up and run. I hate confrontation, and this discussion is beginning to take a turn that I know is going to be difficult for me to navigate around. I brace myself for the storm that lies ahead.

'It got me thinking. It's been five months but we still act as if we're only friends. If I hadn't met you at a Muslim matchmaking event, I would be certain that you're not interested in pursuing this further.'

'It was a networking event,' I mutter under my breath, for want of a better comeback.

'Oh, come on! Everyone knew it was really a matchmaking event for singles and their matchmakers. Anyway. You looked horrified when I called myself your boyfriend in front of what's-his-name – Adnan?'

'Adam. And I wasn't horrified, I was surprised. I mean, come on. We weren't there yet, were we?'

'So are we there now?'

Shit. I walked right into that one.

'We've barely spoken in the past month, and you were pretty pissed off with me for talking to Mo.' I shift nervously in my seat. 'And now you're asking me if we're there?'

'Look, Zara, I don't want to play games. That's not who I am. I like you. I *really* like you. If I didn't, I wouldn't trek all the way up to North London to catch a glimpse of you. But whenever I try and move things up a notch, you retreat. I want to know why.'

Fear spreads through my body like water leaking into a ship. My hands begin to tremble and I clutch on to my glass to steady them. All this time, everything that was left unsaid gave me the freedom to get on with things without having to make the most difficult decision of my life. Who knew how Hamza felt about me? I wasn't about to place all my ageing eggs into a basket with holes in it. But now that he's forced me into a corner, I'm going to have to reveal what's on my mind.

I can't keep looking down at my plate full of uneaten, stone-cold chicken, so I force myself to meet Hamza's penetrating gaze.

'Um,' I begin hesitantly. 'I like you too . . .' My voice trails off as I look down again. This is horrible. *Horrible!* I feel like a monstrous bitch. Why couldn't I be in love with him or, at the very least, like him as much as he likes me? Life would be so much easier then. We could get married; have a bit fat Bengali-Egyptian wedding with tasty Indian food and lively Arabic entertainment; move into a comfortable, affordably trendy one-bedroom flat close to Central London, maybe in Camden or King's Cross; I wouldn't have to work as I'm pretty sure Hamza's on big bucks, but I would anyway, at least until we had kids. Then we'd move out to the suburbs, if not Highgate then Crouch End, and have the cutest, chubbiest mixed-race kids you've ever seen, all golden skin and curly black hair, with their dad's happy-go-lucky temperament . . .

I gulp. This is beginning to sound really, really tempting.

'There's going to be a "but", isn't there?' Hamza interrupts my daydream at precisely the right moment because my little fantasy was becoming a bit too appealing, and I was *this* close to telling him we should go for it.

I open my mouth to tell him that there's no 'but', and then close it again when I see his defeated expression tinged with a smidgeon of hope. I can't lead him on. Not after he's been so open and honest with me. It's not right.

'There is a "but",' I admit, too afraid to look at him. 'I really like you too, Hamza, but I don't know if I want to marry you.'

I was hoping that once the words were said, a weight would automatically lift off my shoulders. But it doesn't.

I feel awful. The fact that Hamza doesn't reply doesn't make the situation any easier. I'm still too scared to look up so I continue talking.

'There's so much that I lo—like about you. You have the purest and most sincere heart. You're successful. Kind. Honourable. Thoughtful. Funny . . .' My throat goes dry and I reach for my drink only to find the glass empty.

'If I'm so great, then what's the problem?'

He's not going to make this any easier for me, but I owe it to him to be truthful. I can't feed him some bullshit about him being too good for me and deserving better. But how can I tell him I don't fancy him without completely trampling over his ego?

'I don't think there's any . . . chemistry between us.' I wince as I say this and continue to avoid looking at him. There is a silence that is magnified by the enormity of what I've said. It's the loudest damn silence I've ever experienced, and in the absence of a response, I hear my heart pounding in my ear, almost deafening me.

'Why? Because I'm fat?' His voice is flat, devoid of any emotion, and it makes me finally look at him in surprise.

'Don't be stupid!' I exclaim, horrified by his accusation. 'You're not fat! And if you were, it wouldn't matter.' This turns out to be the wrong thing to say, because colour floods into his cheeks and he looks even more affronted.

'So now I'm fat *and* stupid?'

'Please don't be like this!' I'm mortified that I've offended him. 'You're putting words in my mouth!'

'Be like what? How did you expect me to react? We've been getting to know each other for five months and only now do you decide to tell me that you're not attracted to me, and only because I've practically forced it out of you? Why the hell have you been stringing me along all this time?'

My own face turns pink under his accusatory stare, and I squirm uncomfortably in my seat, completely unsure of what to say. I'm trying to be honest but his response, albeit justified, is making me wish I never opened my trap. This is not the reunion I was envisioning after our month-long break.

'That's not fair. One of those months was Ramadan, and we've only met like, three or four times. It's not that simple.'

'Simplify it for me then.'

Everything about his tone and his body language is the complete antithesis of the Hamza I thought I knew. I thought I liked assertive men who had a rough edge, but now I'm not too sure.

'Tell me what's been going on, Zara. And don't feed me any crap, please. If you have any respect for me, be honest with me.'

This is it then, the moment of truth. I can go in either direction right now, but he's right, I owe it to him to be honest.

'Wallahi, Hamza, I swear, I think you're really special, and I've been going along with this despite the lack of chemistry because I was hoping that, with time, it would

235

grow. But it hasn't. There's still no chemistry. No tingles. No buzz, you know?'

Instead of looking angry, or shocked, Hamza looks absolutely crushed. But the worst part is, he also looks like he understands.

'So that's why you flinch whenever I touch you?'

The enormity of what I've offloaded onto him hits me, and that's when I know I have to tell him *everything*. I can't let him think that my issues are purely about him, when it is to do with me as well. He doesn't deserve that.

'No, that's not why. There are some things you don't know about me,' I begin hesitantly, nervously twisting the ring I wear on my forefinger over and over. I stop to see if he's listening, and although he can't meet my eyes, I know that he is.

'I was engaged once. His family knew my family, but he and I had never met until they brought the proposal round. We liked each other instantly and my parents let me get to know him before I made my decision. I fell for him hard. It was difficult not to, he was so charming and good-looking and we got on so well . . .'

My voice really begins to shake now, so I stop talking for a bit. I need a drink, but my glass is still very empty, so I grab Hamza's and down the rest of his Coke. I don't look at him, though. I can't bear to see his expression right now.

'We had been talking for about three months when he started trying to get physical with me. I was twenty-four and had never had any proper male friends, let alone an actual boyfriend. My idiotic friends used to tease me and call me a lesbian because I wasn't interested in anyone.'

'That's so messed-up,' Hamza interrupts. 'I hate all these stereotypes about women, created by a scorned man, no doubt.'

I smile a sad, shaky smile then, despite what I'm about to tell him. 'That's the reality of being a woman. If you mess around with boys you're a slut, and if you don't then you're gay, or frigid, or a tease. You can't win either way.'

I take another deep breath and continue. 'Anyway, throughout uni, they all had boyfriends but I was having fun with my girlfriends, going to restaurants, movies, musicals and exhibitions. I didn't feel that I was missing out on anything. Besides, my whole life, my nani has gone on and on about how precious your reputation is, and how once it's shattered, you can never repair it. So, I didn't go there. It wasn't worth it.

'It started with his arm around me at the cinema. At first, I felt uncomfortable but then it actually made me feel warm and safe, so I let him. Then it was hugs whenever we said goodbye. Then we started to hold hands. I kept telling myself that it was minor, everyone did it, most people did more. Then, one day he was supposed to be dropping me home after dinner, and we stopped in Alexandra Palace to take in the view and chat. He started getting close to me and it felt wrong, so I told him to stop, but he wouldn't. He kept laughing and telling me to stop being silly, that we were going to get married anyway, that it wasn't a big deal.'

The tears that have been welling up in my eyes spill over, and I brush them away angrily, annoyed with myself for still letting him affect me like this. I've tried so hard to forget that day, but every feeling, every word, every smell, will be forever etched in my memory.

We had driven up to the top of the hill and he stopped on the side of the road next to the palace, so we could look down at the whole of London at night, with a million lights twinkling in the cold, winter darkness. There were no other cars around so we sat there for a while, talking about random stuff; friends, work, uni. He was doing his Master's at the time, in architecture. And then he suggested we move to the backseat where we could be more comfortable.

We sat in the back, cuddling while we talked. His arm was around me and I was nestled into the crook of it. I had never felt so safe, so secure, so loved. But then he started to get closer, his fingers lifting my top and caressing my skin. I pushed his hand away and tried to laugh it off, telling him that we were going to get married in a few months so he could wait until then. He laughed too, and then tried it on again, turning the whole thing into a joke.

Until suddenly, it wasn't funny anymore.

He became a different man that night, as he pulled at my clothes, pawed at my flesh, held me down with his hands and knees so that I was trapped beneath his weight. I was petrified and kept struggling, but I could barely breathe, let alone move. The windows and doors were locked, and I remember taking huge gulps of air, trying to stop the bile from rising up my throat. He kept laughing and whispering that he knew I wanted it, how beautiful I was, how I was his and no one else's, to stop playing games. He acted like we were having a laugh together, even though I was sobbing. To this day, I just have to catch a whiff of Versace's Blue Jeans and I begin to retch.

'Did he . . . ?' Hamza's voice trails off into a whisper, his face ashen.

'No,' I reply shakily. 'He very nearly did, but then someone suddenly knocked on the window. It was a policeman – we were parked in the wrong place. That seemed to break the daze that he was in. We went home in silence.'

The tears are pouring freely down my cheeks now, and I can't wipe them away fast enough, so I give up and let them flow.

'He called me the next day but I didn't answer,' I croak, my throat hurting too much to speak any louder. 'I couldn't. I felt disgusted with myself, and so, so ashamed. I couldn't tell anyone what had happened. Who would believe me? They'd think I was asking for it, somehow. And maybe I was. Maybe I gave off the wrong vibes?'

'Don't *ever* blame yourself!' Hamza slams his fist on the table, and his ferociousness makes me look up in surprise. He's furious but concerned at the same time, and the relief I feel at not seeing disgust in his eyes is palpable. I begin to cry more, loud, wracking sobs, but this time because I feel so relieved to have finally told someone and have them empathise instead of blaming me. I'm vaguely aware that we're in public and people are probably wondering what the hell is going on, and to Hamza's credit, what others might think about him right now is the last thing on his mind.

'It's *not* your fault,' he continues vehemently. 'You said no. That's enough. He had no right to force you. And I know you, Zara. There's no way in hell you implied that you wanted it. And even if you did – you're allowed to change your mind.'

'I should never have got into the back seat,' I whisper, wiping my nose with my sleeve.

Hamza looks so angry that I'm worried he'll suddenly knock over all the plates on the table. He runs his hand through his hair and shakes his head in disbelief as I continue the story; of how, after a couple of days of ignoring his calls, Tariq stopped calling altogether. And exactly two weeks later, we heard he got engaged to his cousin.

I never told my parents what had really happened between us. Only Yasmin knows the truth. Everyone else thinks he cheated on me . . . and I suppose he did, kind of. I mean, we never actually broke up. I thought that he would try and call me again, and then we'd talk about what happened, he would apologise, and I would persuade myself that it was a mistake, that there was no malice involved. We'd get married and that would be that. That night would turn into a distant memory, a hiccup in what would eventually be a lifetime together.

But he never apologised. In fact, we never saw each other again. He chucked me aside like a used, dirty old rag, and I had to pick up the pieces of my shattered heart and crushed soul, with only Yasmin by my side. All it was for him was one moment of pleasure – something he could have had with anyone – yet a moment was all it took for him to strip me of my dignity, my self-respect, my self-worth, my strength.

For over a year, I barely left the house. I pretended I was busy with work, but the reality was I couldn't face my friends. They had no idea what had happened and thought I was nursing an ordinary broken heart. I stopped going to weddings or events where his family might be present. And not only because of them, but because the rumour mill was spinning fast. As people speculated about what happened between us; gossip turned to rumours, rumours turned to lies, my reputation and honour was questioned.

I stopped wearing clothes that would make me attractive, and I gave away everything that was slightly revealing. I started putting on weight. Someone asked if I was pregnant.

My mum was livid and fell out with his mum over the deceit and all the gossip. My sisters were heartbroken for me. They tried their best to cheer me up and then gave up when they could see that I wasn't responding to their attempts. My nani was practical, telling me that I would find someone better, it was his loss and Abbu was . . . Abbu. He didn't say much at all.

And me? I've spent the last five years making sure that I never give off the wrong impression again. That any guy I speak to knows his place and *my* limits. I've built walls so high around me that you'd need more than a ladder to climb over them, you'd need military intervention. And since I have first-hand experience of how vicious some people in my community can be, I'm more careful about my reputation than ever. Yes, we live in London, but sometimes it feels like we never left Sylhet . . .

'I'm sorry for not telling you any of this sooner,' I say, rubbing my eyes. I'm pretty sure I look like a raccoon right now, with black rivers all the way down my face, but I get the feeling that Hamza doesn't care. I look around the restaurant and there are a few people giving me curious sidelong glances, in that very British 'let's pretend we haven't noticed' kind of way. But there's nothing I can do about that. It's too late; it's all out now. And I feel oddly lighter.

'You don't have to apologise. It was never my business to know. But I'm glad you felt you could tell me. I can't believe you've kept this all to yourself all this time. You should have got help. Justice.'

'Justice? For what? He didn't get to finish the job he started. I would have been a fool to tell anyone the rest. Can you imagine what people would have said about me if it got out? They chatted crap about me when they didn't know anything! No one would have blamed *him*. They all would have said that I was asking for it, or that I led him on, or worse, that I'm lying, that I made it up because he ended it with me. It would have broken my parents and they would have had to deal with the rumours and whispers for the rest of their lives. I couldn't do that to everyone, or even myself. It wasn't worth it.'

'Our society is f***ed up isn't it?' Hamza says with a grimace. I smile a small smile back at him because it's the first time I've heard him swear, and it doesn't sound as out of place as I thought it would.

'It is what it is. So yeah. Now you know why I don't let anyone near me.'

Hamza insists on walking me home afterwards, although my house is only five minutes away.

'Zara,' he begins gently when we get to the bottom of my road, 'I get why you don't like physical contact now, and why you've been reserved with me. I even understand why you needed to cast a wide net. Sort of . . .'

We carry on walking, me examining the cracks and gum on the pavement while he continues to talk.

'. . . But what you said about not being attracted to me is still true. If this isn't going anywhere and you only want

243

to be friends, you need to tell me. I need to know so I can move on. I want to get married and have kids. You're not the only one getting older, you know. I'm going to be thirty-three soon, and my parents are pressuring me. But I want to marry someone who wants me as much as I want them. Not someone who's settling for me.'

We stop walking and, as I look up at his earnest face, I feel a pang in my heart at the thought of never seeing him again. I open my mouth to speak, but nothing comes out. Instead, a lump forms in my throat and it hurts to swallow.

'You don't have to decide today, but you need to decide soon, OK? Please don't leave me hanging forever.' He draws me close to him and gives me another gentle kiss on the top of my head. This time I don't recoil. In fact, I tentatively return the hug. We stand there for a few seconds, our hearts pounding away in unison, while he softly strokes the top of my head. Then he brushes away the last tear trickling down my cheek and walks away.

Chapter 18

A week later, my sisters and I are outside the Alexandra Palace ice rink, waiting for Hamza to arrive. I've taken Layla's advice on board and decided that in order to gain some clarity on my situation, I need my sisters' perspective.

I'm thankful that coming up here doesn't make me feel nervous anymore. It took a good few years, but I managed to overcome my anxiety. This place holds so many positive childhood memories for me; skating at the rink, rowing on the lake, fireworks, picnics, weddings ... I couldn't let Tariq taint all those special moments for me. I'd already lost nearly a year of my life because of him; all the weddings and parties I was too afraid to attend, all the nights I stayed at home locked in my room, too broken to go out. And as I stand by the wall and look down at magnificent London spread out before me, I'm glad this beautiful piece of my history – and perhaps future – isn't forever lost to me.

'Salaam Alaykom!' Hamza's booming voice startles me out of my morose thoughts. I smile back and wave shyly, my insides a bundle of nerves, like my dad's cable drawer with its countless phone chargers, laptop chargers, USB cables and other wires, all tangled up beyond redemption.

'Wa Alaikum Salaam,' I reply when he gets closer, unsure of how to greet him in front of my sisters. Hamza seems to sense my dilemma and gives my arm a quick squeeze before extending his hand to Amina first, and then Yasmin.

'Ah, the formidable Choudhury sisters. I've heard a lot about you! It's so nice to finally meet you!'

He shakes hands with them enthusiastically, pumping their hands up and down as if the harder he shakes them, the more they'll be inclined to like him. I see that Yasmin is trying to supress a smile, whereas Amina's expression is more difficult to read.

We make our way around the building to the ice rink entrance, where Hamza insists on buying our tickets, all the while keeping up a steady stream of conversation with my sisters. Well, with Yas anyway. Amina looks more uncomfortable than I imagined. He tries to engage with her but she responds with closed answers, which makes it challenging for him to continue the conversation.

When we finally get onto the ice, Yasmin whizzes away like she always does, gliding and spinning like a pro. She used to take lessons when we were kids and likes to show off her skills to anyone willing to watch. Hamza looks at me in awe.

'Can you skate like that, too?'

'No,' I mutter, carefully stepping onto the ice and promptly falling down hard on my backside. Whose stupid idea was this? Probably Yasmin's. She's always stealing the bloody show. Today is supposed to be about me. I stare at her as she pirouettes at the centre of the rink, in her leggings that show off her legs for days and her slouchy sweatshirt casually rolled up to her elbows, her perfect hair swishing about in time to the music. The pang of envy hits me hard in my gut, and I feel bad straight away. She's my sister. What kind of lowlife feels jealous of her younger, sexier sister? Hamza laughs, though, takes my hand into his gigantic paw and pulls me back onto my feet as if I'm no heavier than a feather.

'Well, it's nice to see that there's something you're not perfect at.' He smiles, before letting go of my hand and also gliding away. 'Catch me if you can! You're it!'

'Hey, I wasn't ready!'

It doesn't take me long to find my footing on the ice and when I do, I start having fun as we play a lively game of 'It'. Amina also seems to be enjoying herself, despite her aversion to most things physically challenging, as she desperately scuttles across the ice like a cockroach. I catch her straight away, colliding into her hard and sending both of us sprawling.

'You're "It",' I groan, rubbing my hip as I try to stand again. Hamza appears like a guardian angel, pulls me back up and I smile gratefully at him.

After our painful but exhilarating skating session, we go for lunch to one of my usual Turkish hotspots nearby. I know that Hamza will insist on footing the bill so I don't want to take advantage by going somewhere expensive. By this point, Amina has warmed up and they're bantering away like old friends. He's surprisingly good at manoeuvring his way around conversations with my sisters and has this uncanny ability to read between the lines and quickly but subtly switch topics he can sense are contentious. They talk politics, finance, international affairs and policy, and all sorts of other stuff, half of which goes over my head and the other half . . .? Well, I lean back and let them talk. Today is about *them* getting to know each other.

At one point, as I watch them talk about the British occupation of Egypt and Bangladesh, Hamza suddenly starts to look quite handsome. His green eyes sparkle as he gently teases Yasmin about her lack of knowledge of British history, his smile bright, straight and friendly. And it's at that moment, that I realise that knowledge, intellect and good manners are almost as attractive as good looks and sex appeal.

When he books an Uber for us to go home in because, 'Taking the bus after all that ice skating will be too tiring,' both my sisters seem to be won over.

'Omigod, Z, he is *perfect*,' Amina gushes on the ride home, as we sit back exhausted, bruised and stuffed from the day's activities. I can't help but raise an eyebrow as I take in her elated expression. I'm not used to Amina gushing about anyone or anything. 'What? Don't look at me like that! He is!'

'Really? How so?' I lean back against the seat and rest my head on Yas's shoulders.

'He ticks all the boxes, sis. He's tall. Striking. Highly educated. Good job. Intelligent – emotionally and intellectually. Friendly. Everyone's going to love him and he's crazy about you. What more do you want?'

'Erm . . . A bit of a spark?'

Yasmin remains worryingly quiet throughout the ride and it's only when we get back home and we're in the safety of my bedroom that she tells me what she really thinks.

'Look, Z, I can't tell you what to do,' she begins, plonking herself on my bed and kicking all my decorative cushions to the floor as she tries to get comfortable.

'But . . . you're going to anyway?'

'Is he a nice guy? Yes. Does he tick most of the boxes? Definitely. But you need to be attracted to him.'

I sigh and look away, unable to bear her worried stare any longer. She's right. I know she's right. But what about that spark I felt today when I saw how engaging and smart and interesting he is? I confess this to my sister, but instead of understanding where I'm coming from, she rolls her eyes.

'This is so typically you, Zara. You're clutching on to straws now. How long has it taken for you to feel this spark? Six months?'

'It's not the first time, though. I'm slowly seeing different sides of him that I'm attracted to.'

'Look, you asked for my opinion and I gave it. It's up to you to make the choice.' Then, when I don't respond, she softens and adds gently, 'Why don't you ask to meet his sister? Seeing his family might help you make up your mind?'

That night I struggle to fall asleep as the day's events roll around in my head like a chicken on a rotisserie. I thought Hamza meeting my sisters would help clear up this cloud of doubt, and maybe it has a little. Seeing that dynamic side of him has shifted my perspective and it's good to know that Amina at least has my back if we decide to go ahead with things. But still, it's not enough, is it?

Chapter 19

It's Friday night and, although it's been a quiet week at work, I'm feeling really drained. I've been out nearly every evening this week despite my half-hearted efforts to chill at home: gym, cinema with Layla and Ezra, who I haven't seen much of lately because she has some fancy new job that has her working all hours. I've seen Hamza twice. I had to; we went for dinner on Wednesday and he mentioned that he was planning on buying his sister a blender for her birthday. A blender! So I made him meet me in Selfridges on Thursday and picked out a pretty silver bangle instead.

Mo, by the way, unblocked me long enough to send me another text before blocking me again.

I can't believe I wasted so much time on you, you giant freak. You'll never find anyone as good as me. Bitch.

I still feel pretty shaken by the whole thing, to be honest. But I also feel as though I deserve it for speaking to him behind Hamza's back. I don't reply.

Tonight, I want nothing more than to curl up in bed with a film and a tube of Pringles and give my mind and body a chance to recover, but I can't. My eldest cousin Sabina is here from Dubai for four days and if I bail on a night that's been in the diary for months, she's going to murder me. Or worse, tell my mum about the dodgy things we got up to as teenagers.

I put the final touches on my makeup and then spray myself generously with all sorts of chemicals; fix spray, setting spray, hair spray and perfume, before stepping back and checking out my reflection in the mirror. Sabina is a famous makeup artist in Dubai, so I'm extra conscious of my face today. After Mo's 'giant' comment, I'm tempted to give heels a miss. I know Sabs will be in at least four inches; she's almost as tall as me and she always wears heels with confidence, so why do I let the fact that I'm the tallest Bengali girl in London bother me? It's better than being the shortest. Pushing Mo and his parting words out of my head, I slip them on and then complete my look with a rich red lippy. For the first time in a long time I feel good about myself.

The roar of a powerful engine, together with pounding bass, indicates the arrival of my cousin. I peer out of my bedroom window and, sure enough, there's a shiny white Range Rover struggling to fit into the space right outside our house. It goes forwards and backwards about ten times at various angles and I smile to myself, excited nerves brewing in my belly numbing the pain from earlier. I'm in dire need of some fun – and judging by the loud hip-hop that's causing our entire street to vibrate, it looks like she's ready to party too.

'Amina! Yas! Sabs is here!' I yell to my sisters as I grab my bag and head down the stairs. I hear the doorbell ring and the sound of squealing as Sabs greets and hugs Mum and Nani, towering above them in her heels.

'Ahlan wa sahlan habibti!' I call out in Arabic, grabbing my cousin in a bear hug. I'm looking forward to catching up with her and getting her perspective on the Bollywood drama that is currently my life.

'What's happening, tart?' she replies with her trademark, blinding smile. 'You're looking good!'

'Thanks.' I shrug modestly, hearing the thundering steps of my sisters running down the stairs.

There are more hugs and shrieks, then much to Mum and Nani's dismay, we head out soon after. Nani grumbles about us choosing to go out for dinner instead of eating home-cooked food, and Mum looks put out at being unable to catch up with her niece. We assure them that Sabina will be staying over tonight and they can feed her and gossip as much as they want in the morning. They reluctantly let us go, making us promise to behave and not stay out too late.

'By the way, Samia's going to meet us at the restaurant and will come back with us and stay at yours too,' Sabs says as we climb into the car.

'Yeah, cool.' I shrug, although truth be told, I'm not sure how I feel about seeing Sam after she lied to me, but

I say nothing and grab Sabs' ancient pink iPod and flick through all the old school hip-hop and R & B tracks instead. She stops me, making us all recite the travelling and protection prayers first, and I gulp, hoping she still remembers how to drive on this side of the road.

Windows down and music blasting, we sing and dance the entire drive into Central London, screaming every time Sabs takes a corner too fast or slams the brakes too hard. People are looking at us disapprovingly, but we don't care. In fact, the more the car swerves and shudders, the more I let go of my worries and my fatigue. It's summer, the weather is amazing, we're young, we're healthy, we're attractive. We have so much to be grateful for.

Our first stop of the night is to an Indian restaurant in Covent Garden; not exactly the place to party but the food is amazing. Samia is already there waiting for us, a scowl on her face because we're half an hour late, so we all hug her and compliment her on her new outfit to soften her up before making our way to the table where we order every halal item on the menu.

'So! What's been happening since I was last here?' Sabina asks, touching up her siren-red lipstick, so I copy her and do the same. I look around the table and see that my sisters and Sam are also pulling their lippies out. As well as being a hugely successful makeup artist whose client list includes members of the Dubai royal family, Sabina is also beautiful and always looks flawless. Back in the day, she was approached by a modelling agency, despite wearing a hijab. Now she's in her mid-thirties but she still looks fabulous and she's always being gawked at, stalked or stopped by random people; men and women alike. Whenever we're around her, we all make an extra effort with our makeup because if we don't, she's bound to look at us with a pained expression and murmur, 'Are you sure you blended your eyeshadow properly today?'

'Erm . . .' I flounder, not sure where to begin, or how honest to be with Samia right there, ears wagging. I don't really want to spend the evening dissecting my marriage prospects, but then, having been married for donkey's years, Sabs is the right person to explain my dilemma to. It all comes out: Mum's threat on my twenty-ninth birthday. Hamza. Dr Farook. Mr MoneyMaker Mo. The rejection from the Tower Hamlets man I never even met.

I go through the events as succinctly as possible, with Yasmin and Amina chiming in every so often, until the food arrives. Then they're all too busy munching away on the gorgeous grills and fragrant curries to bother. I can tell that Samia is paying close attention, though. I find her silence off-putting, but I can't exactly stop talking, not if I want Sabs' perspective on things.

'Let me get this straight,' Sabina says, picking up a lamb chop with her hands and biting into the tender flesh with her teeth bared. That's the endearing thing about her; she looks like a Muslim supermodel and then she does something uncouth like fart in public.

'OK . . .' I prompt her as she loses her train of thought, grease all around her mouth as she savours every last morsel.

'Yeah. As I was saying. Let me get this straight. You rejected the doctor, and now you're going out with the unattractive one?'

'I wouldn't class it as "going out",' I interject hurriedly, while Amina and Yasmin roll their eyes. They've heard this a million times already. 'And he's a bloody dentist, not a doctor. And Hamza's not unattractive. I'm just not madly attracted to him.'

'Whatever,' Sabina says dismissively. 'So, you don't know if you want to marry him because you don't fancy him?'

'Er, I suppose it could be simplified like that, if you decide to leave out all the detail and nuance,' I concede reluctantly. When she puts it like that, I sound like a right flaky floozy.

She looks at me incredulously. 'What I don't understand is: why the hell are you going out with a bloke you don't fancy?'

'You'd understand if you met him,' Amina pipes up. 'He's really intelligent and well spoken—'

'He is,' Yasmin agrees. 'He's also one of those genuinely decent guys.'

'See what I mean?' I tell Sabs. 'I really like him and get along with him. He's funny. He's smart. He's respectful. He reminds me that not all men are bastards.'

'Yeah, yeah, that's all well and good, Zara, but you can't marry someone you don't bloody fancy. How are you going to do the dirty with him? How are you going to have kids? Lie back and think of England?'

'What does that phrase actually mean?' Samia muses. 'Like, why would you think about England when you can think of other stuff, like what you need to do at work the next day?'

Sabina looks at her as if she's crazy. 'Why would you think of work in the middle of the deed?'

'Why would you think of England?' Samia retorts, her expression serious.

'Er, can we change the subject? All this vulgar talk is putting me off my food,' Amina groans. I look at her wiped-clean plate and so does everyone else, and we all burst out laughing while she turns pink.

'I meant my next helping!' she wails, covering her blushing cheeks and making us laugh harder.

The rest of dinner and dessert passes by in a similar fashion with Sabina bestowing her wisdom on us in the way only she can, with her strong London accent and tactless comments; Amina moaning about her colleagues in the Muslim charity she works for and cracking us up with her impressions of the chairman; Yasmin telling us all about her friends in uni and all the wild things they get up to, and Samia finally filling us in on her trip to Zimbabwe. By this point, I've nearly forgotten the animosity I felt towards her and I decide to try and let it go.

You can't force someone to confide in you and it's up to her who she wants to share her business with. It has, however, made me more mindful of how honest I am with her about my own life and problems.

'I can't believe you lived without a washing machine for two months,' Sabina says, part-awed and part-horrified. 'You never used to even change your own sheets, so how did you manage to hand-wash your clothes?'

'Washing my clothes was the least of my worries,' Samia admits. 'There was no hot water. I took a cold bath every morning with one bucket of water. Even after two months I never got used to the sensation of ice-cold water hitting my hot, sweaty body. It was hard.'

'It must have been amazing, though,' Amina says wistfully.

'It was,' Samia affirms, eating the last spoonful of chocolate cake. 'It taught me a lot about myself and gave me a lot of perspective. Before I went, I started obsessing over getting married, if I would find someone, or would I be still single at almost thirty like Zara.'

Ouch. Even when I'm trying to be zen and trying to move on from all this marriage malarkey, the Universe still goes and plants comments like that right in my face. I wait for her to reveal the agreement she made with her dad about meeting suitors, but she doesn't.

'Sorry, no offence, Zara,' she continues. 'Anyway. When I got there, the fact that my First World Problems are super-trivial really hit me. Babies crying themselves to sleep out of hunger? Now that's a real problem.'

There's a long silence after that. I mean, what could anyone possibly say?

After dinner, we climb back into the Range, the vibe slightly more subdued than it was earlier on. Until Samia starts moaning that she has to sit squashed between Yasmin and Amina instead of riding shotgun, and my sisters nudge each other and murmur, 'First world problems.' This naturally has the rest of us (minus Samaritan Samia) in hysterics and, once again, we're in the mood to party.

Since Sabs and Sam are hijabis, we can't exactly hit a club next, so we head for where every other Not-Overly-Religious Muslim girl goes for a bit of a laugh; a shisha café. As we sing at the top of our lungs, Sabina weaves in and out of the Friday night Central London traffic, almost colliding with other road users too many times to count.

'We're heeeeere,' she finally calls out, coming to a screeching halt outside one of my old haunts in Bayswater.

'You can't park here, it's a double yellow,' I tell her as she gets ready to leave the car right there on the main road.

'Oh, bloody hell,' she huffs. 'Why isn't there valet parking anywhere around here?' She's obviously become a bit of a diva after all these years in Dubai, and of course, the rest of us scream, *'First world problems!'* and start laughing all over again.

'I haven't been here in years,' I murmur when we walk up to the joint, Arabic music emanating from the open door. We step inside, inhaling the sweet, fruity fragrance of the hookah floating in the air, and with it comes a wave of old memories.

I've been avoiding this place because Tariq and I used to come here every week and I'm terrified of bumping into him. I don't want to mention this, though, so I plaster a grin on my face and follow my sisters and cousins through the restaurant to the outdoor area. Pretty Ottoman-inspired lanterns and fairy lights twinkle amongst the shrubs, and Gulf-style red and black upholstery covers the low sofas. It reminds me of the Middle East, but where exactly in the Arab peninsula I'm supposed to be, I'm not sure, because there's a little bit of everything in the eclectic décor.

It's nearing the end of June now and the weather in London is warm and muggy, so I take my blazer off as we sit down and am immediately greeted with 'oohs' from the girls as they all lean in to touch my newly toned biceps. I push them away and laugh uncomfortably, looking around the restaurant to see if he's here. The garden is crowded and noisy with the hum of voices, occasional laughter, and Lebanese pop music playing in the background. The tables consist of mostly Arabs and Asians in their twenties enjoying their Friday night, but I don't see *him*.

Once our orders are taken, we settle back and chill. We've gone for two pipes between us; pineapple and coconut, and grape and mint, and after a few puffs I feel relaxed and a tad woozy. It's been so long since I've smoked this stuff that I've become a bit of a lightweight. Yasmin, however, is somewhat of a connoisseur it seems, because she handles the tongs like a pro and blows out perfect rings.

'How's Fufu doing? She seemed a bit down when I came to the house,' Sabina asks once we're all comfortably settled in, smoking lazily and sipping on our mocktails.

My sisters and I exchange glances and Amina decides to fill Sabina in.

'Mum's completely stressed out with trying to Zara a husband,' she reveals, doing her best to avoid my stare. 'She's scared she's never going to get married because she's too fussy.'

This is news to me. I've been so absorbed in my own dramas that I hadn't noticed a change in my mum's usual neurotic behaviour. I look away.

'Too fussy?' Sabina raises a perfectly shaped eyebrow.

'Because she keeps saying no to everyone,' Yasmin butts in, blowing another smoke ring. I'm tempted to lean over and ruin it.

'The atmosphere at home is pretty tense right now,' she continues. 'There've been no new proposals and with each day that passes, another hair on Mum's head turns grey. She's terrified that one of us will end up like Ruby – forty-one years old, unmarried and probably unable to have kids.'

Oh yes. Ruby. The family example of what happens to women who focus too much on their careers and don't focus enough on finding a husband. The women who have dared to spend their twenties and early thirties studying hard, working hard, living abroad and experiencing life. The women who are 'too fussy', 'too unrealistic' and 'too experienced'; who aren't willing to compromise because they've already tasted the finer things in life and anything less than perfection isn't worth settling down for. Women who want partners who will complement their already fulfilled lives; not bring them down.

Well, you know what? If Ruby's happy, and living her best life, then good for her. Only . . . I don't want to be single, and childless, forever.

'Right. So, Sam, what do you make of all this?' I say to shift some of the attention away from me and to see if Sam will finally reveal what's going on with her.

Samia shrugs, as though she hasn't made a deal with her dad to get her biodata sorted. 'I'm open to meeting people.'

'Just open?' Yasmin probes, nudging me discreetly. I nudge her back, harder. *Shut up!*

'Well, yeah. I mean, obviously I have a lot more time than Zara so it's not exactly a pressing concern right now . . .'

'Are you actively looking then?' Yasmin asks, and I take a long drag of my pipe and wait for the answer.

'Not really. I'm not on a quest like Zara.' She laughs uncomfortably and looks away, while steering the discussion back to me. As I struggle with how to shut this conversation down, I spot a familiar gait sauntering over to us. Although I know it's him, for a second, I see him as though it's the first time; tall, slim, with thick, dark brown wavy hair and a smattering of a beard caressing his strong jawline. He's wearing a black T-shirt that shows off his toned arms and I drag my eyes away from all that golden skin and look into his amused face.

'All right, Z?' Adam grins cheekily down at me. 'I couldn't help but notice all the racket you ladies are making, although to be honest I almost didn't recognise you. You scrub up well. Mind if I join you for a bit?'

I don't know if I'm relieved or annoyed by the surprise appearance. I had a feeling I was going to bump into someone I know today, but I wouldn't have guessed it would be Adam. I'm grateful that it wasn't Hamza, or worse, Tariq, and I'm also glad that it's interrupted Sabina's line of questioning . . . but there's something about the way the others are eyeing him up like he's a juicy steak that makes the hairs on my arms bristle.

'Ooh, of *course* you can, please take a seat,' Sabs coos before I can open my mouth to refuse, scooting up and offering him a seat between us. Although Sabina is happily married, she likes a good flirt with a hot guy every so often. That's not my main concern, though. I know it's stupid, but I can't help but hope that Adam is immune to her beauty and prefers me over her.

Ever since our bike ride back in the spring, Adam and I have become a lot closer and I'm beginning to see him as a real friend. He's changed a lot since the days he would constantly berate me and I've realised that he's not as immature and annoying as I thought he was. Hanging out with him is never boring.

Even so, we rarely spend time together outside the office, unless it's a quick Turkish after a long day at work, so seeing him here amidst my sisters and cousins, while I'm dressed to impress and cradling a shisha pipe in my hands, is a tad unnerving.

I grudgingly move up and as Adam settles in between us, Sabs looks over at me and mouths, '*Who the hell is that?*' and I glare at her, hoping he doesn't notice. He has a big enough head as it is, without all this extra female attention to inflate it further.

Adam's presence changes the vibe of our little table completely. The conversation has thankfully steered away from me and my (lack of a) love life and on to other topics, like work and family. All of a sudden, Samia has become deep and insightful, with her little rendition of how she tried to save the children of Zimbabwe; Yasmin is being sexy and aloof, barely talking but smiling her wide, seductive smile every so often; Amina has gone completely quiet and keeps checking him out from the corner of her eye when she thinks no one is looking; and Sabs is her usual outgoing self, laughing loudly and joking away with him like they're old mates.

And me? I don't know what they're talking about half the time because I'm completely distracted by the fact that his bare bicep is touching my own. His skin is smooth and every time he laughs, it slides up against my arm creating instant goosebumps. This is a completely different experience from the night I rode on the back of his bike when there were at least six layers of clothing between us. Now, there's just his cotton T-shirt and my flimsy silk top, and I can feel his warmth radiating through the fabric and setting my skin alight.

Bloody hell, I think I need a cold shower – and it has nothing to do with the temperature outside. I don't know what's wrong with me. I don't usually get like this around Adam of all people. I see him every day, for God's sake! So why is this happening now, at the worst possible place, with the worst possible audience? Is the shisha getting to my head? Or is it because I've been celibate for so long – my entire life, in fact – that anyone with a bit of facial hair and tanned skin gives me the kajeejees?

Everyone suddenly turns to look at me, and for a second I'm petrified that they've somehow read my thoughts. Did I say something out loud by accident? OH MY GOD. I did, didn't I?

'I was joking,' I croak, grabbing my drink and taking a big swig, hoping they believe me.

'Joking about what?' Sabina replies, confused. 'We were asking Adam how you two met and he said that we should ask you?'

'I figured you could tell the story better than me,' Adam adds, turning to look at me. As his eyes meet mine, something in his expression shifts and I wonder if

265

he can read the desire scribbled all over my face. I shuffle my body away from his as much as I can and look away.

'I hate this story!' I moan, elbowing Adam. 'Why would you do this to me?'

'Right, now we *have* to hear it,' Yasmin insists and the others agree.

Taking another gulp of my mocktail, I tell them all about the day I met Adam.

'So, it was my first day at work and I didn't know a single soul, or where anything was.' I pause and look at my captivated audience. I take another swig, wishing, not for the first time, it were something a little stronger.

'At lunch time, I got up to go to the loo and whilst sitting in the cubicle getting on with my business, I heard a male voice.'

'That was probably my voice, by the way.' Adam grins.

'For a second I thought someone had come into the ladies by accident . . . until I heard the sound of weeing, and more male voices and realised I was in the men's toilets!'

'Shit!' Samia gasps.

'Yeah, thank God I wasn't doing one of those.' Everyone laughs and I let them, not revealing that my heart had stopped and my knees started to shake as I sat there, my knickers around my ankles.

It was excruciating. I stayed sitting in that cubicle for absolutely ages, well past my lunch hour. My stomach was grumbling because I'd missed lunch and I was late returning to my desk on my very first day, but I was too embarrassed to make my escape in case I was seen.

'When the lunchtime loo runs were finally over and all was quiet, I tentatively opened the door and peered out. The toilets were empty thank God, so I decided to leg it out of there without washing my hands before someone else came in. I ran over to the door and yanked it open the same time someone was coming in—'

'And walked right into me,' Adam interrupts with glee. 'She knocked the wind out of me and fell backwards onto the nasty, dirty floor.'

'And banged my head. Pretty badly, in fact.'

'I came to your rescue, of course, being the gentleman that I am.'

I shove him. 'Gentleman? Instead of bloody discreetly helping me back up, you started shouting for help as if I'd been shot! And the next thing we knew, the whole office appeared, watching me lie there on that filthy floor, wondering what I was doing there in the first place.'

The girls are in stitches and I survey them, unimpressed. Adam is laughing too, and he nudges me with his elbow playfully.

'Remember how everyone called you "toilet girl" for about a year afterwards?'

'How can I forget?' I groan, covering my face with my hands. 'It was mortifying!'

The others carry on giggling and talking about embarrassing encounters, and as they do, Adam touches my bare arm gently to get my undivided attention. The contact, as innocent as it is, electrifies me and I turn to look at him, trying my best to focus on his eyes instead of his lips.

'You know, it didn't quite happen like that,' he murmurs so the others can't hear.

'What are you talking about? Yes it did!' I whisper back.

'Sort of. But there's a part of this story I haven't told you before.' He looks almost embarrassed as he admits this and I narrow my eyes, waiting for him to explain.

'I actually came into the toilets before we bumped into each other,' he confesses. 'It was my voice you must have heard. I dropped my phone and when I went to pick it up, I saw your shoes from under the cubicle doors and I sort of guessed what had happened.'

'No way! How could you tell it was me by my shoes? I don't believe you!'

'Uh, pink ankle boots? They weren't exactly inconspicuous. You used to make more of an effort with your outfits when you first started.'

'OK, fine. Then what? You left me in there?'

'Well, I waited a bit, and I could hear that nothing was going on in the cubicle so I figured you were waiting for everyone to leave.'

'And . . .?'

'Well, I left the toilets and was trying to figure out how to get you out of there unseen, but people kept going in and out. In the end, I stuck an out-of-order sign on the door so no one else would come in. I wanted to give you enough time to make your escape.'

'Are you *serious*?' Until recently, I thought that Adam's preferred pastime was watching me squirm.

'Yeah.' He shrugs again, fiddling with the shisha pipe that has found its way to him. He takes the mouthpiece between his lips and inhales deeply, still looking at me. My heart thrashing against my chest, I let myself stare at his lips.

And then he blows a plume of smoke right in my face. Coughing, I shove him, thankful that the intensity of the moment is over.

The rest of the night flies by. The girls begin to loosen up in Adam's presence and start acting more like themselves, which initially was a good thing, until the shisha really gets to their heads and they start going a bit wild, like asking him intrusive questions about his dating life. Sabs becomes tactile with him, pushing and nudging him playfully. He takes it all in good humour though, and tells them all loudly and proudly that he's, 'Single and ready to mingle.'

I'm also loosening up, but that's not a good thing. Adam has his arm on the back of my chair and, as the night progresses, I find myself nestled into the crook of it with my entire right side pressed against his left. At one point, I see Amina and Yasmin elbowing looking pointedly at our proximity, but it feels so right that I don't move away. I don't look at him, though, and barely talk to him because I'm scared of what he'll see in my eyes if I do.

Every so often Hamza's smiling face comes to the front of my mind, and when it does, guilt nips at my ankles. I tell myself that I'm not doing anything wrong, Adam and I are purely platonic, and even if I fancied him – which I don't when I'm in the right frame of mind – I would never go down that road. How can I? I'm his manager, after all.

When midnight comes and goes, we reluctantly call it a night. Adam's friends have long gone and he doesn't have his bike with him, so Samia the Samaritan tells him he can hitch a ride with us. It makes sense as he lives in Haringey too, but it means he'll be sitting in the back squashed up next to them. The thought of Sam getting kicks from his muscular arms really pisses me off. I can't exactly give up my place at the front, though, as it will make it all too obvious, so I smile and agree.

The journey home is raucous, as we blast old school tunes with all the windows down and the sunroof open, dancing and singing like we're at a gig. Until Will Smith's 'Boom Shake the Room' starts playing, that is. At first, we all sing along with it, screaming, 'Tic-tic-tic-tic BOOM.' Suddenly, Amina yelps and switches the stereo off, the abrupt silence shocking us into stillness.

'What's wrong?' I whisper, looking around furtively. 'Are the Feds chasing us?' We have four people in the back which is enough to get a fine at least.

'No! But we can't listen to that song!' she whispers back, her big eyes wide with fear.

'Why not?' Adam asks from his position squashed between Samia and Yasmin – something he's pleased about, no doubt. I note that this time Sam isn't complaining about riding in the back.

'Because it's too risky!' she squeaks. 'What will people think, a bunch of Muslims shouting, "Tic-tic-tic-tic BOOM?" Use your common sense!'

There's a pause while we struggle to comprehend her reasoning and then all of us – with the exception of Amina – burst into uncontrollable laughter.

Chapter 20

I don't know about you, but after I've had a fab night out, I feel on top of the world. My friends who drink beg to differ. They claim that following a night of unadulterated partying, they're usually one of three things: glued to a toilet bowl with vomit trickling down their chins; in bed with a brain-crippling headache; or in bed with a stranger, wondering how to sneak out without having to make awkward conversation. And occasionally, all three.

As for me, I'm beginning to feel like my old self, the one I was before all this marriage drama, before Tariq. Who would have thought that a bit of quality time with my sisters and cousins, good music and shisha was what I needed to pick myself up?

After we dropped Adam off outside his house – a small terrace on the Harringey Ladder – the girls wouldn't stop hooting and singing about Zara and Adam sitting in a tree and other such adolescent nonsense. Samia was particularly enamoured by him and kept asking me questions about him. From general things like what he does for a living and who he lives with, to random questions like what his favourite food is (doner kebab), what sort of music he listens to (old school hip-hop), how he drinks his tea (black and with heaps of sugar). What she plans to do with that information, I have no idea.

The rest of the weekend passed with loads of eating, laughing and catching up. Nani spent the entire time fussing over us all, Sabina in particular. She's always been Nani's favourite, with me coming in at second place and Samia at third.

But amidst all the chaos and curries, I found my mind constantly returning to Adam, and not just about how I felt cocooned against him, but the fact that the first time we met, he tried to save me by sticking that sign on the toilet. And what is most astounding is that he had successfully hidden it from me for three years, instead of reminding me of his chivalry at every available opportunity.

It's while I'm sitting with my family, quietly minding my own business and wondering if Adam ever thinks of me outside the office, that my mum decides to launch into one of her marriage tirades.

'Listen, Zara, I don't know if you've noticed, but things have been a bit quiet on the biodata front,' she says on Sunday night, after my cousins have left and it's the six us of once again, curled up on the sofa watching a cooking show. Rather than reply, I rest my head on Nani's shoulder and stoically continue to watch Nadiya Hussain travel through Bangladesh eating all this stuff I've never heard of, let alone seen.

'Well, anyway, I don't know if you met your Bilquis Aunty at that wedding we went to? She's looking for her son, Tony, and wanted me to share his picture with you.'

I glance over at my sisters to gauge their reaction. Yasmin's scrolling through her phone and appears to be ignoring the exchange and Amina is watching us curiously, probably wondering if I'll 'fess up about Hamza.

'Er, right,' I say, noncommittally.

'You could show a little enthusiasm!' She huffs, glaring at me with eyes as big as mine.

'It's hard to be enthusiastic when it's probably not going to go anywhere,' I reply, my tone neutral. I look over at my dad for backup, but as usual, he keeps out of it. To be fair, contradicting my mum is akin to throwing oneself in front of a bulldozer.

'Well, it's that winning attitude that's getting you nowhere!' she retorts, her voice soaked with sarcasm. 'We have less than six months before your birthday, but riding motorbikes and going out with your friends is more important than finding a husband, isn't it?'

Yasmin stops looking at her phone and Amina sits up straight, the tension in the room so thick you can almost touch it. I woke up this morning feeling like I was in a good place, mentally and emotionally. But my mum's accusation lands heavy, and it hurts.

'How can you say that?' I exclaim, my voice rising. Nani places a hand on my leg but it makes no difference to the rage that's simmering inside. 'I've done everything you wanted me to and more! I wrote your stupid bio-data, I'm going to the weddings, I've lost weight, I signed up to a marriage app, I've been to events! I dressed up like a granny and met Dr Fool after completing that humiliating questionnaire of his! I've even let you send my details to people I'm not interested in, against my better judgement, and they've *rejected* me! And now you turn around and throw it all in my face?'

By this point I'm standing up and waving my hands around manically. All four feet nine inches of my nani is trying to pull me back to a sitting position, but I shake her off as I feel the telltale prickling sensation behind my eyes.

'Mum, you're being out of order.' Amina sounds as indignant as I feel. 'What else is she supposed to do? Promote herself on a street corner?'

'Or take out a billboard ad like that Muslim guy did once,' Yasmin adds.

'Khobor dhar, amar Jara reh bezar khorbai,' Nani joins in, accusing Mum of talking too much and telling her that she better not dare upset me. 'Tumi beshi matoh!' I look over at my mum to see her staring daggers at poor Nani.

'All right, everyone needs to calm down,' Abbu inter-jects feebly.

'I am calm, thank you very much,' Mum snaps. 'Tell your beloved daughter to calm down. She's the one gallivanting around North London on the back of a motorbike, and rejecting all sorts of decent proposals, like she's still twenty-three! At this rate, Samia is going to be married before her!'

'Decent? Are you telling me that Dr Strange was *decent*?' I shout at her. 'And so what if I'm twenty-nine? I'd rather be twenty-nine and single than twenty-nine and married to a psycho!'

'I'll show you psycho if you reject another perfectly decent proposal!' Mum shouts back at me, pointing her knitting needle at me menacingly. 'Six months, Zara! We've got six months and then I'm booking you a one-way ticket to Bangladesh!'

Unable to take any more of the accusations, I run out of the room and upstairs to my room. Despite the door being closed, I can hear the muffled voices from down below. Sticking my earphones into my ears, I squeeze my eyes closed and try to remember how settled and at peace I felt the entire weekend, up until this storm.

The next morning I leave the house extra early to avoid seeing anyone in my household and work out my frustration at the gym.

'Zara, you're smashing it,' Jordan tells me, impressed as he feels my bicep while I beat the shit out of the punching bag. 'You look incredible. Well done, babe.'

'Thanks,' I pant, wiping my sweaty hair out of my face. Jordan's good looks barely affect me these days. I mean, I'm not blind, I can still see them but I've developed immunity to them. I carry on working out with his firm encouragement, my mum's words ringing in my head over and over, like the most annoying song ever on repeat. I can't believe she thinks I've been sitting on my backside for the past six months . . . and then hit me where it really hurt by pitting me against Samia.

Argh! I give the bag one last kick and then chuck off my gloves and go and get ready for work.

After I've showered and changed into my usual summer uniform of cropped trousers, an oversized T-shirt and sandals, I stick big sunglasses on to hide the bags of rage that developed under my eyes overnight and get into the office way before I'm supposed to start working. To my surprise, Adam's already there, steadily working away on his Mac. He turns around when he hears me come in and the sight of him makes me stop in my tracks as Friday's memories once again come flooding back.

'All right, Z?' He smirks, looking me up and down. 'Good night, Friday.'

'Yeah, it was OK.' I cough without making eye contact, hurrying over to my desk, dumping my bag down. 'What are you doing here so early?'

'Fancied it after the gym. You?'

'Same. Do you want some tea?' Leaving my sunglasses on so he can't look at my panic-stricken eyes, I go over to his desk and pick up his mug

'I was about to make one. You log in, I'll bring it over.' He takes the mug from me, and as he does, our fingers brush and I feel a current of electricity shoot through my arm. Snatching my hand away and avoiding his piercing stare, I go back to my desk and busy myself with shuffling folders and papers until he returns.

What the actual hell is going on here? OK, so we had a bit of a moment on Friday but surely that shouldn't warrant such an intense reaction? It's Adam, for God's sake, I rationalise. Adam who takes the piss out of me all the time. Adam who comes into work with creases and holes in his clothes. *Adam who makes you laugh,* the other part of my brain adds. *Adam who rescued you from your unfortunate toilet mishap, all those years ago.*

A few minutes later, he's back with our teas and hot buttered toast, and to deflect from the turmoil that's going on in my head, I grab a slice and stuff it in my mouth. He laughs.

'You looked a bit hangry so I thought you could do with a some nourishment,' he says, sitting on the end of my desk. *Adam who brings you breakfast.*

'Thanks,' I mumble, my mouth full. 'That's sweet of you.'

'I can be a nice guy when I want to be.' He grins, looking ultra-pleased with himself.

I roll my eyes. 'More angry than hangry to be honest.'

'Why, what's up?'

The part of me that now feels weird around Adam, doesn't want to answer. But because I don't want him to notice the subtle change in our relationship, I take a deep breath, calm the tingles in my gut, and give him a brief rundown of my conversation with my mum. He listens without interrupting. That's another thing I've learnt recently about Adam. He's a pretty good listener.

'I take it they don't know about your boyfriend?' he says wryly, watching me scoff down the second slice.

'There's nothing to tell them,' I retort, gulping down my tea.

'If you say so.' He shrugs, getting off my table and putting our breakfast stuff back on the tray. *Adam who tidies up after you.*

'What about you then? How was the rest of your weekend?' I ask, anxious to change the subject.

'Busy. I was out most of the time.' A shadow passes over his face when he says this. He's made a couple of comments like this, implying that he's avoiding going home but I don't feel like I can ask him why outright.

'Doing what?' I ask lightly, trying not to sound too nosey.

'You're an inquisitive little thing, aren't you?' He raises an eyebrow, before looking down at the napkin that has fallen by my feet. I reach over to get it, but he crouches down to do the same, and before I know it, his face is so close to me that I can feel his warm breath on my nose. My own breath catches as we both stop, mid-reach, and stare right into each other's eyes. Nerves ripple through my body and my mouth turns dry. Once again, my body betrays me and I lick my lips. His eyes flick down to them. My heart is thrashing now, so loudly that he must be able to hear it.

'Like I said, I get curious,' I say quietly, trying to tear my eyes away from him.

'Well, so do I, aşkım, so do I,' he replies, his voice low and gravelly as he continues to look at me through hooded eyes.

'Morning everyone!' The office door is thrown open and we both jump away from each other, the spell broken.

I clear my throat and return the greeting to Alex from Housing before turning back to Adam. 'I really needed that toast and tea. Thank you.'

'You're welcome, aşkım.' He smiles at me, and I'm reminded of how handsome he looks when he's not being rude to me. He's in a plain T-shirt and ripped jeans, the white fabric a brilliant contrast against his permanent tan. I look down at the crumbs on my own T-shirt and brush them off self-consciously.

'Aşkım? Is that Turkish? What does it mean?' I keep my voice loud and bright, as if the louder I speak, the quicker we can forget what nearly happened, and go back to how we usually are with each other.

'"Loser",' he replies and I laugh, relieved that the fire from a moment ago seems to have been doused.

'You can't stay nice for long, can you "aşkım"?' I tease in my best Turkish accent.

'Well, where's the fun in being nice all the time?' With a wink, he turns around and lopes off to his desk and I let out a breath as quietly as I can.

The more people that enter the building, interrupting the stillness of the morning, the more I decide that our 'moment' was merely a result of our Friday night flirtations. Things were bound to be weird after we spent most of the night physically glued to each other's side. In fact, by the time Kevin and Francesca get in, Adam's back to his usual sarcastic self and I've never been so relieved. I have enough on my mind with trying to figure out if Hamza is the one, without throwing Adam into the spice mix. If Adam was a spice, he would be paprika. A little smoky, a little spicy, the perfect spice to give a curry a depth of colour. Hamza, on the other hand, is more like turmeric. Plain but dependable. You need it in every curry, but you don't really know why.

As soon as it hits five o'clock, Adam's out the door like a flash, with Francesca right behind him.

I loiter. I can't bear to go home right away and face my mum's accusations. And besides, it's been a while seen I've seen Hamza, and I can't exactly decide if he's the one if I barely see him. I bet if I worked with him every day, and rode on his motorbike, and went for shisha with him, then I'd start fancying him too.

Free for a catch up? I send the text while I'm still at my desk. Luckily, he replies immediately and, with relief, I grab my bag and head out into the hot, summer's evening.

Hamza's already waiting for me outside Nike at Oxford Circus and greets me with the biggest bear hug of my life and I lean into it and let him wrap his arms around me. His embrace feels so safe and comforting that I'm almost disappointed when he finally lets go to grin down at me.

'Salaams, habibti,' he says, his eyes full of warmth. 'How are you?'

'Better now that you're here,' I reply truthfully. 'It's been mad.'

'Tell me about it over dinner?' He takes my hand and, once again, I don't resist.

The days are long and warm now and we stroll hand in hand through the cobbled Soho streets while he fills me in on his weekend and day at work. Everywhere I look I see happy couples stuck to each other like conjoined twins in their flirty summer outfits and sunglasses, and I realise with a start that we must look exactly like them. Hamza's in aviators and because he's come straight from work, he's had to make do with unbuttoning his shirt collar and rolling his sleeves up. I look at his pale arm next to my brown one and the strangest thought enters my head. I wonder what our kids would look like.

We go to a little Malaysian restaurant that serves fully halal meat, and while we wait for our food to arrive, I casually mention that I bumped into Adam on Friday night whilst out with my cousins.

'Hmm,' he replies noncommittally. 'Is that why you had a bad weekend? Did you guys have a fight?'

'No. My tiff was with my mum,' I say miserably. 'She's getting really stressed out about me still being unmarried with my thirtieth birthday coming up.'

'If you need me to save you from spinsterhood, say the word,' he responds, wiggling his eyebrows. I must look alarmed because he sighs and rolls his eyes.

'Relax, I was joking.'

'I know you were!' I say brightly. 'Obviously we're not about to get married when we barely know each other.'

'Well, "barely" is an underestimation, wouldn't you say?'

'OK, maybe not "barely" but not enough to decide that we want to live with each other forever. I don't even know how many kids you want,' I add as an afterthought.

Our food arrives; a sticky barbecue platter for two, ho fun noodles with beef, sambal morning glory, chilli prawns and a beef rendang, and I hope it's enough of a distraction that Hamza will forget that we're talking about marriage, and start talking about food instead.

'I don't care how many kids I have, so long as there's at least one,' he says between bites of the deliciously sweet and spicy barbecue lamb, not forgetting our line of conversation at all. 'What about you?'

'Three,' I admit, deciding to go with it. The whole point of us meeting today was for me to try and suss out our compatibility. 'I've always wanted three, like me and my sisters. You guys are three siblings too, right?'

'Yeah. It's a good number.' He smiles, reaching for the king prawns.

The conversation moves on to work, and Hamza starts talking about some new financial project thingie. I tune out and I think about how there's so much more to maintaining a marriage than how many kids we want. According to Sabina, the beauty of an arranged marriage is that you get to find out all the important stuff before your judgement is clouded with love. We've all heard too many stories of women who haven't done their due diligence, only to be in for a massive shock after marriage.

I somehow need to find out exactly what Hamza wants from me, without making it too obvious. Does he want me to wear hijab? Live with his parents? Stop working? I have no bloody idea, and I need to find out ASAP, before things get more complicated than they already are.

When he finally stops talking about work, I gesture over to his chin. 'You've got some sauce on your chin,' I begin casually. As he wipes it, I continue, 'Good thing you don't have a beard, huh? Imagine how much food would get stuck in it!'

He laughs and takes the bait immediately. 'I might grow one, one day. Do you like beards?'

'They can be pretty sexy sometimes. Would you do it for religious reasons or fashion reasons?'

'Uh, a bit of both maybe?'

'What about hijab?' I quickly ask, thrilled that the conversation is going the way I want it to.

He looks up from his food, a little taken aback. 'What about it?'

'Does your mum wear it? Would you expect your wife to?'

'My mom and sister wear it,' he replies with a shrug. 'But what my wife does or doesn't wear is her business. It's between her and God, not her and me.'

As the night progresses, I manage to elicit more answers from Hamza. He has no intentions of living with his parents after he gets married. In fact, he already owns a flat in South London that he's planning to move in to. He also says that he wouldn't mind moving to North London, so long as he can commute into work easily.

He tells me more about his family and how his younger sister Hiba was engaged once but it didn't work out. I'm interested to know why, but I decide not to ask, it's not my business. Besides, she's around the same age as me and he's probably sick of the stick she gets about being unmarried, like I am.

His answers are textbook perfect. But then, isn't that how all men are at the beginning, when they're still wooing you? I know too many women who thought they were marrying kind, considerate and generous men, but the moment they moved in together, they learnt the hard way that it was all a farce. Sometimes I wish it was acceptable in our culture to try before we had to buy.

I have one more question, and I don't know how to sugar coat it, so while we wait for dessert I blurt it out as nonchalantly as possible.

'Would you want your future wife to stop working?'

He looks a bit surprised, but then shrugs. 'Uh, it's up to you. I mean, her. Islamically, I have to provide for her – financially I mean. So, I'd pay for the mortgage, bills, food and her own expenses. But if she wanted to work anyway, I wouldn't mind. I mean, what else is she supposed to do all day?'

'What if I wanted to go for coffees and brunches all day?'

'I thought we were speaking hypothetically?' He laughs. 'As long as we can afford it, why not? If I could brunch all day, I would.'

We both laugh at this, and I feel the tension pulling at my neck start to ease.

'And what about after kids?' I remember to add, before I get too comfortable. There's still time for him to make a wrong move.

'If you wanted to work after kids, we'd find a way to make it happen. There are nurseries and childminders for a reason.'

'OK . . .' I say slowly after a short silence. 'So what exactly are your expectations of a wife? It doesn't sound like you're fussed about anything. Where's the catch?'

'Look, Zara, the way I see it, marriage isn't about having kids and living together. I want a life partner. Someone

I can laugh with and have fun with when things are good, but someone who will help pick me up when things are bad. I don't expect you to cook and clean for me all day, but if you weren't working, then honestly, it would be nice to come home to a cooked dinner. But I don't see it as it being your duty as a woman. I want to take care of you, and I'd hope you'd also do what you could to take care of me. And we'd take care of the kids together, you know?'

'Makes sense,' I say pensively. There's no way for me to be certain that his answers are genuine, but I get the feeling that they are. He's given me no reason to think otherwise. Sure, he can be pushy at times, but I don't think he's a liar.

'So do you mind me asking what would be completely unacceptable to you in a marriage?'

'Lying,' he says without hesitation. 'Honesty and trust are everything.'

That night, as I ride my Uber home, I mull over Hamza's responses to my not-so-subtle questions, and I feel at peace. If things continue the way they're going, maybe I won't feel this unsure for long.

Those were some pretty intense questions, Hamza texts me when I'm home and tucked up in bed.

I know, I reply. *Thanks for humouring me. And you know you can ask me anything you want, right?*

His response comes through as I'm about to drift into slumber. *I already know what I want.*

Chapter 21

It's Friday night and instead of going to the cinema with Layla and Ezra as I was supposed to, I'm stuck in the office with Adam, finalising the artwork for the revamped community magazine that's due for approvals first thing Monday morning. By the time we finish and send the files off to Kevin, it's gone seven and I'm itching to get out of there.

'Right. That's it. I'm out,' I announce as I shut my computer down and pack my bag. 'I've had enough of this place. I've been here way past five every day this week.'

'Yes, I know, I've been right here with you,' Adam replies wryly, as he scoops up his helmet and keys. 'I could do with a drink.'

I resist the urge to roll my eyes. 'Well, enjoy the pub then.' I switch off the lights and start heading towards the lift, and Adam follows me out, closing the door behind him.

'What are you up to tonight?'

'Nothing interesting,' I admit reluctantly as we wait for the ancient, rickety contraption to appear. 'My friends are about to head into the cinema and I won't make it in time. My family's gone to visit some relatives and Hamza's got a work shindig so I'm actually thinking of going to the gym, that's how lame I am. It's better than going straight home, I guess.'

Adam looks horrified. 'Er, no it's not. You can't gym on a Friday night after the week we've had. That's it, you're coming out with me.'

'Oh, Adam, don't start that pub stuff again,' I implore as the lift pings its arrival and we step into it.

'I'm not. We won't go to the pub. We'll go for shisha at our place in Bayswater.'

'"Our" place?' I raise an eyebrow.

'Yeah, you know, where we bumped into each other that time.'

'That doesn't make it "our" place.'

'Oh, whatever. Come on, let's go.'

'Hang on, I can't go looking like this!'

I look down at my coffee-stained T-shirt, faded jeans and scuffed trainers. My face is barren too, devoid of even a lick of Vaseline and my hair is bordering on greasy. Look, it's been a tough week.

'You have a point,' Adam agrees, as he surveys the hot mess in front of him.

'Oi!' I shove him a little harder than intended and he teeters, grabbing on to the handrail in the lift.

'I'll drop you to your house and pick you up after I've showered and changed. You have forty-five minutes to get ready, not a minute more, all right?'

'OK! Fine! Let's go!'

Riding on the back of Adam's motorbike isn't as scary as it was the first time, and I only squeeze my eyes closed for half a minute or so until I get used to it and start enjoying the thrill of it once again. I also love the fact that we don't have to sit around in traffic. In fact, I'm home in ten minutes which is otherwise impossible. Maybe I should invest in one of these bad boys myself.

The house is dark and silent and I'm glad. I've spent most of the week avoiding or ignoring my mum and I don't intend on breaking my vow of silence today. I shower in record time, spray loads of products in my hair and decide to side-plait it. Anything else is a waste of time because the helmet will flatten it out anyway.

My phone buzzes while I'm in the middle of getting ready and it's a text from Adam telling me that he's bringing a car, not his bike, and he'll be here in fifteen minutes. Flippin' 'eck, that changes everything. I pull the band out of my hair and tousle it up to give it some volume and hurriedly work on my face. I don't have much time so I do the basics and then put on a grey silk top tucked into black leather trousers, a studded belt and an equally chunky bangle. I look at my shoes and, as I'm reaching for my usual flats, I change my mind and grab a pair of stilettos instead. I'm not walking tonight or riding on the back of a motorbike, so why not?

While I'm getting ready, I start to wonder if Hamza would have a problem with me going out for a casual shisha with Adam after all that drama at the event. It feels wrong hiding it from him, especially when there's nothing to hide.

'Hey, Hamza,' I begin brightly, recording a quick voice message. 'I know you're at your work thing and I've just finished up myself. Adam's suggesting we go for shisha to unwind after a mad week . . . I think we're going to Bayswater. Call me if you fancy joining us after you're done. But if not, I'll see you and your sister tomorrow!' There. See? Nothing shady going on.

Yes. I'm seeing his sister tomorrow Not only is the clock ticking with my mum's ultimatum, Hamza's vague one is looming over my head as well, and with the help of Yasmin, I've decided that the next course of action should be to meet his family. Well, one member of his family, anyway. I'm not ready to meet them all yet! I can't say I'm looking forward to it, but it has to be done. I'm not going to be one of those girls who blindly agrees to marry some guy, only to find out that his mother's a dragon, his sister's a psycho, and they're both hell-bent on making my life miserable.

Adam calls to announce his arrival as I'm putting my diamond studs in (a twenty-first birthday present from my parents), so I spray some perfume, grab my clutch and then walk down the stairs slowly and carefully. The last thing I want right now is to buckle and break my leg. Especially as I didn't have time to shave. No paramedic wants to catch a glimpse of these gnarly thighs right now.

Parked outside my house is a swanky black Porsche, and I'm about to walk past it when Adam rolls the window down and wolf whistles.

'How the hell can you afford a Porsche on your salary?' I demand, opening the passenger door and then trying to get in as elegantly as possible in six-inch heels.

'All right, talk about ruining the mood. I was going to tell you that you look bloody gorgeous, and then you talk about my tiny . . . salary?'

I laugh. 'Come on, it could be worse. But seriously. How?'

'It's not mine, it's my brother's,' he admits. 'He sprained his knee playing football the other day and is stuck at home until it heals.' He says all this with a massive grin, and I laugh at his uncontained glee.

'You're terrible!' I chuckle, and then hurriedly do up my seatbelt as he puts his foot down and speeds away, the force sending my head back. I'm about to scream at him for being such a reckless driver but he slows down without me saying anything and the rest of the journey resumes at a normal pace.

We spend the car ride listening to our favourite old school garage and hip-hop tracks, windows down and singing and dancing along to all the tunes. Well, I sing and dance. He nods his head here and there, giving me the occasional 'You're crazy' look.

And he's not the only one giving me looks. I never knew how seductive a sports car can be. Clearly, I've never really had the luxury of travelling in them before. Every time we stop in traffic or at the lights, whoever is in the car next to me turns to stare. One guy even winks at me. At one point, Adam gets annoyed and threatens to close the window, accusing me of egging on their advances.

'How am I egging them on?!' I exclaim in bewilderment. 'I'm not looking at them!' He grumbles an incoherent response, but leaves the window open.

We finally get to our destination and Adam has to help me climb out of the car because my legs have gone numb. Sports cars are so overrated. The seats are tiny and you're so low down that your knees ache from being in that position for too long.

'Hang on, this isn't Bayswater!' I exclaim, looking around at the imposing glass skyscrapers towering above me as a steady stream of traffic whizzes by.

'No shit, Sherlock,' Adam says, casually linking his arm through mine. 'It's Liverpool Street.'

'Oh yeah,' I blush. 'I was wondering why we were passing through Whitechapel a minute ago. What are we doing here?'

'I figured that this opportunity was too good to waste, so I managed to bag us a table at a cool restaurant where my mate works. The waiting list is insane. I think you'll like it.'

He goes up to one of the bouncers and they hug and chat for a few seconds. Adam introduces me to him and I smile shyly as the man shakes my hand and welcomes me to the restaurant, before directing us towards a glass lift that will take us all the way up to the thirty-ninth floor.

The lift begins its ascent and I inhale the magnificent view. From this height, all the other buildings are tiny, and it's almost like someone has spilt glitter all over a black carpet; there are twinkling lights everywhere.

'This is incredible,' I murmur as the lift comes to a stop at our floor, unable to tear my gaze away from the view, a tingly sensation spreading across my body. 'You're full of surprises, aren't you, Turkish?'

Adam looks surprised for a second and then laughs. '*Lock, Stock*? Can't believe you've seen that movie. You're full of surprises yourself, aşkım.'

The hostess takes us over to a table right by the window so we can enjoy the view throughout our meal. We order a selection of cooked seafood and sushi dishes because the meat and chicken aren't halal, and for a second, I'm pleased that Adam respects my feelings about halal food and doesn't decide to start munching pork in front of me. I know he's going to order wine or something with his meal but I'm not going to say anything. It's none of my business – and even if it was, I don't want to ruin the mood.

'I'll have the same mocktail as my friend,' he tells the waitress and I try to hide the look of pleasant surprise on my face.

The food is as amazing as the whole setting. Adam is also being delightful company and, if I didn't know better, it would feel like a date. But it's not. Of course it's not. It's Adam, my immature, irritating colleague; but despite my brain knowing this, the rest of me feels super-attracted to him right now. It doesn't help that instead of sitting across from me, he's right next to me and every so often, our knees touch. With his crisp white shirt unbuttoned at the neck, and the sleeves rolled up to expose his gorgeously tanned, strong forearms, I feel like I'm seeing a completely different side to him.

'How's it going with your boyfriend?' Adam suddenly asks. 'Everything all right? And what happened to that guy from your Instagram?'

I shuffle uncomfortably in my seat. 'Erm . . . about that . . . That wasn't actually anyone. That was my personal trainer, Jordan.'

He stares at me in surprise. 'What? I mean, I thought you said—'

'You were intent on jumping to conclusions about that picture and that whole night, so I let you think what you wanted.'

Adam goes quiet for a moment and then smiles apologetically. 'I was a complete dickhead. The stuff I said to you was terrible. I'm sorry.'

I let him stew in his discomfort for a moment and then give his arm a reassuring squeeze. 'It's OK. You've come a long way since then.'

We sit there for a bit, my fingers still dangerously close to his arm. I think back to how our relationship was before and resist the urge to let my fingertips graze over that silky skin.

'Why did you go off on me that day?' I ask tentatively. 'Say I had slept with who you thought was Hamza? I mean, so what? You probably sleep with a different girl every week.'

'All right, welcome back, judgemental Zara.'

'I'm not judging you. But that day, you were judging me for doing something you do all the time. Why?'

'Because you're different from me. And most of the girls I know. You're . . . I don't know. Innocent. But not in a stupid, ignorant way. You have boundaries and don't compromise them for anyone. I know I didn't act like it back then, but I respect that.'

Wow. I don't know what to say to this admission, so I sit with an astounded look on my face.

'And I guess I was a bit jealous too. I mean . . . why him? Why not me?' He says this with a simple shrug, like it's the most normal thing in the world to confess. But I feel as if I've had an ice-cold glass of water thrown over me and the first thing that comes to my mind is Hamza's smiling face.

My expression must give away my thoughts because Adam laughs an empty laugh and then downs the rest of his drink before swiftly changing the subject. 'By the way, there's this guy at the next table who keeps staring at us. At first, I thought he fancied you, even though he's with a girl, but now I think he might know you.'

I barely register what he says. *He was jealous?* I mean, I thought it was in a protective, big-brother sort of way, not in an 'I want you for myself' sort of way. My heart contracts, painfully, and I stare down at my empty plate, too afraid to look up and see what's lurking in his eyes. *This changes nothing, Zara,* I remind myself as I take a swig of water to wet my dry throat. *He's still Adam. He's not what you want in a husband. And there's Hamza to think about, too. Perfect, sweet, Hamza.*

'All right, enough about me, tell me what's going on with you?' I change the subject, taking a large gulp of water to cool myself down.

'What do you mean?'

'Tell me to piss off if it's not my place, but I've got the feeling something's going on with you at home.'

'Oh. How could you tell?'

'You've been avoiding going home after work. Or at least, that's what I assumed.'

He sighs. 'Yeah, there's some stuff going on.'

'Do you want to talk about it?'

He pauses for a bit, and he looks so disheartened that I wish I hadn't brought it up. 'Remember I told you my aunt lives with us? She's sick. Really sick. Cancer.'

I breathe in sharply and place my hand on his arm. 'I'm so sorry, Adam.'

'Yeah. Shit, isn't it? The thing that's upsetting me the most is that she's suffered her whole life. She got married to an arsehole who used to beat her up. She got married again, kept having miscarriages, and then became a widow. And now this.'

'Can I ask what type it is?' I whisper, my eyes filling with tears as his do the same.

'Breast cancer. They've given her just a few more months. The chemo didn't work, nor did hormone therapy, radiotherapy or surgery. There's nothing left for them to do.'

We sit in silence, my hand still on his arm. He stares out the window at London spread below us, and then takes my other hand into his.

'Adam,' I begin tentatively, 'if your aunt doesn't have much time left, then shouldn't you be spending all your free time with her, instead of avoiding her? I can't imagine how painful it is to watch her deteriorate, but I get the feeling that you'll regret it one day if you don't.'

Adam doesn't reply and continues to hold my hand, stroking it with his thumb. The touch is sending currents through me and I know I should remove my hand, but how can I, when we're talking about his dying aunt?

After a while he pulls away and finally looks at me. His eyes are watery and he smiles wryly at me. 'This is why I have a hard time believing in God. If he's really out there, why do so many awful things happen to good people? I wish I could have the same level of faith as you, but I can't get my head around it.'

The waitress starts clearing away our plates and I welcome the respite from the complexity of this conversation. I still feel on edge, though, almost as though I'm waiting for the next surprise to come and hit me.

'Oh bloody hell,' Adam says once the plates have been taken away. 'That guy's still staring at you. I'm tempted to go over to him and ask him what his problem is.'

'Fine, let me see him.' I whip my head around, even though I suspect that it's a diversionary tactic. It takes a moment to absorb my surroundings as the place is packed with people and I have no idea who the Peeping Tom is.

Then I see him. He's right there, two tables away. Our eyes meet and I'm twenty-four years-old again, sobbing in the shower as I try and wash away the bruises. My head starts to spin like the fast cycle on a washing machine and I hear Adam's voice in the distance but I can't make out what he's saying. My chest begins to tighten and every breath becomes a struggle, so I gulp, trying to fill my lungs with oxygen, but nothing helps the dizziness.

'Zara, what the hell's going on?' Adam demands, getting up from his seat and coming over to me. He crouches down next to me and takes both of my hands in his. 'Calm down. Please. Breathe in slowly, aşkım. I'm here, OK? I'm here.'

He stays like that until I start to breathe normally again. I don't know how long it takes but I finally manage to calm down.

'Do I have mascara streaks down my face?' I croak when I get my wits back and realise that this is not the time to look like a panda.

'Er, no, you don't. Just a little smudge under your eyes. Here, let me.' He leans over and cleans it off with his thumb. The gesture is sweet and tender, but unlike a few minutes ago, I feel nothing towards him. Seeing Tariq has completely crushed me.

What is he doing here? Why did I have to bump into him today, after all these years, when I had finally stopped stressing about him and started living again? Who's that girl with him? His wife? Is she the one he dumped me for, after he . . .

My skin prickles and I rub my arms in an effort to smooth out the goosebumps.

'Do you want to tell me what's going on with that bloke?' Adam asks after a while. The waitress brings us our desserts but they sit in front of us, untouched.

'Not really.' I can't bring myself to tell another person what happened, who he is, why I am the way I am. I hope Adam realises this and stops asking questions.

'But he did something bad to you?' he probes. His voice is gentle but there's a steely undertone to it and I can sense that he's itching to get up and confront Tariq.

'Yeah.'

'Did he hurt you?' His voice is fiercer now, so I realise I'm going to have to tell him something otherwise he won't stop. I take a deep breath and decide to give him the condensed version. One without details, one that won't derail me right here in this restaurant with that demon mere inches away from me. I take a deep breath.

'We were engaged and he took that as a sign to force himself on me. He was interrupted. And then he disappeared and got engaged to someone else a few weeks later without having the decency to tell me it was over.'

'F***!'

'Yeah.'

'How long ago was this?'

'Five years ago. But it messed me up for a long time, Adam. I can't believe he's here and he's living his best life after he effed up mine.' I look down at my plate as tears well up in my eyes again. I hate the way he still has this effect on me.

'Watch what I do to him,' Adam growls, moving to get up, and I stop him hurriedly.

'No, don't, I don't want to look at him.' I take a few more deep breaths and manage to offer him a shaky smile. 'See? I'm fine.'

'You have really shit luck when it comes to men, don't you?'

'The worst.'

'Come on, let's eat our dessert before it fossilises.'

'You know about fossils?'

'What the hell, Zara? I did go to school, you know. I'm not some thug off the streets!'

'Yeah, I know, sorry.'

We start to laugh and I thaw slightly, in Adam's warm, strong, presence. I can't relax though, not with Tariq right behind me, watching me.

'You know, if you face your fears now, you'll probably feel a lot better in the future,' Adam says after a while. 'Maybe it will give you some closure? Some control?'

'Maybe,' I concede. 'But I couldn't look at him without turning into a hot mess, how am I supposed to talk to him?'

'I'm right here with you. He tries anything, I'll knock him out till next week.'

I know he's right. But I also know that I don't have it in me to speak to him. I can't. Not after everything he did to me. If I close my eyes and focus, I can feel him pawing me all over again. No. I can't. I want to get the hell out of here. Screw Tariq for ruining this night for me, the way he ruined the last five years. I was having the best time, and now, when I look back to this evening, I won't remember the delicious food, the stunning view, my handsome date, the sexy car, or how special I felt. I'll remember that bastard showing up and reminding me that I'm a total failure.

The bill comes and it's a lot more expensive than I expected. I attempt to pay my half but Adam gets really offended when I try, so I let it go. He gets up and offers his hand to help me up. I take it, knowing that Tariq is watching us right now, and I'm glad I did because my legs are like playdough.

We have to walk past the Devil's table to get to the exit. I try to ignore him, gripping on to Adam's hand like it's a lifebuoy, hoping to pass him and get out of here without any drama. But Adam suddenly stops, so abruptly that I stumble into him.

'All right?' Adam looks down at Tariq and his date, his features hard. SHIT. What is he doing? I want to turn and run, but Adam is still holding on to my hand. And I can't let that bastard know his presence has affected me.

'Um, h-hi,' Tariq stammers nervously. Oh God, that voice. *Shhh, I know you want me to, babe.*

My head starts to spin again. Round and round and round.

We're getting married, babe. What's the big deal?

I hold on to Adam tighter, my nails digging into his arm, but he doesn't even flinch.

'Zara mentioned that you two were engaged back in the day? I'm Adam, her husband.'

'Engaged?' the girl blurts out in shock. 'Tariq? You never told me you were engaged before!'

Tariq ignores the girl and stares at Adam. 'Husband? Oh. Congratulations,' he croaks, his voice strangled.

'Yes, four years now,' Adam continues proudly. 'Your loss, my gain. Anyway, see you around.'

With his hand on my waist guiding me, we walk away, my breath still caught in my throat, my nails still embedded in his flesh. Did that really happen? Did I really come face to face with Tariq without collapsing? We're only a couple of metres away when Adam stops and stares down at me.

'I bet he's still watching us,' he murmurs, a playful smile on his lips. 'Let's give him something to remember you by that isn't from five years ago.' Without waiting for a response, he draws me close and wraps his arms around me, pressing my still shaky body against his firm, strong chest.

'Hey—' I protest, as he holds me there for an eternity, until I stop shivering and melt into his embrace. I can feel his heart beating, matching the pace of my pulse. Blood is pounding in my brain again, but this time, for completely different reasons. Then, he pulls back enough to look down at my bewildered face. With his palm against my cheek, he leans in slowly, still staring into my eyes, daring me to pull away. I know I should, but I don't. I know this is an act, something to taunt Tariq with, but even so, I feel myself falling into a different dimension in a different universe as his lips press down on mine.

It's like nothing I've ever experienced before. And everything. It's all my emotions and sensations together; clashing but complementing. Contradicting but connecting. I feel so weak, but so, so strong, as my hands creep up around his neck and I start to kiss him back.

He tastes like chocolate and strawberries and, as his mouth continues to explore mine, something explodes inside me and I pull him closer, kissing him so hard I shock him into stillness. And then his pace matches mine and for the first time in five years, I feel unchained. I'm on fire. I want to drink him in, melt his body into mine and stay like this forever. But there's something I need to do first while I have the courage. I pull away and stare into Adam's eyes, his pupils dilated with desire, his breathing heavy with wanting.

'Give me a second, Turkish,' I say, stroking his face. And then I turn and walk back towards Tariq, the adrenaline coursing through my veins. Sure enough, his gaze is still on me while his date lays into him about something. She falls silent when I approach the table again.

'You tried to break me,' I tell him, the fire that's been ignited within me giving me the courage to look him straight in the eye. 'You tried to rape me. Destroy me. But does it look like I'm destroyed? You're *nothing* to me. An ugly memory that's fading more and more each day.' I can see shame in his expression, but there's also a little bit of defiance. So, before I lose my nerve, I pick up his drink and pour it over his head.

'You stupid bitch!' he snarls, making to get up as the bright orange concoction drips down his face. I move back as fear begins to take hold of me again, but he's barely out of his seat before Adam is beside me.

'Don't ever speak to my wife again,' he growls, and then draws his arm back and punches Tariq right in the face with all his strength. There's a cracking noise and a river of blood trickles down Tariq's face, over his lips, merging with the orange. The girl starts screaming and people rush towards us.

'Let's go before he calls the police,' I implore, pulling Adam away as the security guard bursts into the restaurant. Thank God it's his bouncer friend, because all he does is shake his head and usher us out, saying something incomprehensible into his walkie-talkie.

'Bro, is this what I get for getting you a last-second table?' he moans as he pretends to escort us out of the restaurant.

'Sorry, but that's been five years coming,' Adam replies, rubbing his sore hand.

The barriers between us torn down forever; I take his bruised hand and kiss it gently right there in the lift and in front of his friend, and bring it to my chest where I hold on to it. I know what happened upstairs started as acting, but I feel closer to him than I've ever felt to anyone. I feel as though I've known him forever, as though he's mine. A blush creeps up his neck and I wonder if it's with embarrassment or because he feels the same.

'Thank you.' I whisper, tears filling my eyes again.

'Anytime, aşkım,' he replies with a sad smile, slowly taking his hand back and stuffing it into his pocket. 'Come on, let's get you home.'

Chapter 22

The journey home is painfully quiet, with neither of us knowing what to say. I keep wondering how to break the silence, but the atmosphere is so charged that I'm too scared to. What if he kisses me again, this time for real? Then I'll be forced to make a decision on whether or not to let Hamza go.

Adam says nothing either, and every time I sneak a look at him, I see him staring straight ahead with a grim expression.

When we finally pull up outside my house, I'm relieved to see that my dad's car isn't parked in its usual spot, and all the lights are off. I bid Adam a hasty goodbye and clamber out of the car as quickly as I can, given the fact that I'm wearing skyscrapers on my feet. The car speeds away before I get to the front door.

Around three I finally give up on sleep and take a long, hot shower. For the first time since Ramadan, I'm awake for Salaatul Fajr – the dawn prayer – so I wrap a pashmina around my head and seek solace in pressing my forehead on the prayer mat. The repetitive and rhythmic Arabic words manage to calm me down, and when the prayer is over, I continue to sit there for a while, beseeching God to help me and guide me towards what's right for me.

When I collapse into bed, I glance at my phone for the first time in hours to find three missed calls from Hamza and a few messages to go with them, asking if I still wanted to meet up. I stare blankly at the screen for a moment, trying to pull up the memory of Hamza with all his kindness, stability, decency, from the depths of my Adam-induced stupor.

All this time I've known that something's missing in the relationship, but I've struggled to articulate what it is, beyond 'chemistry'. Now that I've kissed Adam, I know exactly what's absent. Fire.

I type out as my eyelids begin to droop with sleep:

Hey, Hamza, Sorry for missing your calls and messages. Got home just before 12 so wouldn't have made sense for you to meet us. Been in bed, just got up for fajr. Hope you're OK. x

When I finally awake around eleven, still emotionally and physically exhausted from the previous night's action, I find his response, reminding me that we're meeting his sister at one thirty.

Shit! His sister. How could I have forgotten?

Every single part of me wants to back out, but instead, I reply 'Of course, let me know where,' to erase some of the guilt I'm experiencing. It doesn't work, though.

I keep reminding myself that not only did I NOT initiate the kiss, it wasn't even real. It was acting. Actors do it all the time. It means nothing. Except Brad did fall in love with Angelina after all their 'acting'. Shit! How am I supposed to face Hamza AND his sister when I look like death and feel like a two-timing bitch?

As I get ready, I realise that my features reek of betrayal; from my sunken sockets, to my glassy pupils and my swollen lips. I get to work concealing the bags under my eyes and brushing some colour onto my sallow complexion, whilst trying not to look overdone. It works, sort of. If only I could brush away what was going on inside me as well.

I pick up my phone at least twenty times to back out of the meeting, but each time I start writing the text out, I imagine Hamza's crestfallen face and how embarrassed he would feel in front of his sister, and I delete the whole message. I can't let him down like this. Plus, he knows I was out with Adam last night and I can't do anything that will make him suspect that something went awry.

An hour later, I'm sitting on the Westbound Piccadilly Line train in sensible pale denim jeans and a simple white cotton blouse. I look like the picture of serenity, but my insides feel like scrambled eggs. What Hamza's super-successful and intelligent doctor sister thinks of me is way down on my list of things to stress about, though. The first ten pages of the list revolve around Adam. Is he as torn up over the kiss as I am? Could he sleep last night, or was he up most of it, thinking about me? Is he beginning to see me as more than a friend? Does he view me differently now that he knows about Tariq? I hope he doesn't pity me.

The fact that I haven't heard a whisper from him makes me inclined to believe that the kiss meant nothing, even though he said I was different from all the other girls. He kisses people every weekend. Snogging comes as naturally to him as eating comes to me. It's a good thing, I tell myself. Fancying me is one thing. He fancies everyone. But Adam actually *liking* me will complicate things further.

As the stuffy carriage gets closer and closer to my destination, the Adam-inspired worries merge into full-blown nerves about meeting Hamza's sister. Whose name I can't for the life of me recall.

I keep reminding myself that he had the guts to meet both my sisters at the same time, and he did it beautifully. I only have to meet one of his siblings (he has a younger brother, too), so how hard can that be? I get along with most people anyway.

But what if she takes one look at me and can tell that, a mere thirteen hours ago, I was in another man's arms? OK, the chances of her being Mystic Meg are slim, but what if she's good at sussing people out and she can tell that my heart isn't 100 per cent in this? What if it's *Hamza* who can tell that something's up with me? What if he can smell the unintentional betrayal on me?

When I get off the train at Rayners Lane, I want to throw up. How am I supposed to keep it together in front of him AND his sister? All I want is to cross the platform and go back in the direction I came from, and I'm about to do so when I see Hamza hurrying towards me, beaming from ear to ear.

'Zara! Ahlan wa sahlan, habibti! Welcome to my neck of the woods!'

Now that he's seen me, there's no going back. My stomach twisting and flipping over and over again, I lick my dry lips and smile a wobbly smile back as I make my way over to him. He hugs me, I stiffen, and then he grabs my hand and pulls me towards his car. Which, I'm surprised to see, is a massive BMW 4×4. I remember Adam's brother's Porsche and guilt swishes inside my belly like a gone-off seafood pasta, ready to come out at any moment.

'Nice car,' I croak as he opens the passenger door, waits for me to climb in and then closes it firmly behind me, almost as though he knows I want to make a run for it.

'Thanks, I bought it last year with my bonus.' His response is casual, and not boastful in the slightest, but even so, I find myself sinking lower into my seat. Bonus? Seriously? I have no idea how much these things cost but I'm pretty sure it's more than my entire yearly salary.

Hamza puts the car into gear and starts driving through leafy suburban streets and I stare out the window longingly, wishing I could throw myself out of it. I don't know

311

where he's taking me and where we're meeting his sister, and I don't ask because I'm scared that if I open my mouth I'll throw up all over the beautiful leather interior. Instead, I let him ramble on about his work event last night, and 'mmm' in what I think are the right places.

After about ten minutes which feels more like ten hours, he pulls up outside a large, single-fronted detached Edwardian-style house with a front garden that could do with a bit of a weeding. I presume this is where we're picking his sister up, but instead of waiting for her to come out, he kills the engine and turns to look at me with a guilty expression.

'Er, so . . .' he begins, shamefaced. 'So, uh, this is where we're going to meet my sister. At my house.'

'Mmm,' I reply absentmindedly. 'OK.' And then my breath catches in my throat as I realise what he's said. 'Did you say *at your house*?'

'Uh . . .'

'She's there alone, right?' I demand. 'No one else is home? You haven't ambushed me, have you?' My voice rises to a shriek as the weight of the bombshell he's dropped on me threatens to crush me.

'Not exactly,' he confesses, looking more and more fearful by the second. 'You see, when my parents found out that Hiba was going to meet you, they wanted to meet you too and they wouldn't take no for an answer, and then my aunt—'

The bomb explodes.

'*Hamza*! I swear down I'm gonna kill you!' I cry, covering my sweaty face with my clammy hands. 'How could you do this to me? I'm not going in! Take me back to the station!'

'I can't! I already texted them and told them we're on the way. They're waiting for you!'

'*Hamza*!!!!!'

'I'm sorry! It was my sister's fault! She told my mom she was meeting you, and then my mom insisted she got to meet you too!'

With one last wail, I give Hamza my fiercest glower before hastily rummaging around in my bag for things to help me look more presentable. In about thirty seconds flat, I manage to dab away most of the sweat, touch up my powder and lipstick, run a brush through my hair and spritz on some more perfume. And I don't finish a second too soon because as I'm about to get my deodorant out, the front door swings open and a cheery girl in jeans, flowery blouse and pink headscarf bounds out and peers into the car before knocking on the window and waving frantically.

This, quite clearly, is Hamza's sister; a smaller, female version of him.

I take a deep breath, plaster a shaky smile on my face, open the door and climb out of the car as elegantly as possible, my legs wobbling with nerves.

'Hi! Assalaamu Alaikum, I'm Zara,' I manage to say with realistic-sounding enthusiasm, extending my hand as she comes towards me. She pushes it out of the way and instead grabs me in a massive bear hug, before planting three alternating smackers on my cheeks.

'Zara! 'Alaikom Salaam! I'm Hiba! Oh, you don't know how thrilled I am to finally meet you!'

Hiba has the same American-ish accent as Hamza and it suits her. She's too full of life to be British. Then, grabbing the hand she pushed away only a moment earlier, she half ushers, half drags me towards The Front Door of Fear. I look back at Hamza in a panic, but he shrugs sheepishly and follows us into the house.

Oh Allah give me the strength to get through the next hour with dignity, grace, intelligence and sanity, I pray desperately as I misjudge the two steps leading up to the door and trip, nearly pulling Hiba down with me. *Allah, please get Adam out of my head and show me whether Hamza is suited to me.* Thankfully she's nice and sturdy and helps steady me before giving my hand a reassuring squeeze.

'Look, don't worry, everyone is dying to meet you. You have nothing to worry about,' she stage whispers as we enter the hallway.

'Everyone?' I croak. Who's everyone?

I soon find out because a second later, we walk into the sitting room. The hum of voices stops abruptly and about ten people all stare at me with a mixture of curiosity and excitement.

'Everyone, this is Zara!' Hiba announces proudly, as if we're old friends.

'Zara! Habibti! Ahlan wa sahlan!' A round woman in a white headscarf comes up to me first and engulfs me into her ample bosom. She feels warm and smells like honey and hand cream, and I know immediately that this is Hamza's mum. OMIGOD I'm trapped in Hamza's mum's arms!

'Assalaamu Alaikum, Aunty,' I reply timidly as she takes hold of my shoulders, pushes me back and looks at me intensely. 'It's very nice to meet you.'

'Haraam, look at you,' she says in a strong Egyptian accent, frowning deeply as she takes in my startled expression, my clothes, my everything. Haraam? What does she mean by that? Is it because I'm not wearing a hijab? I feel my face heat up with humiliation.

'Haraam, you are so small, so skinny! We will have to feed you today. But still, Masha'allah, helou.' Then, as if she realises that I don't understand Arabic, repeats, 'Helou! Beautiful! Masha'allah!'

I let out a breath. OK, maybe she wasn't insulting me, although I still don't know why I'm haraam. I make a mental note to ask Hamza later. But now I'm being shoved towards somebody else as Hamza's mum says something in Arabic, and judging by the wrinkles, I'm guessing it's his grandma.

And it goes on and on. I meet his granny. His aunt. Two cousins. His brother. Some kid his aunt's looking after. His mum's best friend. And then, finally, his dad, who greets me quickly with a reserved smile and firm handshake, welcomes me to his home, and then swiftly leaves the room with the brother. I'm offered a seat on a sofa so soft that it practically swallows me whole and when I think I've got my balance, Hamza sits down next to me which makes the whole thing lean in his direction and I fall onto him. I try to shuffle away to the far end, but it's difficult when I'm that sunken into it.

'Ah, don't worry, everyone gets confused by that sofa,' one of Hamza's cousins says with a shy smile when I finally manage to drag myself to the safer end, cursing it in my head. I swear to God, if I end up being part of this family, this is the first thing that's going into the skip. 'Our grandfather bought it before he passed and so it's too sentimental to throw away. It's become the lucky sofa now.'

Oh.

I smile back, embarrassed. 'It's OK, it's comfy,' I lie, giving Hamza a subtle glower when I hear him suppress a chuckle.

As the women continue to analyse me, I try my best to pretend that firstly, I haven't noticed, and secondly, that I'm not furious at being duped like this.

I remember Francesca asking me weeks ago if Hamza had ever pushed me into things and I tried to defend him. But he's done it again. He could have told me earlier what had happened with his family and then left it to me to decide if I still wanted to go ahead. Instead, he waited until it was too late for me to back out without looking like a complete cow and essentially taking the choice away from me.

In an attempt to distract myself from what Hamza has done, I surreptitiously glance around the room instead to try and get a feel for the place. As sitting rooms go, it's pretty big, with high ceilings and what looks like an original Edwardian fireplace complete with coal and poker. And it reminds me of my own living room, only slightly bigger. The furniture is a bit too ostentatious for my taste, all curvy, engraved wood and floral upholstery that matches the maroon floral curtains. There's a dusty chandelier hanging from the ceiling, and a faded proper Persian rug – not the fake Persian patterned ones you get, but a real, silk one.

And there are lace doilies everywhere. There's one on the mother-of-pearl encrusted coffee table in front of me, spoiling its beauty. About three along the mantelpiece, one on each of the nesting tables, and I can see one on every shelf of the glass cabinet housing fine china and crystal ware. There is also an overabundance of ornaments; candles, vases, bowls with potpourri in them, fake flowers. It's like being thrown straight into Cairo, circa 1979.

Hamza's mum and Hiba walk back into the room carrying two ornate-looking silver trays weighed down with cold drinks and some sort of savoury pastries, which they place on the coffee table in front of me.

'You must be thirsty after the long journey,' Hamza's mum says, handing me the drink. 'Lunch won't be for another half an hour, so please, have some snacks while you wait.'

'Lunch? Oh no, I couldn't—'

'What? Of course, you must! I'm making koshary, it's Hamza's favourite! It's not something I would make for a special guest really, but Hamza asked for it. Anyway, it's nearly ready, habibti.'

With that, she bustles back to the kitchen and Hiba loads up a plate with three different pastries and forces it into my hands. I'm too nervous to eat, but at the same time, I don't want to offend anyone, so after a long swig of juice, I take a couple of dainty bites of the lamb mince one. It's deliciously subtle with very few spices, and different to the Bengali samosas we make at home. I polish off the rest of it and wonder if I would have to change my style of cooking (well, eating, since I barely cook) if I married Hamza.

All this time I've been getting to know Hamza, I haven't given much thought to the fact that he's Egyptian, and I'm Bengali. I've been too preoccupied with the whole attraction thing to really ponder what it would mean to marry outside my culture. But now, as I sit here in this ostentatious sitting room eating food I've never had before, feeling confused about Arabic terms being thrown at me, I wonder how easy it would be to slot into the chaos. Would I be expected to change my ways and conform to theirs? Will it be a problem if I don't? No matter how different our cultures may be, I know for a fact that it would be easier to mesh with Hamza's family than Adam's. As lovely as Adam is, he's not a practising Muslim and doesn't pretend to be. If I went to visit his family, I'd feel uncomfortable about the drinking, unsure if the meat is halal and constantly worried that they'd think I was an extremist.

Hiba and the cousins start making small talk with me; what I do, my family background, how many siblings, what my parents do, etc., and as I start to open up, I slowly become more comfortable in their presence. They're really friendly and personable, just like Hamza, and I'm relieved that they don't ask anything too intrusive.

It's obvious from the way they talk to each other, even when taking the mick, that Hiba and Hamza are close, and have a lot of love and respect for each other. It's nice to see but it's a bit unnerving as well, if I'm being honest. I mean, yeah, she's acting all nice and stuff now, but what if she's unnaturally protective over her brother and no other woman can live up to her expectations? Or what if they're the type that tell each other everything and she ends up becoming the third wheel in our relationship?

And then a sickening thought crosses my mind. What if he's revealed my secret to her? What if, right now, she's actually disgusted by me, and is pretending to be nice to spare her brother's feelings? The thought makes me nauseous and for a good few minutes, I'm lost in a maze of 'what ifs' created entirely by my paranoia.

'Yallah, kids, lunch is ready,' Hamza's mum announces with a flourish as her tomato-red face appears from behind the door. 'Come through to the dining room.'

We go back into the hallway and then into the room next door. Immediately, I'm hit with the scent of cumin, tomatoes, chillies and onions and my stomach growls in response, as if I hadn't gobbled up all those pastries.

Hamza's dining room is a similar size to the sitting room, and has the same high ceiling, fireplace and old-school furniture. The dining table is a glossy mahogany and the matching chairs have oval-shaped backrests engraved with intricate designs. There's a sideboard full of gold frames containing photographs of Hamza, Hiba and their younger brother, Hussain, when they were kids, and by the patio doors there are a couple of fancy two-seater sofas. The room is completely different to my own family's dining room, and then I notice the plastic sheet over the table and suppress a giggle. Maybe it's not that different, after all.

'Tfaddil, take a seat, habibti,' Hamza's mum says as she ushers me into the chair next to Hamza.

As everyone starts to pull out chairs and sit down, Hamza's dad reappears and takes his place at the head of the table and then there's a flurry of activity as Hamza's mum and Hiba start serving everyone the koshary, salad and kibbeh, which is a deep-fried bulgur wheat thing stuffed with mince and pine nuts that I've tried before in a Lebanese restaurant. I stare at my plate with interest.

I've never seen this koshary stuff before, let alone eaten it, and it looks fascinating.

'Koshary is traditionally a Cairo street food,' Hamza's mum explains once everyone has been served. 'I wouldn't usually make it for a guest, but, as I said before, Hamza loves this dish and he wanted you to try it.' She looks a bit embarrassed and I smile reassuringly at her and try and put her out of her misery. She was obviously reluctant to serve this, and I'm guessing it's the Bengali equivalent of serving up daal and rice to a guest.

'It looks and smells amazing, Aunty,' I say genuinely.

'Hold on, let me get a picture,' Hiba says, taking out her phone. 'Sorry, Zara, I have a food Instagram. Do you mind if I take one of you as well?'

'Sure, go ahead,' I say, because it's not as if I can decline. I smile brightly as Hiba takes a picture of me holding up my spoon with the dish of koshary in front of me, and I spot Hamza rolling his eyes good naturedly.

'Don't mind her,' he groans. 'She always does this.'

Once she's done, I take a big spoonful of the concoction and stuff it straight into my mouth to experience what I can only describe as an explosion of flavour and texture. The red sauce is spicy and garlicky, the onions are perfectly crispy, and I think the lentils and rice have been cooked in some sort of stock because it's bursting with flavour. There's also pasta and chickpeas in it. I never thought that such a carb overload could be so tasty. I glance over at Hamza and he's too busy eating to notice me watching him. He looks like he's in heaven.

'This is absolutely delicious, I can see why it's Hamza's favourite.' I look around the table and based on Hamza's mum's pleased expression, it's obviously the right thing to say.

'Saha wa afia,' she replies with warmth and promptly loads my plate up with another massive spoonful. I have no idea what she said to me, but I'm pretty sure it was something nice.

'So, Zara, Hamza told me you work for the council?' This is the first time Hamza's dad has properly looked at me and spoken to me apart from the brief 'salaam' earlier, and he chooses the moment my mouth is full of food to do so.

I don't want to keep him waiting so I try and swallow everything that's in my mouth, but I end up choking and coughing manically, so much so that I'm petrified I'm going to throw up. Hamza frantically hands me a glass of water which I guzzle down as quickly as a thirsty horse in a desert oasis. My eyes brimming with tears and my face flushed from the exertion, I determinedly manage to croak out an explanation of what I do, and everyone listens with pained expressions. I try not to crumple in shame.

'Hamza said your father is an accountant?' Dr Hegazi continues kindly, as if I haven't just made an utter arse out of myself. I smile gratefully at him.

'Yes. He's the director of finance for a housing associating in North London.'

'When did he come to the UK?'

'Oh, in the early seventies. And my mum came here when she was a child, so all my maternal family live in the UK, but my dad's family is more spread out. When did you come over?'

'I came in the seventies myself to continue my studies, but Om Hamza arrived after we married in the eighties. We moved immediately to the States for more than a decade and came back to London in the late nineties.'

'Yes, and I hated it,' Hamza's mum adds with a laugh. 'It was so cold and so grey and boring. But to be fair, I felt the same when we moved to the States. I missed Cairo's heat, the vibrancy, the food, the nightlife. Here, unless you went to the pub, there was no life after five o'clock.'

We carry on talking and I put my fork down, not wanting to risk being caught with a mouth full of food again. Now that my coughing fit has subsided and I'm getting over the embarrassment of it all, I'm actually feeling rather relaxed. His family is so much more peaceful than mine. There's no Amina getting offended every five minutes, no Mum being condescending, no Dad tuning out and not contributing. The only thing that remains exactly the same is a lost grandmother trying – but not quite managing – to keep up with the conversation.

As the afternoon progresses, I almost forget about Adam and all those mixed emotions I was struggling with. There's too much happening in front of me, and while the guilt is still there, the rawness and intensity of the kiss has started to diminish.

After lunch we move back to the sitting room and enjoy some fresh watermelon with our tea, followed by a big tray of baklawa and little cups of Arabic coffee. I make the mistake of calling it Turkish coffee which they're all extremely affronted by, and I'm promptly given a lesson on how the Turks and Greeks are always trying to take credit for Arab inventions, like hummus and stuffed vine leaves and baklawa and coffee.

'Shakespeare is Arab as well,' Hamza's dad says with a completely straight face. 'Sheikh Zubeir. Shakespeare. You get it?'

And then, as the coffee runs out and the tray of sweets gets barer, the day winds to a close. I thank everyone for their hospitality and kindness, lavish more praise on them as they hug me tight and kiss my cheeks over and over again and I'm told that their door is always open and to come and visit them whenever I like.

They all come to the driveway to see us off, like we're newlyweds about to embark on our honeymoon, waving and blowing kisses until we disappear from sight. It's only when we've turned the corner that I dare to exhale and lean back into the seat. I think I must have a weird look on my face because Hamza keeps glancing at me, his own expression a mixture of pride and nervous anticipation.

'Well? What did you think?' he asks, when the silence becomes too much for him to bear. I let him stew for a moment to get back at him for springing all this on me.

'Firstly. How could you do that to me? That was really out of order, Hamza! You completely deceived me and lured me here on false pretences!'

Hamza looks abashed. 'I'm sorry. But if I had told you, you would have refused to come! And say by some miracle you agreed, how stressed would you have been all week? You were a wreck when you thought it was only my sister!'

'All week? So you've known about this for a *week*?'

Shamefaced, Hamza nods.

'I should have been given a choice,' I continue. 'Meeting your whole family is a massive deal and one I should have made an informed decision about. You completely took that choice out of my hands. That wasn't fair.'

'I'm really sorry. I didn't think of it like that.'

Turning my face away, I stare out of the window, pissed off. I can't believe he hid this from me for a whole week. It makes me wonder what else he's capable of hiding to get his own way.

'Hey, you're passing the station,' I say when Rayner's Lane passes by.

'I want to drop you home.'

'But it's over an hour's drive!'

'So?'

'Er, OK. Thanks.' I'm still too annoyed with Hamza to talk much more. I continue to stare out the window and I can feel him looking at me from time to time. I check my phone to see that Hiba's added me on Instagram and has tagged me in the picture she took of me eating. I accept the request and repost the image to my stories, busying myself with my phone so I don't have to engage with Hamza. The silence goes on for a while before he finally breaks it.

'I'm really sorry, Zara. What I did was out of order. Can you forgive me please?' He sounds so despondent that I sigh and nod.

'Fine. But only because your family were so nice. But why did your mum keep calling me "haraam"?' I remember to ask, still puzzled. 'Is it because I don't wear hijab?'

'Huh?' Hamza looks as confused as I am, then starts to chuckle.

'What is it?' I groan, covering my face. 'What did I do?'

'Nothing, habibti. It's an expression in Arabic, it doesn't literally mean "haraam" as in forbidden. It's more like the equivalent of "oh dear", or "oh my goodness".'

'Phew,' I sigh, leaning back in my seat. 'That had me worried for a moment.'

'Anyway.' Hamza gives me a sidelong glance as he continues to drive down roads I've never seen before. 'Did you honestly like my family?'

'I really did. They were so warm and genuine and welcoming. And it's really easy to talk to your sister and cousin, too.'

'They liked you too.'

'Really? Even though I choked and nearly died because I don't know how to eat properly?'

'Ha ha, Baba and Hiba are doctors, they've seen a lot worse than a coughing fit. But yes, they think you're amazing. And beautiful.' Hamza stops at a red light and turns to look at me, his eyes bright with happiness. 'I knew they would love you.'

A sudden shyness comes over me and I look away. Hamza doesn't say anything further, but he reaches over and takes my right hand into his left. We stay like that for the rest of the journey, holding hands in silence. And all the while I feel like a complete and utter bitch because the previous day I was in someone else's arms . . .

Chapter 23

It's gone noon on Sunday and I'm still in bed, the weekend's events playing in slow motion in my head. I've been checking my phone every ten minutes or so, to see if there's been any contact from Adam, but it's still radio silence. I keep telling myself that there's no reason why I should have heard from him. It's not as though that kiss was real, was it? But it *felt* bloody real. It was the most real thing I've experienced in years. It made me see colours I didn't know existed, gave me strength I didn't know I possessed. Surely he felt some of that? It couldn't have all been in my head.

But then, this is Adam. Adam who sleeps with women like he's training for the Sex Olympics. Maybe it meant absolutely nothing to him and, for all I know, he hasn't given me, Tariq, or our kiss, a second thought since he dropped me home on Friday night.

Ah yes, Tariq. A smile spreads across my face and I get out of bed and stretch as if I've woken from a five-year slumber. I've finally done it, I've faced him. And I did more than face him, I emptied an unknown, orange-coloured drink over his head and Adam punched him.

The invisible chokehold he had over me all these years has finally been broken.

And then there's Hamza and his lovely, welcoming and completely sane and functional family. I prayed hard on Friday night, for God to steer me towards the right path and almost immediately he took me to Hamza's house. That must be a sign, right?

I call Layla and give her the lowdown. She doesn't know the extent of my issues with Tariq but she's still as furious as Adam was, and screams when I get to the kissing part.

'I can't believe Adam kissed you! What was it like? Tell the truth.'

'Bloody amazing,' I admit.

'So what? Do you like him now? Because you know it will never work, right?'

I sigh. 'Because he's irreligious?'

'Partly, but also because he's a player and he's not exactly successful, is he? I mean, you manage him! How would that work?'

'You know I don't care about stuff like that!' I reply, annoyed. I get that she's a fancy lawyer married to another fancy lawyer, but not everyone cares about world domination. So what if we both work for local government? So what if I manage him?

'You're saying you don't care now, but you will, when you're on maternity leave and you can't afford all those nice things you like to buy yourself! Don't act like you're simple and ghetto just because you tell everyone you grew up in Finsbury Park. You and I both know it's really Stroud Green. You're as boujie as they come, with your expensive shoes and bags living in your fat house. It's all well and good now that you don't have to contribute financially, but is Adam *really* going to be able to support you and your lifestyle?'

'All right, I get it,' I say from between clenched teeth.

'Hamza is a much better catch,' she concludes decidedly. 'He's successful *and* nice and has a decent family. Don't you want your kids to be brought up with a stable extended family?'

I hang up, feeling worse than I did before I called. I love Layla, I really do, like a sister, but sometimes she's too much like a *real* sister, with no filters and boundaries. She has a point, though. Not about Adam being less successful than Hamza, but about the type of upbringing I want my future children to have.

There's a knock on my door and Yasmin peeks her head around. I nod for her to enter, and not only does she come into my room, she climbs into my bed next to me and pulls the covers around her. She looks uncomfortable and I wait for her to tell me what's going on.

'What's up?' I ask when she still doesn't say anything. 'You OK?'

'Yeah. Don't flip out though, OK?'

'Why would I flip out? What's going on?'

'Well . . .' She stalls, biting on a fingernail. I swat her hand away from her mouth.

'Don't do that. It's a terrible habit.'

'I saw Samia and Suto Mama in Green Street,' she blurts out.

'So?'

'They were looking at wedding gold. They didn't see me.'

'Oh.'

I ponder what she says and laugh a fake, high-pitched laugh. 'Not all gold is wedding gold, you know,' I say, my voice tight.

'I guess,' Yasmin says dubiously. 'Even big, fancy sets with tiklis and everything?'

Samia has been acting shady lately, but would she really be buying wedding gold without mentioning anything to me? I pick up my phone and decide to call her and sort this out once and for all. All this speculation is ruining our relationship and it could be nothing. The phone rings and rings until it goes through to voicemail.

Yasmin gets up and pads towards the door. 'Let me know what she says when she calls back.'

While I wait for Sam to call back, I check Adam's various social media to see if he has updated anything but there isn't even a new story, let alone a post.

I try to spend the rest of the day lazing around in bed, waiting for Sam to call me back and Adam to update his social media, but my plan is short-lived when my mum phones me – yes, *phones* me from downstairs – and tells me to get my butt in the kitchen and learn how to make a Bengali fish curry.

'Mum,' I groan. 'I'm tired and I don't want to stink of fish! I'll have to have another shower!'

'You're happy to eat it though, aren't you? Come down right now. Who's going to marry a woman who can't cook basic curries?'

I want to tell her that Hamza isn't fussed about Bengali curries in the slightest, but I obviously can't since she doesn't even know that he exists. When I drag myself downstairs, I find a huge scaly fish resting on a tray by the sink. I stare at it queasily and the one eye that's facing me stares back.

'What am I supposed to do with this?' I ask her, swallowing nervously.

'Scale it,' she says. 'Like, this, look.' She grabs the fish and a knife and starts scraping it so the scales fall off, and then hands me the knife and waits for me to do the same.

'Right. OK,' I say bravely and tentatively reach out to stop the slimy fish from sliding off the tray while I attempt scaling it with the other hand, all the while trying to conceal my shudders.

'I have another biodata,' Mum begins casually, deftly dicing up onions into tiny pieces like she's Jamie Oliver.

'No thanks,' I respond lightly.

There's a pause and for a second I'm fooled into believing that the silence indicates the end of the conversation.

'"No thanks"?' she mimics me in a threatening tone. 'Unless you've found a potential husband, I believe the correct answer is, "Sure, Mum, please send it to me".'

'I have, actually,' I mutter under my breath.

'What?' Mum spins around and stares at me.

Shit. She heard me.

'There's someone I'm interested in,' I say, keeping my voice steady, my gaze fixed on the fish.

'And you're telling me now?'

'When was I supposed to tell you? When I wasn't interested?'

Mum sighs and I know she's struggling to bite back whatever sarcastic response that's on the tip of her tongue.

'OK,' she says stiffly, as she starts adding various ground spices to the onion, ginger and garlic mixture that's been melting away in the pan. The kitchen instantly fills with the intense fragrance of curry. 'Tell me about this person you're "interested in" then.'

'His name's Hamza,' I begin slowly as I continue to descale the fish, wincing as a bone pricks me for the tenth time. I decide to lead with the stuff my mum would be happy about before telling her that he's not Bengali. 'He's thirty-two. A chartered accountant for a top firm in London. His dad's a doctor, so is his sister. His mum's a teacher. They live in West London.'

'Hmmm,' Mum says, pondering all the positive information I've given her. 'How tall is he?'

'He's over six feet, around six feet two I think,' I reply.

'Does he live with his family?'

'Yes, for now. But he already owns a flat in South London somewhere, I think London Bridge, which he's been renting out.'

'Smart,' Mum muses. 'All this sounds fantastic, Zara, but you know the main thing is his bari and zaath. I can't have you marrying anyone from any old azeh bazeh family. Where in Bangladesh are they from?'

This is it. The moment of truth.

Marrying outside our culture isn't as big a deal as it used to be. When my distantly related 'cousin' got married to a white guy twenty years ago, all hell broke loose. Her parents threatened to disown her, her mum called my mum in tears, various uncles and aunts vowed to boycott the wedding to show their displeasure. Since then, things have changed but no one in my immediate family has broken out of the mould like that.

'That's the thing,' I begin nervously, putting down the knife and turning to face her.

'I knew it!' she wails, slamming a lid onto one of the pans so hard that I'm surprised it doesn't splinter into a thousand shards of glass. 'I *knew* that you'd go and find a khom zaath! How many times have I told you that family background is *everything*?'

Mum starts going off on the wrong tangent and I let her, hoping that once I reveal the truth, she'll be so relieved that the guy isn't from a 'low class' family that she won't care that Hamza's Egyptian.

'You know I don't agree with any of that classism crap,' I say, winding her up further. 'It's so antiquated. No one from my generation cares about all that.'

'Oh, really? You don't care? You don't care if your mother-in-law has a village mentality and expects you to wait on her and the entire family all day and night?'

'That's a pretty big generalisation, Mum. Even so-called bala manush do stuff like that.'

My mother ignores me and carries on her rant, waving around her chopping knife so vehemently that I take a step back in case she accidentally lets go of it. I tune most of it out. I've heard all this before, a million times. Tariq was, supposedly, from a 'top class' family according to Mum. I rest my case.

'He's not Bengali,' I cut in as soon as she pauses for breath.

'What?' She stops in her tracks, her relief obvious in the long breath she's just exhaled. I do the same when she puts her knife down.

'He's Egyptian.'

'Oh!'

My mum isn't often rendered speechless. She comes over to where I've butchered a perfectly good Bengali river fish whose breed I have no intention of remembering and sighs again.

'What have you done to this poor fish? The skin is supposed to remain intact. I guess it's a good thing you've found a non-Bengali mother-in-law. A village hori would have sent you right back to your dad's house.'

As Mum tries to salvage the bloody fish, I fill her in on Hamza and she is surprisingly cool about it all. Sort of.

'You know I can't agree to anything until I've met him and his parents,' she says before I head back upstairs. 'We can speak to your dad then, and not before. He'll be on the phone to all his relatives in Desh and I don't want anyone to know anything until it's concrete.'

Mum's relatively positive reaction comes as a surprise to me. I thought she would have at least a few negative things to say about him, but I think she was relieved that he isn't a khom zaath. It's quite mind-boggling how she would rather I marry a non-Bengali than one from the wrong side of town.

Later that evening, I realise that Samia hasn't returned my call, so I send her a message asking her how she is and what she's up to. Her reply comes back in the early hours of the morning, and it's the first thing I see when I wake up:

All good, sorry been busy. Nothing interesting to report. Catch up soon!

I have no idea how Adam is going to act with me when I get into work the next day. I make sure I'm the first one in so I have a good half hour to myself to gather my thoughts before he and Francesca arrive.

By mid-morning it becomes apparent that I needn't have worried because Adam has decided that the best course of action is to pretend I don't exist.

He hasn't uttered a single word to me all day or looked me in the eye. He grunted once, when I asked him a question about one of his designs, but that's the closest we've got to conversation. I think Fran's noticed the tension in the room, because she's been giving me worried looks every so often. When I catch her eye for the umpteenth time, she mouths, 'Are you OK?' and I shrug and mouth 'Headache' in return.

By lunchtime, I think I'm going to go crazy. I can't stop staring at him, willing him to look up from his screen and catch my eye. I want him to know that I don't want us to ruin our friendship either, but we need to talk about what happened so we can both move on. But it's like I'm invisible.

By three I can't take it anymore and before rhyme or reason can talk sense into me, I text him.

Hey. Are you OK? You're being weird.

I hit 'send' and hear his phone vibrate instantly. He picks it up and I watch him as he reads my message, aching for some sort of expression on his face. Speaking of his face, he looks pale, and his usually bright eyes look dull and tired. Something inside me stirs – and it's not my loins. With a start, I realise that I'm actually *worried* about him. Maybe something happened to his aunt over the weekend?

ADAM: Yeah, fine.

ME: You don't look fine.

ADAM: How am I supposed to look?

ME: Not like this. You look tired. And stressed. Is everything OK at home?

ADAM: I said I'm fine!

ME: Why are you ignoring me then?

ADAM: I'm not.

ME: Adam! Can you stop being like this? I thought we were friends????

ADAM: So that's it then. We're friends?

ME: What are you getting at?

ADAM: Nothing. That's all I needed to know.

ME: Adam! Wtf are you on about?

I watch my phone as he starts and stops typing about ten times. And then he gets up, grabs his jacket, and walks out of the office.

I check my phone like a teenager for the rest of the day and long after I get home.

'All this obsession with your phones is terribly unsociable, not to mention rude,' Mum huffs later that night as my sisters and I all sit there in the living room staring at our individual screens while Abbu and Nani watch the news on Bangla TV, and Mum does the same whilst getting on with some mending.

'Khali bokh bokh khoro . . .' Nani mumbles something about Mum constantly nagging and I smile gratefully at her before continuing my stalking of all Adam's social media, rotating between Facebook, Instagram and Snapchat. But still, deadly silence.

'You know they're using your phones to control you, don't you? All those biscuits storing your information, tracking your every move online . . .' Mum continues with one of her usual conspiracy theories. We continue to ignore her. After a while, she tries again.

'Did you hear about Samia? Your uncle called me earlier. They're fixing her wedding.' That gets our attention and we look up and stare at Mum in surprise.

'Are you serious?' Amina asks. 'She didn't mention a thing to me!'

'Nor me,' Yasmin chimes in. They both turn to look at me as I'm supposedly closest to her. I shake my head.

'I can't believe she never told me,' I say quietly. 'Why the hell would she keep it a secret?' I don't add the fact that she literally texted me last night saying she had no news. It's too embarrassing.

'You know how she loves her secrets.' Yasmin shrugs, squeezing my arm reassuringly. 'Don't take it personally.'

'I'd take it personally if I were you,' Amina counter argues darkly. 'She obviously thinks you're going to be jealous and give her nazar.'

'I'd never do that!' I exclaim indignantly. 'I'd be happy for her!'

'Are you, though?' Mum chimes in. 'You don't sound very happy right now.'

'That's because she hid it from me! If she had told me herself I would have been!'

'Well, maybe she didn't want you to be upset,' Mum reasons, continuing with her mending as if we're having the most blasé conversation in the world.

'Why would I be upset?' I demand, gritting my teeth and very obviously upset.

'You know, because it was that boy who said no to you.' I stare at Mum's needle weaving in and out of the fabric and get the sudden urge to grab it and stab it through my head.

'What boy?' I ask quietly.

'That one from Tower Hamlets. The one who thought you were too old. Well, Samia is only twenty-five so I suppose it's more suitable given that he's thirty.'

'Great,' I manage to choke out. My sisters exchange worried glances, so I excuse myself and head up to my room.

Dangerously close to tears, I get into bed and resume scrolling through social media because if I don't, I'll end up phoning Samia and saying something I'll regret. I don't know what hurts me the most; the fact that she's getting married to someone who rejected me and therefore thinks she's a better option than I am, or that she's hidden it from me. All of it. She obviously met him and got to know him over the past few months, and didn't breathe a word, all the while pretending that she wasn't looking, and that she wanted me to get married first.

As I continue to scroll, I see that Francesca has updated her stories: a bunch of them out drinking, a mirror selfie of her outfit, and then a selfie of her and Adam with their arms around each other and him planting a slobbery kiss on her cheek.

They're friends, I remind myself, chucking my phone to the side and closing my eyes.

At five the following morning, I give up trying to sleep and turn to my phone instead to find that social-media-obsessed Fran has updated her stories once again. This time there's no mistaking what happened as she stares sleepily into the camera, her golden hair illuminated by the morning sun and a sheet loosely wrapped around her. The man still asleep in the background is blurry and out of focus, but I would recognise those arms anywhere.

Chapter 24

I screen-record Fran's story and then watch it over and over again, the pain growing with every view. I try and shake out of it – telling myself that he was never mine, that the kiss was an act, that he has every right to do whatever he wants, that I'm into Hamza and not him. My brain repeats this on a loop, but my heart doesn't get the message and it constricts painfully every time I watch the video.

How am I supposed to go to work like this? How am I supposed to plaster on a professional smile and act like I'm OK for eight whole hours, knowing what I know, feeling what I feel?

I can't do it. I can't face him. Them. Not after he told me he wasn't into her and that he would never go there. Not after our kiss.

The plan formulates while I'm scrubbing away all the pain and hurt, and when I get out of the shower, all I know is that I need to get the hell away from here. I need to get away from Adam, Francesca, Hamza, Samia and even my parents.

Tiptoeing down the stairs to Yasmin's room, I tap on the door lightly and when there's no response, I push it open. She's sprawled out on her single bed, an arm and leg hanging off the edge. I don't want to wake her up so I decide to go ahead with my plan without her advice.

Back in my room, my hands clammy from what I'm about to do, I text Kevin that there's been a family emergency and I need to take the week off. He replies immediately, telling me to take the time I need but to email across a handover as soon as possible. Next, I text Sabina to find out if I can come to visit her for the week. She replies fairly quickly, while I'm looking at flights in fact, so I book the next available flight from Heathrow to Dubai International. Now I have less than an hour to get ready, pack and be in on the Westbound Piccadilly Line if I want to make it on time.

I move fast, packing a small suitcase with whatever summer clothes I can grab quickly; dresses, T-shirts, sandals, linen trousers. In my gigantic tote I stuff my sunglasses, a book, makeup, AirPods and other aeroplane essentials like hand sanitiser. I'm fairly certain I've forgotten things in my haste, but I'm not fussed because Sabina and I are a similar size in clothes and shoes, and I can also use it as an excuse to go shopping.

The stairs creak when I get to the landing outside my parents' and Nani's rooms. I pause for a moment, wondering if I should tell them what I'm doing. I can hear my mum's gentle snores alternating with my dad's rumbling foghorn ones; a geriatric symphony of sorts. But if I wake them up now, there'll be shouting and possibly tears, accusations and questions I can't answer, and I might miss my flight.

I know I'll get a right telling-off when they wake up and get my text, but I'd rather deal with that over messages than face to face.

'Sorry, Mum, Abbu, Nani,' I whisper. 'Don't murder me when I get back.'

Then, I pick up my suitcase so it doesn't thump down the stairs and head outside to the Uber that's waiting to take me to the station.

The journey to Heathrow is long, more so because I don't have the energy to read or listen to music. My head is throbbing, and continues to do so until I get to Duty Free and down two ibuprofen. I usually love looking at all the designer goods, makeup and perfume at Duty Free, but today I don't have the heart.

When I finally get on the plane, it's so quiet that I have the entire middle row to myself. Dumping my stuff on the seat next to me, I take off my trainers, slump into my seat and watch Francesca's video again and again, until we have to switch our phones off. I send a message to the family WhatsApp group telling them what I've done and then put it away.

At least now I can't keep torturing myself, I think as I scroll through the entertainment system and try to find a film to watch. Only it's not as simple as that, because now that I can't get online, I'm desperate to know if either of them has updated their social media, and what they're doing now.

The entire journey continues in this manner, and by the time we land at quarter past ten at night, UAE-time, I'm an emotional wreck.

Dubai International is as clean, glossy and vast as I remember it to be from my last trip a few years ago, when I came with Nani, Mum, my sisters and Samia. I stumble through passport control and customs in a daze, shivering involuntarily. I tell myself it's because it's chilly in here with the air-conditioning on full blast, but deep down, I know it's because I feel empty.

When I turn my phone on, a million texts from my family come through, responding to the message I put up on our WhatsApp group before boarding the plane. I don't read them, but just tell them that I've landed and I'll call when I can. For once I'm relieved that you can't make WhatsApp or Facetime calls in Dubai; it will make it all the easier to avoid my family.

Sabina is waiting for me outside in the pick-up area, so I make my way to the revolving doors and as soon as I exit the airport, I'm hit with a welcome burst of heat, like I've walked into an oven.

'All right, tart?' She grins, striding up to me and swallowing me up in a massive hug. Up until this moment, I never realised how much I needed one of these and I will myself not to burst into tears. I think she senses my heightened emotions because she hurriedly lets me go and then leads me to her VW 4x4 parked up close by with the hazard lights on.

'Where are the kids?' I ask, turning to find the back-seats empty.

'Asleep. It's nearly eleven, you know.'

'Oh yeah. My head's all over the place.'

'Do you want to tell me what's going on now or later?'

'Later, please.' I love that she knows me well enough to give me the option.

We drive to Sabina's house in comfortable silence, the radio on quietly in the background. The roads are still relatively busy and I stare out the window as we cruise down the huge twelve-lane highway, dotted with the occasional date palm and unfamiliar signs in both English and Arabic. She's a lot better at driving here than in London, but I still clutch on to the door handle when she swerves into the exit lane so fast that the car almost topples over. We drive deeper in to the desert, leaving the gargantuan highway far behind us until we pull into a gated community with massive Spanish-style villas, lus-cious greenery, countless palm trees, playgrounds and water features.

'Wow, is this where you bought your house then?' I ask in awe. The last time we came to visit they lived in an apartment by the beach.

'Yeah, we've been here for three years now. When we first moved in after the house was built, the grounds were literally just sand, but they've finally sorted the landscaping out and there are shops, a supermarket, salon, everything you need, really.'

'It's gorgeous.'

Sabs parks up in the open garage adjacent to the house and we enter quietly, mindful of the fact that the kids are asleep. Her husband, who I respectfully call 'Dhulabhai' in Bengali, is also asleep by the looks of things, sprawled out on the beige L-shaped sofa with his laptop still whirring on the coffee table.

'Go and have a shower and change and I'll get you some food,' Sabs instructs, showing me to the guest room where I'll be staying for the week. Like the rest of the house, it's beautiful, with designer wallpaper, a plush cream leather bed and mirrored side tables. I do as she says and ten minutes later I'm digging into roast chicken, veggies, crispy roasted potatoes and delicious home-made gravy. It seems that everything my cousin touches turns to gold. I say this to her, and she guffaws loudly, not caring that Dhulabhai is trying to sleep a few metres away.

'Yeah, I have magic fingers,' she says with a not-so-humble shrug. 'You should see me at work and the stuff I have to do to make these brides presentable.'

'Like what?' I ask, intrigued.

'Like last week, my bride made me put foundation on her knees because she didn't want her husband to see her dark knees on their wedding night.'

'Are you for real?'

'Yep. And covering up bacne is, like, a given on most days. I have to disinfect all my brushes and sponges between each job.'

And there's me thinking being a famous makeup artist in Dubai was a glamorous job to have.

The next few days pass by in a blissful blur of shopping, eating, pampering and playing with the kids; ten-year-old Maaryah, eight-year-old Ibrahim, or Ibby as we call him, and three-year-old Musa. Maaryah's the sweetest tween ever, who sews and bakes and sneaks into my room for chats and makeovers. Ibby's really quiet and sits around gaming whenever he's not at school but likes snuggling next to me when we watch movies together. It's the first time I'm meeting Musa, and he's nothing like his older siblings. He can't sit still and if he's not jumping up and down on the sofas, then he's cannonballing into the pool.

All the food in Dubai is halal so I go to town eating anything and everything I want – to hell with Jordan and his meal plan. Beauty treatments are also a lot cheaper so Sabs and I spend an entire day at a beautiful ladies-only spa getting a hammam treatment done (the craziest bath experience when you get scrubbed to death until you turn a lighter shade), a full-body massage, a facial and mani/pedi. I get a haircut too, and some much-needed high and lowlights, and by the end of it, I feel absolutely amazing. Not quite a new woman, as the emotional scars I have run a lot deeper, but I'm getting there.

Adam hasn't got in touch with me at all. You'd think he'd text me to see if I'm OK, ask why I'm not at work, but nothing. He has no idea where in the world I am because I'm not posting anything on socials (this is supposed to be a family emergency, remember) but it's as though he doesn't care. In fact, it's beginning to feel like I dreamt up the kiss, the punch, the restaurant, everything. It obviously didn't mean much to him, so I've decided to put that entire night into a locked box and throw away the key. I'm not going to let 'what ifs' get in the way of my life anymore. I need to focus on the here and the now.

Hamza, the sweetie, has been messaging constantly to check if I'm OK. At least there's someone who still cares about me. For now, at least. I'm still in two minds whether or not to tell him about the kiss.

'Don't you bloody dare!' Sabina shrieks when I tentatively confess how guilty I'm feeling. We're at the spa, chilling in the relaxation room and sipping on green tea after all our treatments. Thankfully we're the only ones here because her scream shatters the silence. Relaxation, it seems, is over. 'You can't tell him!'

'But it's like I cheated on him,' I explain. 'I'd be a lying snake if I didn't.'

'You haven't cheated on him,' she insists. 'It wasn't real. It was an act.'

'I know, but I was completely into it.'

'So? Adam is bloody gorgeous. If he suddenly appeared in this spa and snogged me as prep for an upcoming movie role, I would be into it, too. Trust me. Hamza does NOT need to know. It will unnecessarily complicate *everything*.'

'Hiding this from him now that I've met his family doesn't feel right,' I say, looking down at my freshly painted toes.

Sabina sighs. 'Before I got married, Tel wanted to know about my past and you know what I told him?'

'What?'

'Nothing. I told him nothing because he didn't need to know. All it would do is make him paranoid and jealous about things that were completely irrelevant. And by the way, Islamically you don't have to reveal your past sins to your husband. Did you know that?'

'Er, I didn't,' I admit, wondering where this sudden religious knowledge has come from. Sabina wears hijab and prays five times a day, but I sort of assumed that it was a habitual thing.

'Yep. I learnt it in the Islamic Studies class I go to every week.'

'I can't believe you go to Islamic Studies classes.' I giggle, imagining her in a room full of abaya-clad women with her red lipstick and heels.

'That's not the point. The point is, men – especially Arab men – are paranoid, jealous and often irrational creatures. You tell him this and he'll never forget.'

'That's a pretty harsh generalisation of Arab men,' I mutter.

'There's no smoke without fire, babe.'

We spend most of the next day Asian-clothes shopping in a place called Meena Bazaar, where Sabs persuades me to not only buy two sarees, but gold bangles as well, because it's so much cheaper out here. Apparently gold is an investment and the prices are always rising. I listen to her advice and invest in a beautiful pair of bangles with intricate designs etched along the rims.

On the way home we pick up cheap but delicious shawarmas from a roadside joint and then sit by the pool in the garden to eat them. It's so quiet and peaceful out here, with the sound of the water lapping against the edges of the pool. The sky is pitch-black, dotted with a million stars, more than I've ever seen in London, and it's lovely and warm at this time of the night. I take a moment to sit back and enjoy the serenity while it lasts.

Just as I'm about to eat the last morsel of juicy, fatty lamb encased in a soft flatbread, my phone beeps. I glance down at it to see that it's a text from Hamza. I figure it's probably him saying goodnight, so I wait until I've finished before I open it up.

I'm here.

My heart stops for a second. What the hell does he mean, he's here? Where? I look around the garden nervously, half expecting him to be hiding in a date palm.

Where? I hastily type, getting grease all over my phone screen.

In Dubai.

What!!!!! Why??? How come???

I was supposed to come for a meeting next month but since you're here, I thought I'd bring the meeting forward and take the opportunity to surprise you.

Shit shit shit shit! Coming out here was supposed to be an escape from all the crap going on in my life, all the difficult decisions I need to make. This was supposed to be my safe haven. And now he's here.

Say something then. I thought you'd be happy?

I try to speak, but it's more of a squeak that comes out. 'Sabs! He's here!'

'Who?' she drawls lazily, stuffing more shawarma into her mouth.

'Hamza!'

Now *that's* got her attention. 'What?' she sits up so suddenly that she drops her sandwich into the pool. Muttering profanities under her breath, she tries, and fails, to fish it out and it sinks sorrowfully to the bottom. 'Is he stalking you?'

'No! I don't think so . . . He said he was meant to come out here for work but moved his trip so he could see me.'

Sabs looks unimpressed. 'Sounds like stalking to me. What if you didn't want to see him, or had plans?'

I stare at her miserably. 'This is the least of my concerns right now. How am I supposed to face him after what happened with Adam?'

'I thought you already saw him when he "surprised" you with meeting his family? He likes surprises, doesn't he?'

'That was different. There were loads of people around. We weren't alone. I can't face him alone!'

'Well, now that he's here, you're going to have to, aren't you? Better to get it over with now so you can go home with a clear head and start afresh.'

I lie and text:

I am happy. Shocked that's all! Breakfast tomorrow?

My meeting's tomorrow morning. Let me take you out somewhere nice for dinner?

Great!

The next day, after a long lie-in, I get up and spend the rest of the morning hanging out with my niece and nephews in the pool. It's hot and I know my tan is bordering on barbecued, but we're having too much fun to go back indoors. Mum will be horrified when she sees how dark I've become, but I don't really care what she thinks right now.

At around five I trudge upstairs to get ready for my execution/date! I brought one nice dress with me, an emerald-green silk maxi dress with a low back. I took it out of my suitcase this morning so I could iron it later, but when I get out the shower I find that Dolly, Sabs' live-in helper, has already ironed it and hung it up for me. She's been making me breakfast every day as well, and my niece has been making me snacks and keeping me company whenever her mum's not around. I could seriously get used to this.

I do my makeup quickly and keep it simple because it's way too hot for full coverage and I don't think my foundation matches my complexion anymore, so it's literally a layer of mascara, a dusting of bronzer and a swipe of tinted lip gloss. I keep my hair up too because the back of my neck is constantly sweating, creating little rivulets that trickle down my back. I take it back – I don't think I could get used to this life after all. Slipping my feet into Sabina's designer heels, I go downstairs and wait for Hamza to arrive, thankful that Sabs is at work and a) can't criticise my makeup and b) can't meet Hamza and give him the third degree.

The nerves intensify while I wait. I think back to Sabs' reaction at his 'surprise'. He's ambushed me *again*.

I know he was trying to do something nice, and possibly romantic, but does the intention justify the means?

When he texts, I slip out of the house quietly so as not to disturb the kids, my stomach buzzing with nervous anticipation – and not in a good way. He's at the wheel of a tank of a car and he jumps out to greet me before opening the passenger door for me, being the gentleman that he is. My stomach twists into a knot.

'I've missed you, habibti,' he says with a smile as he drives away confidently.

My heart twists, mostly with guilt but also with the realisation that I've missed him too. Is surprising your sort-of girlfriend in another country really that bad? As far as sins go, it's pretty minor. Nothing compared to what I've done to him, anyway.

'I've missed you too,' I reply sincerely, after a beat. 'But what on earth are you driving?'

'It's a Hummer,' he reveals, his eyes sparkling. 'I've always wanted to drive one of these! Do you like it?'

'It's a bit big,' I reply, unimpressed, and he laughs at my reaction. His good mood is contagious and I finally lean back in contentment. As always, his presence is comforting and I feel safe with him; safe in the knowledge that he'll not only protect me but he'll always put my needs first. Given my recent experience, this isn't something to take lightly.

Am I being a complete idiot for not instantly choosing Hamza? As we fall into easy conversation, I'm beginning to think that I am. I'm also very aware that, contrary to

Sabina's advice, I need to tell him what happened with Adam . . . and when I do, there's a chance that he won't want me anymore.

We exit the monstrous highway Sabs lives next to and we're now driving down a smaller road – which still has three lanes on either side, by the way.

'How do you know your way around?' I ask in awe as he smoothly takes another exit until we're close to the beach and all the gorgeous five-star resorts along the shoreline. 'I would never be able to drive here.'

'I come here for work a lot. And I lived here for a year after uni.'

'What? You never told me that.' I look at him in surprise. I had no idea that stable, responsible Hamza had this adventurous side to him. OK, it's hardly backpacking through Cambodia, but it's not like I'm the camping-in-the-wilderness-peeing-in-a-bush type, anyway.

'Didn't I? Well, it's no biggie. I have an uncle who lives here so I stayed with him. It was a pretty crazy time of my life. I've always wanted to live here again in the future, for a couple of years or so.'

'Wow, really?'

'Yeah. You up for the challenge?'

I look at his profile as he continues to drive, one hand on the steering wheel and one hand casually draped along my head rest and I begin to think to myself that maybe a lifetime of adventure with Hamza wouldn't be so bad after all.

We pull up at a luxury hotel where the valet attendant hurries to open my door before taking the keys from Hamza. If I lived here I'd become such a lazy prima donna.

'Where are we going?' I ask Hamza as we walk through the plush hotel with its ornate marble interior and traditional Arabic accents, until we're at the back of the resort by the pool area.

'You'll see,' he replies loftily, slipping his hand into mine. I take it, but I'm attacked by another stab of guilt. I open my mouth to blurt it all out to Hamza, but when I turn to face him, he looks so happy that I close it again. I can't ruin this night for him.

'By the way, I forgot to tell you that you look beautiful,' he says shyly as we continue to walk through the exquisitely landscaped grounds, hand in hand.

'Thanks,' I respond, his nerves rubbing off on me. 'You look nice too.' And he does, in his tailored shirt and trousers. In fact, this whole night is transpiring to be super-romantic, not at all what I expected when he dropped that he was here in Dubai. It's difficult for me to enjoy the romance, though, when guilt is simmering beneath the surface.

'Where are we?' I ask, but he doesn't reply, just smiles and leads me along the pier which is gently illuminated by lanterns. We're quite a distance from the shore now and coming up to what looks like a small, intimate restaurant in the middle of the Arabian Gulf, black waves dancing beneath us.

The rest of the evening is equally as spectacular. We have a delicious dinner whilst listening to the waves crash against the pier. Hamza is sweet and attentive as always, but also cracks jokes every so often so the mood isn't too intense; it's comfortable but also romantic, and so different from the night out with Adam. Adam is exciting, dangerous, unpredictable. Hamza is sweet, funny, stable. But obviously, the major difference is that the latter actually *wants* to be with me. For now. There are a couple of moments when the conversation halts and I know I can use the opportunity to tell Hamza what happened. But I don't. I don't want to ruin a night that he's obviously put a lot of thought into. In fact, it's beginning to feel like he flew all the way out here just to see me, not for work as he claimed. Sabina told me the other day that the power balance in a relationship is never completely equal; there's always one person who loves the other more, wants the other more. It's pretty obvious that in this scenario, it's Hamza, but if I'm being completely honest, the sensation of being wanted this badly is pretty intoxicating.

After dinner we start walking back to the main hotel, stopping midway to stare out into the sea again. It's so calm out here, away from the city lights, the traffic, the noise. I close my eyes and breathe in the salty air, enjoying the sensation of the sea breeze brushing against my skin. It's the calmest I've felt all week and I wonder if it's because of where I am or who I'm with.

As we stand there in silence, Hamza turns to me and draws me in for a hug. I snuggle up to his chest, my eyes still closed, inhaling the scent of his aftershave. With his arms firmly around me, I feel protected and safe and I know that if Hamza and I got married, I would never feel as alone and as let down as I have felt this week. Yeah, there'll be other problems, but what is a bit of sex appeal compared to a lifetime of easy companionship?

'Zara?' he whispers into my hair, still holding me tight.

'Hmm?' I keep my cheek pressed against his chest, listening to the steady beating of his heart. He smells good, like cinnamon and the sea.

'I don't want this moment to end.'

'Me neither.' And I don't. Wrapped in his warm, comforting embrace, I feel like I'm home.

'I don't want anything between us to end,' he continues to murmur, his breath tickling the nape of my neck. 'Ever. I know you're still not 100 per cent sure about me but I've never been surer about anything. I want you, all of you; your complicated mind, your kind heart, your generous soul. I even want your crazy temper.'

I swallow nervously, my pulse racing, my stomach somersaulting.

'You sure about that?' I try to joke, the tremble in my voice betraying how I really feel.

'Will you please do me the honour of becoming my wife?'

'*What?*' I try to pull away from him but he refuses to let go and I'm stuck here, in his unrelenting embrace. I try again and this time he lets me, his eyes full of fear as we stare at each other.

'Are you serious?' I whisper, looking up at him in shock.

'I've never been more serious,' he replies solemnly. He reaches into his pocket and takes out a small velvet box. My heart is racing so fast that I'm scared it will jump out of my throat and drown in the sea. I stare at him wordlessly as he opens it up to reveal a striking diamond ring.

I look at the man in front of me, usually so confident and self-assured but right now so nervous and afraid. I look at the lengths he's gone to, to build up to this moment: flying out here, this spectacular setting, the magnificent ring. I think about his warm, loving, stable family and how they welcomed me into their home and their lives. I remember his reaction when I told him about Tariq and how supportive and protective he's been of me since. I remember how good-natured he was when I cross-examined him, and how perfect his answers were. I remember how he found it in his heart to forgive me after Mo showed up at the event. Adam crosses my mind too . . . and how he not only disappeared after our kiss, but he shagged my friend and colleague two days later. Then I think of my mum and how desperate she is for me to get married . . . And lastly Samia, who is about to marry a guy who thought I wasn't good enough.

But as I stand here with this man who is madly in love with me, and who I'm beginning to fall for, I have an epiphany.

I'm *not* desperate. My mum might be, but I'm not. If I was desperate, I would have run off with the first man who came my way, but I didn't. If I was desperate, I would have said yes to Hamza long ago. I don't need a man to complete me. My life's already complete – with my big fat family, my friends, my job. A man would complement it, not complete it.

I've taken my time to get to this point because I've been waiting for the right man, the right moment, and now I know, with all my heart, that the right time is now.

'Yes,' I whisper, my eyes brimming with tears. 'Yes, I will.'

Chapter 25

Last night, I slept like a log, the most soundly I've slept in a really long time. When I finally woke up at noon, I wasn't overcome with regret as I thought I might be. I was worried that once the romance wore off, once I was off that pier in the middle of the sea and back on dry desert, the magnitude of what I agreed to would hit me and I'd go back to that pier and throw myself off the edge. Instead, I awoke to a pleasant tingle in my gut; a happy-but-nervous tingle, not a regretful gut wrench.

'*What the bloody hell is that on your finger?*' Sabina screeches when I finally wake up, flying out of her seat at the dining table and grabbing my hand so that she can stare at my brand-new engagement ring.

'Erm, yeah, about last night . . .' I smile, handing over the ring so she can inspect it properly.

'That is one serious diamond,' she says, almost giddy with desire. 'It looks like a D clarity, and I love the princess cut and setting. Platinum band too. And it's *massive*. If he got it from here, it probably cost him at least five k. In England, it would have been ten.'

'Dirhams?'

'No, *pounds* you useless idiot! Gosh, this diamond is wasted on you. You don't get how spectacular it is.'

'I do, thank you. It's very pretty and shiny.'

'See what I mean? But anyway, tell me exactly how this ended up on your finger.'

I launch into everything that went down last night as Dolly rustles about in the kitchen, emerging a few minutes later carrying a tray with toast, tea and a Bengali-style omelette, but I'm too wound up to eat. The kids are splashing about in the pool and I'm glad my niece isn't within earshot; she doesn't need to hear the ins and outs of my love life. Sabina listens intently, sipping on her special extra-strong tea from her secret stash of Yorkshire Tea: she leaves the tasteless Lipton out for everyone else.

When I finish recounting it all, she leans back and shakes her head. 'Bloody hell, that's a lot to take in.'

It's not quite the congratulatory reaction I was hoping for, but I know she has her doubts. I also know it's not going to be the last time someone reacts like that, so I might as well get used to it.

'Look, I know you're not convinced,' I begin, my face turning pink with defensiveness.

'Hey, you don't have to convince me.' She shrugs, examining the ring in one hand and holding her mug of tea in the other. 'So long as you're truly happy and this is what you really want, and you're not doing it because Samia's engaged or because you're approaching thirty, or because he has a lot of money and he knows how to wine and dine and woo you, and not because he railroaded you into it by showing up here uninvited, then I'm happy for you.'

That's a lot of ifs, buts and ors.

'I appreciate you looking out for me, Sabs, but don't worry, I'm doing it for the right reasons,' I say with growing confidence. 'It's nothing to do with Samia getting married and I'm *not* trying to prove a point. Because amidst all the shit I'm going through, have been going through, Hamza has been a rock.'

'OK, and what about the attraction part of it?' she asks, raising an eyebrow doubtfully.

'Things are different now. Now that I've really got to know him, the attraction has grown. It's there, you know?'

Sabina nods. 'Fair enough. It sounds like you know what you're talking about. I'm happy for you.'

'Thanks.' I take the ring back from her and slip it onto my finger with a small smile. 'Anyway, what are your plans for today?'

'I've got a bride later, but I'd really like to meet Hamza before you leave tomorrow as it looks like the next time I'll see you will be at your wedding. Shall we all go for shisha tonight, after I'm done with work?'

Er, no thanks, I think, but do not say. Sabina has no filter, and I have no idea what she may or may not say that will completely ruin the impression Hamza has of me.

'What?' she demands when I don't reply. 'Don't you want me to meet him?'

'I don't know,' I respond weakly. 'I don't know if I'm ready to introduce him to everyone yet.'

'Uh, firstly, I'm not everyone. Secondly, Yas and Amina have met him already. Thirdly, you've accepted a ring from him, so you *should* be bloody ready.'

'And fourthly?' There's always a fourthly with Sabs.

'Fourthly, don't make the same mistake others make.'

'Which is?'

'Muslim girls these days wait until they're ready to marry their man before introducing him to the people who know her well enough to offer some perspective,' she explains, wrinkling her nose in distaste. 'Instead, they do it when it's too late and they've already made up their minds. At this point, no one can persuade them otherwise as they're too in love to think logically. Don't be that girl, Zara. Let everyone meet him so you can make a more informed decision about your future.'

I give in weakly. 'Yeah, OK, sounds good.' She has a point, I suppose. But still, having everyone and their cousin input on my love life is bloody draining.

That night, Hamza picks me up again and we meet Sabs at a really cool Moroccan restaurant hidden away in the farthest corner of a mall. The shisha lounge is at the back, and when we walk through the doors, it's like stepping into Marrakesh. The walls are almost cave-like in texture and colour and the ceiling is adorned with countless Moroccan lamps of all shapes and colours. The DJ is playing chilled out Berber beats mixed with US chart-toppers and all around me are gorgeous people cradling shisha pipes or sipping on colourful mocktails.

Sabs is already at the lounge and I'm surprised to find Dhulabhai there too. I guess Dolly is looking after the kids. She's dressed like she usually does when she's been in work – as though she's been for a stroll down Camden, in ripped jeans, Converse and a long jersey top. I've also dressed down compared to yesterday, but since I'm a new fiancée and all that, I made a little bit of an effort in heels and red lipstick. It's really weird but I suddenly care about what Hamza thinks of me, and I want to look good for him.

'All right, Hamza? I'm Sabina, Zara's one and only older cousin,' she announces with a flourish and a grin. 'This is Tel, my husband.'

Dhulabhai gets up and shakes Hamza's hand and then we both sit down at the table, opposite them and next to each other. Unlike when Hamza met my sisters, I can sense how nervous he is, though he does a good job at hiding it as he starts to engage with my brother-in-law.

I squeeze Hamza's knee under the table in reassurance and he tries to suppress a grin as he takes my hand and laces his fingers between mine. A tingle runs up my spine and I'm so shocked that I nearly spill my drink.

When it's time to get up and go home, I find myself reluctant for the night to end. I'm too embarrassed to admit that I would rather Hamza drop me off than leave with my cousin, so I bid him a chaste goodbye and make my way to the car park with Sabs and Dhulabhai, while Hamza waits for the valet to bring his car.

'Well? What did you think?' I ask them both the moment we're out of earshot.

'I was pleasantly surprised,' Sabina admits. 'He's actually got a really nice face, good teeth, a full head of hair, and nice hands. If he grew some facial hair he would be quite hot.'

'Nice hands?' Dhulabhai pipes up in confusion.

'Not as nice as yours, babe,' Sabina reassures him, slipping her arm through his.

'Er, that's not what I meant. I'm surprised that you noticed stuff like that. I was going to say I thought he was smart, hardworking and respectful. I liked how he spoke to you, like an equal.'

'Thanks, Dhulabhai,' I say sincerely, my cheeks heating up.

'Do you get why I've been so confused all this time?' I ask Sabina later that night, after we're home and she's sneaking in a quick fag in the garden. She's not a chain smoker but she likes a menthol now and then.

'Yeah, I get it now. I still don't know if I could marry someone I didn't fancy.'

'That's the thing . . . every time I see him I'm begin-ning to fancy him a little bit more.'

'If that's the case, I'm happy for you. And I can't wait for your Big Fat Bengali Egyptian Wedding!'

'Omigod! I completely forgot that there'll be a wed-ding!' I gasp, grabbing her fag out of her hands and taking in a drag. I've wrongly assumed that smoking a cigarette is the same as shisha and I begin to cough, the ash burning the back of my throat. I hand it back to her and she rolls her eyes as I take a gulp of water.

'What the hell are you going on about? How could you forget?' She laughs as I try to compose myself.

'All this time I've been so focused on the actual marriage that the fact that I'm going to have to parade myself in front of hundreds of people slipped my mind,' I explain fearfully. 'I *hate* being the centre of attention!'

'Well, you'd better get used to it.' She grins, stubbing the cigarette out. 'Because once I'm done with your face, no one will be able to tear their eyes away from you.'

I spend the entire plane journey back to London staring at my ring and praying I've made the right choice. Adam crops up into my mind every so often. Not because I still want him, it's just that the last time I was on the plane, it was on my way to Dubai and I was in bits over what had gone down between him and Fran. It felt massive at the time, but the week away and my time with Hamza has dulled the pain, so whenever Adam enters my head, I push him out. Hamza is a decent man. He's been bold enough to make his intentions clear and go after what he wants. *That* is the sort of man I want to be the father of my children, not a sexy, funny and unpredictable motorbike rider who disappeared and slept with someone else right after kissing me.

Chapter 26

Arriving in Heathrow, everything looks tired and dingy compared with gleaming Dubai. Even so, I'm happy to be back in London, grime, cold and all. It might not be as shiny and glamorous as Dubai, but it's real, and it's home.

Both my suitcase and hand luggage are twice as heavy as they were when I flew out, and I'm wondering to myself if I should brave the Tube or splash out on a taxi home when I see familiar faces standing in arrivals, anxiously scanning the crowds of people. My heart soars and I realise that I've missed them, and judging by the looks on their faces, they've been worried about me. Mum's frowning as she surveys the crowd and Abbu is saying something soothing to placate her.

'Mum, over here!' I call out as I struggle to wheel my heavy trolley through the crowd. I wave frantically at her and the relief on her face when she spots me is palpable. She nudges my dad who breaks out into a huge grin as he hurries over to me, engulfing me in a big hug before taking my trolley from me.

'We've been worried sick because of you!' Mum admonishes me when I reach her, throwing her arms around me. I stiffen slightly at the dramatics which makes her tell me off more. 'How could you run off like that? What were you thinking?'

'I didn't "run off", I went to stay with my cousin for a few days because I needed to get my head together.'

The traffic is crazy on the long journey home, causing Abbu to mutter something about Tubing it being faster, easier, and cheaper, and what's the point of being on the Piccadilly Line if you didn't use it to travel to Heathrow? Thankfully, Mum is sitting in the back with me so I'm hoping that the noise of the traffic and radio will prevent him from overhearing the gory details of why I went to Dubai.

'Why did you disappear without telling us? Your nani hasn't slept the entire week!'

I inhale deeply. 'I didn't disappear, Mum, I texted you.'

'A text is *not* the same as asking for permission! Until you're married and you become your husband's problem, you are *our* responsibility! Don't you dare pull a stunt like that again!'

With a deep breath and a prayer, I start with, 'That might be sooner than you think.'

'What are you talking about?'

'Remember I told you about Hamza?' I realise then that I'm still wearing my ring, so I subtly move my hand and squeeze it under my thigh. I don't want Mum to see it until she actually knows who it's from. 'He flew out to Dubai to see me and it made me realise that he's a really decent person and I think this might be it.'

For the first time in my life, my mother is stunned into silence.

'Are you saying you want to marry him?' she clarifies, her voice strangled and her eyes wide.

'Yes, Mum,' I groan, covering my face.

'Oh my goodness me! Alhamdulillah! Alhamdulillah! I thought it would never happen!' Mum's eyes well up and, before I can continue, she bursts into tears. I eye her warily, unsure of how to respond. This definitely wasn't the reaction I was expecting, so I reach over and pat her shoulder awkwardly.

'Mum, stop crying,' I plead, catching Abbu's eye in the rear-view mirror. He raises an eyebrow and we smile at each other. I think he heard what's happening but he's too embarrassed to say anything.

I hand Mum a tissue to wipe her face and blow her nose. When she finally calms down, I proceed to give her a summary of how he proposed.

'I'm still not sure about him being Egyptian,' she says, sniffling. 'That's something different. Of course I need to meet him and his family before anything else can develop. I need to see who these people are that want to take my daughter.'

'Absolutely,' I agree. 'They're really nice people, Mum, much nicer than most Bengali in-laws would be.'

'We need to do salat-al-istikhara as well,' Mum muses, referring to a special prayer that Muslims do when they want guidance from God.

'OK. But I need to show you something as well.' I take out my hand from where I was hiding it and show it to her. It takes a second for her to clock on, and when she does, she gasps.

'*Oh my goodness!*' she cries, her voice rising to an impressive soprano. 'It's absolutely breathtaking!' She grabs my hand exactly like Sabs did and stares at it. 'I never thought I'd see you with a ring on your finger again, and such a beautiful ring as well! Much nicer than that tiny rock Tariq gave you!' Then she starts crying again. I sigh and lean back, but as much as I'm feigning exasperation, I'm secretly quite pleased. It's nice to be the bearer of good news for a change, instead of constantly being the source of disappointment.

When Mum calms down, she takes my hand and studies my ring. 'He's quite well off, isn't he?' she notes with appreciation. I roll my eyes.

'He has a good job and he works hard.'

'Well, he'd better look after you.'

I catch Abbu's eye again and this time, there is a sadness in them. I guess there's one person at home who's not quite ready to let me go. I lean forward and squeeze his shoulder, and he takes one hand off the steering wheel and places it on top of mine. We stay like that for a long time.

Part Four

Autumn

Chapter 27

I feel nervous going back to work after that life-changing week in Dubai, and not only because I'm suddenly so out of sync with it all, or even because I'm engaged (!!!) but because it's finally time to face Adam. It's been seven days since I saw him last; and during this time we haven't exchanged a single message. I don't know what he's thinking, feeling or doing (other than Fran, of course) and the fact that I still care makes me feel foolish.

I haven't been able to work up the courage to tell Hamza about the you-know-what, and as more time goes by, I'm beginning to think I don't need to. The pressing urge to confess has passed and Adam ignoring me has made it easier for me to pretend it never happened.

It's only quarter to nine when I finally enter the office, and I'm pleased to find that I'm the first one in. I'm about to set my bag down on my desk when I notice that it's covered in a sheen of dust, so I give it a quick wipe first. Apart from that, everything looks exactly as I left it.

After I've brewed myself some tea, I power up my computer and start the tedious task of going through all 397 of my emails.

'Hi, Zara! Welcome back!' Francesca is the next person from my team to arrive, at exactly twenty-eight minutes past nine, looking like she's the one who's returned from holiday, not me. 'I love your tan! I wish I could turn that brown but I never get darker than this.' She gestures to her caramel skin and I smile through gritted teeth.

'Glad to be back,' I lie, still unable to look at her the same way now that I know that Adam has gone where he said he never would. And whatever happened to Nathan, anyway? 'There are some sweets and stuff in the pantry that I picked up for you guys. Please help yourself.'

'Thanks, will do. Where did you go? Kevin said something about a family emergency?'

'Dubai. Family business stuff, but we sorted it out.' I didn't want to tempt fate and say that someone had died or was seriously ill, so with Sabs' help, I decided to keep it vague with 'business', which is hopefully uninteresting enough for anyone to probe into.

The door swings open and my heart leaps into my throat, but it's Kevin. We make small talk and I say the 'family business' thing again, and I'm about to get up and make another tea to calm myself down, when the door opens once more and this time, it's *him*. I get a whole second of staring at him unabashedly, before he raises his eyes from fiddling around with his helmet and notices me. He looks gorgeous, golden and dishevelled, in a white T-shirt and khaki combats.

Our eyes connect and my heart squeezes as I drink in all the emotions swimming at the surface of his pupils; the confusion, the worry, the anger, the desire, the concern. And then it all dissolves into complete indifference and I can see him physically shut down, like I'm watching a computer turn off.

'Hey, welcome back,' he says smoothly, tossing his helmet onto his desk and sliding into his chair.

And that's it.

No, 'How are you?' no, 'Where have you been?' no, 'Is everything OK, I heard there was an emergency?'

My stomach plummets to the bottom of my pumps, the disappointment excruciating. My eyes begin to sting so I turn away and hide in the pantry, where I can take a moment to compose myself. I know I'm being a sensitive wimp for feeling like this, I have no right to expect anything from Adam, especially as I'm betrothed to someone else. But what you're supposed to feel, and what you actually feel, are sometimes contradictory sensations, battling for space in your already muddled mind.

As the water in the kettle bubbles away, I get my act together and decide that the best thing to do would be to follow Adam's lead. I force myself to keep my demeanour impassive and professional, all the while wilting inside.

I call a team meeting, instructing them all to get their updates ready beforehand. I keep it concise and professional; there are no jokes, no irrelevant conversations, no concessions. When Francesca admits she hasn't sourced a venue for the autumn book fair when it was supposed to be done two weeks ago, I call her up on it. And when Adam reveals that he's late on a poster design for no good reason, I do the same. By the end of the meeting, the mood in the office is sombre but instead of feeling like a powerful bosswoman, I feel like crap.

The rest of the week passes by in a similar manner. Without anyone to gossip with or take extended coffee breaks with, I'm flying through all my work. I haven't been wearing my ring to work, though. For starters, I don't want my 'emergency' week off to look like I really disappeared to get engaged. I also don't think I'm ready for the grilling I'll get from Francesca. At this point, I doubt that Adam will even care.

Hamza's been so busy all week that we've barely had a chance to catch up, apart from a few texts here and there. I want to tell him that I've told my mum, but don't want to do it by text while he's in a meeting or client dinner, so decide to wait until we talk to each other.

He calls me while my sisters, Mum, Nani and I are watching an old episode of *Married at First Sight*. They've been making me watch marriage-related movies and shows all week. Yasmin seems to think that I could use all the expert opinions on marital issues that I can get. Every time I enter the room, one of them will start humming the 'Wedding March', or 'Chamiya' from the movie *Dulhan Hum le Jayenge*.

'I still can't believe you're getting married.' Yasmin sighs woefully as we watch a beautiful bride walk down the aisle to meet her match for the first time. 'It's not going to be the same without you.'

'When I take your room, I think I'll go for a more dramatic colour scheme,' Amina the scavenger says, earning a scowl from me. We haven't fixed a date and she's already planning on taking my place.

'Look at these women, marrying men they don't know,' Mum muses, enthralled by the TV programme. 'It's exactly the same as it was back in my day, when marriages were more successful and there were less divorces. These days you girls have it so much easier, all this getting to know each other nonsense, yet the divorce rate is higher than ever.'

'The only reason people didn't get divorced back then was because of the stigma, not because they were happier,' Amina argues. 'The success of a marriage is based on happiness, not how long you stick it out for!'

Hamza calls then, saving me from my family, and my sisters whistle and cheer as I answer the call and leave the room.

'Guess what?' I tell him once I'm safely away from prying ears and he's filled me in on his week.

'What?'

'I told my family about you.'

'Finally!' he cheers, and I imagine him beaming down the phone. 'What did your mum say?'

'She's happy. But she wants to meet you and your family. Like, ASAP.'

'I'll sort it out, habibti. I can't wait to meet everyone.'

'Don't get too excited. My mum's a bit of a handful.'

'Why am I not surprised?'

Hamza wastes no time in arranging a meet-up between both families the following weekend. He suggests a restaurant in West London and I agree. It's much less formal than meeting up in either of our parents' houses.

The week flies by with the usual work, gym and a dinner out with Layla and Ezra, who I share my news with. Layla, predictably, is relieved that I didn't let Adam derail my marriage plans. She doesn't say it in so many words, but I can see it all over her face. Ezra, on the other hand, is upset that she hasn't met him. She and I used to see each other all the time, but she's been so busy with her new job as a communications manager for a national charity that I've barely seen her this past year.

'I can't believe you're marrying a guy I've never met!' she wails. 'I don't even know what he looks like!'

'Inshallah we'll arrange something soon. He can't wait to meet all of you.' I take out my phone to show her a picture the two of us took together in Dubai and both Ezra and Layla peer at it, zooming in to our happy faces.

'You both look great together,' Ezra says. 'I'm so happy for you, Zara.'

I stare at the picture long after the conversation has moved on, and I realise she's right. We do look nice together, but more importantly, we complement each other with the important things; our values, character, interests. I wish I had realised it sooner.

Saturday soon comes around and it's time to introduce our families. Hamza is on his way over here, having insisted on picking us all up and taking us to the restaurant (I've discovered his car can be adapted into a seven-seater), despite it being completely out of his way. Mum, Dad, Nani, Amina, Yasmin and I are sitting in the living room waiting for him to arrive. Everyone's in good spirits, including my mum, which is a nice change from her usual stressed out/angry vibe.

'I wonder what they all look like,' Mum muses to no one in particular. I mean, if she asked me, I could have told her.

'Like Cleopatra,' Yasmin teases her. 'And Mo Salah.'

'Oh, stop it!' Mum slaps her arm in jest. 'I'm not one of those—'

'Village mums, we know,' the three of us groan in unison.

She carries on chattering away and I sit there and tap my feet nervously. I really, really hope that today goes well and our families like each other. Families getting along is so important in our culture. We don't just marry our partners, we marry their families as well. If they don't get along, our whole engagement could be called off.

Amina the Perfectionist has tidied the whole house in preparation and there's now a scented candle burning away in the living room, emanating an oud-like fragrance reminiscent of my time in Dubai. Everyone is dressed to impress and I feel like bit like an old school Hollywood actress with my maroon lipstick – and a lot more confident than the day I went to his house in all my casual North London glory.

The doorbell rings and I get up from my seat to answer it, my mum right on my heels.

'Hey, Salaams,' I say shyly upon opening the front door. 'Come in and meet everyone.'

Hamza looks nice in a pale-blue shirt paired with dark trousers, and he smiles warmly at me before extending his hand to my mum. She ignores it and gives him a hug instead, beaming and gushing about him being the son she never had. I gape at her. Who knew that all I had to do was to get engaged for her to thaw out?

She leads Hamza into the living room where he greets my dad, Nani, Yasmin and lastly Amina. After a few minutes of polite conversation, we all bundle into his car. My sisters climb into the back while I sit in the middle row with Mum and Nani, observing Mum's subtle pleasure at the physical evidence of Hamza's wealth.

Abbu's in the front with Hamza, gently interrogating him the entire journey to the restaurant: what he does, how he got there, why he chose Finance, how often he goes to the mosque, everything. At first I feel bad for him, but as the journey progresses, I realise that I'm actually enjoying discovering more about Hamza and I really like how he deals with the questioning – with respect and intelligence, taking a moment before answering the difficult ones. He never once appears annoyed or irritated and my heart swells with pride; this guy is definitely one of a kind.

'How many children do you want?' Abbu asks when we're almost there and I nearly die of shame on the spot.

'Uh, well, I know I'd definitely like kids but so long as it's at least one I don't really mind how many. It's up to Zara, really, she's the one who has to grow them inside her body.'

My heart melts again. How could I ever have doubted him? I'm pretty sure it doesn't get better than this.

'This boy is perfect, too good to be true,' Mum whispers loudly, and I nudge her sharply.

'What?' she continues, still 'whispering' loud enough for Hamza to hear. 'It's true! He is too good to be true! I hope all this isn't an act!'

'Mum!' I hiss, glaring at her and then switching to Bengali for obvious reasons. 'Ekhon ita matyonah!'

'Fine!' she huffs in English, folding her arms and snorting. 'We'll talk later then!'

I swear to God, sometimes I think I should have emancipated myself from my family a long time ago.

The chosen restaurant is a famous Pakistani one and as we enter the venue with its various banqueting suites and main restaurant, we come across scores of Pakistani people dressed up to the nines in all their finest wedding attire.

'How come you chose this place?' I ask Hamza as we wait for the usher to lead us to the table where his family are already sitting and waiting. He blushes.

'My mom thought you guys would prefer it over an Arabic restaurant,' he admits sheepishly. 'I did try to tell them you're Bengali, not Pakistani, but . . .'

I smile at his discomfort and put him out of his misery. 'It's OK, it's sweet of her to try and make us comfortable.'

We find our table and then it's the whole awkward introduction thing all over again. Clever Hamza has the idea of all his family sitting along one side of the table and us opposite them, which will give us a chance to talk to each other properly. Abbu sits opposite Hamza's dad, Ammu opposite his mum, then Nani across from his grandma, etc. I'm not comfortable with having someone between, me and Mum because I really want to keep an eye on what she's saying and stop her from coming out with anything too dodgy, but there's nothing I can do about it so I try to relax and enjoy the night.

'Zara, you look absolutely stunning.' Hiba beams, reaching over the table and squeezing my hand. 'Honestly, you're going to be such a gorgeous bride.'

'Er, thanks,' I mumble, my face heating up. 'I guess I scrub up well.' As soon as I say it, I remember Adam saying the exact same thing to me once, and my gut churns.

'No, it's not the makeup, you have amazing features. Your eyes are huge, your nose is straight, your skin is clear, you're tall and slim. Masha'allah, Allah yah'mik.' She says this in all seriousness and I want to hide under the table. I'm not used to people being so upfront. It's not a very British trait, is it? I wonder if it's an Egyptian thing. Or maybe an American one.

'Thanks,' I reply, struggling for an appropriate response, my cheeks still emanating heat. Hiba is cute, but she's not what you would call beautiful. 'Er, you have nice skin too. And perfect teeth.'

There's a snicker from Hamza's direction and I glare at him, mortified. I look at Hiba but instead of being offended, she laughs, leaning over and thumping her brother on the shoulder. I breathe a sigh of relief. Honestly, this whole Getting to Know In-laws thing is Bloody Hard Work.

Despite the odds (two loud families from two completely different backgrounds), the dinner goes well. The Arabs find the food too spicy but they tuck in regardless, downing glass after glass of water to put out the fire in their mouths, and I'm struck again by how sweet they were to choose this restaurant. Us Bengalis love the food, the heat nothing but a mere tingle on the tongue, and we eat everything, with Abbu and Amina going up to the expansive buffet for thirds and fourths.

The night ends with Mum inviting them to our house the following month for a formal get-together with our extended family, and they agree.

I watch them all talk, smile and laugh, with a growing sense of joy. It's really happening, isn't it? I, Zara Choudhury, serial singleton, am actually getting married before I'm thirty. And not to any old freshie with a degree from a fake immigration uni, but to a decent guy with a top job and a loving family. Alhamdulillah.

Later that evening, after Hamza has stayed for a cup of tea and then gone home, we change into our PJs and dissect the entire night, word by word. This is a bit of a tradition in our family whenever an important event has taken place. Amina makes us all more tea and we sit huddled on the sofas going through our impressions of the Hegazis.

'They're a decent family,' Abbu says once he's changed into his lunghi, a Bengali-style sarong that men wear at home. 'Educated, intelligent, well-off. I think it's a good match.'

'What did you think of Hamza?' I ask nervously, dipping a cake rusk into my tea for a second too long and then watching it all collapse into a sludgy mess at the bottom of my mug.

'Very sensible man,' Abbu replies succinctly, doing the same to his biscuit.

'He was paler than I expected,' Mum chips in. 'Egypt being in Africa and all that, I expected him to be darker.' She looks around the room; anywhere but my frowning face. 'But he seems like a very honest, respectable sort of boy. It's a shame he's not Bengali.'

'He's Muslim, Sunni, he prays and goes to the mosque regularly, that's enough for me,' Abbu says, and I feel a surge of relief that he feels that way. When I first told them about Hamza, he was also hesitant about the cultural differences so I'm glad that Hamza and his family have won my dad over. Mum, of course, is a different story.

'It's not all about going to the mosque, you know,' she mutters.

'What is it about then?' Amina pipes up from across the room. 'I thought you liked him? You were all hugging him and telling him that he's the son you always wanted a minute ago.'

'I do like him. I'm concerned about them being Egyptian and all that, though. What do we know about these people and their ways, after all?'

'Didn't Ruhel's wife's nephew marry an Ethiopian?' Nani chimes in.

'No, Amma, he married an Estonian.' Mum huffs impatiently.

'Oh. Well, I liked the boy and his family,' Nani continues. 'They're not Choudhurys, true, but you can tell they're a good family. I'm not sure how I'll explain the match to everyone, though; how can I tell people that Zara found someone herself? It's bejjoti.'

'Nani! How can you say that!' I glare at Nani and she shrugs helplessly. 'How is it shameful?'

'Hasa toh, mansheh kita khoybah?'

'Who cares!' Amina snarls. 'Who cares what people think? So long as Zara's happy, that's the main thing!'

They go back and forth for a while, with Nani still not convinced that her world will not come crashing down if she tells people that I found my own husband. Mum Googles 'Egyptian weddings' on her phone and nearly has a heart attack when she comes across a sexy belly dancing video. Abbu, however, seems content in the knowledge that I'll be going to a family that genuinely seems to want me, can provide for me and will look after me. For him, that's enough. And for me, it's more than enough. For the first time in a long time, I'm truly at peace.

Chapter 28

Our engagement date has been set. In exactly four weeks, Hamza's family will be coming over to our house to officially ask for my hand. The whole 'hand asking' thing is an Egyptian custom, I guess, but it's not dissimilar to our own paan chini tradition. This is when the groom's side comes over to the bride's house armed with sweetmeats, paan, gold and a ring, to set a date for the wedding. It's challenging, trying to merge both of our cultures, but Hamza is being wonderfully accommodating and doesn't mind what we do, so long as we do it.

In traditional Bengali culture, the groom's side not only brings the bride gold and a ring (which he's already given me, but I've returned it so he can re-gift it to me in front of everyone), he also chooses her engagement dress. I was reluctant to tell Hamza this as I'd rather have bought my own outfit, but it tickled him and he insisted on following this tradition. I'm dreading what he'll conjure up, so I'm going to buy something myself as a backup.

Mum, Abbu and Nani have been busy calling everyone and telling them that I'm getting married. The reactions have been mixed, with some of Abbu's more traditional cousins outraged at the prospect of me marrying a non-Bengali, and others truly happy for us. The same goes with Nani's relatives. Although most of them are accepting, it's the ones who aren't that Nani goes on and on and on about. They're not all coming to the engagement anyway, it's going to be a small ceremony for close family and friends at my house, and the main event will be later on in the year. If Hamza has anything to do with it, it's going to be the Biggest, Fattest, Begyptian Wedding Ever.

I've told my close friends the news and they're all ecstatic of course. At first I was going to let Samia find out from her dad, like I found out about her from my mum. But she finally texted me the other day, letting me know she's getting married, weeks after Mum told us. I swallowed my pride and my annoyance and called her back to officially congratulate her and tell her my own news. It rang for ages before she answered; almost as though she was debating whether or not to pick up. The days we used to speak to each other daily feel like forever ago, and I'm not entirely sure how and why we got here.

'Hello?' she said when she finally answered, a nervous edge to her voice.

'Hey! Congratulations!' I replied, injecting my voice with so much enthusiasm that I sounded like those dodgy telesales people who pretend you've won something only to try and sell you printer cartridges later. (I was one of those people back in uni.)

'Thanks!'

'How are you feeling? Mum said that the nikah's in December?'

'Oh, right. No, we've changed it to January now. Fufu already told you then?'

'Yeah, she told us weeks ago.'

'Oh.'

There was a short pause and then she said, 'I've heard about your news as well. How come you didn't call me sooner?'

What. The. Hell? She'd been hiding shit from me for *months* and now she was angry at me for calling her a couple of weeks late?

'How come you didn't call me yourself to tell me you were getting married?' I snapped. 'Why did I have to hear it from my mum?'

Samia inhaled loud enough for me to hear, and I waited for her explanation. An apology. Something to acknowledge the fact that she messed up. I didn't want to hold grudges. I wanted to move past this, but I felt like I couldn't until we talked about it.

'I didn't know how to,' she said after a while. 'I knew it was a biodata that you had looked at and it didn't work out, so it felt weird.'

'I get that,' I replied evenly. 'But how do you think I've felt, knowing that you're planning to get married without telling me? You know pretty much everything about my search, but not only did you hide yours, you lied about it!'

'I didn't lie!' she exclaimed, a defensive edge to her voice.

'You told me that you weren't looking at all, and that you wanted me to get married first. And then that same afternoon I find out that you had been sending your bio-data out!'

'Well, *sor-ry* for not telling you every minute detail about my personal life! It's a bit hard to get a word in edgeways with all your dramas!'

'Excuse me?'

'It's one thing after another with you! First there was Tariq. Big deal, you broke up. But instead of getting over it, you wallowed in your drama for *years*.'

'You don't know what you're talking about! You're such a bloody know it all, you think you know every-thing but you don't!'

'I know that you *feed* off being dramatic!' she hissed back. 'Admit it, you like the attention!'

'You think my reaction to Tariq was about attention?' My voice was quiet now, as I fought the urge to cry.

'Of course it is! It always is! You have boys throwing themselves at you, like that Adam and that Hamza, and yet you mope around acting like you have no options. Grow up!'

With that, she hung the phone up on my face. It felt more like a punch.

The conversation replayed in my head the rest of that evening and the next morning. I keep hearing her voice hissing at me to grow up, that my reaction to Tariq was all about attention.

I'm devastated that my cousin, who was once one of my best friends, thinks so little of me. And beneath the disappointment is anger. How dare she twist it all on me? What have I ever done to her to deserve such a diatribe?

And deeper down, I'm ashamed because a part of me wonders if there's truth to what she's saying. Maybe I *do* behave like a drama queen. Maybe I am self-centred, so wrapped up in my own life and problems that I overlook everyone else's.

Things at work have been really quiet. I haven't told anyone I'm getting engaged, and since I've returned the ring to Hamza, no one will guess. Adam is still acting off and it's beginning to feel as though I dreamt that night up completely or, at the very least, imagined the electrically charged emotions. I must have, because the way Adam completely switched on me makes me wonder if he ever felt anything for me at all – even as a friend.

I do see the benefits of his multiple personalities, though. If he hadn't turned cold, a silly, stupid, immature part of me would have entertained the hope that maybe there was something special between us, and it would have messed up what was developing with Hamza.

*

The Wednesday before my official engagement party, I arrive to work earlier than the rest of my team. My phone rings as I'm walking up to my desk, and I'm surprised to see it's Hamza.

'Hey, what's going on?' I demand, as soon as I answer.

'Salaam habibti, how are you?' His voice sounds normal enough, but I know that something's up.

'Salaams. Fine. What's wrong?'

'Nothing's wrong. Why would you think something's wrong?'

'You never call me this early in the morning! You had me in panic mode, man. I thought something bad had happened!'

Hamza chuckles. 'You're so paranoid. I wanted to talk to you about the engagement.'

I'm pleased it's not bad news, but I'm still on edge. I sit down at my desk and brace myself. 'OK. What is it then?'

'Right . . . so, think about what I have to say, OK? Don't be rash.'

'Come out with it, Hamza!'

'OK. Um. So. You know how it's our engagement on Saturday?'

'Hamza! You better not be calling it off!' I stand up abruptly, the sudden movement causing the chair to topple backwards with a crash. I leave it there as I wait with baited breath for him to continue.

'I'm not calling it off!' His voice is exasperated but I don't care. Relief pours out of me and I bend down to pick up my chair so I can sink back onto it. But then he continues. 'In fact . . . I was thinking . . . How about we do the kitaab on Saturday instead of the engagement?'

OK, now he's thrown me again. 'What the hell is a kitaab?'

'You know, the katme kitaab? The Islamic marriage ceremony?'

'What, like the nikah?'

'Is that what you guys call it?'

'Stay on point, Hamza!'

'Right. So yeah. Let's do it, habibti. Let's do the Islamic marriage on Saturday and then do the main party later.'

Woah! My emotions swing from one side of the spectrum to the other. It was all well and good getting engaged so quickly, but actually getting *married*? It might not be the legal one, but for Muslims, the Islamic one is the more important ceremony and it's really simple. You need an Imam and two witnesses, and that's it. No making an appointment at the registry office and waiting three months for an available slot. It's also the one that makes you married in the eyes of God. It means you can live together as man and wife, do everything together as man and . . . oh. I see. *That's* why he wants to speed things up.

'Hamza, is this your way of legitimising our relationship so you can get into my pants the halal way?' I demand in righteous indignation.

'No!' He laughs, but I can hear the guilty undertone. 'Filthy mind or what! I just want us to be married.'

'Before you change your mind?' I'm joking when I say this. Kind of. Obviously judging by my earlier reaction, it's a very real fear of my subconscious.

'More like before *you* change *yours*!'

I pause to think for a moment. There's no good reason to say no, really. Aside from the fact that he still doesn't know about . . . well. You know.

'OK, let me talk to my parents and see what they think.' I agree with hesitation.

'So, it's not a "no"?' I can tell that he's smiling his massive, beaming smile and his enthusiasm is beginning to rub off on me, as it always does.

I laugh. 'No, it's not a "no".'

Hanging up, I put my phone away and turn on my computer, a silly smile on my face. I have no idea what my parents will say about this, or if I want to go ahead with Hamza's crazy plan, but it's kinda romantic, right? And it's nice to have someone want me this badly.

'Hey, aşkım, what's got you smiling like a Cheshire cat this morning?' Adam says, striding into the room and grinning at me lazily, the morning sun highlighting the golden strands in his hair. I gawk at him like he's walked in wearing a saree, my blood turning cold with anger. So now he's deciding to treat me like an actual human being, then? *Now* he's deciding to call me 'aşkım' again? After weeks of ignoring me, he decides that today – the day Hamza has asked me to bring forward our wedding date to THREE DAYS FROM NOW – is the perfect time to turn on that stupid, captivating, knee-weakening Adam charm?

'None of your goddamn business,' I snap, turning my face away in time to feel that bloody tingling sensation in my eyes. *Don't you dare let him see you cry,* I tell myself ferociously, blinking rapidly to stop the tears from falling.

'What's wrong, babe?' he asks, his face full of fake concern as he comes over to me and squats by my desk, turning my swivel chair around so I'm facing him. I resist the urge to kick him where the sun doesn't shine and make do with turning my face away instead.

'Don't effing "babe" me, all right?' I snarl, refusing to look him in the eye. 'Now, if you don't mind, I have work to do.' I spin my chair back around and open up my emails to signal the end of this particular exchange, but he refuses to move.

'What's your problem?' he demands, grabbing my chair again, and I hold on to the desk to stop myself from turning in his direction. I can't deal with him spinning me to and fro whenever he bloody wants to, so I get up and face him, my arms crossed defensively. There's an unreadable expression on his face as he towers above me, and it's almost as if I don't know him anymore. I take a step back, but I don't back down.

'My problem? *You're* the one who turns hot and cold faster than the British weather!' I say sharply. 'I thought we were friends but friends don't freeze each other out whenever they want. Well, I'm done, OK? I'm done with you thinking you can charm me one second and ignore me the next!'

'I froze *you* out?' He looks at me incredulously, like I'm speaking Bengali, not comprehensible, digestible, simple English. 'You're the one who didn't show up to work and disappeared for an entire week!'

'I didn't disappear! I had an emergency!'

'Oh really, how convenient.' He raises an eyebrow mockingly and I resist the urge to slap his stupid, arrogant face. '"Family business" problems, right?'

'What are you saying?' I retort, crossing my arms. 'That I missed work for a week to avoid you? Why would I want to avoid my *friend*?' I emphasise the word 'friend', my voice thick with sarcasm.

'I don't know, maybe because I kissed you and you felt something but you were too scared to admit it?' He's standing right in front of me now, so close I can smell him, a dark glint in his eyes. His scent – the freshness and spice – transports me right back to the night I finally got to feel his lips on mine. I stumble backwards. This isn't like before. I'm engaged now and there's no way I'm going to make the same mistake twice. I know this, *of course I know this*, but I can't stop the goosebumps from forming as I watch his eyes move away from my stare and down to my lips.

Time stops – and so does my heart – as I wait for him to either break the spell or lean into it and into me.

The door opens and in walks Francesca. I leap backwards and Adam does the same, crashing into the desk behind him and then swearing.

'Am I interrupting something?' She walks over to her desk and then sits on it with her legs crossed, her skirt riding up and exposing her beautifully smooth, toned legs. I see Adam's eyes flicker to them for a microsecond, and I snort. Just the wake-up call I needed.

'No, nothing important,' I reply smoothly. 'I need to pop out for a bit. Please let Kevin know if he asks.' With that, I grab my phone and head to the fire exit so I can get out of there before my head explodes.

The weather has started to turn chilly in the space of two weeks, the blistering summer sun already a thing of the past, and the autumn wind whips through my hair as I sit down on the steps by the fire exit and pull my hoodie close around my body. First I curse Adam for choosing this moment to start talking to me again, then I curse Francesca for having her way with him, and then I run out of people to curse so I curse myself for being the cheating cow that I am. I've been telling myself that the kiss was a farce, that I didn't want it, that he swooped in on me before I had the chance to say no – but the truth is, I liked it. And if he hadn't woken up two days later with a different girl entangled in his sheets, then right now I probably wouldn't be engaged to Hamza.

But you want *Hamza*, my conscience reminds me. *You chose him because he's right for you. You don't* need *him. You don't* need *anyone. But you* want *him.*

The fire door creaks open and I shuffle out of the way to let whoever it is pass by, but no one does so I turn to see Adam standing beside me. His hands are stuffed into his pockets and he looks as uncomfortable as my bum feels right now on the cold, uneven concrete stair.

'Can I talk to you?' he begins, and I nod my consent in defeat, moving over so he can sit down too. He does, and although there are a couple of inches between us, I can already feel the heat from his body. I shuffle up some more, creating as much distance as I can.

'Look, I need to tell you something.' I can hear the nerves in his voice and I look at his hands clenched in his lap, the knuckles white with tension. I wonder what he wants to say to me that's making him so nervous, and if he wants to hand in his notice. He's been acting so odd at work lately . . . like his mind and heart isn't in it. I always knew he'd move on to greater pastures as soon as he worked up the energy to try something new. He's so talented yet he has no idea.

'I need to tell you something too,' I respond, glancing at him from the corner of my eye.

'Do you want to go first, or shall I?'

'I'll go first.' I take a deep breath and tuck my trembling hands under my legs. I don't know how to say this to him, so I decide to blurt it out as quickly and painlessly as possible because the longer I wait, the harder it will be. 'I'm getting married to Hamza.'

I feel his body stiffen next to mine and I hold my breath, waiting for his reaction.

'When?' His voice is quiet, and I continue to stare at my knees, too afraid to look at him.

'Saturday.'

402

'What the hell? *This* Saturday? *In three days?*' He stands up abruptly and starts pacing in the alleyway, running his hands through his hair. I watch him from the corner of my eye.

'Yeah. The Islamic ceremony. The proper wedding will be later, probably Christmas. I'll let you know when we fix a date. You'll come, yeah?' I try to lighten the mood but it doesn't work and he doesn't respond to my comment.

'Before your birthday, then.'

'You remember when my birthday is?' I don't know why, but the realisation that Adam, who can barely remember what we have planned next week, knows when my birthday is, makes me really, really sad.

'Of course I do. Your dreaded thirtieth, when all your eggs will suddenly expire.' There's a bitterness in his tone, and I bristle at the implication of his words.

'I'm not getting married to Hamza because of that,' I reply defensively, frowning at him as he continues to pace.

'If you say so,' he mutters, kicking a stone on the ground so it flies up and hits the side of the building. I flinch.

'I'm not!'

'I thought you didn't fancy him? And yet you're marrying him?' He doesn't look at me as he says this, but carries on scuffing his boots on the ground.

'I didn't at first. But he grew on me. He earned my respect. He got my attention.' I know I don't have to justify myself to him, but I kind of do. I need him to know that I'm not marrying Hamza out of desperation.

'Where's the ring, then?'

'It's with him. He'll give it to me on Saturday.'

He stops fidgeting and looks at me. His expression is completely unreadable and I have no idea what's going through his head. I break eye contact and look down into my lap.

'So, this is it? You're getting married to Hamza on Saturday and nothing will change your mind?'

'Yep. Are you happy for me?' My stupid emotional eyes begin to water again and I brush them away before turning to look at Adam. His features soften for a second, but I can't for the life of me figure out what he's thinking, or feeling.

'If you're happy, I'm happy,' he says simply, and once more my heart feels like it's going to explode with everything it's holding that cannot be said.

'Thank you. What was it you wanted to tell me?'

'Nothing important. It can wait.' He smiles at me, but it doesn't quite reach his eyes. We stare at each other for a few seconds more, but this time, I can't bring myself to look away. In the end, it's him who breaks eye contact by checking the time. 'We'd better get back to work.' With that, he walks away.

I stay on the steps for a few minutes after he's left, thinking back to earlier this year when I showed him my biodata right here in the same exact place, and the way I felt when he told me that I look better in real life than in pictures. Then there was the time he handed me his jacket because I came down here without one in the freezing cold, and I wrapped it against me and inhaled his scent. Or was that the same time? I don't know. We have too many memories around here, and not just out here, but in the office, in Wood Green, in North London. And after Saturday, it's never going to be the same.

Chapter 29

'What? This Saturday?' Mum gasps when I drop the news at dinner time, her hand freezing near her mouth where she was about to deposit a ball of rice mixed with daal and aubergine bazi. After the exchange with Adam, I was more certain than ever that I wanted Hamza. Hamza knows what he wants, always. He's never uncertain. Never flaky. Always dependable. Exactly the qualities I want in a husband and the father of my future children.

I'm happy to bring the date forward, too; what's the point in delaying the inevitable? Engagements and nikahs are nearly the same thing, we might as well save ourselves the time, hassle and expense and do just one; and then have a big reception later.

'Why?' Amina demands, looking at me as though I'm hiding something. 'What's the rush?'

'I think it's a good idea,' Abbu says thoughtfully. 'Saves us the bother of hosting the nikah a few months later.'

'Ya Allah, people will wonder why we're in a hurry,' Nani splutters in Bengali.

'Don't you want two parties, sis?' Yasmin asks.

'Not really,' I reply. 'I'd rather get this done now and then go all out for the wedding later. Otherwise there's the paan chini, then the nikah, then the mendhi, wedding and walima. Not to mention a bridal shower, and maybe a holud and a sangeet. It's too much. I'd prefer us to have one reception and not bother with a separate wedding and walima.'

'You're our eldest daughter,' Mum says. 'I'm not skimping on anything. People will think we're being stingy.'

'Mum, everyone does it like this now. No one bothers with separate weddings and walimas anymore.'

'That's right,' Abbu agrees, and I can practically see the calculator in his head doing the sums. 'There'll be at least eight hundred people attending, so it's going to be expensive as it is.'

'Eight hundred!' I stare at my dad in disbelief. Do I even know eight hundred people?

'We'll talk about this later.' Mum looks at Abbu pointedly. 'But as for this weekend, if you really want to do the nikah then fine. But check with Kamal to see if he can conduct the ceremony. I don't want any old Imam doing it and messing it up.'

We carry on talking about the event and the logistics throughout dinner. Mum makes it abundantly clear that in no uncertain terms can Hamza and I move in together until after the reception. Not that I want to, anyway. All it means is that, in God's eyes, we'll be lawfully wed and therefore can meet up and do whatever we want without it being haram, or sinful. It sounds strange but it's something a lot of people do, to make the relationship legit while still having enough time to plan an epic wedding.

Gulp.

Anyway. Let's not think about that. Whilst Islamically we will be married, socially, we won't, so as per traditional Bengali customs, my parents don't want us spending the night together until they officially give me away. I tell Hamza this rather timidly, and he laughs and says he's waited to bed me for nearly a year so a few more months isn't going to kill him! Can you believe he said that? Hamza, Mr Sweet and Innocent!

Throughout the rest of the week, every so often I'm suddenly hit by nerves that make my head spin so fast that I don't know where I am anymore, let alone how I got here. It's not that I've changed my mind or that I'm regretting saying yes. I've weighed up the pros and cons a million times and I'm semi-confident in my decision. But it's such a massive thing, isn't it? This is it. The person I'm going to be with forever, and while a part of me feels content, the other part is terrified. What if this is the wrong move? Just because it's happening and it's God's plan doesn't mean it will be a success, does it? What if God's plan is for me to marry Hamza and then get divorced a few years down the line?

I close my eyes and take a deep breath. I can't think like this now, the night before my nikah and moments before my last evening as a singleton.

My sisters and I are meeting Layla and Ezra at a fancy Turkish restaurant that has a modern, fusion fine-dining-esque menu and a boujie, loungey type vibe. All the influencers hang out there and take pictures by the signature gold glitter wall and it's the perfect place to end my single life. I'm wearing a hot-pink off-the-shoulder dress with tights and sparkly gold heels with massive gold hoops and matching pink lipstick. The theme is Essex Glam and I definitely feel a bit *TOWIE* in my outfit, but I don't care. Who knows when I'll be able to tart up like that again? Amina has gone to town in a leopard-print jumpsuit and black strappy heels, her hair scraped back into a sleek pony. Yasmin is slightly more toned down, in skinny jeans, knee high boots and a zebra print top, with lashes so long they look like wings.

The others are already at the restaurant when we arrive so we follow the hostess up two flights of stairs to our table, and as I turn the corner and scan the crowd for my friends, I hear a huge cheer. There, at the furthest corner of the room is a group of people surrounded by golden helium balloons and flowers, all smiling and waving at me. My jaw drops open as I realise that not only are Layla and Ezra among them, but I can see a couple of old uni and school friends, Samia and even Francesca. Not sure how I feel about the last two, but excitement bubbles within me and I push the animosity aside. This isn't the time to hold grudges.

'Oh my God!' I squeal, turning to give Amina a hug. 'Did you do all this?'

'And Yas.' She shrugs. I hug Yasmin too, and then make my way to my friends, allowing myself to be embraced and squeezed to within an inch of my life, while they fire a million questions at me. It's actually a really nice feeling, all this love from people who are genuinely happy for me, and I feel the cloud of uncertainty and sorrow slowly dissipate with every smile and hug.

'I can't believe you're getting married, and it's all thanks to me.' Layla beams as we wait for our starters to arrive. I'm sitting in between Ezra and Shaniqua, with Layla opposite me. Layla's stuck to the *TOWIE* theme and is in a gold lamé top with leather trousers and superhigh sparkly heels. But she's also wearing a gold headscarf that's beginning to slide back like it always does, so it's more Essex meets Beirut, and the combination is odd but it works in a weird Arabian glitz way.

'How's it thanks to you?' Ezra asks her, adjusting her plain cotton headscarf for the millionth time. Despite the careful lengths she goes to, it always looks dishevelled, as if she's just thrown it on. Ezra hasn't tried to dress as per the theme, and I'm not surprised in the slightest. Neither *TOWIE* nor Arab glam is really up her alley, and her charcoal-coloured silk top and matching long skirt with chunky silver jewellery is as dressy as it gets with her.

410

'I'm only the one who dragged Zara to the PwC networking event where she met him for the first time,' Layla replies smugly. 'She didn't want to go but I persisted and now look where we are, at her last supper.'

'No need to call it a last supper,' I interject hurriedly. 'Unless marriage is akin to crucifixion? You would know, Layla.'

'It is a lot of the time.' She sighs, but upon seeing the queasy look on my face, quickly adds, 'But let's not dwell on that now. You're right. This isn't a last supper. It's your last night out before you marry your soulmate, the man you were paired with in heaven before either of you were born, who God put in your path so you could meet again.'

'Is that the Islamic belief then? That God created you in pairs?' Shaniqua, my old uni mate asks curiously. Francesca leans in to listen.

'I'm not a 100 per cent sure, but I have heard that somewhere,' I reply, hoping it's true.

'Yeah, I've heard it too,' Ezra confirms, linking my arm with hers and resting her head on my shoulder. 'So stop stressing, Zara. This is all written, Qadr Allah.'

While my closest friends try to reassure me, the rest of the table is blissfully unaware of the turmoil in my mind and every so often someone says something funny and they all erupt into peals of laughter. I join in as realistically as I can, but no matter how much I smile, I can't control the nerves that are churning so furiously that it hurts.

I glance over at Samia and wonder if she'll bring up her own news. She catches me staring at one point and smiles thinly at me and I struggle to muster up the same level of warmth in my counter smile. It's amazing how, in just a year, our relationship has deteriorated so much. She hung the phone up on me the other day and having her here makes me feel really uncomfortable. Bloody surprise parties. I wish I had told Yasmin what happened, but I was afraid that she'd tell me that Samia was right and that I'm a selfish drama queen who thrives off attention.

The main course arrives, distracting me temporarily from my worries, and we all tuck in, enjoying the twist on the typical Turkish food. It's while I'm eating and finally having a good time, that I see him stroll into the restaurant, his arm around the shoulder of a petite Asian girl with blonde hair. Somehow, the fact that she's brown – the exact same shade as me, in fact – makes the betrayal feel worse. He's wearing a white shirt unbuttoned at the collar with the sleeves rolled up, and I wonder if it's the same shirt he wore when we went out. As I drink him in, a crack forms on my heart and I'm unable to tear my eyes away even when he places his hand on her backside and guides her to their table. Which, for God's sake, is right next to ours. It's not really much of a surprise, him ending up in the same restaurant as me – we both live in the same area, it's Friday night, so why does it feel like the universe has thrown him in my face for a reason?

I look away. I don't want him to know that I've seen him, and I'm hoping he doesn't spot me at the centre of our table amongst all the balloons, flowers and other pretty girls he is likely to ogle.

'Who the hell is that Sex God?' Layla salivates, her eyes wide as she inhales the vision before her. 'Do you know him? Why were you staring at him?'

'Oh, it's Adam,' Fran says the same time as Samia, who's been silent all this time.

'Shh!' I hiss, scowling at Layla. 'I don't want him to see me here.'

'Why not?' Francesca butts in and I decide to be honest, even though she has no idea what's been going on.

'It's been a bit awkward since I told him I'm getting married.'

'Ohhh! This is Adam your colleague?' Layla stage whispers, licking her lips. 'I never expected him to be this bloody hot! I take back what I said about him not being right for you!'

'What?' I hiss, staring at her. She was so adamant that he was too unsuccessful to marry, but yet he's good enough for her to perv on, is he?

'Right, let me see,' Ezra joins in, and before I can stop her, she turns around and gets a good eyeful. 'Not bad for a Turkish guy,' she concedes, like she's not Turkish herself. I'm hardly surprised that she's not as enamoured as the rest of us. Her type is totally different from mine. While I perved on Thor, she was swooning at Loki; when I melted over Jon Snow, she pined over Rob Stark.

'Remember the way he was all over you that night we went for shisha in Bayswater . . .?' Samia adds unhelpfully.

'What? All over you in what way? How come I don't know about this?' Ezra demands in indignation.

'What night?' Fran asks, looking at me strangely. I don't know if anything else has happened between them, or if she has feelings for him, so I don't really want to talk about this in front of her.

'I don't either!' Layla joins in, wiggling her eyebrows. 'Spill the beans! What happened that night?'

'Nothing happened!' I say, shooting Samia a dark look for opening her big mouth. 'And can you guys please stop staring at him? I don't want him to see me here!'

It's a bit hard for him not to notice our table, though, with all the commotion. This isn't even my proper hen night, but my school friend Priyanka, after a cocktail too many, decides it would be a good idea to pull out a tiara from somewhere. She plonks it unceremoniously on my head before wobbling back to her seat, knocking into Adam's table as she does. He looks up and locks eyes with me almost immediately. I see him take in the tiara and, without so much as an acknowledgement of my presence, he looks away and turns back to his date, who's giggling at something he's said. I've already spent the whole day at work with him (albeit without actually speaking to him), but seeing him here, without him even smiling at me, hurts more than I can articulate.

After that, I can't stop watching him. I try not to, I swear I do, but he's right there in front of me. Everything happening on my table goes completely over my head as I watch him laugh with his date, hold her hand, tuck her hair behind her ear. I feel ill.

'Zara, are you OK?' Layla asks in concern, as she takes in my pale face. I nod because I can't open my mouth to speak. She hands me a glass of water and I gulp it down in seconds, trying to sort out my messed-up head. I'm getting married – MARRIED – tomorrow. So why the hell does Adam with a girl bother me so much? It's none of my bloody business what – or *who* – he does. *None.*

Unable to bear looking at them a moment longer, I mumble an excuse and go to the toilets, trying to compose myself.

The door opens while I'm still waiting for my hands to stop sweating and my heart to stop thumping, and in walk Layla and Ezra, looking panicked.

'Zara! What's wrong?' Layla demands.

'Nothing! I needed to use the loo, that's all,' I lie calmly, washing my hands and trying to stop them from trembling. It doesn't go unnoticed and Ezra steps forward, taking my cold, wet hands in hers.

'What's going on with you, Zara?' she asks softly. 'Why has this Adam guy with his date shaken you so much?'

'I don't know,' I mutter, shamefaced. 'But it has.'

This is the first time I've admitted that seeing Adam with other women bothers me. I have no idea what it means. All I know is that it hurts.

'Are you in love with him?' Layla demands, exasperated.

'No!' I bark, wincing at how loud that came out. My friends exchange looks with each other. 'Honestly, I'm not. I fancy him and we did have a special relationship, but that's it.'

'If that's it, then you need to stop this nonsense before you lose Hamza over it,' Layla says, cutting through the niceties and getting straight to the point. 'Seriously, Zara. You're playing with fire here.'

'I'm not doing anything!'

'Good! Because no one's forcing you to get married. If you don't want Hamza, end it now. But if you do, get this Adam out of your head and your system once and for all.'

'OK! Look. It's nothing. You're blowing it out of proportion. Go back to the table, I need to get some fresh air. I'll be there in a bit.'

I half walk, half run out of the restroom and down a million steps in my dangerously high heels until I burst out into the chilly October night, gasping for air. What the hell is wrong with me? Why does Adam have such a hold over me? Was it because of the kiss? My friends are right. I need to snap out of this before I ruin my life and my future.

There's a tall guy in a blazer smoking by the door and he looks over at me with curiosity as I stand there with a plastic tiara on my head doing my deep-breathing exercises.

'You OK, hun?' he asks and I nod at him, still unable to smile. 'Want a smoke?' He holds out his packet to me and although my previous attempts at smoking cigarettes have been a flop, I decide that today would be a good day to try again. Who knows, it might help calm me down. I nod again and he comes over to me and hands me the packet. I take one and he moves in closer to light it with his fancy engraved lighter. As the flame ignites the little death stick, someone violently grabs it out of my hands. I scream and jump backwards.

'What the hell are you doing?' Adam demands, throwing it to the floor. The poor man who was helping me out, backs away and holds up his hands, and Adam turns to me, grabbing my arm. 'You don't smoke! Were you flirting with that guy?'

'Let go of me!' I seethe, yanking my arm away, my heart still racing. I can't believe he's down here. I wonder if he was looking for me or if he was going to have a smoke himself. 'It's none of your bloody business. Why are you here anyway? Go back up to your girlfriend before she comes looking for you.'

'She's not my f***ing girlfriend,' he growls back at me. 'Why were you about to smoke? You don't do shit like that.'

'So what? I felt like it. Maybe I'm sick of being such a goody two shoes. Maybe I want to live a little.'

He goes quiet. 'Don't say that, aşkım. You're perfect. I love that you always do you, without trying to be someone you're not.'

Did he drop the 'L' bomb on me? Not exactly, but he said it about me. What does this mean? I fall silent and we both stand there miserably for a moment, unable to speak.

'I needed something to calm my nerves, that's all,' I say after a while. 'Anyway, I'd better go back upstairs.' I turn to leave but he reaches out for my arm again, gently this time, and stops me.

'Don't go up yet.'

My throat goes dry and I look up at him. Even in my heels, he's still a couple of inches taller than me, and I wonder what it would feel like to have those arms wrapped around me. And then I remember that I already know what that's like. The memory of that night and everything he made me feel floods my mind and I take a nervous step back.

'You're getting married tomorrow and you look like someone's died,' he observes, taking out his own packet of ciggies and lighting one up. I stare at him and he shrugs unapologetically at the hypocrisy.

'Maybe someone *has* died,' I mumble, for want of a better retort.

'What? Who?' Alarmed, his hand freezes by his mouth, just as he was about to place the cigarette to his lips. Oh God, his lips. What I would do to be that fag right now.

'No one. I said "maybe".' Feeling stupid, I kick the pavement with my gold stiletto because I don't know what to do with myself, and end up scuffing the tip. Swearing under my breath, I bend down and rub it with my fingertips before proceeding to wipe my dirty fingers on my tights, realising too late that the move is likely to cause a ladder. The tiara falls off my head. Shit. Shit. Shit! Why am I such a nervous wreck?

'You're a bloody nutjob, aşkım.' Adam shakes his head as he watches the entire scene play out in front of him. Taking his final drag of the cigarette, he chucks the butt on the ground and stamps on it before turning his attention back to me. 'Why are you getting married?'

'What, nutjobs can't get married then?' I grumble, annoyed with myself for ruining my tights.

'No, you idiot. I mean, why are you getting married to *him*? Is it because of your eggs and all that crap?'

'No! I like him, OK! Why is that so hard to believe?'

'"Like"? *Like?* Seriously? You don't love him, but you're marrying him?' His expression is a mix of disgust and pity and I feel like I've been caught out. I cross my arms defensively.

'Oh, shut up,' I scowl. 'What do you know about love or marriage, anyway? What would you rather I did, hop into your bed and everyone's else's bed like that cow upstairs?'

'Watch it,' he warns. 'Don't talk about her like that. You don't know her.'

His scolding me and defending her feels like a slap in the face.

'OK.' I turn to leave, but again, he stops me.

'Why are you getting upset?' he demands, forcing me to look at him. I do, and I'm taken aback by how hard his features are. I stare at him silently, unnerved by his anger. 'You're getting married tomorrow and you have the audacity to get upset that I'm trying to move on with my life?'

'What do you mean, "move on"?' I retort. 'Since when was there anything to move on from, Adam? You think I don't know that you slept with Francesca right after you kissed me? You moved on before we even got started.'

He laughs a hollow laugh. 'You're talking about me going off with Fran? What about you and Hamza? I kiss you on Friday and on Saturday you're posting shit about him on your stories? You were at his house!'

I'd forgotten that I'd done that. So that's why he was ice-cold when I saw him at work.

'Didn't it ever cross your mind that when I kissed you that day, I had to force myself to stop?' he continues, his voice breaking. 'That it took all my self-control not to kill the bastard that hurt you? That having you within arm's reach for the past few months has been driving me crazy? Do you know what it's like to go into work every day and be so close to the woman you want, but can't have?'

It's like I've been punched in the gut. The hardness that alarmed me a moment before has softened into sadness and the raw anguish in his eyes scares me more than his anger. All this time, wondering if he liked me, wondering if I liked him, wondering if it was all hormones . . . now here it is, right in front of me, and I'm so terrified I can't breathe.

'You never said anything. I had no idea,' I whisper, wiping away the tear that's finally snaked out from the corner of my eye.

'You honestly had no idea?' He steps forward until he's so close that I can smell him. It feels familiar, intoxicating, and I have to force myself not to fall on him like a magnet. 'Don't bullshit me, Zara.'

'I didn't! I suspected you might have been attracted to me, but you fancy everyone! How do I know that what you feel is real?'

'Wow, say it how it is, why don't you?' He turns his back to me and paces up and down the strip of pavement outside the restaurant before taking out another fag. The guy who gave me the cigarette observes us from a safe distance with increasing interest, but I'm too far gone to care what he, or anyone else, thinks right now.

'Come on, Adam, take a look through your social media and see how many women you're with,' I continue, my voice getting louder. 'I didn't want to end up as a notch on your bedpost. How do I know that you want me for me? Maybe you only want what you can't have.

You've had over *three years* to make a move, but you choose to do it the day before I get married?'

'It's not like that! Three years ago you were just my manager. A bloody sexy manager, but that was it. It's only since we started hanging out that I felt more for you, but what could I say? You were on this mad quest to find a husband and I'm not ready for all that shit. I've been watching you hunt men and trying to be supportive and it's killing me.'

I can't believe what I'm hearing. Every word is a revelation that has come too late. Why did he wait all this time? Why is he even telling me? What's the point? What am I supposed to do? My head throbs with pain, guilt, anger, regret and confusion.

'I'm sorry I've put you in a shit position today, but how could I let you get married without saying anything?' he continues. 'If I hadn't, I would have regretted it for the rest of my life. Tell me you feel nothing for me, Zara. Tell me, and I swear to God I'll walk away right now and I'll never mention it again.'

I open my mouth to deny feeling anything, but the lie won't come out. I close it again and his eyes widen. He takes my hands into his and the warmth of his skin on mine radiates through me. I know he can feel what's happening to my body, but I can't bring myself to say the words. How can I, when I'm engaged to someone else? I've already betrayed Hamza once, I won't do it again.

'See? I knew it. Don't do it, Zara. Don't marry someone you don't feel anything for.'

I pull my hands out of his, annoyed at the presumption.

'What, you're ready to get married now, is that what
you're saying?' I scoff. 'You can offer me stability, a family? You love me? You'll stop drinking?'

He looks down and his hesitation says it all. 'I'm not
ready for all that. I need time. There's so much I need to
do before I settle down and get married. But that doesn't
mean we can't be together. Does it have to be marriage
or nothing?' His voice is a mere whisper, but I hear the
words as though they're being screamed in my ears. I
squeeze my eyes closed.

'How do I know that after one, or two, or five years,
you'll be ready? What if you keep me hanging for ten years
and then tell me you're still not ready? And then it's too late
for me to have kids? And no one else will want me either.
How can you ask me to wait? You say you want me, but
you don't really. Not enough, anyway. Sorry, Adam, but I
can't give you time. It's the one thing I don't have.'

My heart in my throat, I turn around, walk back into
the restaurant, lock myself in a cubicle in the horrible
black restroom with its horrible dark lighting, and cry
like a baby. The girls have been texting me but my fingers
are shaking so much I can't type out a reply. When they
start calling me over and over, I know I have to answer
or else they'll think I've been murdered and I'm lying in
a ditch somewhere.

When I finally pick up the phone and croak where I am, all nine of them flood into the toilets, taking up every inch of the already tight space. Although I hadn't seen my school and uni friends for a while before today, in that moment, when I see how concerned they all are, I feel that I can confess what's going on. I let it all out; my doubts about Hamza, the attraction towards Adam, the kiss, hiding it from Hamza, Adam's revelation and even Tariq, with the extra sordid details. Fran watches me with her jaw partially open. I catch her eye and there's sadness in them, but no anger or spite. I hope this doesn't ruin our relationship.

Amina and Samia are the most dumbfounded when the truth about Tariq comes out, while I'm sitting on the toilet seat, tears gushing down my face. Layla is the first to rush to me, pushing past the others and throwing her arms around me, her sobs matching my own. I clutch on to her, from the sheer relief of finally being free of this secret. Amina, whose eyes are always dry, is crying, and the three of us hold each other for ages.

Ezra, Shaniqua and all my other friends are completely floored. I see Ezra wiping her eyes and Janine, one of my oldest friends from primary school, lets out a string of colourful profanities and takes out her phone, demanding Tariq's address so her brothers can break his legs. Samia looks as if she's going to be sick, and I can see the regret and sorrow in her eyes, even if she doesn't verbally apologise for what she said about me overreacting when we broke up.

As for my dilemma with Hamza and Adam, everyone has a different opinion and it's confusing me further. They begin arguing amongst themselves; some thinking I should stop the wedding and choose Adam, others thinking I'd be stupid to choose a player who can't offer me anything tangible, over a man who really loves me. Samia and Amina think Hamza has a right to know about the kiss before tomorrow's ceremony, whereas Layla, Ezra and Priyanka think it's something that needs to be buried far away in a lockbox with the key thrown into the English Channel. Fran is quiet, but that's understandable.

'How was I supposed to know?' I sob to Ezra. 'I mean, his nickname for me is "loser" in Turkish! What if Adam is the one I'm meant to be with? What if I'm supposed to wait for him? But I don't even know if he loves me!'

'Loser?' Ezra muses, surprised. 'How did he say it? There isn't a proper direct translation of "loser" in Turkish.'

'He says, "aşkım". What does it mean? Is it worse than loser?'

Ezra falls silent, a pained expression on her face.

'What is it?' I ask with urgency as the overwhelming need to know what it means takes hold of me. She doesn't answer. 'Ezra? What does it mean?'

'Aşkım doesn't mean loser,' she says, catching my eye and then looking away. 'It means "my love".'

Chapter 30

I'm in such a bad state that Layla insists on driving me home instead of letting me take an Uber with my sisters. She and Ezra bundle me into the car hostage-style and I spend the next quarter of an hour listening to them go on at me; I should/shouldn't tell Hamza about the kiss; I should/shouldn't go ahead with the marriage; I should/shouldn't choose Adam; I should/shouldn't choose either. If my head was spinning before I got into the car, now I feel like I'm on an emotional rollercoaster with so many spins, dips and loop-the-loops that I no longer know what day of the week it is. Their words and my own go round and around in circles in my head, and by the time we reach my house, I'm so dizzy that I might throw up.

I know I'll never fall asleep in this state, so I take out an old box of sleeping pills left over from the Tariq days, ignore the expiry date and down two of them, before crawling into bed without even changing out of my clothes, let alone cleaning my face. Just before I succumb to the darkness, I take my phone out and send one final message to Adam. Once I'm married, any communication between us will be more wrong.

It's not long before I fall into a restless sleep, but instead of finding respite, my demons continue to plague me and in my dream I get married to both Adam and Hamza in a joint wedding that no one attends.

The following morning I'm awakened by my phone vibrating over and over and over right next to my face, until it tugs me out of my slumber. I'm actually grateful to whoever it is calling me, because no matter how confusing my life is right now, it's better than the horrors I was experiencing in my nightmares.

I force myself to squint at the screen to see who on God's earth thinks it's acceptable to call a bride at 6 a.m. on her wedding day. And when I see Hamza's name right there in capital letters, my heart drops to my feet. There's only one reason why he'd be calling me incessantly at this hour: he's breaking up with me.

I stare at his name for ages, trying to gather the strength and courage to answer it as it rings again and again. I tell myself that maybe I'm being a paranoid drama queen as usual, and it could be something as simple as the Imam being unable to make it and we'll have to find another. But then I remember that the Imam conducting the ceremony is my cousin, Kamal, so if there was an issue, he would be calling me himself, not getting Hamza to do it.

The phone rings for the fourteenth time and I know I can't avoid it forever, so I sit up in bed, take a deep breath, murmur, 'Bismillahir rahmanir raheem', in the

Name of God the Merciful, the Compassionate, and with a trembling finger, swipe to answer the call.

'Hello?' I croak, my throat still clogged up from last night's events.

'Hey. We need to talk.' Hamza gets straight to the point and although his tone is moderate, there's no warmth in those five words. My heart starts hammering so hard that I can hear it drumming in my ears.

'Uh. OK. What's going on?' I manage to reply as evenly as possible.

'Can you come down? I'm outside your house.'

What? I scramble out of bed and peep out from behind the drawn curtains and sure enough, there's his car parked across the road.

'Hamza, you're really scaring me.' My words catch in my throat. 'What's happening? Why are you here?'

'I need to talk to you about something important.'

I take another deep breath. 'OK. Give me five minutes.'

I don't know how I manage to wash my face and brush my teeth and hair in this panicked state, but I do. If this is the last time I'm going to see him, I don't want to look like a rat that's been dragged through a hedge. After pulling my tangled tresses into a semi-decent pony-tail, I change into joggers and a hoodie, grab my sliders and tiptoe downstairs.

No one from my household is awake yet, so I stuff my feet into my shoes and close the front door quietly behind me. It begins to rain and I can see Hamza's form in the car through the steamed-up windows covered in glossy raindrops. With one final prayer, I walk over to it and knock on the window before reaching for the handle.

'Hey, salaams,' I say cautiously as I enter the car and climb into the passenger seat, my face wet from the rain. I move to wipe it with my sleeve and Hamza stops me, handing me a tissue. I notice that he hasn't greeted me back and my shaky smile falters.

I sit back in the smooth leather seat and turn to face him while I wait for him to tell me what's wrong. He continues to stare ahead, and for want of anything better to focus on, I study his profile. He has a really nice nose; straight, with no bumps, and I wonder why I haven't noticed it before.

He clears his throat, the sudden noise startling me. When he finally turns to face me, I take in his peculiar expression, completely unsure of what he's going to say to me. It could be anything: he doesn't like me anymore; he needs more time; maybe we should get engaged and not married, it was silly of him to suggest it; he's met someone else . . . *Anything*.

'Here, look at this,' he begins, his voice low and serious. 'You'll know what this is about then.' He hands me his phone and I take it from him. Our fingers brush and he snatches his hand away. The snub hurts. A lot. But I push the pain aside and look down at his phone.

It's a text, from me. And when I read it, my blood turns cold.

> I found out what aşkım means. I wish you told me how you felt earlier but you didn't and now it's too late. Forget about me, Adam. Forget about the kiss. Forget whatever it is that you think you/I feel. I'm getting married to Hamza tomorrow and I know it's the right choice. There's more to a marriage than love and attraction. Please respect my decision. x

I read it over and over again. It takes me a minute to understand what happened, because initially, I don't remember writing it at all. Then I get a flashback of myself collapsing onto my bed and sending something to Adam seconds before I fell asleep. Only I sent it to Hamza instead.

Shame and fear wash over me. I'm still too scared to look at Hamza and he's nice enough to give me a minute to compose myself before he holds his hand out for his phone and I reluctantly pass it back to him.

'So. Do you want to tell me what that was all about then?' he asks, his voice level and steady, betraying no emotions, which only makes me feel more nervous because I have no idea which direction this conversation is going to take. I look at the door handle and wonder if I should run, while I can. Now that I'm actually good at running, he'll never be able to catch up with me.

'Not really,' I joke, attempting a feeble smile. Of course, I can't run. I did this, I need to face it. I should have confessed ages ago instead of pretending it never happened. In fact, it's pretending it didn't happen that has landed me in this position now, teetering between marriage and a second broken engagement.

'Seriously, Hamza,' I continue in earnest, 'it's not important, it really isn't. I want to be with you.'

'Right. You want to be with me. But you don't love me and you're still not attracted to me?' He looks at me flatly, but beneath the restrained exterior I can sense how hurt he is and I have no idea how to make it better.

'I didn't say that!'

'OK, what did you mean by, "There's more to marriage than love and attraction"?' He quotes the message without glancing at his phone, probably because he's read it so many times it's forever etched in his memory.

'I meant that marriage is about more than love. It's about respect. Loyalty. Partnership.'

'OK. Let's say that's true. Why are you telling this to Adam? I thought he was just a friend?'

A shudder runs through my body as I try to figure out how much of the truth I need to tell him. Does he need to know how torn I've been feeling? How Hamza has been tugging on one arm, Adam on the other, and how I feel as if my entire body is about to be ripped in half? No, he won't want to hear that. I decide to offer up the bare bones of the story.

'I thought he was a friend. But I bumped into him last night and he told me that he wants to be with me.'

'And is that when he kissed you?' The indifference turns to anger here, and he practically spits the question out. I flinch, each word like a bullet with no exit, embedding itself into my flesh forever.

'No! Hamza, please, I swear to God there's nothing going on between me and Adam!'

'Tell me about the kiss.' He looks straight ahead, as if my face alone repulses him, and I resist the urge to throw up all over the leather upholstery.

'Hamza, there really is no point. It was a long time ago so please trust me! We can move on from this. I'm sorry, I should have told you. I didn't want to hurt or lose you when it meant nothing to me.'

'Tell me about the kiss,' he repeats, his face completely expressionless, like stone. 'Was it while we've been together?'

'It was a joke, Hamza. A ruse to let Tariq think I was happily married.'

'Tariq? What the hell has *he* got to do with any of this?' Hamza turns red, his fair complexion betraying his emotions. I know I have to put him out of his misery no matter how difficult it is for me, so I tell him about how we went for dinner, how Tariq was there, how Adam told him we were married, kissed me to highlight how I had moved on, how I found the strength to confront Tariq and pour the drink over him, how

Adam punched him. I leave out all the details that will hurt him; how I felt like I was floating after that kiss, the charged atmosphere in the sexy restaurant, the way I dressed up, how he picked me up in a Porsche, the chemistry between us, the emptiness I felt when I went home. The heartbreak when he disappeared. Telling him that would be rubbing chilli powder into the open gash.

There's a long silence after he processes all of this. He sighs, and I can tell that he sort-of understands how it all came to be, giving me a glimmer of hope. Maybe this isn't it, then. Maybe my marriage isn't over before it began. I tentatively reach out for his hand; he lets me take it and it sits limp in my own.

'Hamza, wallahi I am so, so sorry,' I whisper, hanging on to his hand like a lifeline. 'I never meant to kiss Adam, or let him kiss me. I only let him do it because I wanted so much for Tariq to see me happily married. I wanted him to know that he didn't break me, even though he did, for so many years. In any other circumstance, I would never have gone along with it. Please, please believe me.'

Another long, torturing silence follows, and I wait it out, my breath stuck somewhere in my throat. This is it, the moment of truth. All this time I've been so unsure about marrying Hamza, but now that I'm confronted with the possibility of losing him, I know for sure that this is who I want. I want a man who listens to me and processes what I say instead of flying off the handle. A man who knows how to control his emotions and doesn't let himself be led by pride. I want *him*.

'OK,' he says simply and I'm so relieved that I throw my arms around him. My face buried into his chest, I breathe in deeply, inhaling his familiar scent. A tear leaks out of my eye, travels down my cheek and falls onto his T-shirt and I stay like this, as another tear joins it, and another one, until there's a wet patch on his chest. It takes a while but he finally turns his body and puts his arm around me and we sit like this for ages, without needing to speak.

I have to leave eventually, to go back inside the house and get ready, but I feel like shit. I'm well aware of the fact that I've dodged a bullet here and I know it's time to bury any feelings I have for Adam, forever. Unless I want to lose Hamza. He might not be quite as understanding next time.

When I walk into the house it's gone eight, and my mum and Nani are up and cooking up a storm. Today's party is small, literally our closest family and friends only, but even then, there will be around fifty people and Mum has insisted on cooking for them herself. Yasmin and Amina are also up, decorating the house and garden with flowers, balloons, streamers and fairy lights. It's coming along nicely and by the time the guests start arriving at six, I'm sure it will all look amazing.

Since I'm the bride, the only thing that's expected of me is to look good, but right now it looks like I won't even manage that. The glimpse I caught of myself in the hallway mirror was pretty shocking; I'm more like the corpse bride with massive dark circles, blotchy skin and greasy hair. I don't have the energy or inclination to do anything about it, though. How can I, after everything that's been going on? Hamza nearly broke up with me! And I know things seem to be on the mend, but I can't shake the feeling that I'm not completely in the clear.

'What happened to you?' Amina asks, emerging from the living room and then stopping in her tracks when she sees my face. 'Are you still messed up after last night?'

She follows me as I proceed to tell her what happened with the text and she listens intently, her eyes wide with horror.

'Holy shit,' she breathes. 'Thank God Hamza has forgiven you. Can you imagine if he called the whole thing off?'

'I don't want to imagine that, thank you very much! I'm stressed enough as it is!'

'So you've finally chosen him, then? Adam is out of your system, once and for all?'

'He's out. It's taken me a while, I know, but I finally get it.' I say this firmly, but as I do, my heart hurts. I may have chosen Hamza, and I may know that it's the right decision, but that doesn't stop the pain of knowing that I've lost Adam, as a friend more than anything else.

'Good,' she says, frowning. 'Now what are you going to do about your face?'

'I don't know!' I wail, covering it up with my hands.

'Leave it to me.' She turns around and heads back downstairs, while I continue to my room and throw myself onto my bed. The sheets need changing, the carpet needs hoovering, and everything else needs a good dusting, but I don't know where I'm going to gather the strength from. All I can do is think about what I've lost – and gained – and everything in between.

I don't realise I've fallen asleep until Yasmin comes into my room a couple of hours later, carrying a tray.

'Hey, how are you feeling?' she asks gently, perching on the edge of my tousled bed. 'Here, drink this, it will make you feel better.' She hands me a mug of coffee from the tray and I pull myself up and take it. She's also brought up a bowl of porridge, a glass of water and a box of paracetamol, and I thank her gratefully.

The nap seems to have revived me. It has certainly helped clear my mind. For the past year, while I've been searching for Mr Perfect, I've realised that I have a lot to be thankful for, and just because I was single didn't mean that I was lonely. Far from it. I have a loving, albeit dysfunctional, family. I have amazing friends. I have a good job. I'm fulfilled. Marrying Hamza will be the icing on the cake, not the cake itself.

And if he hadn't proposed when he did – well, that would have been fine as well. I don't need a man to complete me. No one does. Our whole lives we're taught that marriage is half of our religion, and we take it so literally that we feel incomplete until we achieve it. Yes, it's part of our religion to find a partner and become a parent, but only if the right person comes along. It doesn't mean that without it, we're less, or worse – that we should settle for less.

'Eat up,' she instructs me, pushing the tray towards me. 'I've booked a mobile beautician to come and she'll be here in about half an hour.'

'What!' I exclaim. 'Why?'

'Er, have you seen the state of you? You can't get married like this. You need to hop in the shower because first you're getting a massage, followed by a body scrub, then waxing, a facial, mani/pedi, hair treatment and blow dry. I figured you'd want to do your own makeup. Hopefully by the time she's done with you, you'll look normal again.'

'Oh Yas!' I start tearing up again. 'I don't know what to say.'

'Don't say anything. Eat, shower and wait here in your robe until she gets here.' Yasmin untangles herself from my grip and I hold on as long as possible. When she finally manages to escape, I wolf down my breakfast and jump into the shower, scrubbing away all the sweat and grime from last night.

True to her word, thirty minutes later there's a knock on my door and in walks a pretty, petite Asian girl with glowing skin who quickly sets up her portable bed and unloads a case full of products and equipment. She talks me through the various things she has planned, takes my medical history and then starts off with one of the most relaxing massages I've ever had. She even has speakers with her which she connects to her phone and plays soothing spa music while she works on kneading out all the knots and tension in my muscles.

Though my body is relaxed, it takes a lot longer for my mind to follow suit. I keep thinking about my lucky escape. It's taken forever to get here but Hamza's finally under my skin. All our lives we watch movies and read books that perpetuate the myth that there's such a thing as 'love at first sight', but the reality is, there isn't. There's lust at first sight, sure, but love takes time to develop. It isn't always groundbreaking and earth shattering like you think it's going to be. Sometimes it's a slow and steady stream of good vibes, good experiences and good memories that grow, until there's enough to make you want to hold on to forever.

As for Adam, he'll always hold a special place in my heart. He's been a really good friend to me over the past few months, and I can't help the fact that I'm attracted to him, but I know that it's nothing more than that. Losing his friendship is what's going to be hard to deal with. I'm going to miss him like crazy, but I know I need to keep away from him if I want my marriage to succeed. It's not going to be easy, given the fact that I work with him, but it will be possible. Until last night, we successfully managed to avoid each other for over a month.

I feel reborn once the therapist is done with me. The last stage is blow drying my hair into soft, bouncy waves, and after she packs up and Yasmin parts with half her student loan to foot the bill (I do try and pay for it myself but she insists), I get to work on my face, which feels so much cleaner and refreshed after the facial.

I take out the dress bag that arrived last night while we were out, along with a suitcase full of other goodies. True to his word, Hamza stuck to Bengali tradition and chose my dress, shoes and accessories himself, as well as perfume and makeup. I can't believe that last night's drama made me forget to look in here.

I undo the zip and gasp as I find the most gorgeous Pakistani-style long white dress with delicate pearls and threadwork along the neckline, sleeves and hem. It's simple but stunning, and exactly what I would have chosen for myself. My eyes well up again. He knows me better than I thought he did. The shoes are another surprise; sparkly Louboutin's with red soles and again I can't believe that he went to all this trouble for me. Lingerie is also part of the bridal trousseau, which his sister probably bought. It was really embarrassing when she texted me asking for my size.

By the time I've finished my makeup, it's almost five, so not long left for the guests to arrive. Mum and Nani have finished all the cooking: a gigantic pot of spicy lamb biryani, a hundred pieces of moist tandoori chicken, a vat of vegetable curry and countless juicy lamb kebabs, all home-made. Abbu has bought naan and samosas from a restaurant and we've ordered a fresh cream cake adorned with pink flowers from a local bakery. The ceremony will take place in the living room, with Kamal giving a short speech about the sanctity of marriage, his brother Ridhwaan reciting a chapter from the Qur'an in Arabic, and then the actual nikah will take place, including setting the dowry amount that Hamza will offer me. This could be any amount, from £200 to £100,000 or more. My dad prefers going with the Prophetic tradition of a smaller amount so it's manageable for the groom and not a burden. Abbu and Hamza's dad will serve as the official witnesses. It will be a simple affair, but that's how we want it, especially as we're planning to go all out for the reception.

Nerves begin to brew as I spray myself with the perfume that Hamza chose and take a couple of half-hearted selfies and then sit back on my bed and wait. I can hear the guests start to arrive; cars pulling up outside the house, loud voices and laughter, the doorbell ringing, more voices and laughter. Soon, I hear footsteps coming up the stairs and my bedroom door is thrown open.

'Omigod, you look sensational!' My sisters, Samia and my younger female cousins – Jannah, Madiha and Ameera – all troop into my room and start squealing and taking photos. I oblige and try to smile but after the near miss from this morning, I find it difficult to get into the spirit of things. No one notices, though, they're all too excited. Someone starts playing Bollywood wedding songs, and I half-heartedly dance along with my cousins as they continue to take pictures and make TikToks. We Zoom call Sabina and she gives my makeup the thumbs up, and makes Sam promise to call her during the actual vows so she can watch.

'You did it,' Samia says. 'You're getting hitched before you're thirty *and* before me.'

'It was never a race, Sam,' I reply. I see Yasmin rolling her eyes and I decide to leave it at that. I don't want any ill-feelings, especially not today. After some more giggling, the girls head back downstairs to sort out the final touches before the groom's party arrives.

This is it. I'm getting married in an hour. Everything that has happened over the past year has led to this moment: Dr Farook, Mo, being rejected by the Tower Hamlets guy. It was all part of the maze that is my life, pushing and pulling me in different directions until I found the middle. I realise I've left Adam out of this list and I feel another wave of sadness. No more banter, no more chocolate biscuits in the pantry, no more late dinners in Wood Green, no more motorbike rides, no more confessions by the fire exit, no more Adam.

It's almost without thinking that I take my phone out and check his social media profiles for updates. I tell myself that it's innocent and there's really nothing wrong in what I'm doing . . . right? I go to Instagram first but I can't find his profile. Weird. I head to Snapchat next, but again, he's disappeared. Same with Facebook. He's still there on Twitter, but he hasn't tweeted anything since last month.

Panic sets in as I try to access his profiles over and over again. I don't know if he's deleted me, blocked me, deactivated his accounts or if something has happened to him. His picture has disappeared from WhatsApp and I feel sick with worry and sorrow as I sit there, trying but failing to find out how he is.

Desperation takes over and I call him, only for the phone to go straight through to voicemail. My stomach plummets and I get the overwhelming urge to cry. But I can't, or I'll ruin my makeup.

It's while I'm still holding my phone that it rings. It's Hamza, probably calling to tell me that they're almost here. I take a long, deep breath and try and compose myself before I answer.

'Hello?'

'Hey. So. We need to finish our earlier conversation.'

'I thought it *was* finished?' I reply, panic setting in all over again. Why? *Why* is this happening again? Is God punishing me because I feel upset about Adam? Of course I'm upset! He was a friend! He was important to me! I can't turn off all these feelings with a switch. It's going to take time!

'I had more questions but when I'm around you . . . your presence affects me. I couldn't do it with you right there in front of me, looking at me as though you were about to break. I've been trying to let it go all day but I can't until I know more. I can't marry you until I know.'

I close my eyes and try and gather my thoughts. What else does he need to know? I thought we already went through everything. Why can't he let it go? Anger starts to simmer in my gut, and I try to douse it with positive thoughts. He needs reassurance. It only just happened and he hasn't had enough time to process it all.

'What do you need to know?' I manage to choke out, trying to keep my voice neutral.

'Did you like it?' He says this so quickly that I think I've misheard him.

'What?' I ask stupidly.

'Did you like the kiss?'

'Are you serious?'

'Deadly. Did you enjoy the kiss?'

'Hamza, come on, we're about to get married—'

'Answer the damn question, Zara. Did. You. Enjoy. The. Kiss?'

I want to shout 'NO' but I'm scared that it won't sound convincing. I'm not a good enough liar to be able to persuade him that Adam's kiss didn't send me to another galaxy, another dimension.

'Hamza . . .' I try again, weakly. 'Please let it go.'

'OK, so you did. Thank you for not lying to me.'

'It didn't mean anything! If some gorgeous, sexy model came up to you and kissed you right after you came face to face with a demon from your past, are you telling me you wouldn't have enjoyed it?'

'Adam's gorgeous then? Better looking than me, right?'

'Hamza!'

'What? What, Zara? How do you want me to react? Am I supposed to take all this lightly? I *knew* something was up when I saw the two of you together at your event, but I believed you when you reassured me! And now you've gone and kissed him, all the while feeding me this bullshit about not being able to get physically close to anyone!'

'That's not fair . . .' My voice starts to tremble, matching my hands. I squeeze my phone so tightly I wonder if the screen will crack. I'm scared, no, *petrified* of what this conversation will result in, but at the same time, I'm devastated. How could he throw what I confessed in my face like that?

'No, Zara, what's not fair is that you let him kiss you when you've been pushing me away. What's not fair is that you told me he was only a friend, but now he's gorgeous and sexy and you've been meeting up with him behind my back?'

'It's not like that!' I interrupt, pacing up and down the room to try and calm down. 'Firstly, I didn't go behind your back! I told you we were going out and invited you to join us! Secondly, you *know* that kiss wasn't real, it was a show for Tariq. And lastly, we stopped talking immediately after the kiss and we haven't met up at all since then!'

'And how can I believe you?'

'Because I went to Dubai straight after!' I cry, my voice getting louder. I feel like curling up into a ball and hiding away somewhere until this horrible conversation is over. Yesterday I was an excited bride about to get married and now here I am, struggling to hold back the waterfall of tears ready to gush out of my eyes.

'Hang on – is that why you ran off to Dubai? Because of *Adam*?' Now it's Hamza's turn to sound incredulous.

'No, of course not! I went to Dubai because my family were pressuring me too much after my cousin got engaged to some guy who rejected me!' As I continue to pace the room, I catch a glimpse of my reflection in the full-length mirror and I stop in my tracks. The juxtaposition of my ashen face against the beautiful bodice of my bridal gown is so jarring that for a moment, time stops.

'Hamza,' I plead, my knees buckling as I sit down heavily on the bed, unable to stand for a second more. 'I told you I want to be with you. I've told you I'm sorry and I've explained how the kiss happened. I didn't initiate it. I've told you I'm not friends with Adam anymore and I want *you*, not him. I don't know what else to say or do.' I'm close to hysterical now and it's taking everything I have not to collapse into tears. The effort is exhausting and, in the end, one tear pushes its way out of my closed eyes and trickles slowly down my cheek.

There's a pause on the other end of the line and I hold my breath, waiting for his response. *Please, Allah, give him understanding*, I beg to God, over and over again. *Please. Let him understand and forgive me.*

'I . . .' His voice cracks. 'I want you to tell me that it was always me, that after I proposed, Adam didn't cross your mind. Tell me you weren't torn when you chose me.'

'I w-wasn't t-torn,' I lie in desperation.

'Don't lie to me, Zara! Please! I don't want a relationship built on lies, so if you feel anything for me, do me the courtesy of telling the truth. Were you torn? Did a big part of you want to choose him over me? Was it a difficult decision?'

I want to tell him what he wants to hear, but how can I lie to him after he's begged me to tell the truth? He's right. I wouldn't want a relationship built on lies either. I need to be honest and he needs to make an informed decision about whether or not to proceed.

But the words won't come out of my mouth.

'I-I . . .' I choke, my face turning beetroot from the pressure. 'I . . .'

He laughs. A hollow, empty, laugh. 'It's OK, habibti. I get the picture.' He sounds so completely broken that I release the floodgates and cry like I've never cried before. He stays on the line with me, in complete silence, listening to me weep.

'Is this it? Is it over?' I sob. 'Please, Hamza, please, I didn't mean it. I couldn't help how I felt. Does it matter that it was difficult? I still chose you in the end!'

'It matters to *me*, Zara,' he whispers, so quietly that I can barely hear him. 'I want to marry someone who loves me as much as I love them. I wanted to be your everything, like you were mine. But I'm not. I never was. You *settled* for me, and I can't accept that.'

Were mine.

Were.

The past tense drives home exactly what this means. I open my mouth to beg, every shred of pride and dignity disappearing as the prospect of losing Hamza right here, right now, weighs down on me. But before I can speak, he hangs up. I stare at my phone in horror and call him back immediately, but the call goes straight to voicemail.

This can't be it. *It can't*.

I call back, again and again, and each time, it goes to voicemail. I try sending a text, but it doesn't deliver. With a wail that crushes my core, I throw my phone across the room and it smashes into my mirror. The glass cracks, and so do I.

Footsteps come running up the stairs and Yasmin bursts in, followed by Amina. They take in my wild expression, the black streaks and stains on my face and clothes.

'What's happened?' Yasmin demands, the blood drained from her face. 'What's happened?'

'It's over,' I weep, clutching on to her so I don't fall. 'It's over. The wedding's off.'

Part Five

Winter

Epilogue

The icy air and the harsh wind swirls around me as I pull my heavy woollen coat and thick scarf tighter around my body, a flimsy protection from the cold. It's the middle of January and it's been the toughest winter in a long time. As I wait at the bus stop, large flakes of snow start falling from the heavens. I squeeze myself under the shelter and everyone else does the same; freezing sardines inhaling each other's warm breath.

A motorcycle zooms past me, its rider all in black with a matching helmet. I know it's Adam on his way home from work. I stare at his back, but he disappears in seconds. For a second, I stop breathing, as I always do whenever I catch a glimpse of him.

It's been two months since Hamza broke off our engagement. I wanted to tell Adam what happened. I desperately, desperately wanted to. I called in sick for an entire week after the weekend I was supposed to get married. The day I returned to work, I decided that I would ask him to meet me by the fire exit and tell him then.

But he wasn't there. He had booked emergency leave and was gone for a whole fortnight. I tried calling him, but I soon realised that he had blocked my number. Then I found out from Kevin that an opening had come up in Marketing when I was off, and Adam had applied for it. When he came back to the office, it was only for a day to pack his stuff and hand over, and then he was gone without so much as a glance in my direction.

I don't think he knows that I didn't get married and I've lost the urge to tell him. My head is still pretty messed up, and I don't see much point in dragging Adam into the rubble when I don't really know what I want. Whenever we share the same lift, I feel an immense sadness; I lost more than a flame, I lost a friend, and his absence has left a gaping hole in my life.

As for Hamza . . . well. We don't have to deal with running into each other seeing as we're in completely different social circles, different sectors, in opposite parts of the city, which I suppose is a good thing. We spoke once after that day, but it wasn't a good conversation. He was angry and bitter and he said some things that cut deep; that I was selfish, a narcissist and a cheat. I decided to hang up before the memory I had of him being inherently good became too tainted.

The bus finally comes, and we all trudge onto it. I sit behind the driver and close my eyes, hoping I don't fall asleep and miss my stop. I can't be home late today because we're going out and I barely have enough time to get ready as it is. It's going to be the first social occasion I've attended since Hamza, and to say I'm dreading it would be a massive understatement.

It's Samia's nikah today and, once again, she didn't tell me about it herself, I had to find out from my mum. She's always been secretive but the way she hid this from me after I told her all about Adam and Tariq really, really hurts. Yas said not to take it to heart, she did it to spare me pain, but I know that the truth is she was scared I would be jealous of her and give her the nazar, the evil eye. Bengalis are big believers in black magic and the 'eye', the way someone can have bad feelings towards you and their negative thoughts destroy the good things in your life.

'Finally, Zara, you're home! Hurry up and get ready, we're leaving in half an hour!' Mum shoves me towards the stairs, barely giving me a second to take my snow-covered coat off. I glare at her and kick off my wet boots before dragging myself up to my room. I honestly don't know why I'm bothering to go tonight. Sam obviously doesn't want me there and my presence will put a downer on the celebrations. After all, I've had two broken engagements now; either I've got a really shitty personality that scares away suitors, or I'm cursed. My sisters say that it's neither, I've just got back luck. I love them for always trying to make me feel better, but it's going to take some time before I can fully love myself. I think I'm on the right track, though.

Amina and Yasmin are ready by the time I get to my room, having taken the day off work, so they keep me company (more like distract me) while I grudgingly take a quick shower and get dressed. At first, I decide to keep my makeup simple for fear of looking like I'm trying to outdo the bride, but then I get annoyed and stick on super-glam lashes and go for a vampy dark-red lipstick. *Ha, take that Samia*, I think to myself as I open my wardrobe to take out the simple, gold-coloured dress I've chosen to wear tonight. That's when I see the gown I was supposed to wear on my own nikah, and my heart stops. I yank out the gold number and slam the door closed, making a mental note to get rid of it. I don't need it around, constantly reminding me of what could have been.

'You look amazing, sis,' Yasmin says, coming up to me and giving me a small hug as I stare at my too-thin reflection, my cheek and collarbones jutting out of my flesh like blades. She looks beautiful as always, in a navy ensemble, and I hug her back. Arm in arm, we make our way downstairs and trundle into the car.

The nikah is being held in a small events venue in East London, so it doesn't take long to get there, which is a good thing too, because we spend the entire journey listening to Mum telling us what to say when people ask us about Hamza.

'Say it was because of cultural differences,' she decides in the end. I stay silent.

To be fair, my mum was a rock after everything with Hamza unravelled. During my week off work, she really took care of me, bringing me food in bed, stroking my hair, running me baths, buying me magazines and snacks.

And then she told me something she'd never mentioned before, not even after Tariq. She was engaged to someone before my dad and the man broke it off the day before the wedding. For a whole year afterwards, she felt she couldn't show her face in the community because of all the gossip that ensued.

'Everywhere I went, people would whisper. Your nani was too embarrassed to leave the house. It was the worst year of my life, and things only changed when the proposal from your dad's family came.'

The confession stunned me and I wished she had told me this before, especially after Tariq disappeared. Her obsession with what people think, or might say about us, all made sense now. When my week off came to an end, though, she firmly told me to get my act together and get on with life and the softness she had shown me was once again replaced with her usual stoicism.

The hall is sparsely decorated with a small stage on one end. There are no flowers or balloons, just candles on each table and a white backdrop with fairy lights. Amina asked Sam what she was going to wear but she didn't tell her; apparently she wants it to be a surprise. Well, let's hope it's not gold because that would be pretty awkward.

I'd be lying if I said that I'm not bothered that she's getting married before me. I'm only human, after all. But that doesn't mean I'm not happy for her. I'm glad she's met the right person and I will always pray that God keeps them happy. I just wish things would work out for me as well.

My uncle spots us and comes over, giving us all bear hugs. He doesn't ask what happened with Hamza and I'm grateful for it.

Guests slowly spill into the hall. It's already almost nine but there's still no sign of the bride and groom, nor any food. My stomach rumbles, as it does a lot these days, but I doubt I'll eat much. Eating has become something I do because I have to, not because I enjoy it.

Samia's family is quite religious so there's no music or dancing, only a cappella Islamic nasheeds playing quietly in the background. All in all, it's a pretty boring event so far. With a yawn, I tell my sisters that I'm going to the toilets to check my makeup, and then slowly get out of my seat. At least it will give me something to do.

I hang around in the bathroom for a while, remembering the last wedding I attended when I tripped on my way to the loo and made Samia's saree come undone. And now, almost a year later, here I am. Still single and still alone, at her nikah.

'You OK?' Yasmin asks me when I return to the table and I nod and rest my head on her shoulder for a second. Because I *am* OK. I just need time.

Samia finally enters the hall. It's a subtle entrance, with no fanfare announcing her arrival. She looks beautiful in a maroon saree and I breathe a sigh of relief that she's not wearing gold. I try to make eye contact with her so I can smile at her and try and let my expression reassure her that I'm not giving her nazar, but she keeps her gaze down like a traditional Bengali bride. She slowly makes her way to the little stage where the groom is waiting for her, along with Kamal, who will be performing the ceremony. They both look embarrassed when Kamal starts off with a short speech about the sanctity of marriage and then starts the actual vows.

I watch all this unfold in front of me and my eyes well up for so many reasons. Seeing the groom is unnerving but at the same time, reassuring. I'm *glad* I didn't end up with him but even so, it sucks that he got to reject me when I didn't even *want* to meet him; I agreed to placate my mum.

When it's time for Sam to say 'I accept', she looks absolutely petrified. It takes a lot of coaxing from Kamal, to get her to say it and I glance over at my uncle to see that he's starting to get teary. His reaction gets me all emotional. Samia chokes out her consent and then Kamal raises his hands and launches into a long prayer, asking God to bless the happy couple. The guests also raise their hands, with most of the non-hijabi women covering their hair loosely with their dupattas as a sign of respect for the sheer holiness of this part of the ceremony. My sisters and I do the same as we hold up our hands in prayers, only I add in a few prayers of my own, asking God to give me peace and contentment, in this life and the next.

When the prayers are over, the serving staff quickly start dishing out the food but I don't feel like eating. Samia is now sitting at the head table and everyone is going up to her one by one to offer their well wishes, so I compose myself and do the same, approaching her table with trepidation. When she sees me, there's a flash of guilt in her eyes before she plasters a phony smile on her face.

'Zara! So glad you made it!' she cries, like I'm some stranger that may not have made the time and effort on a week night.

'Of course. Congratulations! You look beautiful,' I say simply. I can feel my smile falter as my lower lip begins to tremble, so I mumble something to her husband and hurry towards the exit. I need some fresh air. But of course, this is a Bengali nikah so things are never as simple as leaving the building. I'm accosted by three different aunties on my way out; two of them ask me why my engagement broke off and the third obviously didn't get the memo because she congratulates me on 'finally' getting engaged.

Bursting out into the freezing night, I inhale huge gulps of the frosty air. I miss Hamza and Adam so, so much. I know that Hamza was right to break it off with me; knowing that my heart wasn't fully his because there was a huge piece of it that belonged to Adam.

And probably always would. Yes, Hamza ending things temporarily crushed me, but one thing I realised, throughout all this, was that I was looking for Mr Perfect and only found Mr Perfectly Fine. He's a good guy, but he wasn't the one for me.

The night of the kiss will forever be a monumental moment in my story, and not only because of the kiss itself, but because it was the moment that Tariq lost the power he had over me. It was the moment I faced my worst fear right in the face and came out on top. It was the moment I realised I was free, I was strong, and I was happy. I can never thank Adam enough for his role in freeing me from the shackles of my past. And as for the kiss? That was the whipped cream on the hot chocolate, wasn't it?

I manage to make it through the rest of the wedding with my dignity intact; smiling at all the right places and not bursting into tears every time I think of what I've lost. I think I do a pretty good job, but later that night, Yasmin tells me that my misery was obvious from a mile off and then I really do start to cry. No matter what I do, it's never good enough. I'm always one step behind . . .

As the days turn into weeks, I wait for the pain and emptiness to ease and it does, a little. My birthday comes and I turn thirty. The sky doesn't come crashing down. My eggs don't rot overnight. My mum doesn't book me on a Biman Bangladesh flight to Osmani International. Life continues regardless of pain, or loss, or anything else that is important to me but so insignificant in the universe.

One evening, a couple of weeks after my birthday, I stay in the office late to get through a mountain of work that has become harder with Adam's absence. We've got a temp graphic designer who doesn't really get me, or my style, and I find myself having to go through rounds and rounds of edits before I'm happy with anything. Kevin's asked me to speak to HR and start recruiting for a permanent role, but I haven't been able to bring myself to.

It's almost seven by the time I wrap up, and I yawn as I wait for the lift to arrive, debating whether or not to take an Uber home. A bus journey feels so unappealing, more so now that it's started to rain. Mum's been on at me to learn how to drive and I decide to add that to my list of things I need to achieve; before a husband, even. A car is probably more useful than a man, anyway.

The doors creak open and there he is, standing in front of me with his helmet in his hands, a smattering of stubble on his jaw and dark circles under his eyes. His gaze meets mine for the briefest second but it's enough to stop my world from orbiting for a moment. He doesn't say hello. He never does. I nod an acknowledgement and step into the lift, my heart thudding so insistently that he'd have to be deaf not to hear it. The doors close and then it's just us, and his intoxicating scent of soap and spices.

I want to say something to him, but he's made it so abundantly clear that he wants nothing to do with me, that I'm afraid to. What if he tells me off, or worse, ignores me?

The seconds tick by and Adam shifts on his feet. It's been weeks since I was last in the lift with him, and we weren't alone that time. I need to make this moment count.

'How have you been?' I finally mumble, my voice trembling with nerves. There's a silence and I hear him inhale shakily.

'Fine,' he replies tersely and my heart soars at his response. Well, not the response itself, but the fact that he responds.

'Do you like your new department?' I continue, like the two of us conversing amicably in the lift is the most normal thing in the world. Like he didn't leave our team to get away from me. Like he doesn't think I married someone else after he confessed how he felt about me. I sneak a glance at him, and to my horror, he looks as if he's about to cry.

'My aunt died this morning,' he whispers when he realises that I'm staring.

'Oh my God! Adam, I'm so sorry.' I place a hand on his arm and he turns towards me properly when I do, his expression one of pure anguish.

'Why are you talking to me, Zara?' he demands, pulling his arm away as if I'm contagious. 'You're *married*.'

'I-I'm n-not,' I stammer, my face turning beetroot. 'We called it off. It's over.'

'*What?*' If he looked pained before, now he looks completely floored. The lift pings its arrival on the ground floor but neither of us moves. We stand there, staring at each other. The doors open, and then close, and we remain standing there.

'I'm sorry for your loss,' I say eventually, not sure what else to say. 'Is there anything I can do?'

Adam's shoulders sag. 'Thanks. And no. Just your prayers. I need to go. My mum's waiting for me. I shouldn't have come to work today.'

'OK.'

We look at each other for a few more seconds and then he turns and walks away, his shoulders slumped, as though walking is a task that's requiring too much from him. I watch his retreating back and exhale.

He spoke to me, and it's a start.

Acknowledgements

To Ammu, who taught me how to read and instilled in me a love for books. This was the beginning of my journey, and I owe that to you.

And then there's Abbu, who bought me my first computer and told me to write stories with it; who paid for my son to go to nursery so I could have time to write this book. I will never be able to thank my parents enough for all they have done for me.

To my boys and husband; thank you for pushing me in this direction and putting up with me occasionally disappearing (physically, mentally and emotionally) while I wrote this! I know it hasn't always been easy, and I appreciate your patience!

To all my friends and family who read chapters of the first draft of this book; Khalamoni, Affa, Aaysha, Yasmin, Emma Bhabi, Sumaiya, Faaria, Shaheen, Sev, Shakila, Suhalia, Lija, Mitali, Merium and everyone else. Your unwavering encouragement and excitement gives me life! Seriously!

To Jodie Kim at Birkbeck. You taught me the importance of respecting our culture whilst owning our stories and identities. As a woman and writer of colour, you saw me in a way that I'm not always seen. Thank you.

To Jodie's Cat Writing Group. You barely knew me at the time, but you helped me more than you will know. I'm so grateful to everyone at our amazing workshop group for helping me develop my story. Thank you.

To all the lovely ladies from Muslim Mamas. Your support and eagerness to know what happened next made me carry on writing this, no matter how hectic life became. A special thanks to the admins, Nafisa and Nargis, for letting me shamelessly promote chapters of the book on your online platforms. You are a true example of women supporting women, the sisterhood, the village. Thank you.

And then there are the people who supported me once my book was written. Salma Begum. You read this book when it was twice the size it was supposed to be, but instead of rejecting it, you saw something in me, and my story, and you helped me cut it down and make it presentable for Abi. Fate brought my book to you, and I am eternally grateful to you.

To Abi Fellows, my wonderful agent at the Good Literary Agency, Gyamfia and the rest of the team. You went above and beyond the call of duty when it came to getting the book ready for publishers. Without you, they would have run for the hills. Abi, thank you for your patience and your calm, zen energy. You always know what to say!

To Sarah Bauer, my editor, who fell in love with Zara's story as much as I did and took the book to the next level. I don't know what magic you did, but just when I thought it couldn't get any better, it did.

To the rest of the wonderful team at Bonnier; Katie Meegan and Lucy Tirahan in editorial; Jenny Richards in design; Vicky Joss and Holly Milnes in marketing; Jenna Petts in PR; Alex May and Eloise Angeline in production; and Mark Williams, Stuart Finglass and Kate Griffiths in sales. You guys are amazing. Thank you for bringing *Finding Mr Perfectly Fine* to life, getting it on the shelves and getting readers hyped up about it!

And lastly, a massive thank you to every single person who has worked on this book, read draft versions, inspired characters, listened to me go on and on about it, given me constructive and destructive criticism; shared their own arranged marriage stories, followed me on social media, let me sit in their coffee shops: Without you, *Finding Mr Perfectly Fine* would have remained an idea and I wouldn't be writing pages of acknowledgements right now. Thank you ♥

Dear Reader,

Thank you SO much for deciding to read my debut rom-com, *Finding Mr Perfectly Fine*. This book has been in the making for almost two decades, ever since my friends and I reached a marriageable age and we began going through the arranged marriage process; from creating biodatas to attending events, to signing up to apps/websites, to volunteering for causes and taking up strange hobbies, between us, we've done it all to find Mr Perfect. I can't believe it's finally here, in print. A true dream come true!

I was in uni doing my undergraduate degree when I first realised I wanted to write this story, but as usual, life got in the way and I focused on other things instead; travelling, my comms career, living abroad and then finally getting married and raising kids.

I revisited the idea when my younger son was six months old. I was awake most of the night in those days, feeding a clingy baby and wondering how I got to this stage without achieving more of my dreams. Those new-baby months are hard. I had a toddler as well, and it felt like my days and nights were an endless cycle of feeding, nappies, vomit, tears (often my own), cleaning and cooking. I loved being a mother but some days it felt like that was all I was; I was rapidly losing every other part of my identity. So, I began to write, reaching over my baby's body as I fed him.

This book saved me in so many ways. It made me feel like a writer again. It gave me a purpose outside of child-rearing. It made me apply for a scholarship and go back to studying and completing a Master's in Creative Writing. And later, when I got this amazing publishing offer while I was working full-time and struggling with life in the pandemic; this book made me decide to leave my job and focus on my passion instead.

When I first wanted to tell this story, back in 2004, I thought that even if I did manage to write it all down, no one would ever publish it. I consumed thousands of books when I was growing up, but none of them featured characters that looked like me. I was desperate to write a book that captured what life is like for women like me; who grow up in London but have their feet in two cultures. Who practise their faith but go against the mainstream media narrative of a Muslim. I wanted to write a book that was fun, funny and light but that touched upon deeper topics like race and faith. Publishing has come a long way since then, and as a woman of colour, as a British Bengali born and raised in North London, I'm thrilled to have been given this opportunity to share Zara's story with you all.

There's a little piece of everything and everyone in this story; my nani, who inspired the character of Zara's nani. My mum, my dad, the house I grew up in. My friends and their husband-hunting experiences. I hope that you also find something here that you can relate to or connect with.

Zara's journey towards love and self-discovery is one, I believe, that transcends cultures and I hope you resonated with some of it. I also hope you understand why I ended it the way I did! I feel like too many of us compromise what we want or need in a partner just to settle down and do what society tells us to, when we're worth so much more than that. We don't need a sub-standard partner to be happy, and Zara learns this in the end, albeit in a pretty painful way.

Thank you again for choosing to pick my book up; I hope you enjoyed reading it almost as much as I enjoyed writing it! If you did, I'd be really grateful if you could leave a review on Amazon, Goodreads, social media or anywhere else, or just tag me on Instagram: @tasneemarashid and use the hashtag #FindingMrPerfectlyFine. I can't wait to hear what you think!

Thank you again,

Tasneem xx